THE ANCIENT BOX

J B BONHAM

Disclaimer:
This is a work of fiction. All characters, locations, and businesses are purely products of the author's imagination and are entirely fictitious. Any resemblance to actual people, living or dead, or to businesses, places, or events is completely coincidental.

The Ancient Box by J B Bonham

ISBN: 978-1-7343672-0-1

Many thanks to Cindy, Diana, Herb, Cindy, Randy, Bill, Mark, and my wonderful wife Becky

CHAPTER ONE

"Dammit, God," Adam Garrett screamed, looking into the vastness of the dark heavens above. "Where is it?"

He glanced at Enrico's tent. A breeze rustled the flaps, but his companion hadn't stirred. He resumed his back-and-forth walk through the narrow passage between rock formations, his way lit by a full moon hanging ten degrees above the horizon. He flung a stone as far as he could. He heard the splash but didn't see it hit the water.

"You wouldn't have led me here if somebody already found it. What did I miss?" More stones entered the sea. He looked at the stars again. "No one else on the planet knew it existed. This is no hot spot. Nobody comes here unless they're lost. There's no record of its discovery—I would have heard about it. So, where is it? The ground's too hard to dig, so he didn't bury it. He hid it in a cave or under a pile of rocks, right? But I've looked everywhere. It's just not here." More rocks hit the water. "I'm out of ideas, so unless I get an epiphany, I'm going home. Maybe someday you'll tell me what this was about."

He trudged back to his tent and pulled his sleeping bag out. He liked to look at the stars before falling asleep. Usually, with his head resting on a pillow outside the opening of the tent. If it rained, he could wiggle back inside and close the flaps. He crawled into the bag, which barely held his lanky frame and rested the back of his head on his interlaced fingers. He surveyed the massive universe overhead, said a half-hearted goodnight to its creator, and fell asleep.

*

"Dr. Garrett, are you awake?"

"Hmmm? What? Oh, Enrico, good morning. What time is it?"

"Time to hit the road. Sun's about to come up."

"Do you know what that means? Do you see a road to hit?"

"Oh, I see. I mean, I don't see. Anyway, time to rise and shine."

"That's better."

"Sorry this trip did not go good for you."

He stared at the ground. Where did I go wrong? At least I only told Mom and Dad about this—well, other than Brad. Glad I don't have to explain this epic failure to anyone else.

"Do you believe in God, Enrico?"

"*Si.* Don't you?"

"I thought I did. I'm not sure anymore, not after this wild goose chase. He put me up to this. He sent me here, or so I thought. He could at least have talked me out of it. We were barely on speaking terms. Maybe He tried, and I didn't listen. It's not the three wasted days I mind; it's the years of research and the anticipation of a big payoff. This possibly could have made my career. What a letdown."

"I am so sorry, Mr. Adam. I hoped for you. You were kind to give me this job. Our economy is uncertain these days, and with the baby due next month, this helps *tremendamente*, uh, tremendous, or however you say it."

"I got it. Even though I didn't find what I came for, you've been a big help. Thank you, Enrico."

He broke down his campsite and hauled his gear to the boat for the trip back to the Italian mainland while the young man he'd hired cooked breakfast one last time. Maybe he won't burn the bacon this time.

"Ready to go," he announced on his return. "Coffee any good?"

"Of course. Help yourself. Breakfast ready soon."

He poured a cup and walked to the middle of the island to take a last look at the place. He drank the hot brew, then spat it out. How can anyone ruin a pot of coffee? He poured the rest on the ground and looked toward the eastern horizon, where the nascent sun floated on the edge of the Mediterranean Sea. Finally. A sunrise. My last morning. He observed the effects of those first rays of sunlight hitting the rock formations around him—the hues, the shadows. I need pictures.

He retrieved his camera from the boat and snapped away. Satisfied he'd captured the best shots he could in that rare lighting, he walked toward the north side of the island to photograph Enrico on the southern end burning the bacon one last time. He found himself next to a skull-shaped rock formation he'd named "Old Man." He called it that because it reminded him of an artist's rendering of a Neanderthal, whom he'd nicknamed Old Man, that hung on a wall in his office. Whenever a student came to see him and asked an incoherent question, he would point to the picture and suggest they rephrase it. Old Man stood a few feet in front of another large rock he'd named "Old Lady."

"I suppose you two have been together for, what, a billion years? So you were here at the time. Where'd he hide it? It can't still be here, can it? You'd tell me if you knew, right? You're about as talkative as God. I should spray paint a face on you. If I gave you a mouth, would you tell me? By the way, your pictures don't do you justice. You're actually a fine-looking rock. But, is it me, or do you look different today?"

"Mr. Adam, breakfast is ready."

He turned off the camera and headed for the boulder he usually sat on at mealtimes. Enrico handed him a plate of bacon with eggs and the last biscuit from the bag they'd brought from Messina. He thanked him and stared at the crisp, black bacon strips. He shook his head and looked at Enrico.

"Aren't you hungry, Mr. Adam? Did you get good pictures?"

He turned the camera on and navigated through the menu options to find his recent photos. He paused at one of Old Man, and studied the LCD screen, then turned his gaze and focused on the large rock across the island.

"Here, look at these." He jumped off his perch and handed Enrico the camera. "I'll be right back."

He returned from the boat with his satchel and

searched through it until he found two photographs with Old Man in the background. The first had been taken by the German Navy during World War II, the second by the American Navy after they'd run the Germans off. Something puzzled him. "Enrico, do you see the difference?" He held the two photos for his companion, who examined them with keen interest.

"Uh, *si*. The two large rocks, the one in the back is different in the second picture. The top is not there."

"That's right. I'll bet the Americans blew it off in the war. I don't know how I missed that, but I need to go take a closer look."

"Now? Don't you want to finish your breakfast?"

"No."

He ran to Old Man and climbed it, then jumped over to Old Lady. He peered at the ground between the two rocks and spotted what had to be her top, resting against the back side of Old Man. He scrambled down and found a handhold. With arms flexed and feet firmly planted against the base of Old Man, he pulled with all the force he could muster. A budge. Enrico? If I compliment his breakfast, he may help.

The young man scarfed down the rest of his breakfast and accompanied him back to the rock. Together, the two managed to tilt it back about a foot, but when they let go, it fell back to its original position.

"I have a pry bar on the boat. I'll get it."

When Enrico returned, they pulled on the rock again, and when it moved, he thrust the steel bar beneath it. On the count of three, they lifted upward on the bar and angled the rock another foot away from Old Man.

"Can you hold it there?" he asked.

"I'll try."

He jumped behind the rock and grabbed the handhold he'd used before. He felt his neck veins bulging as he strained to move the obstruction. When the massive rock gained momentum, he hopped out of the way and watched it fall. What Old Lady's crown had hidden since the 1940s now lay exposed.

"By God, Enrico—that's got to be a cave."

A stack of rocks had been skillfully wedged into the opening, forming a barrier that might have prevented most people from gaining access to the cave, but not a determined archaeologist in a bad mood. After clearing out the impediments, he knelt in front of the entrance and extended his right hand inside and let it wander, but found nothing. Undaunted, he lay down on the ground against the bottom of Old Man and repeated the effort. When he felt something other than rock, he stopped.

"What is it? Did you find something?"

He tapped it with his fingertips. "I think it's wood."

He contorted himself into a new position on the ground that allowed him to reach further inside. He grasped a corner of the object and worked it toward the opening in a zigzag fashion. When it failed to slide out, he backed away and studied the situation. The solution he arrived at was to lift it with one hand while tilting it with the other. It worked. It barely made it through, but it was free.

"That looks like an old box. Is that what you were looking for?"

"I believe it is." He stared at it. "I believe it is."

"*Congratulazioni.*"

"Thank you, Enrico. You know this means a big bonus for you."

"No, I did not know that. Thank you so much. Now, can we open it?"

"Not here. I'll open it when I get it to my workbench." He smiled and looked to the heavens. "*Tremendamente.* But why do you always have to make things so difficult?"

CHAPTER TWO

D r. Mary Walsh found a parking spot in the lot
behind the biology building. The darkened skies
had finally come through on their ominous
threat and sent raindrops downward, hitting the hood of
her car with an accelerating, monotonous beat. Newly
formed puddles on the pavement expanded, becoming a
greater nuisance by the minute. She'd have to negotiate
several to get to the entrance of the building. Or wait a few
minutes. Nah. She threw the door open and bounded out
of the car, dancing her way to the steps, which she took
two at a time to reach the portico. She pushed the door
open and flew up the stairs leading to the second-floor
office of the chairman of the Baylor biology department.
She stepped through the open door and greeted the
secretary.

"Dr. Walsh, you're wet."

"Nah. It's nothing. Is he in?"

"Yeah, he's here, go on in."

She tapped on the open door and stared inside.

"Dr. Walsh. Hello. Come in. How are you?"

"Great. Glad to finally be here full time."

"Have a seat. Welcome aboard. This is a formality; you know your way around. I do need to discuss something with you, though."

"Shoot."

"A complication, I'm afraid."

"Oh?"

"Raymond Adkins. He wants his job back."

"His job? You mean the one I'm here to take over? The one I've unofficially been doing since May? The job for which I have a signed contract that states I officially start today? Yes, that is a complication."

"Look, Adkins was still at the top of his game when he retired to care for his wife."

"And since it's been, what, three months since she passed, he wants to come back to keep busy and be among friends?" she asked. "That about it?"

"Her death devastated him. She'd responded to treatment, then took a sudden turn for the worse. It happened so fast. Anyway, now he says he wants to come back."

"And, you told him…what?"

"I told him I'd try to figure something out. He thinks being around colleagues and the students would be good for him. He also thinks getting back into the lab would help. You know him, he's always been passionate about his research."

"Of course he didn't work in the lab, he supervised a few technicians and postdocs," she said. "But, I get the point. Still, how would this work?"

"Raymond was, *is* one of the foremost authorities on

mitochondrial gene expression. You know that. He's well-liked and respected by everyone in the department. He brought grants and prestige to Baylor. He knows the university president, the provost, the dean of arts and sciences. And he knows them well. If he wants his job back, he'll get it."

"And I'd be out of mine? I mean, I don't see the need for both of us. We do the same research; we teach the same subject. I have his grant, and I'm listed in the course catalog as the instructor for cellular biology this fall. Did he propose a solution?"

"No. He left it to me."

"Well, the easiest remedy for this is for me to step aside. Just so you know, I turned down two other offers. Both allowed me to do research in this area and teach cell bio."

"I'm not asking you to do that. You're a bright and promising young scientist. I'd hate to see your career here aborted before it got started. Then again, I'd love to have Raymond back. We all would."

"Yes, we would, and I'd love to work with him. Can we do that? Split teaching duties, run the research together?"

"Hmmm. That may not be a bad idea if we could make it work. Let me look into it. I'll see if he can get by on his retirement pension, as the grant pays for only one teaching and research salary. And, if we can expedite the request to make him Professor Emeritus, he could teach whenever he wanted, without feeling obligated. Though I'm sure he'd want to be in class a good bit."

"I'd sit in on his lectures."

"You wouldn't learn anything you don't already know."

"I might learn something about teaching. He gets great evaluations."

"Yes, he does. That's another reason I want him back. So, let me look into this. Meanwhile, get situated, let Personnel know you're here, talk to Ed. For now, you're still his boss."

"Yes, sir." She stood and turned for the door. "I'll go see him now," she said over her shoulder.

"Oh, before I forget, we provide a service for the anthropology department. Whenever they need radiocarbon dating analysis, we facilitate it for them under a contract we have with a company in Houston. Basically, you take their samples and send them off."

"How often do we do this?"

"Not often. Several times a year. But, apparently, someone over there needs it. They'll contact you soon."

"I take it this is one of those extra-duties-as-assigned?"

"It is, and it's yours because you're the new kid. You'll have it until the next assistant professor arrives."

"Great. Thanks."

"You're welcome, rookie."

She made her way to the familiar second-floor lab and office. Officially hers, for now. She greeted Ed, her research assistant, and two of Adkins' six graduate students who happened to be in the lab.

"Ed, when you get a sec, can you bring me up to date on the mitochondrial experiments?"

"Sure thing, boss. Are you here for good now?"

"I'm not sure. Adkins wants to come back."

"What? How will that work?"

"I don't know."

"Darn. Just when I thought I had the new boss broken in. Okay, ten minutes?"

"Perfect."

She logged on to her computer and dispensed with new emails. Brightened skies greeted her when she opened the window blinds. The rain had ended, and the sun appeared to want to make its presence felt again. I should go for a run. Two boxes in the corner caught her eye— Adkins' old journals. The secretary can find a place for them. Or throw them out, they're online now anyway. And free.

She pulled her preliminary fall cell-bio syllabus from a folder on the desk and checked off two more days. First four weeks in the can. This is so cool. This is what I was born to do. Too bad it may not last. She wrote the title of the Monday lecture for week five on the notepad and added five keywords on the next line. She glanced at the door when she heard the knock.

"Hey, Ed, come in."

She stopped writing and studied the two pages of graphed data he handed her.

"You sure this is right?"

"I read the plates twice, so, yes."

"One of the reagents is bad. Why don't you make a mock plate and change out reagents one at a time and see if we can pinpoint the problem."

"Will do. Good to have you here full time, Dr. Walsh. Lord knows I need the supervision."

"Oh, you do not. I'll bet a day's pay you'd already

planned to do this. It wouldn't surprise me if you had a plate ready to go, sitting on ice right now. Well?"

"Okay, guilty as charged. But I'd rather work for you than Adkins."

"Why?"

"You explain the science. And you don't expect me to have an experiment done five minutes after we talk."

"You'll be more interested and involved in an experiment if you know its purpose. And I know how long it takes to do them, because I've always done my own work. Adkins didn't come into the lab much, I take it?"

"Not at all."

"In twenty years, though, I may be like him."

"Well, he forgets that I also have to keep supplies ordered and things organized in there. Plus, it takes time to train new students when they show up."

"Believe me, I understand. Just be aware that Adkins may eventually come back and take over again."

"He is awful smart."

"He is," she said. "He's brilliant, in fact. Okay, you work on that, and since the rain has stopped, I think I'll go for a run."

"I'll try to have answers by the end of the day."

"What? You should have it done by the time I get back from the track."

"Ha, ha."

"Okay, then, just have it done before lunch. Oh, and, Ed, I thought I asked you to call me Mary."

CHAPTER THREE

"Hello, Momma."

"Hey there, Adam. How's my favorite archaeologist?" Alice Garrett asked as she wrapped her arms around her oldest son, squeezing tightly. "I can't wait to hear about your summer."

"Good to see you, Momma." He kissed her cheek and set his bag on the table. "How about we wait until Dad gets home and I tell you both about it? When's he coming home?"

"He said he'd try to get here early."

"Oh, good." He headed for his old room. "Let me put my gear away. What's for dinner?"

"Your favorite."

"Everything you make is my favorite," he hollered back as he looked around the room he'd spent so much of his life in as a kid. He read countless books, built dozens of model airplanes, organized a rock collection, and fought with two brothers in a ten-by-ten bedroom. "Glad you haven't given my room away, Mom."

"Who'd take it?"

"When I'm famous, you can rent it out, and I should get a percentage of that."

"So, you're famous now?" She poked her head into the room.

"Not hardly. And probably not anytime soon."

"If that happens, I'd have to share you with the world. No thanks. Sounds like you found something on your trip."

"I'll tell you about it at dinner so Dad can hear it too. What did you say we were having?"

"I didn't. But it'll be your favorite. So you're staying through Sunday?"

"Probably. David or John coming home this weekend?"

"John is, I don't know about David."

"They doing okay?"

"Yes. And David has news."

"What is it?"

"I'll let him tell you."

"I'm getting precious little information from you, Momma. Why should I tell you what happened in Italy?"

"Because I'm your mother. Now get your old clothes on and go cut the grass."

"Did you forget I'm an important college professor? I'm not little Adam anymore." He found a pair of jeans and a T-shirt in his dresser drawer.

"You were never little. You shot up tall and lean from the get-go."

He kissed her forehead and nudged her out of the room so he could change clothes for the yard work he liked to do when home. After a quick gulp of water, he stepped into the garage. The sloshing sound the mower made meant gas in the tank. He wiped the perspiration from his brow and dragged the mower out of the garage. The engine started on the first pull.

Twenty minutes later, he killed the engine and returned the mower to the garage. He lifted the weed whacker from a ceiling hook and slid a charged battery into its slot, then trimmed around the house, trees, and landscaping. As he knelt to pull an outlaw weed from his mother's flower bed, a baseball rolled past and stopped at the base of a yellow rose bush. He picked it up and inspected it, then went into a throwing motion that would send it into a neighbor's yard. He stopped mid-throw and looked toward the house. "Oh, it's you, I thought the kid next door lost this."

"There's no kid next door. Shut up and throw it back," Carl Garrett said as he lobbed a glove to his son. "How was your trip?"

"Great, Dad. I may have found something."

"That's exciting. Significant?"

"Possibly."

"Your mother said I'd have to wait to find out what it was, but is it a big deal?"

"Possibly bigger than I'd care for."

"Meaning?"

"Oh, you know me. I like to keep a low profile."

After a few warm-up tosses to loosen their arms, the ball took a flatter trajectory and carried more velocity with each throw. The popping sounds as ball met leather grew louder.

"Do you know what Mom's fixing for dinner?"

"Your favorite."

"What's that?"

"We'll find out together. Hand hurt?"

"I guess that's the signal to stop before my fastball does more damage. You probably still have a bruise from the last time we threw."

"No, your mother put ice on it. It healed after a few days. But I do think I hear her calling us in."

*

"Pork chops, small red potatoes, and green beans. My favorite. Thanks, Mom."

"You're welcome, now tell us about your trip or you don't get dessert."

"What is it?"

"Your favorite."

"Of course. Okay. Well, then, how I spent my summer…"

During the meal, he described the six-weeks of work at the site near Florence and the three-day trip to Melnikos that followed. After dinner, he opened his laptop and took them through a slide-show presentation of his best photographs of the trip. While they enjoyed pictures of Italy and Melnikos, the photograph of the box failed to generate excitement in his audience of two.

"Doesn't look special," his dad said.

"It looks old though, right son?" his mother asked.

He nodded agreement, then showed them the last slide. In it, an Italian security agent held a small printout.

"Can you tell what's in the photo? No? I couldn't

either, but I have an idea."

"Are you saying you haven't opened that box yet?" Carl asked.

"Well, no, I haven't. I need to go through the biology department to arrange for samples to be sent for radiocarbon dating. I also want someone to document the chain of custody, so they'll need to help me get the samples. I'm working on that."

"So, what is it? What's your guess?"

He showed them a close-up of the x-ray.

"Hard to make anything out in that photo, so I'd hesitate to hazard a guess. But if it's what I think it is…Look, sorry, I can't say much now, but I'll know a lot more in a week or two. Can you wait that long?"

CHAPTER FOUR

Tap…tap…tap.

Dr. Richard Clark's brow furrowed, and the corners of his mouth drooped as he beat the eraser end of a pencil on his desk. The more he read, the harder he tapped. He rubbed his eyes and refocused them on the charts near the end of the report. Good results for mice, guinea pigs, and rabbits. Not so good for non-human primates.

"Rats," he said.

"You want to test rats now?" his diabetes project manager at Expression Vectors Incorporated (EVI), asked.

"Funny. No, I want this viral vector to work in monkeys. I want you to make it work. The monkeys want you to make it work. Why can't you make it work?"

"We talked about this. It's the pi site."

"I know, I know. Amazing how three little nucleotide base pairs can make that much of a difference in protein expression levels."

"It actually wasn't that big of a difference, boss. We got acceptable insulin synthesis."

"The monkeys needed more. To them, the difference

was important."

"Why can't mice and monkeys be more alike? This could have worked."

"Are you serious?" he asked. "Then we'd be more like mice. And we're men, aren't we?"

"Sometimes, my wife isn't so sure."

"Get her in here; let her make our vectors. Maybe she'd have gotten this one right."

"Fine. We could use two paychecks."

"If we don't get better insulin expression, none of us will have a paycheck. Okay, okay, let's figure this out. We made a decision. Go with a one-size-fits-all vector. It got us through the lower animals, but…"

"We rolled the dice on the monkeys and lost."

"But other expression vectors without pi seem to work fine in monkeys."

"True, but we didn't know how much insulin synthesis we needed for optimal blood sugar levels."

"Apparently, we need more. When do you expect to have the new vector ready?"

"Another week. The pi site is in place. We're waiting for sequence results on the whole vector."

"And it works in tissue culture?"

"Like a charm. We tested three independent clones. They each look good. And we're sequencing all three. We'll know by the end of the week."

"Production can begin as soon as we get confirmation?"

"Yes, sir."

"We need to answer a question."

"And that is?"

"Do we go back and retest it in the other animals first? Or go straight into monkeys?"

"That's your call, sir."

"But do you have an opinion?"

"I'd at least look at it in mice. We don't care if we get reduced expression there. We expect that. But we need to make sure the vector works, at least to some extent, in mice. Monkeys are expensive."

"Anything in the literature about it? Anybody ever make a vector with a pi site and measure expression in mice?"

"I don't know. I'll find out."

"I have a meeting with the New York funding agency in two weeks. We have control mice that aren't too old. Can you hit them with the new pi vector and see what you get?"

"I can do that. I assume you want to use the new batch when it's ready?"

"Let's pick one of the three clones and start production now. We'll infect control mice as soon as it's ready. That'll save us close to a week. If that vector is defective and we have to start over, it won't have cost much. It's worth the risk. We need to show progress."

"And the results we have now, they're not that bad. Would New York be impressed?"

"They might, but we want something marketable. A cure for mouse diabetes isn't in demand."

*

Clark pulled the phone from his pocket and punched in Vanessa's number.

"Hi, gorgeous. How's your day been? Deliver any babies today?"

"Sure did. How about you?"

"No, no babies here. Just nasty little monkeys."

"Yeah? How's their insulin production?"

"A little too low."

"Oh, that's too bad. How do you fix that?"

"We're repairing the vector. Should be ready for testing in a day or two."

"That's the spirit. So, you working late tonight? Want to grab dinner?"

"I can be done by six. Diablo's?"

"Be there by six-thirty, or I'll start without you."

"What if there's traffic?"

"There's always traffic. Besides, you're only two miles away. Take the back roads, or walk, just get there."

"Ooh, I like it when you take charge like that."

"Just get there, goof."

CHAPTER FIVE

"Hey, Goodie, guess what?" Adam asked.

"You found something," Dr. Bradley Goodwin responded. "Tell me you found something."

"Okay, I found something."

"Are you serious? Tell me you're serious."

"I'm serious. I found a box on Melnikos."

"No kidding. Is it old? Of course it's old. What's in it?"

"I haven't opened it yet."

"Why not?"

"Haven't had time. I dropped it off in Waco and went to Abilene for a couple of days. It's still in the bubble wrap from Melnikos."

"Any problem with customs?"

"Not at all. Luigi signed off on my permits in Rome. Sailed through Dallas. We're free and clear."

"Great. When do I get to see it?"

"You can help open it, get samples for carbon dating, take pictures. What do you say?"

"I'd love to, but I can't this week. The grandkids are in town. And next week I have a conference in Phoenix. But you won't be able to wait two weeks. Any idea what's in it?"

"Luigi took me to the airport and asked security to give me a print of the X-ray. So I have an idea, but I'd rather not speculate. I'll know soon enough. And when I know, you'll know."

"I appreciate that. This is exciting. Congratulations. Let's hope there's more than a few trinkets inside."

"Let's hope. And if it's what I think it is, you can help me with authentication."

"Of course. I'm here for you."

"You've always been there for me. I'd have never found it if you hadn't taken me to Florence. You deserve much of the credit."

"You did the work, kid."

"And had luck along the way."

"Don't sell yourself short. You're a good archaeologist. I enjoyed working with you this summer, now that you're a legitimate archaeology professor. I wish I could have stayed longer and gone with you to Melnikos."

"We both didn't need to go. Besides, that was more of a treasure hunt than archaeology. I mean, the only signs of a human presence were the support bracket for the German radio tower and spent ammo. Regardless, let's not get ahead of ourselves. This may not be what I think it is; it may not be much of anything. I'll let you know what I find."

*

Adam found room 204 and knocked.

"Come in."

He pushed the door open and stuck his head in. "Dr. Walsh?" he asked before his mind went numb and his limbs limp at the sight of her. He'd seen other young women who resembled Jill, but the person standing in front of him had to be her twin.

"Yes, but I'm afraid office hours are over, and I'm about to leave for the day. Sorry, but can you come back tomorrow?"

He stood in the doorway, frozen. He tried to speak, but the words stuck in his throat. Oh, wow, this is embarrassing.

"Something wrong?" she asked.

"N-n-no," he finally managed to say, and breathed a sigh of relief. "No, no, I'm sorry. Tomorrow is great. What, uh, what's a good time?"

"Office hours are two to four. Are you taking my class this fall?"

"I teach here. Archaeology."

"Oh, sorry. I assumed you were a student. Come in, come in."

"Thank you. It's my jeans and T-shirt, I guess."

"And boyish looks."

"I'm Adam Garrett." They shook hands. Shivers went up his spine.

"Mary Walsh. Glad to meet you. Is this something we can take care of quickly? The staff at the gym is giving new faculty members an orientation. We're meeting at five o'clock. Then I'm staying for a workout."

"This will only take a moment. It's a request."

"Shoot."

"I need analysis of archaeological artifacts—specifically, radiocarbon dating on an old wooden box. I have to go through one of the faculty here to get that authorized. Apparently, that's you this time."

"Oh, so you're the one. Yes, the Department Head told me to expect you. Sure, I can help. I'm still a faculty member here, but that's another story. Come by tomorrow morning, and we'll take care of it."

"Great. Thank you, Dr. Walsh. Have a good workout."

"I'm curious. Did this box contain anything interesting?"

"I don't know."

"Haven't you opened it?"

"Not yet."

"Seriously? Why not? Don't you want to know if anything's in it?"

"Of course, but I secured it immediately when I found it because I didn't want to risk breaking the hinges or having it fall apart trying to open it. And I want to establish a chain of custody. My helper on the island witnessed me sealing the box. His initials are on the wrapping tape."

"Okay, but is it heavy? Can you tell if things move around when you shake it?"

"No, I haven't shaken it, but there are things inside. I'll find out what they are soon enough."

"I certainly wouldn't have had your patience. How big is it? Where'd you find it?"

"Not big." He held his hands apart, approximating the size of a large shoebox. "And I found it in the

Mediterranean Sea, or, rather, on an island there. Do you want to do this today or tomorrow?"

"Probably tomorrow, but now I'm intrigued."

"We could do it after your workout."

"Hmm. It's in your office, I take it?"

"My apartment."

"Your apartment? It's not here? Won't you be working with it here? What exactly does an anthropologist do with whatever he finds when he finds it?"

"First, I'm an archaeologist. Second, well, the second point would take a while to explain, and you have to get to the gym. So, tell me if you want to do this after your workout this evening or tomorrow."

"Which would you prefer? I'm still trying to settle in. I planned on being here tonight anyway."

"All right, you do your workout, and I'll get the box. We'll meet back here at six-thirty."

*

He returned to his office and changed into running clothes. He considered riding his bike home but decided he needed a good workout, one that would help him forget what just happened. The distance to his apartment measured three miles by the shortest route. A longer, five-mile route wound through campus first and then a path through the woods. He chose five and ran through the picturesque campus toward the woods at a faster pace than usual.

Mary Walsh had brought back the haunting memory of his childhood sweetheart. Her death on her nineteenth birthday devastated him. Dr. Walsh had her looks, her smile, her pleasant nature, her intelligence. Even her hair. It was her. But then, of course, it wasn't her. It couldn't be.

Those memories paraded through his head, one after the other, for the first three miles of the run. In the ten years since her death, the pain, nearly unbearable at first, eventually became manageable. He immersed himself in work to avoid thinking of the heartbreak. His faith took a huge hit, but he figured he had nowhere else to go and hadn't ended his relationship with the Almighty. Instead, he intensified his study of theology with a desire to better understand the tragedy, and someday come to terms with what he considered the senseless loss of the only girl he'd ever loved.

"What's the big idea?" he yelled. "Of all the women in the world you bring one to Baylor who looks exactly like Jill, and then you arrange it so I have to work with her on a project you pushed me into. You've revived the pain, not only for how she suffered but also your refusal to do anything. Sometimes I wish you'd leave me alone. There don't seem to be a lot of perks with you anyway. I mean, what's the upside with you, at least here on Earth?"

He slowed to a walk and let his emotions roil. He kicked sticks and leaves and threw any rock he could find. He shouted at the heavens. He stopped and leaned against a large, live oak tree, supporting himself with both outstretched arms. "You want to find out if I still blame you, is that it? Well, I do. She didn't have to die. You can do anything. You let her die. You let me go crazy for a girl who died in her teens. And she suffered. An innocent girl. She never harmed a fly, and she suffered. You could have healed her. I asked you every day for six months. And afterward, no explanation. Nothing. But now this: someone who takes me straight back to Jill and those horrible days. I don't get it, and I don't get you."

He swayed gently and allowed the mental anguish to subside. He looked through the treetops into the clouds, shook his head, and took in a deep breath. He turned toward home, took a step, then another, picking up the pace until he found himself sprinting. When his apartment complex came into view, he slowed to a trot. When he reached his door, he went inside and collapsed onto the couch, his heart racing and chest pounding as he glared at the Bible on the coffee table. His pulse and respiration rate returned to normal as he thought about that book. He picked it up and fanned the pages with his fingers, then laid it back down.

"What am I going to do with you?"

*

He knocked while pushing on the partly opened door and saw sneakers next to the desk. She's back.

"Ah, Adam," she said, walking in behind him. "What's this?"

"Hamburgers. This could take a while. I thought you might want to eat first."

"I am a little on the hungry side."

"I didn't know what you'd want on yours, so the condiments are in little packets."

"Where'd you get those? That doesn't look like fast food."

"A restaurant near my apartment. Life's too short for

29

fast food. You'll like it."

They divided the food and chowed down.

"So, tell me about the box. Did you find it on the side of a road? Or in an antique shop?"

"Funny." Dr. Walsh had Jill's playful ways about her, which didn't help. "Ever hear of Melnikos?"

"Mm-mm." She swallowed the bite. "That was a 'no.' Who is he?"

"It's not a he. It's a small island between Italy and Greece. Closer to Italy. When I worked at a dig near Florence a few summers back, I happened to find documents that described a box left on Melnikos. It may contain artifacts from the time of Christ."

"That old? That's exciting. I can see why you want carbon dating."

"You and I will be the first ones to look inside it since it was left on the island. I think. I hope."

"Sounds like uncertainty there. But, what the heck, let's get to it."

"Happy to. However, it still has the bubble wrap that I put around it on the island, and I want to record this on video. I have cameras; is there a lab bench we can use?"

"Sure. Across the hall. Want to finish these burgers first? They're pretty darn good."

"I do."

CHAPTER SIX

✠

C lark met Vanessa at El Diablo, a Mexican restaurant they both liked. He ordered chimichangas. She opted for chicken enchiladas. They sipped wine and discussed the affairs of the day while they waited.

"Nice to sit down and catch up," Vanessa said. "Either you're gone, or I'm doing late rounds at the hospital. So, how are things?"

"Things could be better," he said. "I don't like having to start over with the diabetes vector."

"Yeah, that's too bad. I guess that's the nature of science, though. Sometimes living organisms don't behave the way we want them to."

He'd met Vanessa a few years back when she was a graduate student and he a professor at the University of Texas. He admired her intelligence and work ethic and wasn't the least bit surprised to see her successfully clone a ring-tailed lemur using SCNT—somatic cell nuclear transfer technology. With several publications and a PhD resulting from that work, she was off to a fast start in the world of life sciences research when she decided to change course and entered medical school. Now in the final year of her OB/GYN residency, she was eager to set up a reproductive medicine and fertility clinic. In Beverly Hills, if possible.

"I know," Clark said. "But we don't do basic research, and we don't look for breakthroughs. We want to use proven tools and methods to get therapeutic viruses into people."

"Humans can pay for it, and animals can't?"

"Exactly. But the ones who are paying us now are growing impatient. I have to go to New York in two weeks to meet with them."

"To ask for more money?"

"Yes. Seems like that's all I do."

"Well, that's what your MBA is for. Any danger they'll pull the plug?"

"I think I can hold them off with a credible scientific explanation for the delays."

"And that's what your PhD is for. Whatever it takes to make your millions and get the clinic you promised me up and running. Don't fizzle out on me now."

He poured another glass of wine for her and one for himself. "We'll be living the good life then, that's for sure. But I don't want to be your errand boy. This project needs to work, and it needs to work for EVI to survive."

He'd started EVI three years earlier when he left academia for the business world. Preferring project management to work in a laboratory, he relished the opportunity to build a profitable enterprise from scratch. He had little patience, however, for the frustrations that were part and parcel of entrepreneurial endeavors.

"Well, if EVI crashes and burns like many startups do, you could always teach again. Just don't fall for another student like you did me."

"Sure, I could, but I don't want to. Unless I can get a department chairmanship. I'll need EVI to succeed before that happens. And I would never fall for another student. I don't think."

A playful kick connected with his shin.

"Kidding. But if I ever did, they wouldn't be high-maintenance like—"

He felt another kick, one that made him flinch.

"Your meals," the waiter announced as he approached their table.

"Just in time. The gentleman is digging himself into a hole."

"I dig ditches for a living," Clark told the waiter, with a wink.

"I understand, sir." The waiter set their plates before them. "May I get you anything else?"

"Nice fellow," Clark said after dismissing him. "So, where were we?"

"You were harassing another poor graduate student again."

"Oh, yeah. No, those days are over. And I didn't make a habit of it. You were special. Still are. I don't know if you knew it, but you were actually the only student I ever dated."

"I didn't know that."

"I'm getting too old for college kids. Besides, why would I ever want anyone else but you?"

"You won't if you know what's good for you."

CHAPTER SEVEN

Adam retrieved the box from his car and placed it on a bench in Mary's lab.

"Are you ready?" he asked.

"I am, but I don't have anything at stake. I'm only an observer. Are you?"

"I'm a little nervous. This could be big. Or nothing. If carbon dating shows the box is first century, that will make the documents I have that say it belonged to Pilate more believable. And that's big."

"Wait. Who?"

"Pilate. Pontius Pilate."

"*The* Pontius Pilate? The one who crucified Christ? You can't be serious. Is this a joke?"

"No. This is legitimate."

"Something isn't right. I keep up with the news, Professor Garrett. If anybody here at Baylor had discovered something connected to Pilate, I'd have heard about it. You expect me to believe that a first-year archaeology professor visits an island and walks away with something that significant, and no one knows about it?"

"I can go over the corroborating evidence if you like."

"Why hasn't the school made a big deal about it? No announcement? No fanfare? It doesn't add up."

"The school doesn't know about it. Yet."

"So, what, you go to archaeological dig sites as a hobby? You paid for this?"

"Technically it wasn't archaeology. The island has never been inhabited by humans, or much of anything, except maybe a few birds. I merely followed up on a lead I developed in grad school. No way was I going to use grant money to pay for it. I worked on an actual site in Italy this summer. This was a three-day side trip at the end, and I paid for everything."

"All right. Fine. Let's get your samples. If they're old, wonderful. This all just seems a little odd. Pontius Pilate? Okay."

He mounted a video camera on a tripod and set it on the bench behind them. When he handed Mary a second camera for still photographs, she stared at him a moment before taking it.

"Look, this is real; it's not a joke of some kind."

"Okay, I'll play along, but let's speed this up."

"I can get someone else; this doesn't have to be done tonight."

"No, you're all set up. It's the least I can do since you bought dinner."

"Don't let that mean anything. I'd owe you anyway for sending my samples out."

"So, you're saying you have absolutely no idea what's inside?"

"I have an idea."

"Based on what?"

"An X-ray at the airport. The security agent let Luigi and me have a look."

"Luigi?"

"A museum curator from Rome, my Italian liaison. Helped with permits and such. Good guy."

"So, what did the X-ray show?"

"One of the objects looked like a short, rod-shaped piece of wood, and another appeared to be organic matter with an ill-defined shape. There were also strands of something, possibly leather. No metal except for the hinges and latch, though the security screener did say he saw small pieces of lead. He said he'd seen that a thousand times before in the bags of fishermen. And, obviously, nothing that looked like weapons or explosives or he would have made me open the box."

"Too bad. He could have been your witness and spared me."

"Yeah, an Italian TSA worker I'll never see again. That would have been memorable. I have a picture of the X-ray on my phone. Here, look." He pulled out his phone and displayed the image. "You want to guess what's in here?"

"Looks like a bird's nest and a miniature baseball bat. I don't know. Open it already."

"I'll start recording in a minute, but first let me point out that this wrap is taped, and that the tape has Enrico's signature. And mine."

"Enrico?"

"Luigi's nephew. He borrowed a boat and took me to Melnikos. He's my discovery witness."

"Ah. I'd like to see pictures of Melnikos."

"I doubt it. The place is rocky, nothing grows on it, and

there's nothing to do there. No one goes there unless they're lost or have boat problems. But, I'll show you pictures later."

"I meant later. Right now, I'm pretending to be interested in this prank and wanting to see what's in the box," she said, stone-faced.

"Right. Well, you can see under the outer wrap where the inner wrap is taped. There's also some on the sides. They all have our signatures. Get pictures of those. And get close-ups of the wax seal on the latch in case Pilate imprinted his seal into it. I'll try to pry it off intact. I want pictures of all of those things."

He positioned the box on the bench between himself and Mary, then adjusted the video camera on the bench behind, and began recording. He pointed to the tape on the wrap and asked her to photograph it, then gently tore it off and placed it in a clear, resealable bag. Ever so gently, he worked the plastic bubble outer wrap from the box as Mary took more pictures. The pieces of tape across the inner wrap came off next, and each went into the bag. He used a thin, metal spatula to pry the formless wax seal away from the latch. It crumbled into three pieces, each of which went into a separate, smaller bag which he sealed.

"Oh, I almost forgot. I collected ten small pieces of wood from the island. They're in here." He picked up a clear, resealable bag and opened it, and from it poured out ten smaller baggies containing small objects. "These looked like scraps from old ship timbers, and since nothing grows on the island, they had to have been taken there. I'd like analyses on them too. All right, back to the box. The wood seems to be in good condition. And the two hinges look intact."

"Those are hinges? I've never seen anything like that. How clever."

He smiled and asked her to take close-up photos. That done, he dripped lubricating oil on the moving parts.

"Looks like bronze. Okay, I'll lift the lid, and if it doesn't fall apart, I'll rest it against the shelf above it."

He raised it in a slow, even motion. The hinges creaked but worked. The lid moved freely upward past vertical. Its top edge met the shelf above the bench and rested there. The box lay open.

"Wow. I thought maybe…but it is. It's what I thought. Unbelievable."

"Okay, now I'm convinced."

"I thought you wanted to see the carbon dating results first."

"That was sarcasm. Now I'm convinced this is a joke. What, I'm supposed to believe that's the crown of thorns they put on Jesus? And that's the whip they beat him with? Give me a break."

"I don't know if these two things ever came anywhere near Jesus. Probably not, but unless carbon dating proves otherwise, I have to believe Pontius Pilate once possessed them."

"All right. Let's get your samples. I'll send them out for analysis, and that will be that. I may be better off somewhere else. This school certainly has its peculiarities."

"So I'm a peculiarity, am I? That's a first, though my brothers might agree. Do you have sample vials in here?"

"Of course." She retrieved a foil-covered glass beaker full of sterile, screw-capped plastic tubes from the shelf above the bench. "And here's a Sharpie to label everything, for what it's worth. Let's get this done."

"I'll start with pieces of the vine that have broken off. Ah, what's that? It looks like papyrus there on the bottom. I didn't see that on the X-ray. With faint writing. Hard to tell what language that is. Tell you what, let's take the whip and the crown out and get those samples, and then we'll look at it. If it's papyrus, it'll be brittle. Surprised it lasted this long."

"It probably says 'you've been punked.'"

"So cynical."

He placed two sheets of clean paper on the benchtop surface. He eased the whip out of the box and placed it on one piece of paper, and the crown of thorns on the other.

"Do you have forceps?"

She pulled an autoclaved packet from a drawer and opened it. With the forceps, he picked up loose pieces of the vine lying in the bottom of the box. Each piece went into a separate tube and was given an identification number. She photographed each sample with a derisive smile but otherwise made no further comments. He next took a scalpel from the packet and sliced off two small pieces of dried vine from the underside of the strand of thorns. Moving on to the whip, he cut tiny slivers from the wooden handle, then trimmed two filaments of leather that had split from the main portion of one of the thongs, and put each in a tube.

"Looks like shards of rock or bone wedged into the ends of the thongs. If it's bone, we might have a shot at carbon dating, right, Dr. Walsh?"

"If it's bone, but hold on a second."

She set the camera down and put on latex gloves. With the aid of a magnifying glass, she examined one of the gritty shards lodged in the end of a strip of leather.

"These may be bone chips, but…I see something else. Hmmm."

"What do you think it is?"

She removed a sterile needle from its packaging and jabbed at the surface of the shard. "I have my proof. A piece of organic matter is lodged into a cavity of this piece of bone." She took the forceps from his hand and wiggled the rubbery substance until it came loose. "Looks like cartilage, but it isn't two thousand years old. Did these pieces of bone come from a butcher shop?"

"What? No. I don't know. I have no idea how that got there."

"There's certainly no sense sending any of this for carbon dating."

His heart sank as the possibility that he was the victim of a hoax hit him. "I don't see how. Cartilage? I don't see—"

"Because you didn't want to see. You were too invested in the outcome you wanted. Wasn't there anything suspicious about those documents? I don't mean to question your skill as an archaeologist since I don't know you, but something somewhere had to look wrong."

"No, no, those documents were two thousand years old. If it's a hoax, it's…unless somebody translated them, found the box on Melnikos, and swapped the original contents with these things. Who would do that?"

"I don't know, but it would explain the cartilage."

He closed his eyes and grimaced. "Wow, what a profound impression I must be making on you."

"Look, I'm sorry, I didn't mean to impugn your competence. I might have been fooled, too. Tell you what—I'll look at this, this, whatever it is, tomorrow, and try to identify it. That may help you figure out how this happened."

"Thank you. I would appreciate that. In the meantime, would you mind sending these samples out anyway? They may still be quite old."

"Sure, it's your money."

"Thanks. Let's finish up, then. I want to get a look at that papyrus."

"Or whatever it actually is," she said.

"It looks real, so I think I'll leave it in place. Let me see the camera for a second."

He took it from Mary and adjusted the aperture, ISO, and shutter speed until he got the faint writing on its front side bold enough with proper contrast to make it readable.

"You have your writing. What language is it?"

"I don't know. Oh, wait, it's Latin."

"That's not Latin," she informed him. "It's something, but it's not Latin."

"You know Latin?" he asked.

"I studied it in high school, but that's been a while. Do you?"

"Sure. 'E pluribus unum,' 'semper fi.'"

"Clown."

"How about 'mea culpa,' 'a priori.'"

"How about 'ad nauseam.'"

"Okay, okay. No, it's Latin, the writing is just upside down."

He rotated the LCD and tried to translate the text.

"There's what, fourteen, fifteen words? Shouldn't take long. I may have one already. Do you know the Latin word

41

for 'prank'?" he asked.

She smiled. "Latin is a nice touch since that's what Pilate would have used. Is the word for 'prank' there?"

"He probably spoke both Latin and Greek. And, no, I don't know the Latin word for prank, but I do have an idea what this says. And I don't need to translate the name Pontius Pilate."

"Well, that doesn't mean much. I'd expect his name to be there as part of the hoax."

He slipped the end of the scalpel under the sides of the papyrus and gently raised each edge, looking for additional writing on the underside.

"All right, we're finished. Thank you for your assistance and not laughing at me too much."

"I imagine this happens to the best."

He moved the thorns and the whip back into the box and took one last photograph. After lowering the lid, he wrapped it with new bubble wrap and placed it back on top of the Styrofoam peanuts in the bottom of the cardboard box. He filled the sides and the top with more peanuts and taped the top flaps shut. He packed his cameras and thanked Mary for her help.

"Look, Mary, I had good reason to look for this box. If it's a hoax, I have to give credit to whoever did it. He did a great job. And if carbon dating doesn't show these to be first-century artifacts, the box goes into a hole, and only a few of us will ever know about it."

"And keep your fingers crossed that word of this never gets out."

"Exactly right. It'll be our little secret."

CHAPTER EIGHT

✤

"How long will you be gone?" Vanessa asked Clark as they sat at the kitchen table, drinking coffee. Bacon sizzled while scrambled eggs waited their turn for the frying pan.

He looked up from his laptop, having already digested the overseas political and financial news. "Hmmm? Oh, overnight; I'll be back tomorrow. Why, are you inviting your boyfriend over again?"

"I might."

"As long as he's gone when I get back and doesn't leave clothes lying around," he said. "You do know I have this place under surveillance, don't you?"

"Then you know about my indiscretions. Well, you should also know that I'm having you watched by a private detective. Don't think that because we aren't married, I won't wring you dry if we end up in court."

"I love it when you're threatening. Want to go to New York?"

"Right. Like a resident can just walk away from the hospital. But you knew that. Meeting anyone tonight?"

"Nope. When I get back to the hotel, I'm reading reports and making calls. I've decided to get more involved in day-to-day activities. I can't let this project get away from me. It ought to be at a make-or-break point in about six months; how about we plan a vacation?"

"Celebrate your cure for diabetes?" she said. "That sounds great."

She drained hot grease from the pan and added the eggs. She put two pieces of bread in the toaster and retrieved butter from the refrigerator.

"More coffee?"

He was reading again but heard the question, thought about it, and declined the offer. He'd been watching his caffeine intake lately, thinking he might be getting sensitive to it as he neared middle age.

"So, you'll be making rounds today?"

"I am. Want to be my patient?"

"Right now? Let's see how breakfast goes first. Who knows, I may need you to nurse me back to health."

"What? My cooking makes you sick? Take two aspirin and call me in the morning, ingrate."

"Let me rephrase that."

*

Sitting in the waiting area, Clark opened a browser on his laptop and launched an online subscription service that specialized in life science articles. One of the titles piqued his interest. A group of scientists had published their work on the same viral vector EVI was using in the diabetes experiments. Their version also homed to the livers of mice, with the only difference being the therapeutic gene it carried. It efficiently entered hepatic cells and even synthesized detectable levels of the enzyme it expressed. All well and good, boys, but your enzyme doesn't provide relief from a disease. You need the proper transgenic mouse. I suppose you're busy making it. Good work, but we're ahead of you.

He read a text message from Vanessa and grinned, then typed a short reply. Pulling a notepad from his laptop case, he studied the notes and scribbles and hand-drawn charts littering the front page. He put the notepad down. I'm ready.

"Dr. Clark, they'll see you now," the receptionist informed him.

He stood, straightened his tie and buttoned his jacket, then walked toward the room in which the source of his company's lifeblood sat—the financiers. The first two years of grant money carried with it an opt-out clause where either party could dissolve the relationship and walk away, no questions asked. That moment had arrived, and he needed an extension to get the proof of concept he needed for long-term funding. He pushed the door open and walked in, trying to appear calm and confident, as if to tell them by his appearance that they had nothing to worry about. They didn't seem to care much about his appearance. They had concrete questions for which they wanted clear and cogent answers.

"When will a product emerge from the animal studies?"

"When will human trials begin?"

"How long will safety testing take before efficacy can be evaluated?"

"What will the FDA say? Have you begun discussions with them?"

"When will a product be marketable?"

He answered every question, with spreadsheets, charts, and summary tables, and even plain English when it suited, hedging a little at times, not quite telling the whole story at others. He needed more research time, so he gave them answers that would give him that time. When he finished, he thanked them, though not too profusely, not wanting to look desperate. He concluded with words of optimism and assurance and took his leave. On the way out, he thought he detected approval on their faces and in their body language. He won his extension, he thought, and would make the most of it. He would make the diabetes project successful. He would achieve his dream. Whatever it took.

CHAPTER NINE

A dam completed the list of topics he planned to cover during the spring semester. As he reviewed it, the email notification alert chimed. The sender line read, "Mary Walsh, PhD." Ah, yes. The new cell biology professor. Jill's twin. *The one who must think I'm a complete idiot after the Melnikos box debacle.*

Two weeks had passed since the humiliating moments in her lab. The subject line read "carbon dating results." *I guess this puts an end to that fiasco. So much for the big discovery. Goodbye to tenure. Goodbye to a career in archaeology. Maybe I could become a fishing guide in Montana, or Wyoming, or Idaho. Oh, open it and get it over with.* He clicked on the message. It read "call." *What does that mean?* He dialed her number.

"Dr. Walsh, this is Adam Garrett. How bad is it?"

"Are you sitting down?"

"That bad?"

"No, that good. The report says two thousand years. For everything except the wood scraps you thought were ship timbers, and even they range from centuries to millennia. Three of them are two thousand years old, like the box, and one is even older. Now when I say everything, that, of course, doesn't include the little tissue fragment we didn't send out. Hello? Adam?"

"I'm here, but I'm not sure I heard you right."

"Okay, I'll repeat it, but please listen this time. It's the number two followed by three zeroes. In years. I'll send you a scan of the report so you can see for yourself. Adam? You there?"

"Of course. Yes. I knew it all along."

"Liar. I saw it on your face when I showed you that piece of cartilage. You looked devastated."

"Okay, you're right. You had me convinced it was a hoax. Two thousand years old is…is fantastic. Thank you so much for the news."

"I thought you did this as a prank, but the look of disappointment on your face told me you hadn't. In any event, you're to be congratulated."

"But, what about that tissue fragment? How can it be recent and everything else old? You said you'd examine it. Whatever came of that?"

"Nothing. It's still in a vial in the fridge. I've been so busy that I haven't had time to do anything with it. I will now."

"I understand. It didn't make sense to waste time on it, but now—"

"Now, I'll get on it."

"Let me know what you find. And thanks again for your help."

"Adam?"

"Yes, Dr. Walsh?"

"What's this 'Dr. Walsh' stuff? It's Mary, please. Anyway, I'm happy for you. I'm glad you didn't waste your time and money on that trip."

"And the research before that. I spent a lot of time translating Greek language documents to discover that Pilate had left something on Melnikos. And more time figuring out where the tiny island was."

"You have to be relieved."

"Not sure what I am. I need time to digest this."

"Hey, can I buy you a cup of coffee? Now that this is real, I'd like to hear more about it."

"I'll grab my papers and take you up on that. I can meet you at your office in thirty minutes."

"Make it sixty, and I'll take a look at that piece of cartilage before we go."

*

After working on the course syllabus another hour, he gathered his Melnikos papers and photos and tucked them into his backpack. He walked across the grassy quadrangle to the biology department building and climbed the stairs to the second floor. A note on Mary's office door directed him to the lab. When he entered it, he spotted her talking to a technician, so he waited at the door. She'd seen him come in and held up an index finger to indicate she'd be quick.

"Hello, Adam. Where's the nearest coffee shop?"

"Ten minutes. How about a walk-n-talk?"

"Lead the way."

They exited the building and strolled along the maze of sidewalks leading to the edge of campus. A variety of stores and shops catering to the needs of college students lined the thoroughfare that divided the school from the town. Most had down-shifted their retail activity as a concession to the scarcity of students during the summer break. He pointed out a place called Common Grounds and made a beeline for it. He opened the door to the coffee shop, and they moseyed in.

"What'll it be?" the smiling barista asked in a manner that reminded him of the bartenders in so many Western movies.

"Mary? How do you like your coffee."

"Black. No sugar."

"Make it two," he said.

He paid for the coffees and added a generous tip.

"Thank you, sir."

"Thank you for the coffee and the cheerful smile."

He took the cups to the table Mary had selected—she had the pick of the place—and offered her the choice of either cup.

"No, you paid. You get to pick."

"Okay, I'll take this one."

"Darn, I had my eye on that one."

He took off his backpack and sat in the chair opposite her.

"Did you look at that piece of tissue?"

"It's mammalian epidermal and dermal tissue with a bit of the subcutaneous layer and muscle cells."

"Interesting. You don't know what species?"

"No. That would take genetic analysis, like PCR."

"Do you do that?"

"Of course. Do I have time? Not at the moment. Nor

do I have the right reagents. If you want it badly enough, I can do the work at night, but you'd have to buy the supplies."

"That scrap of tissue caused me considerable anguish, so, yes, I'd like to know what it is. I still have startup funds; I can pay for the reagents."

"Good to see you didn't use all your research money this summer."

"That was all out of pocket."

"Oh, that's right. You didn't want it to look like a paid vacation. But, now what? You'll use Baylor money and facilities to analyze it?"

"Now it's real. I can easily justify working it into my research plans."

"What about publicity? When do you announce it?"

"Not for a while. There's still work to do. Like confirming as best we can that Pilate put the box in that cave."

"Who else here knows about it?"

"Just you and me."

"Not even your department chair?"

"Davison? Especially not him."

"Uh-oh. Is there bad blood between you two?"

"Yes. He treats me like the department's token archaeologist. Like it isn't a serious degree. I somehow get left off faculty meeting invitations. He doesn't talk to me, so I don't talk to him. If I see my name in the course catalog, I know I have a class to teach—things like that. Anyway, yeah, I still have most of my startup funds. I can even do the work if you show me what to do."

"Depends on how good you are with your hands. Ever

use a pipettor?"

"Of course. Undergrad microbiology lab. Between that and the biochem labs, I learned to use a pipettor."

"Great, I'll set it up. I'll send you a list of reagents, you get them, and we'll find out what that tissue is. Now, tell me more about Melnikos."

He unzipped a compartment on his backpack and pulled out an envelope. He unfastened the tie string, pulled back the flap, and emptied the contents onto the table.

CHAPTER TEN

Adam picked out a photo from the stack on the table. "This is Brad Goodwin, my thesis adviser at Texas Tech. He has an ongoing collaborative relationship with his Italian colleague, Luigi. That's the two of them standing next to the Tower of Pisa; Brad is on the left. He took one or two students to Italy every summer and worked with Luigi at sites around the country. I was there three years ago when they first worked a site near Florence and still go back every summer. We rented villas and work long hours during the week, but weekends were free. During our free time, we toured the country, sometimes together, sometimes on our own. Luigi knows people everywhere, and whenever I gave him a destination, he'd ask me to contact a friend there. After a while, I figured out he was doing me favors, because every time I called one of his friends, they'd roll out the red carpet. They invited me to dinner, helped me find out-of-the-way places, even suggested local spots that were more interesting than the ones I'd originally planned to see."

"Do you speak Italian?"

"Yeah, a little; enough to get around. Many of the people I came across knew some English, which helped a lot. Anyway, several invited me to use spare bedrooms for the night, which brings me to Rome. I enjoyed it so much that I went back three times. Luigi has a cousin who lives outside the city, and he let me stay at his farmhouse. A short walk into the nearby town got me to the train station. I'd be in Rome fifteen minutes later."

"On my last trip to Rome, he showed me an old equipment graveyard at one end of the farm. He said he'd picked it for his 'dump' site because that's what the previous owner had used it for, and said I could look through it. Naturally curious, I spent time in it before leaving to catch the train back to Florence. The major items were two cool, old tractors, but the place was littered with broken furniture, old bicycles, tires, stuff like that. Well, what did I find under a rusty bucket but an old vase? It had a tight-fitting plug that I worked loose. Inside were rolled up parchments, and that's where this starts. Fortunately, I was able to unroll and separate the sheets without tearing them. They had Greek writing on them. Lots of it."

"You recognized it as Greek at the time?"

"I did. I took two years of Greek in my undergraduate days."

"You took Greek? Who takes Greek?"

"Nobody, but I have a keen interest in the Bible. I took Greek so I could translate the New Testament from the original texts. It's a hobby with me. The language has changed, by the way, and you wouldn't study New Testament Greek if you wanted to speak modern Greek.

Shall I go on?"

"Please do."

"It got late, and I had to hurry to catch the train, so I stretched the parchments out on the ground and took pictures. There were twenty-one pages in all."

"So, what did they say?"

"I didn't start the translations until I got back to school that fall. My Greek grammar was rusty, and I didn't exactly blaze through the project."

"So, what did they say?"

"They said to go to Melnikos and find a buried treasure. And the last page had a map with an 'X' on it."

"No it didn't."

"Okay, it didn't. I wanted to see if you were paying attention."

Her eyes rolled upward, then settled back on him as she took a deep breath, puffed her cheeks, and let it out slowly through pursed lips. "So…what did they say?"

"Do you want the long version or short?"

"Start with short. If I look interested, add detail."

"Those pages were a journal kept by Pilate's traveling secretary. Whoever the guy was, he apparently accompanied his boss on trips abroad, mostly to Rome. I'm sure Pilate had more staff in Palestine to keep daily logs of government business. Why this man in particular traveled with him, I can't say. On one particular trip to Rome, a storm disabled their ship, and severe winds blew them to a tiny island no one aboard knew about. It took a day for the weather to clear, and two more days to make repairs that allowed them to limp to Rome. I'll bet those two-thousand-year-old pieces of wood are from his ship. You with me so far?"

"Yes, Pilate's having a picnic on an island near Italy. Continue."

"It was no picnic. Something happened to him there, though, and I'm thinking he may have had a second encounter with Jesus. He'd been in a state of mental anguish, apparently for some time. The text doesn't describe it in detail, just says he'd been 'greatly troubled.' He spent time alone on the island, maybe two or three days waiting for repairs. When the ship limped into Messina, he caught another boat to Rome and made his report to Tiberius before returning to Palestine. The following year he made another trip to Rome, and another entry was added to the journal. This one mentioned a brief stop at that same island, only this time the secretary referred to it as 'Melnikos.' A single sentence said that Pilate left a small chest there as a memorial to Jesus. Nothing about where he put it. That trip turned out to be the last one described in the documents. So, do you see why I was interested in Melnikos?"

"Yes. I do. Now tell me how you found Melnikos."

"Well, I looked for historical references to Melnikos and didn't find a thing. So, I brought all my years of experience in the field of archaeology to bear and then, well, got lucky."

"Lucky? Come on."

"All right, according to the journal, the island had to be near the route from Palestine to Rome, but closer to Rome, and it had to be small and rocky. I found descriptions of several islands in that general vicinity in the U. S. Navy archives. The one I went to fit the criteria the best."

"How did you know where to look for the box once you got there?"

"The soil is too hard to dig, at least not without a lot of time and effort and tools, so I figured he hid it under a pile of rocks or in a cave. I laid out a grid and searched sectors, then repeated that same search pattern the second day. And the third."

"Let me guess your frame of mind at the end of the third day. Disappointment? Frustration?"

"Yeah, all of the above, and then some. God and I got into an argument that third night."

She laughed. "Really? Who argues with God?"

"Me. You don't? I figured he'd led me to that journal for a reason, so a quick trip to Melnikos to look for the box seemed reasonable. When it didn't turn up, I yelled at Him."

"That's bold. You didn't get struck by lightning?"

"No, but I did find the box the next morning, so we may be back on speaking terms."

"You're an interesting guy, Adam."

"Thanks, I think. Any more questions?"

"Well, yeah, you haven't told me where you found it."

"In a small cave."

"A cave you missed for three days?"

"Blame it on the Navy. They blasted the island to run the Germans off in World War II. When they did, they knocked off the top of a large rock formation near the cave. It fell and happened to cover the entrance. I flat missed it."

"Is that why it hadn't been found already?"

"Partly. Melnikos isn't in a shipping lane, and recreational boating didn't take off until after World War

II, for the most part. If the island had been closer to Italy, someone might have found it first, but nobody goes there. I didn't find one speck of trash. The cave itself is too small for anyone to crawl inside, plus Pilate blocked the entrance with a pile of rocks. After the Navy did their thing, it wasn't going to be found."

"Why were the documents you found in Italy written in Greek instead of Latin?"

"Hey, good question. You know a little history. Latin and Greek were both spoken by the educated in the Roman Empire. Greek must have been the preference for Pilate's secretary."

"All right, the vase. How old do you think it is? And the parchments, were they two thousand years old?"

"The vase dated to the early part of the twentieth century, so it wasn't old, but I knew that when I found it. I had an expert look at photos of it, and he agreed on the age. As for the parchment inside, I had radiocarbon dating done on a scrap at the bottom of the vase. Its shape fit a missing section of the last page like a jigsaw puzzle piece and had no writing on it. It came out the right age, sometime around the first century."

"No anachronisms in the text?"

"No anachronisms, no historical inconsistencies. In fact, there are details that will be of interest to historians. Luigi and I are working on a manuscript to get it published."

"Why didn't you keep the vase?"

"Luigi has it. And the documents. He'll put them on display when our paper comes out."

"Speaking of publishing, since radiocarbon dating on

the box says it's first century, what happens next? Or, hold that thought, let me stay on topic. How did those old parchments end up in a new vase?"

"I'm not sure. Italy experienced turmoil last century. They changed their government several times. Mussolini was ruthless. They saw Hitler burn books in a cultural purification. Someone wanted to protect those documents."

"It took you several years to go to Melnikos. Why so long?"

"My dissertation and job search took priority. I didn't pick the island until this past spring."

"How do you feel knowing you sat on that information for several years? That box would be in a museum by now, and you'd be famous. Where is it, by the way?"

"Not here. But I wasn't sitting on it that long, I don't think. And, I did make the trip the first chance I got after figuring out where to go."

"If you were a good archaeologist, would you have figured it out sooner?"

He stared at her again. Jill had that same teasing way about her. He loved it and always played along.

"Without a doubt, but I've never been able to compete with the best. I realize my career will be a dazzling display of mediocrity, and I'm okay with that."

"Liar."

He laughed. "But, as I said, this was not textbook archaeology."

"I know. I was kidding. Last question. Can you prove Pilate had anything to do with this?"

"Pilate? I'll talk to Brad about that. What we have now

may be enough. But Jesus? I doubt it. Not directly, at least. The symbolism is there, of course, but that's probably all we'll get."

"How would you even begin to try to link Jesus to the crown or whip?"

"God only knows. I'd say it's nearly impossible. Maybe you have some ideas?"

"No, but I do have one more question. This isn't really related to the box. That okay?"

"We'll see. Ask."

"In light of the existence of fossils millions of years old, when did God create Adam and Eve?"

He laughed. "Gee. Nobody's ever asked me that before. The short answer is, I don't know. Do you want the long answer?"

"Can you make it under thirty minutes? I have work to get back to."

"I'll make it under thirty seconds. There are fossils not just millions, but billions of years old. The earth has been here for about four and a half billion years. Life started maybe three billion years ago. Adam and Eve came along around fifty thousand years ago, more or less."

"*Homo sapiens* are older than that."

"They are, but not a whole lot."

"Explain, genius."

"All right. I'll give you my working theory. It's one that lets me enjoy archaeology and trust in the science underlying the estimation of elapsed time while believing in the God who created Adam and Eve."

"This ought to be good."

"Feel free to adopt it if you like it. So, here it is. The

earth is an unusual planet. Not just in the sense that life thrives here, but it's also the focus of an intense drama being played out in a dimension we don't normally have access to. Call it the spiritual dimension. By the way, there are probably thousands of planets capable of sustaining life in the universe, and I'm guessing many of them do have it in some form. How advanced? Who knows. Fun to think about. But getting back to earth, I speculate that what we have being played out before us is a confrontation between God and Satan. We not only have ringside seats, but we're also in the middle of it."

"My theory has God as the only entity capable of creation. He started our universe with the Big Bang and with certain physics constants that make life possible. He is a God of life. Satan may have been created to help administer life in the universe, but his free will brought him down when he entertained and acted on the idea that he could be a god himself. He rebelled and convinced a number of angels to join him. Rather than destroy the rebels immediately, God confined them all to earth. The purpose? To demonstrate the consequences of pride and disobedience. Satan and his cohorts would be allowed to oversee life here while the rest of the universe observed. Would he run the world for the benefit of its inhabitants or his own tyrannical pleasure? Would he ask God for help when things got complicated and needed a course correction? Or would he proudly muddle on and make a mess of things?"

"So, life began. Until I know otherwise, I'll give God credit for life on earth. It started somehow, possibly as simple biochemical replication systems that became more efficient over the vast amount of time and with the rich resources of the earth available. Microbes happened, multicellular life forms happened, plants and animals happened. Eventually, sentient beings arose—hominids who could think and reason and form their own judgments about good and evil. I doubt anyone back then would have considered their world a utopian existence—lots of killing and just plain evil. But life persisted, and the whole universe has watched this drama unfold over several billion years and have seen for themselves whether Satan has been a force for good or evil. The observers will have witnessed firsthand the spiritual changes that happen to a being who turns his back on God. Anyway, this drama is winding down but isn't over, and that's where Adam and Eve come in."

He finished his coffee and asked if she had any questions.

"Do you ever discuss this theory in class?"

"I try not to, but occasionally a student asks the same question you did. I tell them it's a theory that undergoes revision from time to time. It has sparked some interesting discussions. But it's an archaeology class, not religion, so we quickly move on."

"Sounds like Adam and Eve came along *en medias res*. Or maybe at the end of things."

"Aha! You do know more Latin than you let on. Well, yes, this theory has the pair showing up in the middle of things. The authority God gave Satan meant that He wouldn't arbitrarily intervene in the world to change the fates of living creatures, but when *Homo sapiens* came along, things changed. God felt compassion for them and decided to declare humans a special species, and set about to provide whatever hope he could under the rules He'd put Himself under. He chose to create a parallel set of humans whose mission in life would be to go out into the world and live their lives among the world's inhabitants."

"Adam and Eve were trained in the safety of the Garden of Eden before being let loose in the world. They would be under God's authority, however, not Satan's. While they had the advantages of God's protection and bodies with perfect genomes, once in the world, they were exposed to the same hardships as everyone else. When they persevered with joy and flourished, the world would know they were different. When others asked about that difference, they would be told about a God who loved them and had a better way for them. Adam and Eve were the first missionaries. How long that effort lasted, I don't know. Satan reacted maliciously to what he considered a threat to his dominion and threw everything he had at those two. Adam and Eve lost that encounter and, with it, their protection from God. Their DNA gradually degenerated to where they went from living forever to less than a hundred years in just a few generations. If it wasn't UV radiation, it was intermarrying with other humans that brought their kids all kinds of genetic problems. It didn't take long for their offspring to be indistinguishable from anyone else on earth. Great work, Satan. I suspect he forever sealed his fate with that, though it probably already was."

"There is a silver lining of sorts, however. Adam and Eve enriched the gene pool, probably in the area of intelligence and creativity. My colleagues talk about a leap forward in human development that happened tens of thousands of years ago. This could have been it. I give God credit for improving the lives of our species with that, but He didn't stop there. There was a second Adam."

"Let me guess. Jesus?"

"You know your Bible. Paul called him a 'second' or 'new' man. Same deal. Perfect genetics, sent to teach us about God's love. Satan tried to defeat him too. That's another story for another day. We both need to get back to work. Anyway, that's the working theory that lets me do archaeology without worrying about a timeline. I let science tell me what it can, and I let God tell me what He can, at least to the extent I can hear it. I would like to ask Him one day about my silly theory. If I ever see him, I'll do just that."

"You mean *when* you see Him?"

"I stand corrected. As usual."

CHAPTER ELEVEN

Adam drove his '97 RAV4 to Fort Worth the third weekend in September to watch a football game with Brad. He met his former mentor at a barbecue joint near the stadium three hours before game time. They ordered a platter of brisket for two that came with a big slab of cheese, a sliced onion, bread, and drinks.

"Smells great in here," he said. "Must be a smoker out back."

"There is," Brad said, handing him one of the two tickets. "Let me give this to you now in case we happen to get separated on our way to the stadium."

"Wow, forty-yard line, fifteen rows up. Not bad."

"No, not bad. I have friends. Anyway, what shall we talk about?"

"Are you kidding? You're kidding. Let's talk about how you want to help me with the box."

"As I figured. However, all I know is that you brought a box back from Italy. You never told me what was in it."

"That's why I'm here," he said, sliding a packet of photographs across the table. "Take a look."

The Texas Tech professor emptied the envelope and examined each photo, saying nothing until he had finished the entire stack.

"Interesting. Now, what was really inside that box?"

The waiter cut him off as he lowered two long sheets of butcher paper with their food onto the table and spread them apart.

"I'll be right back with your drinks."

He waited until the large Styrofoam cups of tea were placed in front of them before answering the question. "C'mon, you know me. I'm not good at practical jokes. Tell you what, look at this."

He handed him three pages of radiocarbon dating analysis.

"Ninety-five percent probability first century on everything," Brad noted. "So the box is consistent with Pilate's lifetime. And these results apply to the box itself and everything in it?"

"They do. Here, this should convince you." He held his smartphone so Brad could watch a video clip. "You're looking at the box the moment we opened it. And, here— this is a copy of the X-ray image the TSA agent in Rome gave me. Are you satisfied now?"

"Yes, yes, I'm satisfied. But, I'm also, what, astonished, I guess. I don't know what to make of it. Help me out here."

"If you're asking about the crown and the whip, my best guess is that the crown was a replica, and the whip was one of dozens available to Pilate. They're symbolic. Recall the journals. Pilate had a mental crisis on Melnikos when his ship nearly sank in the Mediterranean. That was about three years after the crucifixion. My theory is that he converted to Christianity shortly after that near-disaster and hid the box in a cave on Melnikos on his next trip to Rome."

"A memorial to Jesus?"

"Yes. The items inside the box obviously had special meaning."

"Confessing his guilt?"

"Or acknowledging his role in the whole thing. And mad at himself for letting the Jewish leaders get the better of him that day."

"I suppose that makes sense. What did you think when you saw the X-ray?"

"Oh, you know me. I'm a slow thinker. It didn't dawn on me until halfway across the Atlantic what these were. Then I went through every emotion, including fear."

"Fear?"

"You ever see *Raiders of the Lost Ark*?"

"What self-respecting archaeologist hasn't?"

"Remember when they opened the lid of the ark?"

"Ah, yes, I see what you mean. Open the box, and your face melts. You were afraid of that?"

"No, not really, but God and I have a rocky relationship. And I did consider the possibility this was a hoax."

"You think God plays practical jokes?"

"Sometimes, it seems like I don't know anything at all about Him. But think about it. Who am I to find that box? A novice. Barely out of grad school."

"Yeah, but you learned from the best. Me. You consulted with me along the way, and I didn't see anything that would suggest this could have been a hoax. You're a good archaeologist; don't sell yourself short."

"I appreciate that. Thanks."

"So have you completely ruled out the crown or whip being the originals?"

"Seriously? No, I haven't given it much thought. How would I prove that?"

"I don't know, DNA?"

"Oh sure, we compare DNA on the crown or the whip to…what? Look, technically, I don't even have to prove Pilate put the box on that island. I tell the story as it is and let people decide on their own. The box is old. The documents suggest Pilate put it there. But the Jesus connection? I'll think about it, but I don't know how to get there."

Hungry patrons had filled the restaurant by then, forcing them to speak in hushed voices. They ate a good portion of their meal before resuming the discussion.

"So, what can I do?"

"Help shore up the evidence that the box belonged to Pilate. For starters, can you find out what's available in the historical records about the guy? I've browsed a few sources and didn't find much, but that's your specialty. You know a lot more experts on the first-century world than I do."

"Done."

"And show those pictures of the whip and the box to your contacts. Ask them if they look anything like other pieces in Palestine during Pilate's governorship."

"I can do that too. In fact, I have a friend in Damascus, a curator at the museum there. He can answer that. Do you know what species of wood it is?"

"The box? No, but it has a faint smell of cedar. As for the whip, I don't know."

"Well, try to nail that down; it could be important."

"And then there's the thorny vine shaped like a crown. Dr. Walsh is researching that. She's hoping to find a genetic test to distinguish between several plant species that look like the one we have."

"Dr. Walsh?"

"Yeah, a new professor of cell biology at Baylor."

"No kidding? A cell biologist? How in the world did she get involved?"

"Luck of the draw. We send our samples out for carbon dating through the biology department. She drew the assignment. It went from there."

"This Dr. Walsh, she has time for this? She's an assistant professor who I assume is working toward tenure, and she has time for side projects?"

"That's another story, but, yes, right now, she does. She may not be at Baylor long. Seems the retiree she replaced is coming back."

"Ah, I bet that's a bit sticky."

"It is."

"By the way, how old is she? Is she married or dating anyone?"

"Why do you want to know that?"

"Because you're not married, and I've been working on that for a long time."

"Did I ever show you a picture of Jill?"

"I don't think so. Why?"

From his backpack, he pulled out a large envelope containing documents and photos and found one of Mary holding the crown of thorns. He took the picture of Jill from his wallet and showed both to Brad.

"Oh my God, the resemblance. That's amazing. That had to hit you like a ton of bricks."

"I made a fool of myself in her office. I froze. I couldn't move or speak for what seemed like minutes, though it was only a few seconds."

"So, can you get past that and ask her out?"

"Because she looks like Jill? And because she's nice and helpful and easygoing and intelligent and attractive? Actually, I did buy her coffee the other day when I gave her the background on Melnikos."

"Well, good to have her on board, she seems like a valuable asset. And you should ask her out to dinner."

"And you should stick to teaching archaeology."

"That's what my kids tell me when I give them advice. Anyway, you're making progress. Let me ask you, who knows about the box?"

"Us three. And my parents. I'd like to keep this on a need-to-know basis, and, basically, no one else needs to know. Can your friend in Damascus be discreet?"

"I've known him for twenty years. I think so. I won't have to give him much context. He'll understand, and he'll be able to tell us whether the box or the whip could have been made or used in Palestine during the first century."

The dinner crowd had begun to thin out, most heading toward the stadium, prompting Brad to suggest they leave as well.

"Before we go, look at the writing on the piece of papyrus," he said, pointing to the photo on the table. "Do you know Latin?"

"Sure, well, some, anyway. I'm a little rusty." He studied the picture for a minute. "Looks like something about hands and feet. They've been bathed or cleaned or something. Am I close?"

"Yes. It says, 'I washed my hands, you wash my feet.' It's signed, 'your ever grateful servant Pontius Pilate.'"

"Interesting, but what does it mean?"

"The best I can figure out is that he regretted his part in Jesus' death. Pilate washed his hands during the trial and absolved himself of responsibility for the outcome. The 'you wash my feet' part may refer to Jesus' statement that his disciples didn't need to be washed all over, that his washing of their feet was sufficient."

"Sufficient for what?"

"I think it was Jesus' way of saying that the outward washing of their bodies in baptism was allegorical. It signified that their inner man had been cleansed of sin. The foot-washing suggested that only their feet needed to be cleaned daily, not their whole bodies, as in baptism. In other words, baptism was a one-time thing when they were completely forgiven of their sins. They got their feet dirty walking around the countryside, which represented daily activities when they would occasionally sin. Foot-washing got them back to a clean slate, so to speak."

"So Pilate was saying what, that he considered himself a believer? That he was past the baptism part and was receiving spiritual foot-washings from Jesus? That would seem to confirm your theory that he became a Christian."

"If I'm right about what his words mean, then, yes, it does."

"Send me a scan of that papyrus, and I'll see if there's

a way to compare it to documents in a Roman Empire database. Unlikely to find a match, but it's worth a shot."

"I'll send you a scan. In the meantime, you can have this photo. By the way, do you have time for this?"

"I'll make time."

"All right. Thank you. I guess we'd better get to the game. Who am I cheering for, by the way?"

CHAPTER TWELVE

✛

Adam delivered the first Archaeology 101 lecture of the fall semester and then dressed for a run. On his way to the track, he stopped by the biology building to pay Mary a visit. When he reached her open door, she waved him in.

"Hi, Adam, come in, come in. I was about to call you. Do you know what this is?" She handed him a photo.

"It reminds me of an electrophoresis experiment I botched in biochem lab. You ran my reactions?"

"Very good. You did nice work. Know what it says?"

"Let's see, single bands in some lanes, nothing in others. No, I need to know what was in each lane."

"Here's the notebook."

He looked at the list of reactions and their corresponding lanes on the agarose gel. He put marks next to the positive reactions, then looked to see which DNA primers he'd used on which samples. "My God, that piece of tissue is human. Isn't it?"

"It is."

He stared out her office window, looking at nothing

in particular, feeling his way into the chair behind him.

"Adam?"

"Yes?"

"What are you thinking?"

"Ouch. Poor guy. But it doesn't mean it's from Jesus, of course."

"No, it doesn't."

"What do we do with it, though? How do we explain it?"

"The victim of a brutal whipping had a chunk of tissue ripped from his back, one that resisted degradation for two thousand years. At least it was intact enough to let us do PCR analysis."

"That's hard to believe without a preservative like ice or amber," he said. "By the way, if there happened to be blood on the thorns, is there a chance of finding it after all this time?"

"No, not likely. Certainly not whole cells. Fragments of hemoglobin or human peptides? They may still be detectable. That isn't my field, but I can look into it. And I can see if a microscope can tell us anything."

"I was thinking that if Pilate had made a mock-up of sorts, for whatever reason, there wouldn't be blood on it."

"Unless he stuck himself," she said. "Those thorns are sharp, even after all this time."

"Okay, I'll bring the box in. There were a couple of loose thorns in the bottom, and then there's the rest of the intact crown. Do you have a safe place to store it? A cabinet that can be locked would be nice."

"We do have a flammables cabinet—"

"Flammables? I don't think so."

"If you'd let me finish, I was about to say we have a new flammables cabinet that's still empty, and it can be locked."

"Oh. Okay, good."

"You coming from class?" she asked, pointing to his clothes.

"Funny. No, I thought I'd go for a run."

"You run too?"

"A few miles, several times a week. How about you?"

"As often as I can. I like to alternate short runs with longer ones."

"What's short? What's long?"

"Short is three miles or less. Long is, well, anything longer than three miles. Monday I ran a quick two miles, yesterday I did five. Can I join you?"

"Sure. You free now?"

"I am."

"Well, how about three miles?"

"Sounds good. If you leave my office for a few minutes, I'll get changed."

"I'll be outside, stretching."

*

He found a spot under an old oak tree and did his pre-run ritual. Mary joined him and stretched also.

"Where's your three-mile course?"

"Starts at the center of campus."

They reached the spot and took off together at a leisurely pace, his route taking them mostly around the edge of campus. They passed what appeared to be a daycare, with kids running around and having fun on the playground equipment.

"Ah, the good old days," he said.

"Not too hard to imagine you as a kid. What did you like to do?"

"I dug holes and looked for buried treasure while you dissected frogs."

"Not at recess. I was too busy outrunning all the boys who chased me."

"Running away from the boys. I see. Did you ever get caught?"

"Now that you ask, no, I never did."

"Did you ever want to?"

"Ummm…"

They found their way back to campus and the spot where they'd started. He walked her back to the biology building but stopped first at the oak tree for post-run stretching.

"Thanks for the run. I enjoyed it," she said. "I'd better get a shower and eat lunch. I have a meeting with Ed at one o'clock. I'm glad you stopped by."

CHAPTER THIRTEEN

"Hello, Adam, are you busy?"

"I always have time for you, Brad. What's up?"

"My contact in Syria confirmed that the design and construction of the box are consistent with the early-middle Roman Empire. And that's not all. His museum has a whip nearly identical to the one you found on Melnikos, and it's also from that time period."

"Well, we knew that from carbon dating. What I need to know is whether they were common to that region. Did you ask him that?"

"I did. He said he thought so and would do a little research on that and get back to me."

"Okay, great. So far, so good, sounds like. Thanks for the call."

He found an email from Mary in his inbox. It had been over a week since he'd heard from her. It said she had news, but it came with a catch. He had to beat her in a five-mile run tomorrow. If she won, he had to buy lunch. If he won, she would buy and tell him the news. Nothing about when, or whether, he'd get the news if she won.

Ah, a challenge. Seriously? Well, you're on, missy. I can wait a day. Can't be too important, or she wouldn't have made it conditional. They met at the Baylor track the next day, a Saturday, at nine in the morning. After a brief bit of small talk, they warmed up, stretched, and got psyched for the race.

"Good luck. You'll need it," he said, getting into position at the starting line.

"Thanks. I don't mind buying you lunch. I guess I owe you for the fun I've had on this little project. It's been exciting."

"Well, I owe you a lot too."

"However, I don't think I'll be buying lunch today."

"Is that so?"

"That's so. Hey, what's that over there?"

He turned to look but didn't see anything, and then heard the sound of shoes hitting the all-weather track. "Why you little—" He laughed and took off after her. He chased her around the first curve and caught her on the backstretch.

"You have a nice stride," he said. "I can see you're a good runner. The question is, do you have the endurance? You suggested five miles, so maybe you do. I guess it comes down to your speed. I doubt you can keep up with a guy, though."

She smiled but didn't take the bait. In a counter move, she complimented him instead. "You have a nice, long stride yourself. You make running look easy, effortless. I may have underestimated you."

"A lot of people do."

He picked up the pace after the first two laps, which he essentially used as warm-ups, and built a lead. After the first mile, he looked back to find her. Hmm, she's hanging in there. Only fifty yards back, not bad. The lead lengthened to a hundred yards after two miles. He tried to demoralize her by running a fast third mile, which got him a half-lap lead. Two miles to go. It's in the bag. She's buying. His significant lead allowed him to glance left and follow her progress around the track. So graceful. So agile. He imagined what it would be like to go places with her, do things together, enjoy her company. Wow, I haven't had that feeling since…since Jill. Sorry, honey. Won't happen again. Two laps later, he looked to his left but didn't see her; she'd closed the gap to a quarter-lap. Nothing to worry about, plenty left in the tank. She moved to within fifty yards at the four-mile point. He kept a close watch on his lead, determined to kick it up a notch if she got closer. Which she did. Steadily. Methodically. Two laps to go, and he could hear her shoes hitting the track. With one lap left, they crossed the start/finish line side-by-side. He strained to gain speed, but it was useless. She took off and beat him to the finish line by seven seconds. He crossed it panting, staring at her, his face contorted into a big question mark.

"I ran track in college," she confessed. "Did the fifteen hundred and three thousand meter races at UT. Took third place at the NCAAs in the three thousand my senior year."

"Why didn't you ever tell me that?"

"You never asked. And now you owe me lunch."

"That's not fair. You sandbagged me."

"All's fair when you're a girl competing against a boy."

"Never heard that rule before. Does this mean you won't tell me the news?"

"I'll tell you when you beat me in a race."

"Oh, come on. It's obvious I can't beat you."

"Okay, okay, whiner. Buy me lunch, and I'll tell you what I have."

"It's early for lunch. Why don't we sit in the shade and bring each other up to date."

They sipped their water bottles on the walk back to campus. Near the biology building, they found a large pecan tree that served their purpose and sat down.

"You first, since I won."

"All right," he said and told her the news from Brad's contact in Syria. "That's all I have. Your turn."

"The crown of thorns. It's Calicotome villosa."

"Never heard of it. How did you determine that?"

"I simply looked at images of thorny vines on the internet. Two that look similar to ours are indigenous to the Middle East. So, I did a little research, and it turns out they have genetic markers that make them amenable to identification by PCR. We ordered primers and did the reactions. The results are clear. *Calicotome villosa.*"

"Are you serious? Just like that? Wow, you're good. So, they're native to the Middle East. Do they also grow in Europe?"

"Eastern Mediterranean is what I recall about their habitat. I don't know about Europe, but I can find out. Why?"

"I had a theory that after his shipwreck, Pilate found a thorny shrub in Italy and made a crown out of it. Hung on to it until his return to Melnikos. But, since it grows in Palestine, that point is moot. By the way, you said I had to pay for reagents."

"Primers are way too cheap to worry about. And PCR reactions are trivial, but, I'll send you a catalog number of something we need. You get it, and we'll call it even."

"Fair enough. Thanks. This is progress."

"Wait, there's more. I also looked at the tips of several thorns, the ones I could maneuver under a low-magnification lens."

"And?"

"Some are discolored."

"Can I look at them?"

"Of course. Come by the lab anytime."

"So, when you say discolored, what does that mean?"

"The crown has two kinds of thorns. They're all a dull gray, but some are darker than others at the tips."

"I don't suppose you can tell if it's blood, can you?"

"Possibly, with mass spectroscopy," she said. "Can you talk to your friends in the chemistry department and see if they'll analyze our samples?"

"What will I have to tell them? About the source of the material, that is."

"Keep it vague. They work with unusual samples all the time, but tell them you're interested in human peptides and hemoglobin."

"Suggesting blood. Got it."

"Oh, one more little detail," she said.

"Yes?"

"The thorns with dark tips, well, they all face away from the plane of the crown, and are all on one side pointing the same way."

He closed his eyes a moment and visualized what she'd said. "Wow. Like it sat on someone's head and pierced the scalp. I don't know if I'm ready for this. Are you?"

She didn't answer, having lain back on the ground, looking into the bright blue sky, which hosted a handful of cirrus clouds. Her eyes glistened as they surveyed the vast expanse. He caught her wiping away a tear.

"I guess you aren't either."

"Oh, no," she said, smiling. "No, I was thinking about my parents. I'd love to be able to tell them about this."

"You can. We can't keep this to ourselves much longer anyway."

"No, my parents died when I was eleven. I wish they were here. They would go crazy if they knew what I was doing. Especially if we can somehow prove it's Jesus' blood on those thorns."

"Oh, Mary, I'm so sorry. I'm sure they'd be extremely proud of you, even apart from this project. Don't you think?"

"That's kind of you to say."

He lay back and gazed at nothing in particular. The leaves of the tree above remained motionless beneath the azure sky. The sounds of a few students milling about and traffic in the distance seemed like so much muffled background noise. Time hesitated.

"They died instantly, in a car wreck. Drunk driver."

"Aw, that's awful," he said, sitting back up. "I hope they fried the guy."

"No. In fact, he got out on parole last year. A young guy, pushing forty now. Threw his life away."

"And took yours from you."

"My brother Keith and I went to live with my aunt and uncle. They had a ranch outside Kerrville. Aunt Aubrey died two years ago. Uncle Frank passed away last year. They weren't Mom and Dad, but they were the next best thing. I miss them."

"And Keith? What's he doing?"

"He's in the army. Special Forces. I see him once in a while, but he's gone a lot. He doesn't tell me where he goes. Says I'm better off not knowing."

"Is he older or younger than you?"

"Two years older. His outfit is at Fort Belvoir. He's married and has a little boy. How about you? Do you have brothers or sisters?"

"Two mangy brothers, two great parents. The folks are in Abilene. Middle child David is a state trooper, lives in Sweetwater. Baby brother John is in San Angelo working for the Parks and Wildlife Department."

"Cool. Does he like to hunt or fish?"

"Both. He's a better hunter, but I'm a better fisherman."

"I like to fish."

"You can't. Girls don't like to fish."

"I hunt, too."

"Dadgummit, girl, what don't you do?"

"Windows."

He laughed. "I bet you do those too. You seem to like to work and be busy. I envy you. I tend to be on the lazy side."

"Right. Which is why you just made the most important discovery of all time."

Her words gave him pause. He hadn't allowed himself to think about the possibility that the box he'd discovered actually contained the crown of thorns the Romans put on Jesus' head or the whip they beat him with. Her comment forced him to confront those thoughts.

"Presumptuous?" she asked.

"Yes. Yes, I think so. We can't say that yet. There's still a lot of work to do. Several things have to fall our way. Speaking of which, anything new on that piece of tissue?"

"Oh, I meant to tell you. I cut off a small piece and put it in sterile water. You should see it. It's rehydrating, resuming a normal shape."

"Is that surprising?"

"Well, I've never seen it before. Usually, when tissues dry out, the cell membranes crack, and they don't recover. But these are different. Like they've been preserved somehow, protected from desiccation. If it's okay with you, I may play with them."

"Play?"

"Yeah, like, see if they have residual metabolism. If the membranes are intact, functional proteins may still be present. I can do three or four simple enzyme assays to show that."

"Of course. Do whatever you want. Meanwhile, I've been putting together a manuscript. Like you, I need publications. I'd like you to write a section on the analysis you've been doing. You okay with that?"

"Sure."

"Wouldn't it be odd if the first paper you're an author on from Baylor is in an archaeological journal?"

She smiled, the kind of smile that told him there was

something he didn't know.

"Oh, of course, I should have guessed," he said. "You've already written a paper, probably two since you've been here. You work fast, girl."

"We submitted a manuscript last week. Don't forget I've been involved in research here since May."

"Well, want lunch? I'm buying."

CHAPTER FOURTEEN

Clark fired up the grill and cooked burgers in the backyard while enjoying a local craft beer. Vanessa returned from a shift at the hospital at seven-thirty and greeted him with a lusty hug, then went back inside to change clothes. Off came suit pants and blouse, on went a sleek top and shorts. She didn't bother with shoes.

"How was your day, Richie boy?"

"Sucked. Yours?"

"Uh-oh, new vector not working?"

"It works fine in tissue culture, not so well in mice. Better than the last vector, but I don't know if it'll be enough for diabetic monkeys."

"Do you have a solution?"

He flipped the burgers and stirred the onions and mushrooms sautéing on the side burner, and thought about the question. Vanessa poured a glass of wine, then stood next to the grill and watched him perform his magic. "You ever lose EVI, you could be a chef."

"A little late to change careers. Anyway, we'll probably

test it in monkeys and hope for the best. The promoter we fixed works better in monkeys than in mice. It's supposed to. It was designed for them. We'll have to keep our fingers crossed that it works out that way. I just hoped to see better performance in mice."

"Will you have time for the clinic? We need to start thinking about renting or owning, or even building. Getting permits and financing and all that. I need you and your MBA, big guy."

"It'd be nice to start off in a new facility with new equipment. I have to believe we can get a loan large enough to cover a state-of-the-art facility without going public. Location is important. We could look for an older building in a prime spot, tear it down, and build a new one. Want me to contact a realtor?"

"Yes. I'd like that."

He tested the temperature of the burgers with a food thermometer. "Looks like they're done."

She sat in a chair at the glass table on the patio and assembled her hamburger from the assortment of buns, tomatoes, lettuce, and condiments he'd brought to the table.

"You'll make a killing with those precious little Beverly Hills snobs," he said. "They have lots of money to spend and no brains to tell them where to spend it. You could probably sell them on designer babies."

"Right. And when the little wunderkinds turn out average? I get sued."

"I wasn't serious."

"I know. I won't make promises, just pregnancies."

"That's smart. But you're always smart. I should hire

you. I might get experiments to work once in a while."

"Well, you got the grill to work on your own."

He glared at her, then smiled. "Funny."

"This isn't half bad. Thanks for cooking, handsome."

"You're quite welcome. But you get to clean up, so it was worth the effort. Why don't I help you and then we can relax in the pool with a margarita?"

"You read my mind, sweetie. But this burger is so good it'll take me a while to finish. I want to savor every bite."

"And I want to savor you."

"You will. Later. Hey, wait a sec. Did you go to the gym today? I can't canoodle with a man who isn't keeping himself svelte for me."

"I went yesterday. It isn't good to work out every day."

"Wrong. It may not be good to lift weights every day, but you need to exercise every…stinking…day. Am I not the doctor here?"

"The MD, but I'm the PhD, the one who actually knows a little science."

"Cell biology, maybe. But you don't know jack about physiology. I do, and I'm telling you, we need cardio every day to stay in shape and keep the internal organs happy and healthy. Especially that brain. Which needs help because you forgot I also have a PhD."

She threw a french fry at him that bounced off his shirt.

"See? See what's happened to your hand-eye coordination? You can't even catch a french fry, for Christ's sake."

He tossed one back at her. "Food fight?"

"Oh, God, are we eighteen again?"

"Oh, to be. We're stuck in mid-life, I'm afraid."

"Who's we? You're the one about to turn forty. I only keep you around because you can make my clinic dream come true."

"You're not that far behind, Miss Thirty-five. You're on the downhill slide to forty yourself."

"Do you know how silly that sounds? How many beers did you have before I got home?"

"Working on my second, actually. C'mon, let's go with that burger, I'm getting in the pool, and I don't want you far behind."

"I thought you said you'd help clean up." She took another bite.

"I was until you made fun of my age. Okay, Okay. I'll wait. Tell me how your day went."

"I delivered a baby today."

"Oh, wow, good for you. What's that, your fifth? Sixth? How was it?"

"Fantastic. And it was number seven, but who's counting?"

"Everyone doing okay?"

"Everyone's fine. The dad nearly passed out. But I'll cut him some slack. He worked all day yesterday and helped his wife get through early labor during the night. The mother was a trooper, though. I wish all my patients could be like her."

"Well, that's why they'll pay you the big bucks, for handling the tough cases."

"I'll be happy to take the big bucks, but I'll have trouble if I ever lose a patient."

"So, don't lose any."

"Every doctor loses patients. I hope I can handle it when it happens. You'll have to be there for me when it does."

"I'll be there. But at least you aren't in geriatrics. Most of your patients will be young and healthy."

"Exactly right, and when it does happen, it'll be that much more tragic. A geriatric has lived a long life, often a good one. You don't expect a young mother to die."

"As I said, you're smart. Figure out how to keep them healthy. Work hard to get to know the little darlings. Keep them well, then take their money and send them home."

She took the last bite of her hamburger, chewed it slowly, and stared at the table. "Yeah, I guess that's all I can do."

"I'll take care of the grill and clear the table," he said. "You square away the kitchen, and I'll meet you in the water."

"Ooh. I love it when you give orders."

"Just don't be slow about it."

"I'm never slow. It only appears that way so I don't embarrass you, what with your advancing age and all."

He laughed. "My, but you're sassy."

"Good thing you like sass."

CHAPTER FIFTEEN

✛

A dam downloaded the large file containing the results of the mass spectroscopic analysis of the slivers taken from the crown of thorns. He studied the first several pages of the report and realized he could not surprise Mary with his understanding of any of it. *This is a foreign language. And now I have to wait for the translation—only one thing to do.*

"Hey. I want a rematch. Tomorrow morning. Nine o'clock. Three miles this time. I think I can take you at that distance."

"Hello? Who is this, please?"

"Smart aleck."

"Oh, wait, Adam? Adam Garrett, is it?"

"Quit stalling. You know I can beat you at three miles."

"Hi, Adam. I'm sure that's quite right. What are the stakes this time?"

"You choose."

"Dinner," she said.

"Double or nothing? Dinner and a football game?"

"We both have faculty football tickets, Adam, that wouldn't count. How about if I win I give you credit for a Dutch treat for the football game and you get to pay for the dinner?"

"Fine, but you won't win. If you do, though, we'll make it dinner, football game, and I tell you the mass spec results."

"Really?" she asked, sarcasm dripping. "Oh, I can't wait to go to a fast-food joint, then to a football game I already have a ticket for, and top it all off with a discussion of the mass spec analysis of your archaeological relics. You know how to impress a girl."

"You know I don't do fast food. And you're a scientist, you're into this now, so you know you're curious about the data. As for the football game, okay, that's a freebie."

"Ah, you fell for that one," she said. "You should have said spending time with wonderful you at the football game would benefit me, even if you don't pay for the ticket."

"Don't know how I missed that. So, nine o'clock?"

"Nine o'clock. But what's the news? Why don't you tell me now?"

"I can't tell you now."

"Why not?"

"I don't know what the numbers and letters on these spreadsheets mean."

"It's mass spec data. Send it to me, knucklehead."

"When can you work on it?"

"Now. Send it."

"I knew you were into this. So will I have to win the race tomorrow for you to tell me what it means?"

"Absolutely. So eat a decent meal tonight and get a good night's sleep. And run for your life tomorrow. You might have a chance at the shorter distance."

*

Mary beat him by five seconds. She did let him lead the first ten laps, but then slipped past him at the end and cruised to the win. They walked back to campus and did the cool-down routine under the oak tree.

"Okay, you owe me dinner. Before or after the game? What time does it even start?"

"Afternoon game. It's on TV at two-thirty. We can plan for dinner at about seven o'clock. So, tell me what the data meant. Did they find anything on the thorns?"

"They did. The data you saw was a list of peptides identified by the mass spectrometer. Lots of plant peptides, but guess what else?"

"Uh…blood?"

"No, not blood, but evidence of it. Human hemoglobin peptide fragments."

"No kidding?" he said. "Wow. That's evidence of human blood, though, because plants don't make hemoglobin peptides, right?"

"Right. They also detected fragments of human keratin and collagen, which are present in skin."

"So both blood and skin. Fantastic."

"I gave you four samples. Three were tip-ends taken from thorns that pointed downward, the ones that looked discolored. The fourth came from a thorn pointing the other direction. Only the three pointing down came back positive for skin and blood peptides, the one pointing up did not."

"So those thorns were on somebody's head."

"Or pressed against their body somewhere," she said. "That's what it looks like. I have more news. Remember that chunk of tissue I let rehydrate?"

"I do."

"I cut off a thin section and put it into a cellular growth medium."

"And?"

"Hold onto your hat. It's growing. Those enzyme assays I told you about? They worked. And those cells looked so good after weeks of rehydration that I thought I'd see if they had other metabolic capabilities. I didn't expect them to resume growth. I thought they'd take up a few nutrients through broken membranes and catalyze a few reactions, but not grow to where they start dividing."

"Two thousand years old, and it's growing?"

"We didn't actually do radiocarbon dating on it," she said. "Everything else, but not that tissue fragment. And it's too late, because now that it's growing it's taking in new carbon."

"That's too bad. I wish we'd have thought of that at the time."

"Well, guess what?"

"You have another way to tell its age?"

"No, but I have a lot more fragments to work with. I gave those bone shards a thorough microscopic exam yesterday. There are small chunks of tissue everywhere."

"Really? Did they look anything like the first piece?"

"They're similar. Thin and dry. I even found two or three pieces as big as the one I pulled out that first night. I put a bunch in solution to see if they'd rehydrate, and I sent four off for radiocarbon dating. Last night I did PCR on small slices of all of the ones I collected. They're all human, Adam. Human."

"They beat the tar out of this guy, looks like. Unless it was more than one. I guess we don't know if this is one man or fifty getting whipped?"

"No, but we may be able to figure that out with PCR profiling. My guess is that it's the same guy."

"Or what's left of him."

*

They didn't talk much about Melnikos at the football game. Instead, they discussed their former lives, their families, what they did in high school, friends they'd left along the way. The game had gotten out of reach by the fourth quarter. Baylor ran and threw the ball with little opposition, and the score showed it. When fans began leaving midway through the fourth quarter, they joined them. They headed for his car and the short ride to the restaurant Mary chose. Once again, he would pay for the meal.

"Mary, you could have had your pick of the most popular guys in high school or college. What happened?" he asked, opening her car door.

"I could say the same about you. Why aren't you married or dating, Adam? I take you as someone who needs a mother figure in your life. I bet your apartment is a mess."

He got in the driver's side, backed the car out, and left the faculty parking lot. They headed for Alexander's, one of the better steakhouses around.

"Uh-huh. You answer my question first. Why don't you have a boyfriend?"

"I'll meet someone someday. I'm giving them more time to mature. Your turn."

"Someone like me, then? Mature?" he grinned.

"Yes, someone like you. You put on a good show, but you've matured past the selfish stage. Many guys your age are still a work in progress."

"I put on a good show?"

"Yes, you try to act younger. You make wisecracks, tell corny jokes, horse around," she said. "But deep down, you don't think only of yourself. I like that about you. Now, if your jokes were funny, you'd be darn near perfect. I'm surprised you aren't in a relationship. You're a catch."

"You're too kind. But I like it. And I sort of like you."

"I like you too, Adam, but I don't know if you're my type."

"What is your type?"

"All right, I'll tell you. I haven't had a serious relationship with a guy because I've been so focused on science and my career, but also because no one I've ever met has stood out. So the answer is, I don't know what my type is."

"So, what, you'll know him when you see him?"

"I suppose."

"Don't wait for Mr. Perfect. I hear he doesn't exist."

"You're right there. Except for my dad. He was perfect. At least that's how I remember him."

"I would have liked to have met your dad and your mom," he said, pulling into the restaurant's parking lot. "Here we are. Time for me to pay up. Shall we?"

"Let's. And thanks for being such a good sport about this morning."

"You won by what, two seconds?"

"Five, but that's all I was shooting for. And I told you I'd be happy to go to the game with a loser."

"You sure know how to make a guy feel good. Why don't you order a thirty-two-ounce porterhouse and set me back a hundred bucks to complete the evening?"

"I should, just to teach you to watch that sarcastic tongue. However, I'm a filet girl. Angus, of course."

"Of course."

CHAPTER SIXTEEN

C lark convened a meeting of his top scientists to plan the upcoming monkey trials. He told them that if their diabetic monkeys didn't make enough insulin to control blood sugar levels correctly, the investors who financed the venture would likely cut ties with EVI. His company had funding for only two other projects, both smaller in scope and already fully staffed. Personnel would receive termination notices based on seniority if the experiment failed. They could not afford mistakes in the next three months. He implored them to pay attention to detail and not ignore even the smallest of problems.

"Today I'd like to discuss the calendar, when the monkeys are to arrive, when we inject vectors, when we bleed, and so forth. Think logistics. Think about what you'll need at each stage. If it's supplies, check stocks and order now if you're not sure you have enough. I don't mind a little excess, we have storage space, but we absolutely cannot afford to get caught short."

Back in his office, he woke his cell phone. According

to the log, Vanessa had called during the meeting with his senior staff. She didn't leave a message, so he dialed her number, but the call went to voicemail. He left a hello and a brief message.

That afternoon he put on his rainmaker hat and called the potential funding sources to whom he'd sent proposals. None were ready to commit to EVI; all were in the review and evaluation phase and would not have an answer for him for several weeks. He made calls to former colleagues who might need corporate help with an ongoing project or might know of someone interested in investing with EVI. Nothing. The well was dry. It had never been this bad.

By the end of the day, he found himself in serious need of a workout. On the way to the gym, he tried to reach Vanessa, but she didn't answer. That wasn't unusual. She turned her phone off when she examined patients or otherwise didn't want to be distracted.

At the gym, he started with five minutes of jumping rope, followed by five minutes of stretching, then moved to the weight room. He added extra weight to the amounts he usually lifted at each station, thinking a tougher workout would help get rid of the frustration that clung to him like damp clothes. He didn't like it when business realities interfered with science. Nor did he like not having the time to help Vanessa during the initial phase of getting her clinic off the ground.

When he finished weightlifting, with more energy to burn, he joined a pick-up basketball game. The friendly contest allowed him to forget the issues at EVI, for a while at least. At six feet, three inches tall, he often had a height advantage and played close to the basket where he could physically mix it up with the others. His weight training helped him stand his ground, and other teams could not back him away from the rim. He out-rebounded everyone that night.

A staff member blew his whistle. "Five minutes, league game starts at seven."

"Seven? Geez, how'd it get that late?"

No one answered. They'd run down the court on a fast break, so he gave chase. When the five minutes elapsed, the game ended, and they all shook hands. He headed to the steam room where he could be alone with his thoughts. The problems at EVI came back, but he was in a better mood to deal with them. The workout had done its job.

On his way out, he finally reached Vanessa, who said she was at home, curled up on the sofa with a romance novel and a glass of wine. She accepted his offer to pick up takeout sushi, and when they resumed their conversation at the dining table, she told him about her meeting with a real estate agent during lunch. They had driven to two vacant buildings not far from the part of town where she wanted to locate her practice.

"Neither grabbed me, but I'd still like you to look at them."

"Happy to, dear."

"You're a better abstract thinker than me. You envision renovations better; you know how rooms will look after moving furniture and equipment around or adding new construction."

"And you know what you want in the way of accents, colors, final touches, those sorts of things. I do the grunt work, and you do the finesse work. Right?"

"That's right."

"Okay, I promise I'll find time to look at those buildings."

CHAPTER SEVENTEEN

Clark praised his team during the morning meeting. "Good work, guys. Great work. Looks like this went off without a hitch. We've done all we can. Now we wait. It's up to the monkeys, but I feel good about things. I'm giving everyone a day off, paid. You deserve it. Figure out the best way to distribute the days among your sections, keeping in mind we have to monitor the monkeys. Diets for each group as in the protocol. Bleeds every third day for the first two weeks. We can breathe easier now, but keep your fingers crossed. This one is hard to predict. Okay, anyone have problems? Issues to address? Questions?"

It had been a busy and tiring two months of work. Clark practically slept in his office. This was his baby. He'd done everything to ensure success, but in the end, the vector had to work its magic. They'd know soon, possibly in a few days, how well it expressed insulin.

He could turn his attention to Vanessa, who had to be feeling abandoned, and get more involved with clinic plans. He hadn't liked either of the first two buildings the real estate agent showed them. The third one, a vacant flower shop on the ground floor with an apartment above it, had potential. An excellent location at a reasonable price for something they could tear down. The buildings on either side had undergone extensive renovations, so they'd be around a while. Vanessa didn't care much what they were used for; her clinic would not rely on passersby for business. As it turned out, one was a coffee shop, the other a beauty parlor. Okay by her. Properties turned over fairly quickly in Beverly Hills, so they needed to make a quick decision. Since it fit their criteria and because it just felt right, he put a deposit on the property. He solicited bids for its demolition and interviewed architects for the new design. Vanessa recommended a sales representative who would meet him in a few days for an estimate on medical equipment and furnishings. He was elated to finally be able to help fulfill her dream of owning and running a clinic.

"What's the price tag?"

"A few million, but that's the cost of doing business. You'll have instant equity for a good chunk of it and recoup the rest in a few years. That's how this works, don't get too uptight about it."

"Uptight? Isn't that a sixties word?"

"I don't know where that came from, just don't go there. It'll cost a lot of money to do this right, initially. You want the latest in office and patient room design and equipment, don't you? You'll need to advertise, hire staff. That takes money. We can write off a lot of it, so when I say a few million dollars, think less than that. When you open your doors, a patient will come in, get great care, will like your office, and spread the word. Bingo! Word of mouth will bring in more business. We'll get rich, build another clinic, and we'll get richer. That's how it works. It takes time, and it takes resolve. You're a good doctor; you'll get patients, and you'll help those patients. In return, you'll get appreciated, you'll get respected, and you'll get rich. We'll go to France; we'll go to Italy. We'll buy a home in France; we'll buy a home in Italy. You have to persevere, stick to the game plan. We're almost there, babe."

"This is why I come home to you. You make me feel like all I have to do is leave things with you, that you'll make them happen. That's why I chose you—you make me happy and safe, and someday you'll make me rich. I want to walk over there and grab you and never let go."

"I'm here for the taking, sweetie. I've got nowhere else to go. If you left me, I'd quit. There wouldn't be anything left to live for."

"I'll never quit you, even if we never get rich. Money isn't everything, you know."

They stared at each other a moment before saying "nah" at the same time.

"Hey, it's been stressful lately. What say we take a drive up the Pacific Coast Highway? Can you get time off?"

"I think so; give me a day to set it up. I may need someone to fill in for me."

"Fine. Tomorrow is Thursday. Let's drive north Friday morning and forget this place. Come back Sunday, raring to go into a new week. Sound like a plan?"

"It does."

CHAPTER EIGHTEEN

"Oh, look," Adam said. "Roadkill. You know how many UT grads it takes to eat an armadillo, don't you?"

"Of course," Mary answered. "Three. The other two watch for traffic. Ha, ha. Are we near Abilene?"

"Half-hour out."

"I passed through Abilene when I was a kid. We were on a family trip to Colorado, but I don't remember anything about it except that we got gas and took a bathroom break there."

"You should have looked me up."

"What? How old were you then?"

"When?"

"When I came through Abilene."

"When did you come through Abilene?"

"I don't know, but I did look you up. They said you were in school detention, so we kept going."

"Forget I asked."

"Forget you asked what?"

"Exactly."

"So tell me more about your folks. I want an idea of

what I'm getting into this weekend."

"Dad grew up in Amarillo, Mom in Lubbock, so both are native Texans. Dad runs his own accounting firm. Mom went to nursing school and worked at a local hospital, but quit when she had me. Now she volunteers twenty hours a week at the Regional Medical Center. They attend Oakwood Baptist Church, and when I'm home, we go to the contemporary service.

"And when you're not home?"

"Mostly they go to the traditional service. We'll go to the contemporary service on Sunday."

"Will your parents go with us?"

"Sure, but that's three days away. There's still a lot of fun to be had before Sunday. In fact, we'll be early enough today to go fishing before dinner. White bass can still be caught in October if you know where to go."

"Don't forget why I came along. This is a working trip. We have a paper to write."

"You had nowhere else to go, so enjoy a little family time here with the Garretts."

"I will, and thanks for inviting me. I'm just saying, we agreed to at least get a first draft done. If we go fishing today and if your brothers come in tomorrow…"

"It's a pretty day. Might be fun to get out in it."

Just before the outskirts of the city, they turned north on a farm-to-market road and drove two miles, then turned down the lane that passed the Garrett home a half-mile later. The houses were far enough apart that the only noise came from chirping birds and mooing cattle on John and Sarah Newly's ranch across the street.

"John has a stream running through his property, and

I fish there a lot. Let's say hi to Mom and walk over. Sound good?"

"Lead on."

He kissed his mother on the cheek and introduced Mary. Alice hesitated ever so briefly, then gave her a big friendly Texas hug.

"Momma, We're going fishing at the Newly's. Is that okay?"

She said it was, and that Mr. Newly was doing well, but Mrs. Newly had been sick, and that it would be nice if he took a minute to check in on them. "Do you want to come in and have a snack or iced tea?"

"No, thank you. We brought water and snacks and hit a rest area a while back. Mary, you good?"

"I'm okay."

"All right, Momma, we'll be back before dark."

"You all have fun. Nice meeting, you, Mary."

The two turned and headed to the garage for fishing poles and tackle. He looked back and waved at his mother. She smiled and formed the word 'wow' with her mouth while pointing at Mary, who wasn't looking. He grinned and nodded in agreement.

With fishing gear in hand, the two left the house and walked down the road toward the Newly's place. Along the way, they surveyed their surroundings and agreed on both the beauty of the Texas countryside and the spectacular weather that was theirs to enjoy. Upon reaching the entrance, they crossed the cattle guard, which was nothing new for Mary, and headed for the three-bedroom house in which the Newlys had raised their two daughters. Mrs. Newly rocked on the porch in the gentle breeze and saw them coming. She went inside and returned with a pitcher of iced tea and two glasses.

He waved at her as they approached and greeted her when they got within earshot. "Afternoon, Mrs. Newly."

She waved back, and when they got closer, returned the greeting. "Well, hello, Mr. College Professor. Are you still teaching them youngsters how to dig holes?"

"Ha, ha, ha. How are you? Mom said you'd been sick, but you look wonderful as ever."

"Oh, it was nothing. John finally got around to taking me to the clinic. The doctor there said it was probably a viral infection. I'm feeling much better today, thanks for asking. Now tell me who this Hollywood starlet is you brought with you."

"Mrs. Newly, I want you to meet Dr. Mary Walsh. Mary teaches at Baylor."

"Very pleased to meet you, Mary. I'd shake your hand but give me another day or two to get past this cold. What do you teach at Baylor?"

"I teach Adam's students how to fill in holes."

He and Mrs. Newly looked at each other, grinned, then busted out laughing.

"No, I was teasing; I teach cell biology."

"Beautiful, and a sense of humor. And smart. Course, they usually don't let dummies teach college. Well, John's out with the cows. I see you're here to fish. I believe the bass are still around. You may even catch a few."

"I plan to throw them back, unless you'd like me to bring you some."

"Heavens, no. John has our freezer so full of fish now I don't know how we'll ever be able to eat 'em all."

"How are the daughters and grandkids?" he asked.

"They're fine. I tell you what. You two have some iced tea, and I'll go inside and get my latest pictures. I won't keep you more than a few minutes."

"Sounds good, Mrs. Newly," he said. "No hurry. The fish can wait."

They sat on the porch for the next half hour, sipping tea and talking about grandkids, and him as a boy.

"I'll never forget the time the three boys came over to fish. A storm blew in out of nowhere, so they ran into the house to get out of the rain. Their clothes were soaking wet, so I told them I would put them in the dryer. I had Adam put on a pair of John's pants and one of his shirts, but the younger boys were too small for his clothes. Well, what I did was I found two old dresses in my youngest daughter's closet and had David and John put them on. I assured them that no one would see them and that their clothes would soon be dry. They had so much fun acting silly in those dresses that when the rain stopped, they wore them to the stream and went back to fishing dressed like girls. Now, me being the sneaky sort, I got my camera and took some hilarious pictures. I gave prints to Alice and Carl. I imagine they still show up at family get-togethers."

"I never bring them out," he said with a wink.

"Of course not," Mrs. Newly said. "Okay, you two, go catch some fish. Stop by on your way home and say hello to John, he'll be done for the day by then."

"We'll do that," he said.

"Thanks for the tea, Mrs. Newly," Mary said. "Sometime, I'd like to hear more funny stories about Adam."

"Oh, I do have some. Get him to tell you about looking for buried treasure here on the ranch. Might be how he got interested in archaeology."

They left the house and walked a quarter of a mile to a wide part of the stream and set up the two poles. While the white bass stayed away, a few crappies obliged, which he promptly released. Mary caught something that fought well before spitting out the lure.

"May have been a largemouth bass," he said. "Looked good-sized. Too bad."

"This is nice. Reminds me a little of my aunt and uncle's ranch. Adam, I like your mother, but I saw an odd look on her face when we met. Or was it just me?"

"I think she saw Jill in you. Like I did when we first met."

"Who's Jill? An old girlfriend?"

"Yes."

"Didn't work out?"

"She died. At nineteen. Leukemia."

"Oh, I'm so sorry. I take it you were dating at the time?"

"Broke my heart. Still hurts. My childhood sweetheart. We had plans."

The sun slipped ever closer to the tops of the hills in the west, telling them to wrap it up. He removed the lures from the swivels on the ends of their lines and placed them in the plastic tackle box. He snugged the box into his vest and snapped the swivels onto the loops attached to the rods near the reel clamps. They stopped by the Newly house to say hello to John and then returned to the Garrett homestead for a dinner of chicken-fried steak, mashed potatoes, and green beans. After dinner, they sat at the kitchen table, spread out their papers, notes, and writing pads, and got to work.

CHAPTER NINETEEN

Adam woke to the smell of brewing coffee. The clock said six-fifty. He jumped out of bed and found his robe where it always was—hanging on a hook inside the closet door. Wrapping himself in it, he went out into the family room, expecting to see his mom sipping her first cup of coffee and his dad reading the paper. Instead, his mother and Mary sat on a sofa, chatting.

"Good morning, you two," he said. "Where's Dad?"

"Your father went into town to eat breakfast with friends. Then he's got stops at the hardware store and butcher shop. He'll be back later in the morning. Want some coffee?"

"Thanks, I'll help myself." He returned and took a spot on one end of the couch, resting an elbow on the armrest and holding his cup with the other hand. "What have you two been talking about? Not me, I hope."

"No, no, I don't think your name has come up," said his mother.

"Yeah," Mary said, "do you think the world revolves around you or something?"

"I said I hoped you *weren't* talking about me. You have to pay attention. The way I phrased that suggests I don't think too highly of myself."

"I told Mary about the houses we've lived in since moving to Abilene, starting out in that two-bedroom ranch on Fourth Street. Boy, was that small, but it was all we could afford. When you turned twelve, we moved here. You three boys had plenty of room to run then."

"And a place to fish," he said. "Momma, I'll bet when you first saw Mary the last thing you would have guessed is that she teaches at Baylor, as young as she looks."

Mary blushed. "Adam, stop."

"And I hate to admit it, but she's smarter than me. And did you know she can outrun me in a three-mile race?"

"Why, no. Can she really?"

"She ran track in college. Holds a bunch of records. And, yes, she beats me all the time."

"So you two run together? A lot?"

"Oh, once or twice a week," he said. "I guess we've become running partners of sorts, unless she runs on the side with someone I don't know about. Which is fine, of course. Do you?"

"I'm so busy I can barely make time to run with you. So, no, though I do get to the gym on the other days."

"As do I."

"Seems like you've enjoyed running since you left for college," his mother said. "Have you slowed down now that you're approaching thirty?"

"Probably. But I run to clear my head, mostly. Nothing like a quick five miles to help you put things into perspective. I thought I'd take Mary out past the Johnson place and back this morning."

"Why, that's more than five miles."

"Seven point one, to be exact. We'll take it easy. It's a pretty run, and mostly flat."

"How about breakfast first?" she asked.

"Sure, we're in no hurry."

"Pancakes and sausage sound okay?"

"Ah, Mary, you're in for a treat. Mom makes the best pancakes in the county."

"Sounds good, Alice. Thank you."

"David and John should be here when you get back. You'll like them, Mary."

"As I told you, David's married," he said, "and you'll like his wife, Emily. But watch out for John, he'll try to put the moves on you."

"Adam, you hush that talk," his mother warned. "He'll do no such thing."

He laughed. "That little fart will try anything."

"And watch your language in this house," his mother insisted.

"Oh, like that's a bad word. And the stories I—" His mother's look stopped him dead cold. "Okay, Momma. We'll tell them tonight after you go to bed."

Their run that morning was a jog rather than a race. They ran together about three and a half miles east, stopped before Route 604, rested a moment, then ran back. Arriving at noon, they looked a little tired but were eager to visit with David and John, who waited on the porch with Emily. He introduced Mary to everyone. Hugs accompanied the introductions, and when John lingered too long with Mary, he forcibly pulled him away and gave him a stern reprimand.

"You're forgetting who carries a badge and a gun, big brother," John said.

"Just a game warden, bro," David said. "Keep it real."

"And you're forgetting who can still whoop your behind, little brother," he said. "Don't make me do it." They pretended to fight for a moment, then shook hands again. "Good to see you guys. And thank you, Emily, for taking care of this ornery creature some people call a state trooper. All the while carrying my first, what, niece? Nephew?"

"We haven't said yet."

"And we won't pry, will we, Adam?" Mary said. "Congratulations, you two."

While Carl grilled ribs and chicken and Alice prepared side dishes, the boys and Mary played football. Emily, six months pregnant and not about to join them, watched. When they tired of that, they moved to the shade of the front porch and sipped iced tea. Carl and Alice announced that supper was ready. The sun had moved behind the big oak tree by four o'clock, which put the backyard redwood table in the shade, making it reasonably comfortable for dining. After the meal, the talk turned to his discovery.

"Okay," David said. "I'm not clear on how you knew where to look that last day on Melnikos."

"A stroke of luck, really," he said. "I had actually given up, my gear already packed and stowed in the boat. I wanted a few pictures of the island in the early morning light and happened to see a certain rock formation that seemed a little off. It made me curious, so I studied a photo taken by the Germans during World War II. Turned out to be the rock structure behind it that had changed, and I figured it happened when the Americans bombed the island. The top of that second rock happened to fall and cover the cave entrance. Who knows, that may have saved the box from being found. Enrico and I had a heck of a time, but we managed to roll it back, and the rest is history."

"History, huh?" David said. "You're telling me that for two thousand years, no one found that box until you came along?"

He explained the reasons why the cave turned out to have been not only a good hiding spot but had also provided environmental protection for the cedar box. And he admitted that dumb luck played a huge role in finding the vase containing Pilate's journal.

"Okay," John said, grinning. "You stumbled onto an old box. Anything in it? Gold? Silver? Jewels?"

He described to his skeptical brothers and Emily the analysis they'd done on the three items they'd found in the box. He requested they keep the information to themselves.

"Mom, Dad, is he for real?" David asked. "Are we being hoodwinked?"

"I don't think so," Alice said. "He seems sincere every time he tells the story. What convinces me, though, is Mary. She doesn't seem to be the type to go along with a practical joke this long. So, yes, I think it's real."

"Gee, Mom," he said. "I'm overwhelmed with the vote of confidence. Anyway, who wants to go listen to music?"

"How about a slice of pecan pie before you go?" Alice asked.

"You have to try this, Mary," he said.

"Okay, but only a small piece, please."

"None for me," Emily said, rubbing her belly.

"What music do the Garretts like?" Mary asked.

"There's only one legitimate style of music in Texas," John said. "You ought to know that."

"I do, but does Abilene have an orchestra?" she asked.

"I don't know, but the Rusty Nail does," David said.

"Yeah, you young 'uns go. Your dad and I will put the food away and tidy up," Alice said. "Emily, can you and Mary keep these boys out of trouble?"

"Haven't been able to yet," Emily replied.

CHAPTER TWENTY

As the oldest brother, Adam had felt obliged to shepherd the gang and got them home before ten o'clock. He prevailed upon his mom and dad to assign sleeping quarters before they turned in for the night themselves. David's old room naturally went to the expectant couple, and they gave Adam's to Mary. That left only John's old room in question. He suggested that it be given to the winner of an arm-wrestling match. John countered that it was his room, and there was nothing to argue about.

"You get the couch, Adam," his brother declared.

"Mom, Dad, this is your house, how do you see it?" he asked.

"Well, we were always partial to John," Alice said. John laughed and gave her a big kiss on the cheek.

"But we've always been more afraid of Adam," Carl added. "This is a dilemma."

"You two are a lot of help," he said. "No wonder we turned out the way we did."

"Is this how it was, Alice?" Mary asked. "Look, guys, I don't have to have a bed. I can sleep on the couch."

"Stay out of this," he insisted, then added, smiling, "Please?"

"You just want to argue with your brothers," Mary said. "Okay. I'll stay out of it. But it's getting late. Get it settled. Please."

"It's already settled," he said. "It's John's room. I'm on the couch."

"So, that was an act?" Mary asked.

"Of course."

"The only thing we don't know now is who gets the bathroom first," David said. "Emily is ready for bed now, and since she's pregnant, we'll defer and let her go first. But who gets it after her, well, we'll have to fight it out."

Mary looked at Alice. "You had to deal with this for how many years?"

"Twenty-five-and-a-half," Alice said.

"But when we finally got rid of John, or, I should say, by the time John moved out, it got eerily quiet in this house," Carl said.

"Empty nest?" Mary asked.

"Yes, and was it ever nice," Alice said. "No, we miss the boys; those were fun times. A lot of work, for sure. But, time moves on, things change, we've gotten older. Now we're looking forward to having grandchildren running around here, getting into fights."

"Glad to oblige," David said. "Now, if these other two worthless yahoos would get busy and find someone who'd tolerate them, you might have a few more rug rats coming down the pike."

Pillows flew in David's direction. Carl stepped in before they could be thrown back and explained how things would proceed. "Emily gets the bathroom first. David will be next so they can get to bed. Mary goes after David so she can get to bed, then John, and then finally Adam. Your mother and I are retiring for the night, so there'll be no more fighting and no loud noises. In the morning, we'll have breakfast ready at eight and leave for church at nine-thirty. Adjust your schedules accordingly. Good night, everybody. Alice, say good night."

The rest of the evening unfolded as Carl had decreed. Almost. The boys and Mary chatted while Emily prepared for bed. When she emerged from the bathroom and said her good nights, David took his turn. When David finished and went to bed, Mary offered to let John go next. He started to argue but saw the looks on their faces, so he excused himself and went to get ready for bed.

"That was the funniest evening sitting around a living room I've ever had," Mary said. "You guys crack me up."

"I love those guys to death. They mean the world to me."

"Ready to work on the paper?" Mary asked.

"Are you?"

"Nah. Why don't we relax, take a break? We've made good progress."

"Better than I expected with the family here."

"Yeah, not bad. On the way back tomorrow, I can work on it while you drive. You can talk and drive at the same time, can't you?"

He picked up a pillow. She gave him a look. He put it down and smiled.

*

The next morning, the bathroom was not an issue as everyone woke up at different times. Bacon, eggs, and toast appeared promptly at eight o'clock. They took two cars to church, and afterward, Alice and Carl drove Emily and David home while the others went to get fried chicken and biscuits. Alice put seven ears of corn in boiling water and heated a can of baked beans. Carl made pitchers of tea and lemonade. When the chicken and biscuits arrived, Carl blessed the food, and they commenced eating.

The weather forecast called for rain coming from the west, so Adam and Mary drove back to Waco after lunch. They said their goodbyes and hugged and promised to do it again soon. His brothers left at the same time, David with Emily heading west, John southwest. Adam and Mary started east, well ahead of the weather, and the others might make it home dry.

"That was fun, Adam."

"Which part?"

"All of it. Your family is a blast. Church was good too. More casual than I'm used to."

"Seems to be the trend. Did you like the music?"

"I did. I barely remember Mom and Dad taking me to church, but I do know they didn't have electric guitars and drums. I guess God's okay with rock music?

"Sure, why not? Lots of things are okay with God. More than we think. I think. We make too many rules for ourselves, but we naturally rebel at rules. Something's got to give. I think Jesus would have been at home in our church."

"Is he at home with formal churches?"

"Of course. Now, do you want to work on the paper?"

CHAPTER TWENTY ONE

C lark read the preliminary reports in front of him and confirmed the data with the lab manager. "Not enough expression. Blood sugar levels are better, and the monkeys seem healthier, but not good enough to go into human trials. We're so damn close. Any reason to expect better numbers in the next few weeks?"

"Maybe, but this virus doesn't last long outside cells. More integration isn't likely. The levels of insulin synthesis we've seen at this point in earlier projects are about where they ended up."

"All right, do what you can to try to figure this out. Something isn't right. Sacrifice one of the monkeys and do the biochemistry. Look at mRNAs and preproinsulin in its liver. Do the histology. Do anything you can think of. If we can get another extension, we'll have a good chance to make this work, but we'll have to figure out what's wrong."

"Yes, sir."

Well, that does it. I'm officially in a bad mood. Better not try calling contacts today, they'd sense desperation in my voice. I should call it a day and go home.

He didn't even stop at the gym. When he arrived home, he grabbed a cold beer and headed to the pool with his phone. He called his mortgage broker and asked him to draw up a line of credit for $500,000 secured on the equity in his house. They were buying a building, technically, but it was the lot they were after. He called the Beverly Hills permit office and asked for the status of his demolition application. It had moved along through the approval process with no red flags and should be approved within two weeks. He called the architect and gave him the go-ahead to draw preliminary sketches for the new clinic based on their discussions earlier in the week. He transferred $5,000 into the man's account to get him started. Next, he called a friend who knew how to navigate business loan sources and applications. He wanted to get the largest loan he could for the building, furnishings, and equipment before hitting investor friends for the rest.

Vanessa had left a message saying she'd be late and that he'd be on his own for dinner. That was his cue to swim a few laps, then get out of the water and dry off, get dressed, and walk to Joe's. He rarely went to Joe's Bar and Grill without running into a friend or acquaintance. He beat the dinner crowd, so he ordered a beer and grabbed a cue stick, racked the balls, and worked on his pool game. Two beers later, a couple of regulars showed up. One always had a few good jokes, the other had a remarkable past and often told fascinating stories. He bought dinner for them, figuring it well worth the entertainment value.

One benefit of running a company is that no one calls you on the carpet for getting to work late. He considered that perk when deciding how late to stay out. Nothing currently required his presence at EVI, and if anyone needed him, they simply had to pick up a phone and call. Vanessa had already gone to bed by the time he returned home, so he flipped on the TV and poured a nightcap. He awoke the next morning to an empty house and the clock way too far ahead then called and informed his secretary that he'd work at home unless something urgent came up.

CHAPTER TWENTY TWO

A lmost human?" Adam asked, sitting in the chair in front of Mary's desk. "Sounds like my brothers."

When she invited him by phone to her office to discuss her latest experiments, she'd told him that the four tissue samples sent out for radiocarbon dating were confirmed to be two thousand years old. He couldn't wait to hear more, but as he stared attentively into her eyes, ready for the update, all he could see were Jill's eyes. He struggled to focus on her words and thought he got the gist of it—something about PCR and the samples being human.

"Say that again? I thought I heard you say the stuff in the whip was human."

"I did. Want me to slow down?"

"No. I, my mind was somewhere else. I'm sorry."

She repeated her description of the limited PCR analysis she did on the fragments of skin and muscle excised from the bone shards from the whip. They were clearly human. That led her to take the DNA analysis a step further and conduct a more extensive PCR profile.

"Extremely close to human DNA, but different enough that I don't know how they should be classified."

"Where do they fall on the spectrum of animals, say from mouse to man? Or monkey to man?"

"Oh, they're human, no question. But *Homo sapiens*? A subspecies of *Homo sapiens*? That isn't my field, but before we publish, we should have the nomenclature figured out. We could call him Melnikos Man for now."

"So it's male DNA?"

"Well, yeah. Otherwise, I'd call her Melnikos Woman."

"Cute. So it's not quite but almost human. This gets curiouser and curiouser all the time. What kinds of differences did you find?"

"For the most part, the PCR primers worked as expected on both human and Melnikos Man DNA, but a few didn't or resulted in larger DNA fragments for Melnikos Man. We sequenced the ends of two of those larger fragments, and they are extremely close to human— greater than ninety-nine percent identical. How close is the Melnikos Man genome to the human genome? I'd love to sequence it and find out."

"The whole genome? How expensive is that these days?"

"Getting cheaper all the time. You can afford it since you still have startup money."

"That would be cool."

"Yeah, especially when I tell you that the tissues I rehydrated in growth media are all healthy. So easy to take care of. They're resistant to stresses in heat, salt, temperature, pH. They survive anything I throw at them, even pathogenic bacteria."

"And human cells don't do so well in those experiments?"

"No. These cells survive well past the point human cells die. They easily out-compete them in mixed cultures."

"Out-compete? You put them in little contests?"

"Sort of, silly. You mix these cells with the same number of human cells in a nutrient medium and let them grow. Melnikos Man cells eventually take over the culture. They outgrow all other cells. They're extraordinary."

"The other pieces of tissue, are they like this too?"

"All of them. They all have the same DNA profile, and they all do well in a growth medium. But it gets better."

"It's already overwhelming."

"Put on your scientific thinking-cap; this gets a little technical."

"Well, if I look puzzled by what you say, speak a little louder."

"What?"

"It's a joke. Never mind, go ahead. I'll stop you if I don't understand."

"Okay. We designed PCR primers from the sequence data we got from the ends of those two larger Melnikos fragments. Those new primers only work with Melnikos Man DNA, nothing else. Bottom line is, I can distinguish Melnikos Man cells from human cells. You with me?"

"I think so. But I'm starting to wonder when you sleep. That's a lot of work."

"It's been so intriguing that I couldn't resist. Anyway, that's how I could tell that Melnikos Man cells outnumbered other human cells in the competition assays. Guess what else?"

"I give up, what?"

"It concerns the mass spec data. Remember we analyzed four thorn tips, three that pointed down, and one that pointed up? And only the three that pointed down had human collagen, keratin, and hemoglobin peptides. You remember?"

"Yes."

"We kept back a small amount of each of those samples, so I did PCR on them to see if there was intact DNA and, if so, would it react with Melnikos Man primers? Turns out that all three samples taken from thorn tips pointing down had Melnikos Man DNA, while the one tip pointing up did not."

"Mary, you're amazing."

"Modern science is what's amazing. And, for the sake of completeness, I examined all the other thorn tips by PCR."

"Is this going where I think it might?"

"Hold on, hold on. So I did PCR on seventeen other tips. All thorns pointing down had Melnikos Man DNA, and only Melnikos Man DNA, on them. None of the ones pointing sideways or up had any kind of DNA."

"Suggesting the crown was on someone's head rather than someone having pricked themselves with thorns while fashioning a crown."

"Exactly. And in each case, the DNA belonged to this Melnikos Man, whoever he was. The man who was beaten by the whip also wore that crown of thorns. That's what I conclude from PCR analysis."

He stood and slapped his hands together.

"Absolutely amazing," he said, pacing around her office. "You did it. You connected the whip to the crown of thorns. This is stunning. I never dreamed you'd be able to do that at all, much less so quickly. You are simply astonishing."

He hugged her, the first physical contact with her since the handshake the first day they met.

"Oh, I'm sorry. That, that's embarrassing. I'm sorry, I lost myself there."

"Why would you be embarrassed?"

"Uh, well, it's—"

"It's Jill, isn't it. I talked to your mom about her. She says you've never gotten over her. I understand. It's okay."

He looked at her in silence for a moment, then said, "Thank you, Mary."

He sat back down and stared out the window, trying to take it all in. He struggled to comprehend it, but thoughts flew out of his head before he could put any two together.

"I have to run before I explode. Want to go?"

"I'd love to. The track? Around the neighborhoods?"

"Let's get ready and meet under the oak tree, then decide. If I don't burn off this nervous energy I'll, I'll, well I don't know what'll happen, but it won't be good. See you in ten."

Outside at the designated meeting spot, he paced, he bounced, and he stretched. A veritable ball of energy, he didn't stop until she appeared. "Let's do five miles," he said. "I can take you today."

"Loser buys?"

"Loser buys. You're going down, Miss Super Scientist. I have energy to burn."

"Track or streets?"

"Your call."

"Track. I have a slight heel strain. I don't want to aggravate it.

They arrived at the track and did more stretching, then met at the starting line for the run.

"May I ask a favor?" he asked.

"Sure."

"Do that thing you did before."

"Well, can you narrow it down some?"

"Uh, when you, uh, gave me a hug."

"Adam, that was something that happened in the moment. Don't read too much into that. But as I recall, you hugged me."

"I know, but you hugged me back, and, well…"

"All right. You win the race, you get the meal and a hug."

"Oh, look, your shoe is untied."

"It is not," she said as he reached down and pulled on the laces. She objected when he slipped it off her foot, but by then, he'd launched it some twenty feet away. He grinned and took off running.

"I guess the race is on, then?"

He pretended not to hear and kept running. He moved out to a considerable lead, and she didn't catch him until the last lap. He grinned at her as she sailed by, winning by ten yards.

"Nice try, but you expended yourself way too early," she said as he crossed the finish line panting.

"I…did, but my goal was…was to run off a ton…of extra energy, and I accomplished that," he said between gasps. "I'm exhausted. What…what do you want for lunch?"

"How about we make it dinner? I have exams to grade. I'd like to get them back to the students by Monday. Finals will be here before we know it, and I want them to know where they stand with their grade averages."

"Sounds good. Should I pick you up at your office or apartment?"

"Uh, make it the apartment. If I'm not done by dinner time, I'll take my work home and finish later."

"Six o'clock?"

"Works for me."

*

He pedaled his bike through older neighborhoods on the way to his apartment. A mixture of brown and green leaves dangled from long oak and pecan tree branches overhanging the streets. When he reached his usual turn-off, he went straight instead. Several minutes later, he came to a hilltop with a view of the lake outside town. He stopped, dismounted the bike, and sat on a grassy knoll overlooking the water.

Mary's results had given him so much to think about. He needed to slow his thoughts and let them develop into a plausible hypothesis that would make sense of all the random pieces of information so suddenly dumped into his brain. An explanation for the longevity of Melnikos Man tissues zoomed through his head and disappeared. Hey, hey, get back here. The wayward thought returned and lingered long enough to be captured. He meditated on it a while and then looked up. "Is this from you? Can it be?" He sat, motionless, eyes closed, tuning out the world so he could think. He stood and gazed across the water, then jumped on his bike and raced home. He pulled his Bible and a Bible commentary off the bookshelf and put them on the kitchen table, poured a glass of water, and opened the two books.

*

He pulled into her apartment complex at five fifty-five, found a place to park, and made a beeline to her door. She opened it before he had a chance to knock.

"Right on time. I like that in a guy. Ready to eat?"

"Ready, and I have something I need to run past you."

"Now? Or while we eat?"

"While we eat. What did you decide? About dinner, that is. Where do you want to go?"

"I decided to make you pay," she said with a devilish smile. "The steakhouse."

"Geez, you're draining my bank account with these restaurants, but a deal's a deal. And I must say, you've earned it."

"Well, if you'd win a race for a change, I'd pay."

"You sure know how to hurt a guy."

They ordered their meals and sat back to talk about Melnikos. Adam presented a theory for her to consider. One not scientific, but rather theological in nature.

"Remember I said the Bible was a hobby for me?" he asked.

She nodded.

"There's an Old Testament passage in Psalms, attributed to King David, where he wrote that he didn't want to be abandoned in 'Sheol.'"

"Sheol?"

"Think of it as where you go when you die. I'll have to study it more, but I think the Hebrew usage meant the grave. This is one of those verses New Testament writers later quoted. That means it's important. Fast forward a thousand years from David's time to the days just after Jesus walked the earth, and you have his disciple Peter speaking to a crowd in Jerusalem. He quoted that verse from Psalms and said it referred to Jesus. That Jesus wouldn't be left in the grave."

"I don't understand,"

"How do you think I feel half the time you're explaining science to me? Anyway, certain translations of that verse in the book of Acts use the words 'his flesh shall not see decay.' He said that because Jesus died but didn't stay in the tomb long enough for his body to decay in fulfillment of Old Testament prophecy. We know the tissue samples you found in the whip are bits of human flesh, or extremely close to humans, genetically. We also know they're two thousand years old and can be revived. Well, what if this prophetic verse applied not just to his intact body but also to pieces of his body that got left behind? It would mean they would never decay either. So, that may be why you're able to rehydrate them and get them growing again."

"So you're making the call. 'Melnikos Man' is Jesus."

They stared at each other. They thanked the waiter when he brought their meals, but otherwise sat quietly.

"I know," he said, breaking the silence. "I know, but our food is getting cold. Let's eat."

"I actually had that idea in the back of my head because it was one way to explain the data, but I didn't want to mention it because it's incomprehensible. So, I fashioned theories like Melnikos Man having descended from another subspecies of *Homo sapiens*. Whose lineage died out, and it's why we don't see that particular PCR profile today."

"Jesus was conceived differently and was of a different lineage than the rest of us. In fact, Paul called him the 'second man, Adam' in Corinthians. He could not have descended from the first Adam because that man had fallen into sin and taken every one of his descendants into sin with him. Jesus had to be close enough, genetically speaking, to the *Homo sapiens* species to be considered fully human, but not tainted with Adam's sin. That way, his sacrificial, substitutionary death for justice's sake would be acceptable and would apply to all humans descended from the first Adam. Theologically speaking, that is."

"That's complicated, but I think I followed it. I've never thought about it that way, but it makes sense. Theology is a new area of thought for me. Anyway, without sequencing the genome, we don't know exactly how close Melnikos Man DNA is to ours. But, oh modern Adam that you are, let me hasten to say that your theory won't fly in an academic journal. It's clever, but it doesn't prove it's Jesus' DNA."

"Oh, I know. I'm just always on the lookout for ways to bridge the gap between science and faith. Fun to think about. We'll write this from a scholarly viewpoint. In the discussion section, we can mention the religious implications, but those won't impact the importance of the find. Now, if we can prove Pilate put the box on Melnikos, that's different. Then we have a connection with Jesus through a different route."

"And where are you with that?"

"Goodwin talked to two Roman Empire scholars, and both said there's precious little about Pilate in the historical record. The good news is that none of the few mentions of the man contradict our story. Brad's still looking, but he doubts he'll find much else."

"Anything more I can do?"

"Prepare the data for publication. Get good microscopic images of those cells. And go with me to Abilene next week for Thanksgiving. We'll continue working on the manuscript there."

"You're inviting me to your family's home for Thanksgiving?"

"I am, but if you have a better offer…"

"No, I'd love to. I like your family. I'm in."

They finished their meals and left the restaurant, stopping at a Dairy Queen on the way home. He pulled into a parking spot at her apartment complex and escorted her to the door."

"Been quite a day," he said.

"I'll say. In one day, we figured out we not only had Jesus' DNA, but we also had living cells that came from his body. Unbelievable. How does one know how to act in situations like this?"

"I don't know, but I have an idea."

With that, he gave her a quick goodnight kiss. "Don't

read too much into that," he said as he turned and walked away.

"Adam!"

CHAPTER TWENTY THREE

Adam flipped the switch on the coffee pot and collected his fishing gear. He opened the front door and stepped into the early morning darkness. A light jacket ought to do. He turned on the porch light and stashed the gear in the back of his SUV. When he returned to the house, he found his mother sitting at the kitchen table, sipping a hot cup of the fresh brew.

"What are you doing up, Momma?"

"I was about to ask you the same thing. Then I remembered you'd planned to fish this morning. Taking Mary?"

"I gave her the option of sleeping in or tagging along. If she gets up before I leave, she's going. Now, answer my question, please, Mom."

"It's Thanksgiving, silly. Don't I always start the turkey early?"

"Oh, of course. I forgot."

"Did you two get much writing done last night?"

"We made progress," he said, pouring himself a cup. "It's coming along."

"Very nice of you to invite her for Thanksgiving since

she doesn't have family nearby. Her charm and beauty have nothing to do with it, right?"

"Of course not. It's strictly a working relationship."

"Working relationship, my foot. I saw how you looked at her during supper. And I believe I saw the same thing on her face. You two are headed down that road. I didn't notice it on your last visit. What's happened since?"

"I don't know about her. I'll take your word on that. I'm wondering if I've finally come to terms with the loss of Jill. It seems like I'm feeling free enough to enjoy Mary. She's easy to have fun with, not that I know whether it'll go anywhere."

"Amazing how much alike those two are. We thought the world of Jill, and it broke our hearts to watch you suffer the way you did. Son, look at me. Mary is probably the best woman you'll meet the rest of your life. Mothers know these things. But don't even think about pursuing a relationship with her just because she's so much like Jill. If you want her, want her for being Mary, not a replacement for Jill."

"I know, Momma. I've thought of that very thing. But how will I know if I'm doing that?"

"Emotions are hard to figure out and hard to control, so let me give you two pieces of advice. First, feel free to continue to miss Jill. Mary wouldn't expect you not to. When you start thinking that your feelings for Jill are coming back inappropriately, ignore those thoughts. Let them have their say and then tell them you're dealing with it and move on. They'll go. Second, let Mary help. Trust her. Lean on her. She has what it takes. She'll help you find your way."

He stared at the coffee in his mug. Wisps of steam floated up from its surface in a swirling pattern. He felt her hand slide over his, and then a kiss on his forehead.

"You'll be fine. You're a good man."

"There's a good man here?" Mary asked, rubbing her eyes. "Where?"

"You're looking at him. And good morning to you too. We were talking about—"

"The weather," his mother interjected.

"Momma. We were talking about you, actually."

"Yes, and 'weather' or not you wanted to go fishing this morning," she said.

"Uggh. Like mother, like son," she said, groaning. "So that's where you get your corny sense of humor. Sure, I'll have some coffee, thanks for asking."

"Pardon my manners, Mary," she said, filling a cup and placing it on the table. "Here you go, have a seat. Sleep well?"

"Fine, thanks. We going fishing, or what?"

"I'm ready. Do you need to powder-up first?"

"Adam, shush. Don't mind him, Mary. I never could get him to be polite with girls."

"Oh, that's okay, he just doesn't like it when I catch more fish than he does, which is what's happening today."

"You two run along and let me get this turkey in the oven."

"You do that, and I'll take this other turkey fishing," Mary offered.

"I should go by myself if this is all the respect I get around here."

*

When they returned later that morning, he saw his dad throwing the football in the front yard with David and John. He joined them while Mary took the vacant rocking chair on the porch between Alice and Emily, who looked much bigger than she did on the previous visit. The women rocked and talked about babies while watching the boys play. They moved to the dinner table when Carl clanged a makeshift dinner bell. They feasted on the scrumptious meal and talked about anything and everything.

With the whole family there to help eat his mother's homemade pumpkin and pecan pies and watch football on TV, he and Mary made zero progress on the manuscript on Thanksgiving Day. On Friday, however, work took precedence. And Saturday as well. Sunday morning, they went to church and then returned to Waco, feeling pleased that the paper had made it into the second draft.

*

Three weeks later, the semester ended. Adam enjoyed teaching, but he also liked the five-week break between semesters. It gave him a chance to finish preparations for the spring semester and then catch up on the latest goings-on in the world of archaeology. Mary planned to attend a two-day conference the week before Christmas in Washington, D.C., then spend the holidays with her brother and his family in Virginia. She stopped by his office to say goodbye.

"Hey, you," he said. "I'm wrapping this up. I hope to send it to Goodwin in a day or two. When you get back, we ought to be ready for internal reviews."

"Which means…"

"It'll be out there."

"Reviews are supposed to be confidential. How long do you think that will last?"

"I won't give it to anyone who doesn't agree to keep it that way. My only concern is Davison. I don't trust him, but he has to get a copy too. If it leaks, it leaks."

"I'm a little surprised it lasted this long. It's good you can trust your family. So, have you given much thought to how you want this to roll out?"

"Not much, no. I guess I figured it would take on a life of its own. Get it to the journal, get it reviewed and accepted for publication, then make an announcement. I'll talk to the public affairs office; they can help. They should know what's coming so they aren't blindsided."

"I'm sure they can help, but are we getting a little ahead of ourselves? It could take a while to get this accepted."

"Possibly, but if it gets slow over the break, I may walk over there and pay them a visit."

"I guess it couldn't hurt. Call if you have questions about anything, any of the science, that is. You're on your own with the archaeology parts and the theology."

"Yeah, but is a single Bible verse really theology? We're taking everything together and speculating that the tissues could have come from Jesus. That's what discussion sections are for."

"Still, there could be resistance, because that comes awful darn close to proving his existence. That's a touchy subject for many people."

"If it comes down to it, we'll take it out of the manuscript. The archaeology here can stand on its own."

"As can the cell biology, so if we can't get it into an archaeology journal, we can separate it into two papers."

"All right, see you in two weeks. Have a good trip. By the way, who will I run with while you're gone?"

"How about training on your own, doing fast three-milers? If you ever beat me, it would be at that distance."

"I've gotten too used to chasing a pretty woman to train on my own. That wouldn't work."

"You'd better not be chasing other women."

"Would you be jealous?"

"I might."

"I'm kidding, then. I'll be in Abilene a few days, but much of the time I'll be getting ready for the spring semester. I've neglected that."

"Adam?"

"Yes?"

"I won't see you for two weeks. I've gotten used to you barging into my lab or office, talking to Ed or me about science and whatever. And running. Gosh, we must have run close to a hundred miles together, or, well, not together since I was well ahead of you most of the time. And going to Abilene with you twice, so, my life may have a bit of a void in it until I get back."

With that, she walked over to him, kissed him, and turned to leave. On the way out, she paused and said, "Don't read too much into that."

CHAPTER TWENTY FOUR

Adam spent Christmas in Abilene working on the manuscript. On his return to Waco after New Year's Day, he sent an electronic copy of the third draft to Mary, now back from Virginia, and to Brad. Mary called to tell him she had no corrections. Goodwin had a few revisions and a suggestion, which Adam incorporated into the paper. That done, he gave copies of the latest version to two colleagues in his department and to a biology department faculty member that Mary recommended. A courtesy copy went to Department Head Davison. He requested each to please review the paper and return it in a timely manner, with corrections. When the in-house reviewers were satisfied, it would be submitted for publication to the Journal of Antiquities and Archaeology. In the meantime, he made an appointment to meet with Baylor's chief public affairs officer to make her aware of the details of the find and his plans to publish a manuscript describing it.

*

The call from Davison came later that day. The

Department Chair wanted to meet with Adam to discuss the paper, not unexpectedly. What he didn't expect was the demand that he be a co-author.

"I don't understand. Why do you think you should have authorship on this?"

"Besides being chairman of this department and having given you startup research funds, I have stature in the field and influence with many journals, including this one. I can grease the skids for you and help you get it accepted."

"That's great, but you had no input on the scholarship. You didn't contribute ideas or help write it."

"Look, if you'd hold off on this for two weeks, I'm sure I can help make this a much stronger paper."

"I don't see how. It stands on its own. Brad Goodwin likes it, and he's got a better reputation in archaeology, with all due respect. What would you change or add?"

"I'd take the Jesus part out, first. I doubt they'd publish it with that in there."

"A historical connection exists between Pilate and Jesus. We have good cause to mention him for that alone."

"But saying the tissues are his?"

"It's one sentence of speculation on how a piece of tissue can be alive after two thousand years. We can't come up with anything else."

"They won't go for it."

"If the editors insist, we'll take that sentence out. It's not critical to this story and won't influence their decision to publish it."

"Perhaps, but I can still help with that."

"Okay. I'll hold off for a week. Send me your

revisions, and I'll look them over, but unless you add something that significantly improves the paper, the authorship line stays as is."

He left his office and rolled his eyes. I have work to do. He gets one week, that's it.

*

"I can't believe I let him do that."

"Yeah, that's bizarre," Mary said. "What a blatant power play. I haven't seen that in academia, not that it doesn't exist. But it's only a week. Small price to pay to keep peace in the department. Are you ready for your classes?"

"No. That's my next few days. Now I need to call Goodwin and let him know about the delay. He'll probably chew me out for going along with the guy, but, you're right, it's only a week."

"I'm glad you called. I need to talk to you about Melnikos Man cells."

"Want to go for a run first?" he asked.

"It's raining out, goof."

"I know, but I gained a few pounds over the holidays. I didn't run at all. Played basketball, but that's it. So, did you miss me?"

"No, why?"

"Because you're supposed to. I'm the one who's been pestering you for what, four or five months now? And you got a respite from that. Come on, not even a little? How's your brother?"

"I didn't get to see him. He couldn't get away from an assignment. I spent Christmas with my sister-in-law and her little boy. They would have been alone, otherwise."

"Doesn't she have family?"

"They couldn't make it this year. Her dad lost his job last summer and only recently found a new one. He had no vacation days, and they live in Alaska."

"Too bad. So, what about the cells?"

"I'd like to investigate them more thoroughly, see what makes them tick. We should also go ahead and sequence the genome. Adkins seems to be doing well and has taken over most of the mitochondrial research I came here to continue. We're splitting a cell biology course again this spring, so my teaching load is light. This would be the perfect time to focus on those cells. But, before I do, you need to consider whether you want to patent them, because if you do, you ought to get the application process started. Before we publish anything."

"A patent? On Jesus' cells?"

"Maybe. They're different enough from any other cell line and aren't naturally-occurring. I think you could make the case that no one else will ever isolate these cells, and they have a lot of commercial potential, including therapeutics. You'd have to get the lawyers involved, but I'd say it's worth a shot. It would cost a little. Okay, more than a little, but it would protect you as the owner of the cell line."

"Me, the owner of Jesus' cells? Do you know how absurd that sounds?"

"Think of it as making yourself the administrator of their distribution. You would control who works with them and who doesn't, even if you didn't want to profit from them. We can learn a lot from those cells. Everyone stands to benefit from their study. Possibly enormously. They may change medicine."

"I don't know, Mary. That seems too, too something."

"I can give you the number of an attorney I know. I've worked with him before."

"You have a patent on something? Is there anything you haven't done? Geez, girl."

"It's pending, but it still protects the four of us on it. This guy is good. He'll walk you through the steps and explain everything along the way. He's easy to work with. And he doesn't cost an arm and a leg. If he doesn't think these are patentable he can at least advise you on how to maintain control."

"Okay, I guess it couldn't hurt to talk to the guy. Still, the thought of owning Jesus' cells is strange. Hey, let me ask you something. Is there anything more you'd need from the box? I'd like to get it and take it to a secure location."

"Don't trust my flammables cabinet anymore?"

"I don't trust Davison. There's something about that guy. And now that we know what it contains, and its implications, it's time to move it to a safer place."

"It's where it's been the last few months. Anytime you want to come and get it, you know where the key is."

*

The call to Goodwin for advice on the patent idea convinced him to proceed, so he dialed the attorney's number. A pleasant gentleman from Houston. He needed a small retainer to make him his legal representative before

147

the patent office. Adam wrote a check from his savings, slid it into an envelope, and addressed it. He hesitated at the post office drop box, looking upward for a moment before opening it and letting the letter fall in. He called Mary to tell her that he had spoken with the attorney, and his advice was to allow her to do anything she wanted with the cells under one condition.

"And what might that be?"

"Go to a movie with me tonight."

"I don't believe that. More likely, he said dinner and a movie. And only once? You sure are easy, but, it's a deal, or a date, or a whatever."

"I'll call it a date if you will."

"Have we been on one yet? Officially, that is? We've called them working lunches or working football games or working trips to Abilene. Yes, I'd love to finally go on a date with you, and a movie is fine if you're too cheap for dinner."

"I gave my last dime to the patent attorney, so the movie is whatever freebie is showing at the Student Center."

"You really know how to impress a girl."

"And they have free popcorn, so dinner's included."

*

When the week ended, Davison called to ask for more time. A short discussion revealed that the department chairman hadn't come up with anything substantive, so Adam declined to extend the deadline. Davison threatened to fire him and said he'd try to deny him tenure. After hanging up, he retrieved the Melnikos box from Mary's lab. He wrapped it carefully and drove it north two hours to the Dallas Museum of Natural History, where a friend worked. Two days later, it was en route to Luigi's museum in Rome. There it would go on display the moment their paper appeared in print.

That moment did not want to arrive with urgency, however, as the dreaded rejection letters piled up. Phrases such as "does not meet the purpose and scope of our journal" and "did not generate sufficient interest among our editors to warrant further consideration" appeared in the short replies from the journals. After consulting with Mary and Brad, he removed any mention of the name Jesus from the manuscript and resubmitted it to each of the journals that had previously rejected it. When none bothered to acknowledge receiving the revised manuscript, he submitted it to other journals, one by one. None expressed interest. Frustrated, he talked with Brad, who agreed to look into the puzzling matter.

Meanwhile, Mary had written a manuscript about her findings on the tissues found in the whip and the resulting Melnikos Man cell line. She likewise omitted any mention of Jesus or Pilate. Despite good internal reviews, her experience with rejection letters mirrored his, with no explanation from the journals.

CHAPTER TWENTY FIVE

C lark looked at his lab manager, who sat across the desk from his boss. "Well, what do you have for me?"

"I have good news, and I have bad news. Which do you want first?"

"Bad news."

"The bad news is that the good news comes too late for this project, and, I suspect, to save EVI."

"So, the good news must be that you figured out why we aren't getting insulin production?"

"We have."

"I've been racking my brain on this, and I keep coming back to the vector. But, in your reports, the vector looked good. So, that must not be it. What is it?"

"The vector."

"Well, pardon my French. Explain."

"We sequenced it and found a two base pair deletion in the promoter enhancement site. We also sequenced earlier versions, including the original clone, and they all had the same deletion. This promoter came from a company that sold it that way. Their documentation doesn't show that mistake. They somehow missed it, and since we relied on their product data sheet, we never caught it."

"But it works well in mice, right?"

"It does, but those two bases are only important for high expression in live monkeys. We got expression, but it wasn't enough. I suppose they never notified us of the problem because no one else complained."

"They'll find out about it now, believe me. I suppose everyone else got what they wanted in mice, guinea pigs, rabbits, whatever, as long as they didn't test it in monkeys. Of all the rotten luck. Nobody ever used it in monkeys?"

"Only one that I know of, and he sent me his data. The deletion is not there, so he must have had an earlier version of the vector. His worked well in monkeys."

"How long would it take to correct the sequence?" Clark asked.

"I'll have it done by tomorrow."

"Seriously?"

"In the morning, FedEx will deliver the oligonucleotides I ordered twenty minutes ago. After some PCR magic, we'll have the corrected vector. Of course, we'll have to move it into *E. coli* and pull out a good clone. That's a day. Then it'll have to be sequenced. That's another day. We could theoretically put it into animals next week."

"If everything works right. Look, we still have naïve mice and guinea pigs. We also have a few control monkeys from this project. Why not use them? It won't be a complete study by any stretch, but if we move quickly on this and get those monkeys to make insulin—more insulin, that is—we may be able to hold off the grim reaper. Good work. Remind me to give you a Christmas bonus this year."

"Christmas was three weeks ago."

"Oh, well, remind me to do it next year."

"I can certainly do that."

*

He read the text from Vanessa. Working late. Again? Joe's tonight? Been a while. I should hit the gym first, though.

He turned to the mail on his desk and found one he didn't want to open. Has to be another rejection letter. While your research is important and worth pursuing, we are not in a position at this time to finance this work, blah, blah, blah. One particular letter caught his eye, though. What's this? Handwriting? Who sends mail to EVI with a handwritten address? How quaint. He recognized the name in the return address, "Mary Walsh, PhD." One of my best students ever. Why is she writing to me? He tore it open and read the request asking him to consider reviewing a paper of hers and helping her get it published. He dialed the number listed in the header.

"Dr. Clark, how are you? Thanks for calling. Can you help me?"

"Hello, Mary, of course I can help, or at least try. Send me the manuscript. In fact, I have time this afternoon. Can you email it?"

"Dr. Clark, I must tell you why we aren't getting anywhere with it. It's where the cell line originated."

She told him about Adam and his Melnikos discovery,

about the tissues found attached to bone shards in the whip, and the potential link to Jesus Christ. "Regardless of where it came from, this cell line has remarkable properties. I've never seen anything like it, but apparently, none of the journals can see past the name 'Jesus' even though we're now leaving it out. It's nowhere in the paper, and yet we're still getting grief. You're an editor at a prestigious cell biology journal, so I'm hoping you can look into this and see if you can find out what we're up against."

"Happy to. Email it; I'll look it over and make some calls. Chances are, I can find out what the holdup is."

*

He printed her paper and read it with fascination. This is amazing. I can't believe no one wants to publish this. Makes no sense. He made notes in the margins, looked at several references, made more notes, and put the paper in his drawer for the night. Gym time.

After weights, basketball, and the steam room, he drove to Joe's. Joe saw him coming and got a beer for him, but this time he saw someone new at the pool table.

"Haven't seen her here before, Joe. Know her?"

"That's my sister. You stay away from her."

He watched her make a few shots. "Not bad. Should I join her, or were you serious about staying away?"

"Linda," Joe hollered. "Come here a second. Meet Clark. He shoots a little pool. Neither of you is very good, so you might enjoy playing each other."

"Linda, nice to meet you."

"Nice to meet you, Clark. Is that your first name or last?"

"It's Richard Clark. I'm not sure I remember when people started calling me just Clark. Call me what you like. Want to play a game?"

"Sure," she answered, and walked back to the table. He grabbed a cue stick and followed.

"I get here two or three times a month," he said. "You?"

"I live in Texas. Mom, my other brother Bob, and, of course, Joe are here in LA. I come out and see everybody two or three times a year."

"That explains why we haven't met." He racked the balls and invited her to shoot first. "What do you do in Texas?"

"I sell pharmaceuticals for Ensign Drugs. I work the Austin to Dallas market. How about you?"

"Science. Research. I run a company that tests new therapies for diseases like diabetes, hypertension, something called choroideremia, things like that."

"We're both into therapies, then," she said, raising her glass. "I'll drink to that. Cheers."

*

"How was your day?" Vanessa asked as he came through the door.

"Interesting, very interesting. We figured out why our monkey trials didn't work. After that, I had a crazy experience with a former student about a paper she wrote. Then, after the gym, I finished the day playing pool with Linda. How was your day? Deliver any babies?"

"As a matter of fact...no. I had to stay late and cover for one of the midwives at the hospital."

"What, she go on vacation?"

"No. She had a baby."

"Wow, be careful at work, sounds like that stuff is catching."

"Cute." She scowled. "Who's Linda? You meet someone at Joe's?"

"Linda is Joe's sister. Not a bad pool player."

"Uh-huh. Is she pretty?"

"Not as pretty as you."

"You and her play pool all night?"

"No, just a couple of games. Linda's from Texas. I doubt I'll ever see her again. Nothing to worry about."

"So, what happened with the monkeys?"

"Bad viral vector. By only two base pairs, but it resulted in lower levels of insulin synthesis than we needed."

"Will funding dry up?"

"It might. I have other irons in the fire, though. One of them will come through."

"I certainly hope so. Will this affect loan money?"

"Well, you get right to it, don't you? I suppose it could—not the mortgage, and probably not the business loan. We have three straight years of profit working in our favor. But, if we need investment money, and I suspect we will, this kind of news gets around. It won't help, that's for sure."

She read a text from an OB/GYN doc she worked with and texted back.

"So, who was the crazy student?"

"Not a crazy student. A crazy experience with a former student. Do you remember Mary Walsh?"

"How could I forget Mary Walsh? I saw her in your office every time I came back. Drop-dead gorgeous and hanging around you while I attended med school."

"Oh, c'mon. It was nothing like that."

"Oh yeah? I visited UT three times during med school, and each time she was in your office. I swear."

"You'd already left by the time she got there, so you didn't know her."

"Lucky for her. She'd have met my right hook."

"Oh, for goodness sake. She was a new grad student, and I was on her advisory committee. It wouldn't be unusual for her to be in my office asking questions, getting, you know, advice."

"I'm surprised you didn't go after her with me out of the picture. She was there, gorgeous and vulnerable. Why didn't you?"

"Read me lips, sweetie," he said with a faux British accent. "Because...I...loved...you. You, not her. Well, I did have a brief crush on her. But you said yourself she was gorgeous, can you blame me?"

"Yes, of course I can blame you...you little two-timer."

"But she wasn't vulnerable. She was very bright. Knew what she wanted. Knew how to take care of herself. And she was an athlete. One of the best female runners in a long time to come from Texas. Besides, when she told me her brother was Special Forces, I got the hint. We had a good relationship. That's likely why she asked for help getting her paper published."

"Why? Doesn't she know how to write a paper by now?"

"She knows how to write. She writes well, in fact. It's the cells she experimented on, that's the problem."

"Why? They infected with Ebola or HIV?"

"No, nothing like that. How do I put this? They are…they're cells from God. Or, at least, that's what her collaborator says."

"Oh, is that all?" she said as her face contorted into a sneer. "We come across those all the time. What's the problem with those publishers? Has Mary gone off the deep end?"

"No, I don't think so. I read her paper. She has interesting data, and I must say, I'm intrigued. Those cells are resistant to many stresses. She claims she was able to rehydrate them after they'd sat idle in a cave for two thousand years."

"Two thousand years? That makes it during the time of Jesus. Please don't tell me she thinks she's developed a cell line from Jesus. How bizarre. How could that even happen?"

"Something about pieces of tissue lodged in the thongs of a whip. Her collaborator found the whip in a box on an island near Italy."

"Italy? When did Jesus go there? Didn't he spend all his time partying in Jerusalem?"

"Partying? Jesus partied?"

"Yeah, brought booze to wedding receptions. And he hung out with tax collectors and prostitutes. I'm telling you, the guy partied. I suppose he walked to that island?"

"Apparently, this Pontius Pilate guy confiscated the whip used to beat Jesus and stashed it in a cave there. It's been there ever since. Whatever the source, I want to follow this up. It's too interesting to ignore."

"You're kidding. You just had a disastrous end to the monkey study, and now you want to chase after a funny cell line? It must be Mary. You want to see her again. Admit it."

"I haven't thought about her since Texas. She graduated and took a postdoc about a year after I left to come here. But these cells, if they're for real, they could be huge."

"You mean you want to sell Jesus' body?"

"Hey, if there's money in it, I don't care who they came from. If they've survived extreme environmental conditions, they're worth studying. We're into gene therapies, remember? The genome sequence may give us clues on how to treat heritable diseases. Who knows, this may be the fountain of youth."

"Do you know how ridiculous you sound?"

"Yeah, I know. Look, forget the Jesus connection, I already have. I'll experiment a little and see if they're what she claims. It doesn't matter where they came from."

"Will she let you have them?"

"First things first. I have a list of questions. If I get the right answers, I may pay her a visit."

"Gee, why am I surprised about that?"

"You're incorrigible. I'd need to see for myself. Look at the cells, her experiments, her data. Then see if she wants to collaborate. I'll let her know I can do the work here, at EVI."

"Okay. Go to Texas. See if I care. Don't come back converted and try to get me to become a saint with you."

"You're deliberately misconstruing everything I'm

saying tonight. What's wrong?"

"I guess I'm tired. I've been working late a lot. It's starting to take a toll, apparently. I think I'll shuffle off to bed."

"Maybe I'll shuffle back to Joe's and see if Linda is still there."

"Have fun, jerk."

"You know I'm kidding."

"Good night. Don't bother me when you come to bed."

"Good night," he said, opening his laptop. He checked his emails and then went to a science website he subscribed to and logged in. Let's see, Mary Walsh, what did you publish as a postdoc? The site returned titles for four peer-reviewed articles listing her as first author. Impressive. This is good work, and in Bill Anderson's lab. Not bad. Oh, yeah, that's right, I wrote a reference for her. Well, good for her; she started off well. This Jesus business could be good for her. Or it could be bad. More likely bad. I'd hate to see this drag her down. I'm surprised she's involved with something risky like this. I might be doing her a favor taking these cells off her hands. It may be time for a trip to Texas.

CHAPTER TWENTY SIX

Clark expected the call from New York. The decision had been made. There would be no more extensions. The lawyers would resolve outstanding legal issues such as final payment amounts and intellectual property rights. He thanked them for supporting his company, told them he understood their decision and wished them a good day. And that was that.

He composed the email and addressed it for universal distribution. "EVI will continue operations until our accounts are exhausted. We hope to acquire new investment dollars before serious downsizing occurs. We are looking at other options, including business loans, if our insulin vector continues to look promising. I hope you all will remain with EVI. Let's ride out this storm together. Thank you for the wonderful jobs you're doing."

Personnel would head for the exits, and he didn't blame them. He had been so close to a workable diabetes therapy, only to be stymied by a tiny deletion in the viral vector. The success Travers achieved with the three diabetic control monkeys, now looking as healthy as could be thanks to the corrected vector, might attract new investors. He made flight reservations for Dallas, Houston, Atlanta, and Boston, hopeful that he could interest a venture capital firm to take a chance on his therapy.

*

"You did what?" Vanessa asked.

"I transferred money to EVI to help keep it running a few more weeks."

"What money? Savings? Stocks? Bonds?"

"All the above."

She stood and threw the book she'd been reading onto the seat cushion of the sofa behind her.

"Don't worry, we're not going bankrupt," he said, trying to reassure her.

"That was clinic money."

"We'll have the money when the time comes. We can cure diabetes. I'll find somebody who wants to make a fortune. We'll be back on track soon. This won't delay your clinic. I promise. At the very least, we may have to rent office space and equipment for a short time."

"A short time? We know how that goes," she said, her voice getting louder. "I really don't want to start out renting. You had me convinced I'd have state-of-the-art equipment and facilities. Not sure what it'll do to my reputation to open a clinic that isn't first class."

"Your reputation will come from your medical skills. You fix, people and the crowds will beat a path to your door. You're overplaying the ritzy aspect of being in Beverly Hills. Anybody would want to be treated in a brand new facility, but above all else, they want what's wrong with them fixed."

She walked outside and briefly stopped, then continued down the driveway and into the street, not looking back.

Well, that didn't go well. Women. They don't understand finances. He packed his suitcase and checked his boarding pass. With everything ready for his morning flight and Vanessa nowhere in sight, he got into his car and drove to Joe's, who waited at the bar with a cold one. Must have seen me coming. He took it with a thank you and headed for the pool table.

After a game with another patron, he ambled to the bar and ordered a hamburger. The chef knew what he liked on it and had it ready in no time.

"So, Joe, where does that sister of yours live again?"

"The one I told you to stay away from?"

"Yes, Linda. I know she's in Texas somewhere. I'm flying there tomorrow, be happy to buy her dinner if we happen to be in the same town."

"She lives in Austin but drives the I-35 corridor when meeting clients. On any given day, she could be in Dallas or Austin, or anywhere in between."

"Must put lots of miles on her car."

"She does, but she makes a decent living."

"I'll be in Dallas tomorrow, then driving to Waco and Houston. Be nice to see the wildflowers. And the Texas countryside. Gorgeous in a rustic sort of way. You ever been to Texas, Joe?"

"Never. Sis always flies to LA. She'd be the only reason I'd go there."

"Texas is rugged pretty. I liked it when I taught school

there. Still do."

"Lots of cowboys and cactus?"

"Yeah, and oil wells on most streets. I believe it when you tell me you've never been there. Anyway, why don't you give me Linda's number and I'll look her up. Be fun to shoot pool after a day of twisting arms."

"Aren't you already hooked up, Clark?"

"Oh, I am. With Vanessa. Look, Joe, you know me. That isn't what this is about. The other day during a game of pool, she told me she was divorced and that the road gets lonely. I thought she might like to see a familiar face. Besides, you see me in here. When's the last time you saw me chasing another woman?"

"Got me there."

Joe gave him Linda's number along with the plate the cook had placed on the ledge for pickup.

"Enjoy. Dinner, I mean."

"Thanks. Don't worry. We probably won't cross paths, anyway."

"I'm not worried, Clark. You're a good man."

CHAPTER TWENTY SEVEN

A dam looked up from the pile of exams on his desk to see a Baylor police officer and a man neatly dressed in plain clothes standing at his office door.

"Excuse me, sir. Are you Adam Garrett?" the man asked. He noticed a bulge at his waist and assumed the man carried a holstered weapon under his sport coat.

"Yes," he answered, trying to figure out what trouble he might be in now. "What can I do for you, gentlemen?"

"I'm Deputy U.S. Marshal Ralph Connelly," the man said, holding up his credentials. "Mr. Garrett, I have a subpoena here instructing me to retrieve from you the wooden box and its contents that you recently brought back from Italy. Can you please get those items for me, sir?"

"What? I don't understand."

"The subpoena is signed by United States Federal Judge William H. Harrison pursuant to the matter of a custody dispute."

"Custody dispute? No, there's no dispute I'm aware of. I brought that box back with permission from the

Italian government with all the necessary permits. Who is it that thinks they have a right to that box?"

"You'll have to discuss that with Judge Harrison. Can you get the box, please?"

"I'm sorry, I don't have it and can't get it at the moment."

"I'll need you to sign an affidavit to that effect then, sir," the Marshal said, handing him a prepared document. "Please explain in as much detail as you can where it is and why you can't retrieve it."

"Looks like you expected this."

"It happens enough that I always come prepared. Saves everybody time."

In the space provided, he explained that he'd sent the box to a friend in Italy and signed the form.

"Thank you, Mr., uh, Dr. Garrett. Have a good day."

"Is that it?"

"Probably not. The judge may ask you to appear in his courtroom and explain more fully as to the whereabouts and status of these items. If you do hear from him, it will most likely be sooner than later. Good day."

He pushed the pile of exams away and leaned back in his chair to think. He called Goodwin and informed him of the situation, but Brad had no explanation or insights. He called David next and asked for advice. His brother likewise had nothing to offer, other than to suggest that he may want to hire an attorney, but promised to ask around. Then he called Mary, who didn't answer, so he left a message. Busy in the lab, when she returned the call later that morning, she couldn't help either.

"This can't be related to the manuscript," she said.

"What will you do?"

"I don't have the box, so I can't give it to them."

"So you moved it. Where to?"

"I'll tell you when I know more about the nature of this custody dispute. Remember when I said I didn't trust Davison? It may be better for you and everyone else not to know where it is."

The subpoena to appear in court came the next morning, delivered by the same two men. Nine o'clock, two days hence, U.S. District Courthouse, Waco. He called his patent attorney and asked if he could recommend an attorney in Waco. The man said he knew two Waco lawyers and gave him their contact information. He reached for the phone to dial one of the numbers when it rang. David. He'd learned that the Greek government wanted the box, claiming ownership.

"That's nuts. The island is uninhabited, hasn't been since World War II. Nobody owns it."

"Apparently, they convinced the judge that since it had a Greek name, it belonged to Greece. It's coming through Department of State channels, so you need to get that lawyer. Those boys don't mess around."

"I have two names. I was about to call one."

"Good. I'll call back if I find out anything else."

The first attorney had a court appearance and couldn't take his call. The second agreed to represent him but urged him to contact another local attorney, one with more experience in federal matters. Coincidentally, it was the one he had tried to call first. During a lunchtime recess, that attorney returned his call and arranged to meet him the next morning to discuss the custody dispute.

Feeling antsy, he needed to get up and move around, so he walked to the anthropology department office to check his mail. A copy of a journal, a piece of junk mail, a mailer envelope with department business, and a letter from the Journal of Antiquities and Archaeology. Returning to his office, he read the letter. The manuscript had been rejected for not meeting the purpose and scope of the journal. Again? Still? He reformatted the Melnikos paper to comply with the requirements of the next journal and sent it out that afternoon.

*

Once again, Adam described the Melnikos box, this time for the benefit of the attorney now considering representing him in the custody dispute. From the parchments in a vase near Rome to the box in a cave on Melnikos, he laid it all out. He provided copies of the permits issued by U.S. Customs and by the Italian authorities. He gave him contact information for Brad, Luigi, Enrico, and Mary. Lastly, he provided written summaries of his research concerning Melnikos and photographs of the island.

"I don't get why they would go to this much effort to try to get their hands on a simple box. Are they really after what's inside? Was there anything in it?"

He told him about the whip, the crown of thorns, and the papyrus. He told him how Mary had spotted a piece of human tissue embedded in the end of the whip. And then he told him how Mary had resurrected two-thousand-year-old chunks of tissue, pulled from the ends of the whip.

"What? Are you serious?"

"I know. That's the reaction I always get, though I haven't told many people about it."

"Okay, I'll try to get past my incredulity here, because it seems strangely believable yet unbelievable at the same time. I'll work on that, but in the meantime, tell me something. Since you haven't told many people about this, how did the Greek government know about it?"

"I don't know. Can you find out for me?"

"I'll do what I can. Judge Harrison is a reasonable man and probably only allowed the subpoena because the State Department inserted itself, not wanting to risk offending a U.S. ally. I may be able to get him to persuade their counsel to be forthcoming and inform the court as to the source of the leak. Tomorrow is mostly a fact-finding hearing to determine the whereabouts of the box. Where is it, by the way?"

"I don't have it, and I can't get my hands on it at the moment."

"Look, I can't be forced to reveal anything you tell me under attorney-client privilege, but you will be required to disclose its whereabouts to the judge tomorrow. How did you describe its location in your response to the initial subpoena."

"All right. I promised Luigi that his museum would be the first to display the box if it turned out to be historically significant. So I shipped it to Rome. Luigi has it. He's waiting for the publication of our article before he puts it on display."

"So this could turn into a dispute between Italy and Greece. That would be interesting."

"I'm not worried. The Italians won't give it up.

They'll exhibit it for a while and then ship it back here, though I may have him send it directly to another museum. They won't pay the Greeks any mind over something so blatantly specious."

"You certainly have faith in the Italians. But, at any rate, right now, we need to worry about the American legal system. I'll look into this, particularly the sovereignty status of Melnikos. You seem to have been well-prepared for not only making your discovery but getting it back here legally. I can't imagine a scenario under which you'd lose possession of the box. This may be nothing more than bluster and smoke-blowing by the Greek government to save face when your discovery goes public. We'll move for dismissal tomorrow, but we need to be prepared to discuss your claims for legal ownership. Stay by your phone for the rest of the day in case I have questions about Melnikos. And be in my office by eight tomorrow morning. We'll go over any last questions I have, and I'll drive you to the courthouse. *Capeesh?*"

CHAPTER TWENTY EIGHT

C lark spoke with an old college classmate in downtown Dallas an hour before his meeting with the group of speculators looking for a place to park money. His friend advised them on technical issues and, over the years, became aware of the investment proclivities of each.

"These guys are heavily into oil and real estate and doing well, but sometimes they'll give money to risky ventures. I don't think they've ever capitalized a scientific enterprise, though. I believe yours would be the first."

He greeted the group and asked if anyone objected to his having taught at the University of Texas in his previous life. In a place where college rivalries continue to exist well after graduation, he wanted to score humor points, but at the same time, let them know he'd spent time in their state. Having thus established a degree of rapport, he introduced them to EVI, describing its history, mission, strengths, and accomplishments. He listed therapies EVI had in the pipeline and proudly went into detail about the one they had successfully transitioned to human clinical trials.

Moving on to his latest project, he asked how many of them personally knew someone with diabetes. Everyone did. He walked them through the experiments leading to the monkey trials, then explained the problem with the viral vector that sabotaged their recent experiments and that the repair process was currently underway. He closed with a proposed timeline for the sequence of events that would demonstrate the efficacy of their diabetes therapy.

"All of this could be done in nine months. Since things never go perfectly in scientific research, like many other challenging endeavors, my time frame to complete the work is one year. When the animal testing phase is successfully concluded, we'll contract out human clinical trials to an established and successful firm that works with a number of hospitals around the country. So, gentlemen, that's where EVI is at the moment. Thank you for your time. I'm happy to answer questions."

He impressed them with his understanding of the budgetary aspects of running his company, using the opportunity to remind them that he had an MBA. They seemed genuinely interested in the science EVI conducted, asking him about therapies he might pursue in the future. He mentioned the three potentials highest on his list, then thanked them and said goodbye.

He called Vanessa but had to leave a message telling her the meeting with the Dallas investors went well. He added that he still intended to build her a reproductive medicine clinic—a new building with new equipment and esteemed personnel. He clicked on his phone's voicemail icon. Linda had called to say she'd finished her rounds in Fort Worth but was staying in Dallas that night. She also said she'd love to get together and shoot pool at a popular hangout west of Dallas.

He arrived early and ordered an imported beer. He saw three pool tables in the back, two of them not in use, so he laid a ten on the bar and grabbed a cue stick from the rack. He was into his second beer when Linda walked in, dressed in a leather jacket, miniskirt, and high-heeled shoes.

"Wow, Linda, you can dress up. Can I get you a beer? You ready to shoot pool?"

"Yes, and yes. You get me that beer, and I'll rack."

"The usual?" Clark asked.

"No, tell you what. They have great frozen margaritas here. Buy me one?"

"You got it, be right back. Oh, what flavor?"

"Make it raspberry."

He set two raspberry margaritas on a table near the wall and grabbed the cue stick for his shot, which he missed. "Gonna be one of those nights," he said. "But I had a good day, so who cares?"

"I'm glad you called. I don't know anyone in this town, but I guess that's my fault. I've been coming here for at least a year."

"Yeah? How often do you make this trip?"

"Oh, once or twice a month. I made the rounds yesterday in Fort Worth. Today and tomorrow, I'm here in Dallas. Two hospitals, four clinics, and seven doctor's offices. Three days and two nights usually gets me headed back south."

"You must put on the miles. Where do you stay?"

"Here. The Hampton Inn off the exit. You probably

passed it on your way in. I checked in and walked over. Where are you staying?"

"A buddy of mine gave me a key to his house. He lives in Mesquite."

"Mesquite? That's an hour away, depending on traffic. I hope you don't have an early meeting."

"I did, but they canceled. I'm driving to Waco tomorrow, but at least I get to sleep in. When do you have to be somewhere?"

"If I start my rounds by mid-morning, I can get on I-35 and head south before rush hour."

"Well, then, a free night. Want another margarita?"

"Yeah, but I'm buying this time. You can rack 'em since you lost that game."

*

The sunlight made wiggly lines across Clark's pillow after sneaking past the edges of the blinds into a room he didn't recognize nor remember coming to the night before. He put an arm over his eyes to shield the ever-increasing brightness and tried to piece together the events from the night before. This is a hotel room, but how did I get here? Linda? Did she bring me here? How much did I drink last night? He rolled over and saw a note on the other pillow. Uh-oh. What happened? He read the note. "Enjoyed the games last night. See you in LA sometime." He rubbed his eyes and groaned. Games? He sat on the edge of the bed, still trying to get his bearings. Both beds had been slept in. Whew. That's a relief. I think.

CHAPTER TWENTY NINE

Clark hated hotel room coffee but had no choice. While it percolated, he surveyed the room, looking first for his clothes. The pants lay across a chair next to a desk by the window. Wallet's here, good. Phone not here...ah, on the desk. So far, so good. Next, he spotted his suitcase leaning against the wall next to the headboard of the bed. It appeared not to have been opened. From it, he fished out a small toiletries bag. Inside it, he found a bottle of ibuprofen and washed down two of the little pills with the nasty coffee. He spotted a key he didn't recognize on the dresser. The rental? He slumped into a chair and rubbed his face. A shower might help. It did.

When he finally emerged from the room, he saw a single car in the parking lot near the hotel. When he clicked the key fob, it chirped. A restaurant across the street caught his eye, and after checking his watch, he headed for it.

Two eggs, two pieces of toast, and two civilized cups of coffee later, he felt almost human again. No messages on his phone, but there was an outgoing call to Vanessa. At least I had the good sense to call her last night; too bad

I can't remember it. Hope I didn't sound drunk. Margaritas. I remember now. Linda was right; they were great. He responded to his emails, called a friend in College Station, and figured he'd caught up with everybody. After wishing Vanessa a good day in a text message, he called Mary and headed south.

He'd never been to Baylor, but Waco wasn't Dallas. The campus wouldn't be hard to find. There were patches of bluebonnets and Indian paintbrushes in bloom in the highway median and along the shoulders. The bright sun intensified the colors of the little flowers but didn't do much for his headache.

A half-hour out of Waco, he pulled into a rest stop, took care of urgent business, and sat on a bench away from the Interstate facing a field dotted with more clusters of bluebonnets. A mild breeze made them dance gently, as though they enjoyed themselves despite the generally inhospitable terrain they found themselves rooted in. He marveled at how things of such beauty didn't seem to mind growing where most plants declined to make the effort. He slumped slightly to get his head supported by the top board of the back of the bench, but still angled downward enough to allow him to maintain his gaze on the field in front of him. The sounds of cars and trucks passing by on the highway behind him were hypnotic.

He was awakened by a dog off its leash, panting and staring at him as if to communicate to him that he was trespassing on his turf. An apologetic owner soon appeared and scolded it. He told him the dog hadn't barked and therefore hadn't disturbed him, then congratulated him on having such a well-behaved pet. As the two wandered off, he tried to assess how long he'd napped. It couldn't have been more than a few minutes, but however long it lasted, it had to be one of the most pleasant moments of slumber he'd ever had. He felt refreshed, his head had stopped hurting, and he wished he could bottle and sell such sleep. He stood and stretched, then headed to the restroom for a second visit before getting back on the road.

He parked in a visitor's lot and asked directions to the Biological Sciences building. What a lovely campus. What a beautiful day. These Baptists must be doing something right. He reached his destination and went inside, finding Mary in her second-floor office.

*

Mary heard the light tapping on her office door and looked up. "Dr. Clark. Hello, please come in," she said. "How are you?"

"Great, Mary. And look at you. A professor at a major university. Congratulations."

"I had fabulous teachers along the way."

"You did, but you were a bright student who took full advantage of your education experience. I'm not the least bit surprised you're here."

When the small talk played itself out, they turned to her cell line. She reached into her purse for a key and unlocked a desk drawer. She pulled out a small cardboard box and lifted the lid. Inside he saw a slotted vial container housing a dozen vials. Lifting one of the vials, she set it on her desk in front of him. "Here they are."

"Here what are?" he asked.

"I call these 'J-cells.'"

"You keep them in your desk?" He looked incredulous.

"Why not? They do fine here."

"Oh, that's right. Those cells seem to be content wherever they are."

"Plus, it's a security thing. If you wanted to steal these, wouldn't you look in my freezer?"

"Makes sense. Can I see them?"

"Sure. The lab is upstairs. You need anything first? Coffee, water?"

"No thanks. But can I hang my jacket in here?"

"Sure. There's a hook on the door right behind you."

In the lab, she swirled the vial and took out a few microliters of cells with a pipettor and carefully ejected it into the middle of a microscope slide. She laid a thin, glass coverslip on top of the tiny liquid sample and watched it spread underneath, then topped everything off with a drop of immersion oil. She put the slide in position on a microscope, switched everything on, and brought the cells into focus.

"Take a look."

"Nothing unusual about these. They look normal to me."

"That's the point. They look normal, yet when you stress them with enough salt or acid or base that kills other cells, these survive. You read the paper. We have cell lines that die when you look at them funny. These are highly resistant to killing by whatever means; they only seem to die voluntarily, when it's time to make way for new cells."

"You could autoclave them. I'd bet they'd die then."

"That's true, they do. But other treatments, within

reason, they survive."

"Mary, I reviewed your paper, and after looking at these cells, if everything you say is true, you may have a gold mine here. The research possibilities would be endless. I'd venture to say you could spend years, decades even, working out their metabolic capabilities, regulatory systems, growth characteristics—who knows what else. Dozens of publications could come out of these cells. Did you say you wanted to sequence the genome?"

"We're doing it. We'll have it finished next month."

"Good. That ought to explain a lot. There may be genetic cures for certain diseases; we may learn more about the aging process; we may find mutations that could lead to a variety of therapeutics. Have you thought about generating stem cells from these?"

"I have, but that would be later. I'm too busy with my funded studies to spend much time with J-cells."

"I understand. Do you have a bioinformaticist here you can work with?"

"Unfortunately not. I'll have to contract that out."

"I have an idea, then. Come work for me, and you can work on these cells full time. We'll hire someone and get a complete genome annotation and gene comparison profile. Funding will come in by the millions. By then, you'd be in charge of research teams extracting all kinds of information from J-cells. You'd get countless requests for collaborations from around the world; it'd make your head spin. And if J-cell stem cells prove curative…I'm getting excited just talking about this."

"You—you're serious?"

"I've thought about this a lot since we spoke on the

phone, and I had a chance to read your paper. Believe me, this is Nobel material."

"I don't know about that, but in any event, no one will publish this."

"Save those rejection letters. They'll be priceless someday."

"There is a caveat, however. They aren't my cells. They belong to Adam."

"Ah, yes, Adam Garrett. I'd like to meet that man. I'd like to hear about Melnikos. Sounds fascinating."

"Well, he's offered to buy us dinner if you can make it. Where are you staying tonight?"

"Anywhere. I'm driving to Houston for a noon meeting tomorrow."

"Driving? Why aren't you flying? Aren't you the CEO of EVI?"

"Yes, but I wanted to see the wildflowers. Haven't seen them in years."

"They're peaking; you timed it well."

"So, Adam, has he said what he wants to do with J-cells?"

"You won't believe it, but he says he wants to give them away."

"Wow. I admire his altruism, maybe not so much his business sense."

"At least they're protected. He has a patent pending on the cell line and intellectual property rights for whatever comes out of their research."

"Smart guy. Did you tell him to do that?"

"Sort of. I mainly put him in touch with a patent attorney."

"Good for you. So, when can I meet him?"

"I'll see if he's busy."

She called Adam, who said he had a few minutes to talk but had an appointment with a student and couldn't stay long. He walked into her lab two minutes later. "What did you do, run over here? Anyway, meet Dr. Clark."

"Nice to meet you, Adam; I've heard a lot about you. I'd love to hear about Melnikos when you have the time."

"Telling the Melnikos story is a love-hate thing. But since it's turned out so well, I've gotten over the hate part."

"Okay, should I ask about the hate part or save that for another day?"

"Another day. I have to get back to my office. I'm glad you stopped by. Mary thinks you can help with her manuscript."

"Not only that, I've offered her a job. She's not free to work to her full potential here, what with Dr. Adkins having come back. In my lab, with your permission, she'd have complete freedom to study these cells all day, every day."

"Ah. Are you considering it?"

"I like teaching," she said. "But I like research more. It might be nice to work in the lab full time."

"Look, we can always get you an adjunct faculty position at UCLA or USC. You could teach a class every semester to stay sharp. Either school would love to have you for that. Oh, a call. Excuse me a moment." Clark answered his phone as he drifted out of earshot.

"Is this something you might seriously consider?" Adam asked.

"I don't know. I'd have to think about it. I don't

know. Would you miss me?"

"What do you think?"

"There's a catch, though. These are your cells. He wouldn't hire me if you didn't give us permission to work with them."

"So, if I say no, you won't go?"

"Of course not, what would be the point? He wouldn't hire me for my looks?"

"I would."

"That's you, Adam. You are a little off, you know. But a good kind of off. A fun kind of off."

"But if this is something you want to do, and I say 'no,' I would look extremely selfish. Neither one of us would like me then. So I can't say 'no.'"

"But, you would retain legal ownership."

"I'd give that up to be where you were."

That caught her off guard. She didn't know how to respond, but Clark rescued her.

"I'll have to take a rain check on dinner. I'll be staying in College Station tonight, so I need to get on the road. That's what, an hour and a half from here?"

"About that," she said.

"If I leave now, I should be able to see more wildflowers on the way. Mary, think about coming to California; it'd be a great opportunity for you. These cells are as intriguing as they can be. Adam, nice to meet you. I still want to hear about Melnikos sometime. And I hope you'll consider allowing us to work with J-cells. We have access to the best intellectual property rights attorneys around, and we can get your interests completely protected."

*

He headed the rental car along the Brazos River toward Highway 6. Great setting. Beautiful campus. He reached into his shirt pocket and pulled out a microscope slide, setting it on the console. Well, what have we here? How did that get into my pocket?

CHAPTER THIRTY

"Adam, Brad here. I have something for you. But first, tell me how it went in court."

"It went well. I repeated to the judge what I had reported in my response to the subpoena. I didn't have the box and couldn't get my hands on it right away. The counsel for the Greeks wanted him to compel me to retrieve it."

"What'd he say?"

"He told them that he was confident it was secure and that its presence or absence from those proceedings would not affect his ultimate decision, so he ruled against them. They were furious."

"Good. I guess you couldn't ask for more than that."

"We did ask for a dismissal, but the judge cited diplomatic concerns and denied it. Then we asked how they found out about the box since we hadn't published it. They declined to respond, but the judge encouraged them to be thorough during discovery. He set a hearing date for the end of the month."

"So you have two weeks, then, to get ready?"

"Yeah, and that will cost a little cash. My attorney wants to look at everything I have on Melnikos, in detail. He plans to contact the Greek government and ask for documentation of their claim on the island. This guy wants to be fully prepared for the hearing even though it's a bogus lawsuit. He's sold on the importance of the box, and wants to keep it out of the hands of the Greeks at any cost."

"Of course, since you'll be paying those costs."

"Not entirely. He thinks I have a decent chance of getting damages since this is a frivolous lawsuit. Plus, he says the publicity will more than offset the loss of fees he now plans to waive."

"A lawyer said that?"

"I know. Hard to believe."

"Well, my experience is that they get a bum rap too often. Sure there are shysters, but mostly we need them, or this would be a free-for-all."

"So, you have information?"

"I do. Davison has been sandbagging our paper. He knows the editors at the journals we've submitted to. We haven't had a chance."

"Well, he must also have friends at Archaeological Today because they turned us down. Their letter came today. They must have had the manuscript for all of two minutes before mailing the rejection notice."

"Wow, he got to them too. I knew he was devious, but this is crazy."

"Well, he can't know everybody. I'll try again somewhere else. Say, Brad, can you do me a favor?"

"Sure."

"Whoever you talked to at the journal, was it off the

record, or might they consider signing a statement as to what they know about Davison's involvement?"

"This guy would. There's no love lost between him and the managing editor. I'll get on it. And I have a contact at JA&A; I'll see what she can find out about why they wouldn't publish your paper there."

*

Adam called Mary to inform her of the latest rejection and that he'd send the manuscript out once again. He also relayed the information from Goodwin about Davison.

"That's crazy. He really has it in for you."

"He's nuts. Look, if it gets rejected one more time, I'll make the Melnikos announcement in the school newspaper. Then we wait for the publicity to grow and make it impossible for the next journal to turn us down."

"That's a good idea, but there's just one problem."

"What's that?"

"Your discovery is in today's edition, front page. Ed brought it to my attention. Davison's name appears twice; you aren't mentioned until the last paragraph. He's taking much of the credit. I was just about to call you."

"What? No way. Seriously?"

"Check it out yourself."

"That little snake. Unbelievable. How could he possibly—"

"He used the word 'we' a lot."

"So, what's next? Will this be in the national papers tomorrow? This is infuriating. I need to have a talk with that man."

"Don't do anything rash, Adam."

"Like punching him in the teeth? I'll try. Not to, that is. But we're going to have words, he and I. He'll find out what happens when you screw around with a West Texas boy."

He went to the first-floor office, where Davison stood talking to his secretary in the outer office. Finding a copy of the Lariat, he stood there and read the article. Davison sneered at him. When he finished reading the article, he threw the paper at Davison. It missed the target as the pages flew apart, each gliding through the air to different spots on the floor.

"You glory-hounding twit. I wasn't ready for this to come out. Who do you think you are to not only take credit for my work but time its release to the public? Get ready for a lawsuit, jerk."

"Well, Garrett, you're fired. And good luck with the lawsuit. I'll have the entire Baylor legal office at my disposal. This time next month, that box will be on display in my building, and your name will appear in the smallest font possible. Now, get out of my sight."

Mary waited for him in his office. She hugged him when he came in and asked if he'd calmed down. And had he done anything rash?

"I got fired, is that rash?"

"Davison fired you? On what grounds? Will you fight it?"

"It just happened, I don't know what I'll do."

"You didn't punch him, did you?"

"No, of course not. I did throw the Lariat at him."

"Well, nobody gets fired for that. But he can't have cause. You can appeal this. Will you?"

"I don't know. Maybe. I have to sort this out."

"Do it for me?"

He looked at her a moment, then closed the door and put his arms around her. There was no hurry to release her, and she didn't pull away. He leaned his head back so he could look into her eyes. Then he let her go, taking his seat behind his desk.

"Thanks, I needed that."

"Anytime."

"You have a persuasive way about you. Of course I'll fight it. Hey, want to go for a run?"

"Three miles? Loser buys?"

After the race, they walked to a deli, and Adam bought two sandwiches, chips, and drinks. They carried the food back to their oak tree and ate a leisurely lunch, sitting in the shade. Professor Adkins, out for his afternoon stroll around campus, spotted them and stopped by.

"Dr. Adkins, have you met Adam Garrett?" Mary asked.

"No, but I've heard a lot about him. Adam, I'm Raymond Adkins, nice to meet the man who found the cells my colleague here enjoys working with. Or was it Davison who found them?"

"Oh, you read the article," he said. "Yeah, it appears that Davison made the discovery after all. Melnikos is a small island, though. I believe I would have seen his tent, had he been there."

"That guy has a reputation. I bet you didn't count on publishing your find in the Baylor Lariat, did you?"

"No, sure didn't. I get scooped on Melnikos and fired all in one day."

"Fired? For what?"

"There's no cause. Davison is mad that I didn't include him on the paper. He had nothing to do with it. I couldn't in good conscience make him an author even if it would have bought goodwill in the department."

"No, you couldn't do that. Unethical, even though it happens. I applaud you for that."

"And worse, Davison sabotaged our paper, several times now," Mary said.

"How do you know that?"

"Brad Goodwin," he said. "He's the third author on our paper. He knows the big names in archaeology and talked to a few. Turns out Davison had called in his chits and got our paper rejected at the first two journals we submitted it to. Brad thinks he's been behind the others also, which makes sense. There's no academic justification for not accepting our paper."

"Ouch. What did you do to get on his enemies list, besides deny him authorship?"

"I don't know. Nothing. I'm the only archaeologist in the department. I tend to keep a low profile, do my job, and don't make waves. I don't know what I did."

"Well, I'm so sorry about this. I hope it works out. Nice meeting you, Adam. Mary, I'll see you later."

"My pleasure meeting you, sir. Mary tells me nothing but good things about you."

"I do, I do," she said, grinning. "Have a good walk, Raymond."

CHAPTER THIRTY ONE

"Good news, dear," Clark said. "The Dallas group wants to meet again. We may have dodged a bullet." He leaned to kiss Vanessa, who pulled far enough away to avoid contact. He took his suitcase into the bedroom and emptied it. She followed him into the room.

"Plan to see your girlfriend again?"

"What? What are you talking about?"

"Your girlfriend in Dallas. I heard her in the background. Must have been a pool hall by the sound of things. I didn't understand much of what you said, though. It's on voicemail. It was after midnight in Dallas, by the way."

"Oh, Monday night," he said, relieved he'd made that call from the pool hall rather than the hotel. "Yes, Dallas. I played pool with Linda after the meeting."

"Linda, who?"

"Linda. Joe's sister. You know Joe. He owns the grill over on Wilson Street. I met her at a bar in Dallas. We played a few games, had a few margaritas."

"Ah, so it was the margaritas talking."

"Must have been. I was in a real fog the next morning. She said they made the best margaritas. She wasn't lying. Anyway, she's not my girlfriend. You are. Besides, she lives in Austin. She's a drug rep and drives to Dallas once or twice a month. I doubt she'll be there next trip, so, no, I won't be seeing her."

"There have to be hundreds of bars in Dallas. She happened to be at the one you went to?"

"No, of course not. I got her number from Joe when I decided to go to Texas. He made it clear that I had to behave myself, and he knew I would. I called her after my meeting. She happened to be staying overnight in Dallas, said she'd been to that place a few times. Look, she's a nice girl who's had some bad luck. Her husband ran out on her two years ago. She's working hard to help support her mother, who lives here in LA. We had fun playing pool. That's it."

"If you say so. When do you go back to Dallas?"

"As soon as they meet again. Probably not before next week, though."

"If they're interested, how much are we talking?"

"I'd say we'd be back on track with EVI, shouldn't have to lay anyone off. The Dallas boys are wealthy, and they don't seem as tight as the New York guys. If they jump in, they'll probably back us for at least two years, but that's all we'd need to wrap this up."

"So, you'll get your loan back?"

"Absolutely. Your clinic is back on track, too, if that's what you're wondering about."

"What I'm wondering about at the moment is why

you have a microscope slide in your suitcase," she said, having spotted it in one of the compartments.

"Oh, that. I'm taking it to work to see if there's anything to Mary's J-cells. I took it off the microscope in her lab when we finished looking at it, but it somehow went into my pocket rather than the hazardous waste bin."

"Nice trip. Now you're a cheat and a thief. And J-cells? What the—oh, that's right, the infamous J-cells. The ones that come back from the dead. Well, I'll have to see it to believe it."

"If what she says is true, that would be unprecedented. Normally I'd give someone like Mary the benefit of the doubt, but to claim these can withstand severe dehydration, I'll have to see that too. I've had this slide a week, and any other cell type would have been long dead. I'll see if I can bring them back to life as she did. And I didn't cheat on you. I don't think."

"You don't think? What's that supposed to mean?"

"As I said, the margaritas were really good."

"Well, you better not have, or you'll have to come back from the dead yourself."

"I like it when you tease like that."

"Who's teasing?"

"You."

"Think what you want. And you can't be serious about those cells. Even if you find one intact, it'll fall apart the second you do anything with it. This time, Clark, put it where it belongs. The trash. Don't waste your time."

"I don't know. Her data is convincing. In any event, it'll only take five minutes to pull off the coverslip, add a little buffer, and get them in a culture flask."

*

He rarely found himself in a lab coat at EVI, and then only to observe technicians while they conducted experiments. He arrived early that morning and turned on the lights to an empty lab. Except for animal caretakers who worked in a separate part of the building, his employees rarely came in on Sundays. A scientist would occasionally come in to transfer or feed tissue cultures, but at the moment, he had the room to himself. He mounted his pilfered slide on the stage of a microscope and took a look. The intact cells surprised him. Shriveled-looking things, to be sure, but also visible were discernible nuclei, mitochondria, and other organelles. He carefully worked the coverslip off the glass and pipetted a small amount of sterile buffer on the J-cells. He scraped the slide with the pipette tip and pipetted buffer in and out at that spot to loosen material stuck to the slide, then transferred it to a small flask containing sterile nutrient broth to stimulate growth and allow antibiotics to kill bacterial contaminants. He labeled the flask with his initials and the date, then placed it in a clamp in a shaking incubator that maintained an optimal temperature, humidity, and CO_2 for most mammalian cell cultures. Lab coat off, lights off, still no one in sight.

He walked to his office and sorted through the mail on his desk, looking for anything important. He picked out a letter and an EVI interoffice envelope, but neither appeared urgent. Everything else could wait until Monday. He locked his office and the entrance door to the building, and drove home.

Vanessa had not yet started her day. She caught up on

sleep and read the newspaper on Sunday mornings, then did whatever she fancied in the afternoon. Sometimes a walk on the beach or in the park, sometimes a bike ride, sometimes a drive, usually with Clark. He brought her a cup of coffee. She grunted, sat up in bed, and sipped.

"Want to go out for brunch?" he asked.

"Ask me in ten minutes, after the fog lifts."

"All right, I'll be reading the paper on the patio."

From the chaise lounge, he turned his head at the sound of the shower coming from the bathroom window, then resumed browsing the sports pages. Vanessa appeared by the time he'd finished the editorials.

"Decided on brunch?"

"No, I don't know what I want. When I feel like this, though, it usually means I need a workout."

"Feel like what?"

"Cranky. Irritated at you for going to Texas not to see one girl, but two."

"But I came back. That has to count for something. How about a bike ride? That would get you some exercise."

"Yeah, a bike ride to the beach and then a run on the sand. That would be a workout."

"Or we could put on the boxing gloves, and you could take a few whacks at me."

"That isn't funny, Clark. I'm trying to play the jilted lover, and you crack jokes. It isn't supposed to go like that."

"Because I know you're too smart to think I would fool around with girls in Texas. We've been together for ten years, and I've never once so much as looked sideways at another woman."

"Yeah, because you look straight at them."

"I see the coffee has kicked in. Why don't you eat a bite and we'll go for that bike ride? It'll do us both good."

CHAPTER THIRTY TWO

C lark's text consisted of two words: "They're alive." Vanessa texted back, "I'm from Missouri. Show me." His reply: "Anytime."

At dinner that night, she asked about his knowledge of Christian apologetics. "None," he said, surprised at the question. "I suppose they taught that at your Catholic High School?"

"That's right. An honors class in theology. It was interesting. Tedious and boring, but interesting."

"Isn't that an oxymoron?"

"That's theology. Anyway, one of the explanations that emerged to refute the resurrection of Jesus from the dead was that his disciples had rolled back the large stone blocking the entrance to the tomb, stole his body, and reburied it somewhere else. Then they claimed Jesus had been raised from the dead. Probably to get money, but that's another story."

"Okay, what does that have to do with anything? Anything here in California, anything at all in the world?"

"You don't get it, do you? You stole Jesus' cells from

Mary Walsh. Nobody knows you have them. And now you're hiding those cells, to make money. So you're like the disciples who stole his body from the tomb. Only you're the twenty-first-century version," she explained, then laughed until she cried.

He didn't laugh. "Your analogy breaks down, dear. Mary still has those cells; I only have an aliquot. It'd be like the disciples taking an arm or a leg from Jesus and leaving the rest in the tomb."

"That's silly. Who would only steal an arm or a leg?"

"You're confusing. Forget the stupid analogy. If someday I sell the secrets of these cells to Big Pharma for big bucks, money that will pay for your clinic and your staff and the latest state-of-the-art medical equipment, will you call me Judas Iscariot?"

Her laughter had subsided until that remark. "Judas. That's good," she said when she'd settled down again. "Now you're catching on. That was good. I needed a good laugh. Or a good cry."

"A cry?"

"It seems my clinic depends on a guy who wants to make a fortune with magical mystery cells, supposedly from a Jew who died over two thousand years ago. So, yes, a cry might be in order."

"Okay, Dr. Wonder Woman, how do you explain human cells that are alive a week after being taken out of culture and left to dry on a piece of glass?"

"I don't know. Could the storage medium have had a high concentration of glycerol? Glycerol keeps cells from freezing, probably helps keep them from drying too."

"Well, possibly, but glycerol usually isn't added to

culture medium at high enough concentration to be an antifreeze or antidesiccant. I put them in a glycerol-free medium this morning. At the end of the day, I spotted a sample on a glass slide and left it exposed to air. Tomorrow I'll see if they're still alive. Will you believe it then?"

"I'd still have to see them with my own eyes."

"Doubting Thomasina."

"Ha, another one. You're on a roll."

"Maybe I could get a night gig around here."

"You already have one, playing pool with Linda."

"Will you let that go? I played with her twice. Once here, once in Texas. That's it. Now cut it out. Please."

"Sorry. I'm in a rut and need a change. I'm tired of residency. It's taking forever. I can't wait to get the clinic running. How is everything?"

"Loans are moving along. If I get the Dallas group interested in EVI, I can repay myself. That would mean we'd only be about a quarter million short."

"Time to hit your rich friends?"

"I've talked to a few people. Fifty thousand here, a hundred thousand there. We can get awfully close to what we need."

"We'd still be majority owners?"

"Absolutely."

"Hey, I need a change of pace, and you need to be done with J-cells. How about I spend time at EVI, throwing everything I can at them? I'll find something that brings them back down to earth."

"What, take time off from your residency?"

"Lord knows they owe me the time. Lots of it. No, I thought I'd work shorter days at the hospital for a while and spend afternoons at EVI. I can work weekends at the hospital if they need me, and at EVI if they don't. What do you think?"

"Would I have to pay you?"

"Of course not. The sooner you forget about J-cells, the sooner you can refocus on the clinic."

"I haven't forgotten about the clinic. And you can work in the lab anytime you want."

"Does that lab have a hood and incubators?"

"And a microscope, and I can get anything else you need. I run the place, remember?"

"Things ought to have slowed since the monkey study ended. I shouldn't be in anybody's way. It might be fun to get back into research for a few days, if only to disprove the existence of God, so to speak."

"You do have a way with words, I'll give you that. So, I take it you didn't enjoy high school?"

"So-so. There were a few decent teachers. I really liked the one I had for biology, but you had to keep your distance from the other Sisters."

"I can see you getting in their faces. Did they turn you off religion?"

"Mostly, it was my parents. They'd go to Mass on Sunday and live like the devil the rest of the week. Well, not quite like the devil, but close."

"Hypocrites?"

"Yeah. Dad cheated on Mom. Mom cheated on Dad. She may have only done it to get back at him. But come Sunday, they were in church."

"That's too bad."

"They weren't the only ones, though. I'd look around

church and see people who shouldn't be there. As if they never did anything wrong. So many hypocrites."

"Funny how we've never talked about religion," he said. "I don't even know if you believe in God or not."

"I don't not, and I don't do."

"I recognize female logic when I hear it, and I think I got that."

"I will say this," she said. "Life is amazing under a microscope. Living cells. Embryos developing into living, breathing beings. Then they become people and the evil they do, and it makes you wonder how a God who tolerates that exists. So I haven't ruled him in, and I haven't ruled him out. Mostly out, I guess. What do you say?"

"I agree with that. Some people need religion. I don't. But religion can do much good. I've seen the amounts of money churches spend on hospitals and charities. Too bad it can also cause people to do evil."

"Imagine killing other people in the name of God. Does that make sense?"

"None. None at all. But religion is like a lot of other institutions. It depends on what kinds of people are running things."

"Speaking of running, I think I'll go for one," she said. "Want to tag along?"

"I don't think so; it's late, but how about a swim?"

"I think I'd rather run."

"It's dark out. I'd feel better if I went with you. Can it be short?"

"Sure, good idea. Let's do the Baker Street loop; that's about two miles. Then we can do a few laps in the pool when we get back."

"Then a margarita?"

"That's Lin—never mind," she said, remembering to cut it out. "A margarita sounds good. Let's go."

They changed into their running clothes and shoes. On their way out the door, he asked her if it turned out that J-cells were immortal, could that influence her thinking about God?

"As I said, it won't happen."

"But if they're immortal, we could be rich. You'd have your clinic. Don't you want to root for the existence of God?"

"Damn you, Clark."

The comment perplexed him.

"It's a joke," she said. "You don't get it?"

"No. But it may come to me on our run."

"It will. Think about it."

CHAPTER THIRTY THREE

Vanessa drove to EVI after a morning shift at the hospital. She went straight to Clark's office, knocked on the open door, and allowed herself in. On the phone, he motioned for her to sit in one of the two chairs stationed in front of his desk. He ended the call and announced the news to her.

"Dallas wants me to present a detailed business plan and a formal seminar to them and their scientific consultants the day after tomorrow. I'm going to Texas."

"That's fantastic. Can you go to Texas and stay away from Linda?"

"Didn't we agree you'd knock that off?"

"No, we had no agreement; you only made a request."

"Do you want me to go get the money or not? Or even better, go with me."

"No, you go. Get the money and come back. But make it money business, not monkey business."

"Right. Regular business in Dallas, monkey business here."

"Before I start in the lab, what's my budget?"

"You shouldn't need much, but I'll open a spending line for you." He went over to the door and closed it. "I'll put five thousand in it for supplies. If you need more, we can discuss it, but looking for weaknesses in J-cells shouldn't cost much."

"Want to sequence them?"

"Mary's doing it. We don't need a genomic sequence for you to find sensitivities or deficiencies. You always seem to find them in me. I have faith that you'll find them in J-cells."

"There you go again with the wordplay. Faith?"

"I didn't intend it that way, but I guess it is funny. A little."

"They aren't immortal," she said. "Can't be. Were they genetically engineered to make them more resistant to dehydration and stress? This could be a fraud."

"A clever fraud, if true. How would you even begin to do something like that?"

"Oh, I don't know off the top of my head. Expedited mutagenic evolution? Who knows? Sequencing would tell us."

"I'll be back Thursday, let's see what you've found then. I'll be happy to pay for sequencing if it'll answer questions, but Mary should have that soon. If not, we'll do it. Also, no one here knows about this. I've told others in the lab you're here to develop a new cell line for a future project. I've labeled J-cell vials 'DC1600', so please refer to them with that name in your notes."

"Got it. Are they in a freezer?"

"Yeah, in the 101 lab. You need orientation?"

"It wouldn't hurt."

"And, here," he said, reaching into his desk drawer. "You may as well use the notebook I started."

He led her to the lab and showed her the bench she'd use and the available equipment. She'd have access to whatever chemicals or other reagents and plasticware she needed. He showed her the freezer and the box of DC1600 cells, then explained environmental procedures and what types of waste went where. He introduced her to Bob, a technician who worked in the 101 lab and could give her any help she needed.

"Don't flirt with the staff, dear. I have eyes and ears around here, you know. I'm like God in this place. Now, good luck trying to disprove that other one."

*

Clark flew to Texas Tuesday afternoon and drove a rental car to the west side of Dallas. He found the familiar bar and grill that made terrific margaritas and ordered a beer. He grabbed a cue stick and racked the balls on the far table. A few minutes later, Linda walked in.

"Hi, Clark. Loser buys dinner?"

"You're on," he said. "Want a drink?"

"Usual, but make it lime."

"I'll be back, go ahead and break." A moment later, he returned with a margarita.

"You liked these last time, as I recall," she said.

"A little too much. I have an important meeting tomorrow, so I've reached my alcohol limit for the night. You heading back to Austin tomorrow?"

"Yep. Same schedule as last time."

"So, Linda. What the hell happened last time? I don't

remember anything after playing pool with you, but the next morning I'm in a strange bed in a hotel room that I didn't check into, with a note from you on my pillow."

"You don't remember that night?"

"No, I don't. Tell me what happened."

"You sure you want to know?"

"Yes. I need to know."

"Okay. You really enjoyed the margaritas, but they made you play pool poorly, and you lost $500 to me in bets."

"I did not. I don't bet on pool. I know better than that."

"As I said, you enjoyed the drinks."

"Okay, okay. I'll give you the $500. What else happened?"

"I'm kidding about the bet, but you do owe me for half the hotel room. You had enough sense not to drive to Mesquite, and you let me put you up here for the night. I got you into bed, and when you hit the sheets, you were out."

"Did you take my pants off?"

"Well, you did the work, I just made sure you didn't fall over. Look, Clark, nothing happened, if that's what you're asking."

"That is what I'm asking. Not that you aren't amazingly attractive, Linda, but Vanessa would know immediately if I ever fooled around. On the side, on a trip, she'd know, and that'd be the end."

She looked at him wistfully, and then sank the eight ball. "All right, I'll settle for dinner. Let me know if you ever get back on the market."

"It's a date, or, rather, a deal, I should say. Let's eat."

CHAPTER THIRTY FOUR

✠

A dam sat back in his chair and smiled. He'd returned from Davison's office, where he witnessed a surprising spectacle. The irony. He'd almost forgotten about the letter he'd stuffed in his back pocket. It was from the first journal he'd submitted their paper to. He opened it and read it. Twice. Mary needs to know about this.

"Mary, how are you today?"

"Great, Adam, where are you calling from? This was an on-campus ring, and I thought you'd been fired. So, are you in your office? Do you still have an office?"

"I do, but Davison doesn't."

"What? Seriously? What happened?"

"I don't know. When I went to check my mailbox, campus security was in his office, helping him pack personal things. Then they escorted him out of the building. I saw it all."

"You stood there and watched?"

"Well, I did offer to help when he passed me carrying a box of papers. He sneered and kept walking.

"Tell me you aren't grinning right now."

"Okay, I'm not grinning right now. Are you?"

"A little. So, does this mean you still have a job?"

"Apparently. Want something else to grin about?"

"Let's hear it."

"The Journal of Antiquities and Archaeology re-evaluated our paper. They've decided it fits their readership after all."

"Wow, you're two-for-two today. What made them give us a second look?"

"I don't know."

"Actually, I may know something about that."

"You do?"

"A few days ago, Ed overheard Adkins mention your name during a phone call. It turns out he was talking to Dr. Hardcastle. You know, the University President."

"Yeah, I know who he is. Go on."

"Ed said he heard Davison's name too. He also said Adkins asked him to look into something about unethical conduct. That was it. I guess we know what that means."

"Adkins went to bat for us? He must be impressed with you."

"I guess doing what I could to accommodate his return helped. Our arrangement works. It's not permanent, but it works for now. And I think his coming back to work at Baylor has done him a world of good. He really is a nice guy, and I'm happy for him."

"Looks like your graciousness has paid off," he said.

"I don't like to make enemies under any circumstances, but what sense would it have made to fight for my job with someone like Adkins? Anyway, during exams, I had an idea."

"Shoot."

"I'm thinking of asking Clark if he'd let me work at EVI during summer break."

"Well, then, I'll go with you."

"And do what?"

"Spend time with you."

"I'd be working. There'd be no free time."

"Not even at night? Or weekends?"

"Don't be silly."

"Okay, forget LA."

"Here's what I'm thinking. The J-cell genome sequence is almost finished. When it is, we send it to Clark. He said he'd pay for gene annotations and bioinformatic analysis. When we get that, we look for anything J-cells would be predicted to do that ordinary human cells don't. I go to his lab for the summer and do experiments that confirm the genetic basis for those differences. We publish it, and J-cells are off and running. All that needs to happen soon, though. We should have at least two experiments decided on before I go."

"That sounds perfect because I have a solid prospect for a dig this summer, near Cancun, of all places. I'd be there while you're in California. We'd both be at the beach this summer. Just different beaches."

"Who knows, that might keep you out of trouble. Wait, Cancun? Hmmm. Anyway, would you be okay with sending Clark the sequence and sharing J-cells with him?"

"Fine by me. My idea is to make them freely available anyway, eventually. Even so, I'm sure the patent attorney would insist on a materials transfer agreement. I'll call and have him work one up. When do you expect the sequencing to be done?"

"They're piecing together the last segments this week, should be ready Monday or Tuesday. One more thing I should mention. No doubt Clark is hoping to buy your good will so that when the time comes, you'll consider him on future developments."

"Fine."

"He's offering his expertise, including legal and business advice, so he'll have a head start making J-cells—"

"Profitable?" Before she could interject, he beat her to the punch. "I'm not necessarily opposed to that. If he takes risks and is meeting payroll and helping science and mankind, fine by me. That may be the best way to get J-cell benefits out there. Government doesn't always have to be the only game in town. Let the Clarks of the world have at it, and they'll probably get it done faster and cheaper."

"Sounds like you're familiar with laissez-faire economics."

"I have a lot of time to read on digs. But everyone should know that; it's undergrad stuff."

"Not at many schools. Anyway, we're off track. It sounds like you're okay with me working with Clark this summer?"

"I am. I'll miss you, but go. Do whatever you want with those cells. You know I trust your judgment."

"All right. I'll think about it."

"Want to go out tonight? You buy me dinner for a change? Take in a movie?"

"Aren't you visiting Davison tonight? He could

probably use a friend about now."

"Oh, yeah, right. But that does remind me to call Goodwin and tell him about the paper."

"And Davison getting canned?"

"That might come up."

"Might, nothing; it's guaranteed to come up. Pick me up at six?"

"It's a date."

CHAPTER THIRTY FIVE

Vanessa mulled over Clark's notes. *He did what I would have done. I should first repeat the desiccation-dehydration experiment. Then hit the cells with heat, salt, and a range of high and low pH buffers. No, that's not right. Start cultures today, then when they're nice and healthy, stress them and see how long they survive. Yes, and let aliquots of those cultures dry overnight and try to revive them. That's it, and compare actively growing cells to frozen, to see how they do coming out of frozen storage. Okay, I should get an estimate of starting quantities with a quick count under the scope. Control cells? Oh, yes. Where's Bob?*

The tech had stepped out for a moment, and when he returned, she asked for a stock of a healthy human cell line. He walked her to an ultra-low freezer and showed her where they stored mammalian cell lines. "If you take any out, please record the vial number on this log sheet. And if you have problems culturing them, I can make new working stocks from our liquid nitrogen master seed stocks."

"Will do. Thank you."

She set up an experiment to compare the ability to resist stress between a human cell line known as "HeLa" and DC1600 cells. The wells of nine identical 24-well culture plates containing sterile nutrient broth were seeded with either DC1600 cells, HeLa cells, or a little sterile water. Then she added small amounts of solutions of sodium chloride, sodium hydroxide, hydrochloric acid, or sterile water separately to individual wells containing one of the three test samples. Three plates would be allowed to grow at 28°C, three more plates at 37°C, and the remaining three plates at 40°C, each set placed in its own temperature and humidity-controlled CO_2 incubator. Finally, before leaving for the day, she pipetted a small amount of DC1600 cell stock and the same amount of the HeLa cell line onto the plastic bottom surfaces of two empty, sterile Petri dishes where they would dry overnight. She replaced the lids and put them in a 37°C incubator.

The next afternoon, she collected the nine 24-well culture plates and examined each well for growth. She observed no cloudiness in any of the wells to which she had added only water instead of cells. No apparent contamination. So far, so good. HeLa cells didn't grow in anything except normal growth medium. She saw robust growth at 37°C but less growth at 28°C and 40°C. DC1600 cells, however, grew nicely in every well into which they'd been inoculated, including those to which she'd added salt or changed the pH up or down. Well, I'll be damned. In Clark's notebook, she wrote the following: "DC1600 cells resistant to 0.5M NaCl, growth medium at pH5.5, and growth medium at pH 9.0. HeLa cells lysed or damaged. Triplicate plates identical." She returned each plate to their respective incubators to allow them to continue growing, if they could, for another day. She then set up that exact same experiment, but instead of adding thawed frozen cells to start cultures, she inoculated the wells with freshly growing cells from the HeLa or DC1600 cultures she'd started the previous day. Turning to the dried spots of DC1600 or HeLa cell cultures on the bottoms of Petri dishes, she layered sterile buffer on them and gently scraped the plastic surface with a pipette tip to loosen and retrieve any intact cells. She transferred those cells to small flasks of growth medium. She placed the two flasks in a 37°C shaking incubator and called it a day.

After returning home, she poured a glass of wine and opened the PubMed website on her tablet. The OB/GYN Department had asked her to participate in the establishment of in vitro fertilization services at the hospital, suggesting that she would be in the running for the director's job. Thinking that title would look good on her resume, she launched herself into a review of the latest developments in the field and read articles until midnight. With Clark not around, she'd lost track of time.

The next afternoon, she returned to EVI and examined the two flasks. What the—wow, what is it with these cells? Amazing. She examined them under the microscope. There they were — plump and happy-looking DC1600 cells. HeLa cells? Nothing but debris scattered around the field of view. She printed photos and pasted them into Clark's notebook. Those surprising results stimulated her thinking. She considered a number of other ways to test DC1600 cells, but since Clark wanted to remain discreet, she couldn't call an infectious disease colleague or a cancer specialist friend and ask them to run experiments on this new cell line. So, working with what she had at EVI, she repeated the experiments comparing HeLa to DC1600 cells, only this time with a broader range of salt concentrations, temperatures, and pH variations. That would allow her to explore the limits of environmental stresses DC1600 cells could withstand. Clark would be back later that day, and, despite her initial misgivings, she would have to confirm that J-cells were unique. Like Mary and like Clark before her, she had given in to the inescapable pull of those cells. Their amazing capabilities took her in a hundred different directions as she pondered future research possibilities. Just as Mary had ideas for investigating their remarkable biological properties, and Clark had his own designs on exploiting those properties for profit, she settled in on a purpose for them of her own.

*

Clark stopped at EVI on his way home from the airport to take care of a few administrative chores that had accumulated during his absence. Before heading back, he called Mary Walsh.

"Congratulations to you and Adam. I see that your paper has been accepted; this is exciting. So, is there anything new with J-cells?"

"The genome sequencing is mostly done, pending gaps that appear after it gets assembled. The guy tells me that he's already seen a few alignment issues, so there will be follow-up sequencing. We don't know how much yet.

In any event, now I need someone who does bioinformatics to annotate it. And someone who does comparative genomics."

"Come to work for EVI, and you'll have your bioinformaticist."

"I'm tempted. I find myself wondering at times if I should put my other research on hold and study J-cells full time."

"Come to work for me, and you'll have all the resources you need, not to mention a hefty paycheck."

"Stop it, Clark. Make me an offer I can refuse."

"Why? What's keeping you in Waco?"

"A job I like. The career I want. And don't forget, Adam controls the cells. I can't guarantee he'd let me take them with me if I leave."

"He seems like a nice guy. I'll figure out a way to hire him too."

"He's an archaeologist. I doubt he'd fit in at EVI."

"Well, the job is yours if you decide you want it. If it would help, I'd be happy to hire a bioinformaticist and have him work at our Waco field office."

"You have a—oh, of course, that would be us."

"That's right, and you'd be his or her boss. If Baylor had a problem with them working on campus, we'd let him or her work from home."

"I'll run it by Adam."

"Good, good. Can you let me know one way or the other in a few days?"

"Sure. The semester is winding down. I'll have more free time after finals next Monday."

"I don't want to rush you. It's more for planning

purposes, you know, since we're on a budget here and I have to meet a payroll. Tell Adam I said 'hello.'" Bringing her on board at EVI might be the easiest way to get legal access to J-cells. I may have to give Adam a piece of the action, but if it meant having some of the pie or none at all, a portion of a gold mine is better than nothing.

*

"Anybody home?" he asked. "Is my brilliant scientist-doctor here?" He unpacked his carry-on bag and changed into shorts and a T-shirt, then walked barefooted out onto the back patio. Vanessa reclined in a chaise lounge, reading a JAMA article and sipping a margarita. "There you are. I'm back."

"I can see that. There's margarita mix in the blender. Sorry, I don't have a pool table, but we do have a pool you can use."

"How many of those have you had?"

"This is the first. Sorry, I couldn't resist. I'll stop with the wisecracks. These are good if I say so myself." She lifted her glass toward him. "You should try one."

"I believe I will. And I didn't drink any in Texas. Texas was all business," he said as he headed for the kitchen. "Need anything while I'm in here?"

"Crackers and cheese?"

"Coming right up," he called over his shoulder. He returned shortly and set a plate of snacks on a small table between them and sat in the chair opposite her.

"So, how was Texas?"

"Big. Friendly."

"You know what I mean."

"They want me to submit an informal proposal with a summary statement of work, a timetable, and a budget estimate. They're interested, so, fingers crossed."

"When will you know?"

"I expect them to either politely decline to fund us or ask for a formal proposal in two to three weeks. They won't wait around or keep me waiting."

"Okay. Fingers crossed."

"So, did you work on J-cells?"

"I did."

"And?"

"And I'm impressed. Everything you and Mary said was true. The more I worked with them, the more bewildered I got. I'd like to see the phylogenetic linkages of that cell line. Is the DNA sequencing finished?"

"Mary says it's almost done."

"Will you have access to it?"

"Working on it."

"There's no doubt it's human DNA?"

"No doubt. It has a few anomalies that have caused alignment problems, but it's human DNA. I get the sense she's frustrated with getting it completed and ready for publication."

"Why is that?"

"Partly due to differences with the consensus human genome, and those differences cause delays because they're hard to automate. But also because Adam is paying for it out of his research funds, and she's being conservative with his money. I suspect they sent it to a local biotech outfit who've gotten themselves in over their heads. I offered to get it done here and get it done quickly by paying whatever it costs to hire top people and get the work expedited. Some situations need additional firepower, and money makes that happen. I even offered her a job, told her we'd finish the genomics, and that she'd be able to work exclusively on those cells."

"You offered her a job. Why am I not surprised? Maybe Linda could be her technician."

He ignored the sarcasm.

"Think she might be interested?"

"Not sure, but I would love to get her out here so EVI could take over the research and do the lion's share of the cell biology on them."

"And if she declines? How do you propose to do that with stolen cells?"

"I haven't figured that out yet."

"Does she want to stay in Texas?"

"I think she likes teaching. Enjoys the academic environment. I don't know. I called her again today to let her know the offer still stands."

"Bring her out for the summer. Call it a workshop. I'm sure Baylor allows that sort of career enrichment."

"I'm sure they do too. And that's a great idea. Brilliant, in fact. Those cells would be here legally. And possession is nine-tenths of the law, or something like that. Our lawyers would find a way to keep them here."

CHAPTER THIRTY SIX

News outlets across the state had republished the Lariat article announcing the discovery of the Melnikos box, and Adam could only watch as it quickly became a national, and then global, story. The anthropology department secretary transferred calls seeking more information to him, and he patiently explained that Dr. Davison, the central figure in the article, had recently been terminated by the school. He himself would have no comment until after the manuscript he and his colleagues submitted to the Journal of Antiquities and Archaeology had been published. Internet chatter increased concomitantly, and he and Mary marveled at the attendant speculation ranging from the second coming to the apocalypse. They agreed that when the less-sensational truth came out in a few weeks, many would probably be disappointed.

When a call came from his mother one morning, he was pleased that it wasn't just another call for a comment on the box. He greeted her and asked her to call his desk phone.

"Hi, Mom, what's up?"

"We haven't heard from you lately, so, well, do you know what day it is?"

"Of course, Mom. Of course."

"But you aren't coming home today."

"No, I'm not. I did it for ten years. It's time to move on."

"Would you like me to?"

"Sure, yes, that would be nice. Thanks, Mom."

"Do you still see Mary since you finished your journal article?"

"I do. She's still working on the cells we isolated from the bone shards, so she keeps me up to date on her findings."

"What I meant was—"

"I know what you meant, Mom. Yes, we see each other. A lot, actually. We still run together once or twice a week. We have a twenty-mile bike ride planned for this afternoon."

"Ah-ha. Ever ask her out on a real date?"

"Mom. Aren't you prying?"

"That's my job. Now answer the question."

"Okay, well, yes, I have. Several now. Dinner and a movie, twice. A Baylor baseball game. Church three or four times now, and fishing once. "

"Fishing is a date?"

"It is when the bass are running. And we packed a picnic lunch, so I'm counting it."

"Mary is a wonderful young lady. I hope it works out."

"Yeah, she is."

"Okay, we'll see you soon?"

"Soon, Mom. Love you, 'hi' to Dad."

"By the way, why did you have me call your desk number?"

"I didn't want to be interrupted by Rosalyn. The Lariat article has made the rounds, and she's getting calls asking for quotes and interviews. She sends them to me. I'll probably have a message waiting when I hang up."

"The price of fame?"

"I guess so."

He checked his messages, and, sure enough, another call had come. He dutifully returned it but gave the standard response. He used the time before the ride to prepare for his next lecture, then ate a snack and met Mary at her office.

"Low eighties, partly cloudy, light breeze," he said. "Like you. You ready?"

"What's like me?"

"The weather. Almost perfect."

"Care to spell out my imperfections?"

He did not.

They made their way through the campus and onto the road that worked its way west toward Lake Everson. A few miles out, it took a turn to the north, where they hit a steep grade that elevated their heart rates. When they'd rounded a curve at the top of the hill that took them back to the west, he motioned for a stop. A pull-off there gave travelers a scenic view of the lake and surrounding countryside.

"Have you fished here?" she asked.

"Of course. Next time we ride, we should carry our gear and catch that smallmouth that got away last time."

"This is pretty."

"The creek that feeds this lake wanders by the little town of Henleyville, off in the distance there," he said, pointing due west. "You can make out a church steeple north of that rise yonder."

"I see it."

"Henleyville is right at ten miles from campus, but a half mile before the town is a beautiful grassy spot by the river's edge. I say we stop there and take a break. That okay?"

"Fine by me. I'm in no hurry."

They pushed forward, returning to the road that would take them around the lake and past mesquite tree-lined pastures dotted with cactus and Hereford cattle. Puffy cumulus clouds drifted high overhead, periodically filtering the sun's rays and ever-so-slightly darkening the sky. The two riders generated most of the breeze that provided any cooling. Whether that offset the heat produced by the working muscles in their legs was debatable. Adam convinced himself that it didn't, and when they reached their intended rest spot, he leaned his bike against an oak tree, took off his helmet, shirt, and shoes, and jumped in the river.

"Come on in, the water's fine."

"No thanks," she said when she finally stopped laughing. "Sticking my feet in the water is enough."

She took off her shoes and socks and waded in until the creek reached halfway to her knees. She leaned over and splashed fresh water onto her arms and face, then retreated to a grassy patch and dangled her feet in the cool stream. She leaned back against a large boulder in the shade of a giant live oak tree.

He splashed and dog-paddled a few minutes, working his way to the other side where he found perfect water-skipping stones near the edge. He waved for her to join him, but she didn't move, so after throwing a few rocks downstream, he dove in and swam back.

"Okay, Tarzan, get out of the water and sit next to Jane."

"Sit next to you? I didn't know this was a date. I thought we were just getting exercise."

"Liar. This was your idea, and you picked this romantic spot for a reason. Admit it."

"To be honest, I didn't think of it as romantic. The first time I came here was to fish. But it is idyllic."

He dragged himself up the bank and allowed water droplets to run down his body and drip off onto the grass. He pulled his shirt on over his damp head and shoulders, grabbed water bottles and snacks from their bike packs, and sat next to her.

"I take it you're still getting calls about the box?"

"Yeah, but it's not hard. I tell everyone the same thing, though I did stop giving out Davison's phone number."

"That's nice of you."

"He had it changed; there wasn't much point."

"So when the paper is published, you'll take calls and answer questions?"

"No, I don't want to do that. I'll have the public affairs office schedule a news conference and do it all at once. And you need to be there—you and Brad. And someone from the administration, if they want to. Thankfully, Davison won't be able to worm his way in. But I like Hardcastle;

he's a good guy. If he wants to get publicity for Baylor, I'm all for it."

"Depends on when it is. I may have a class to teach, or an experiment to do, or my apartment windows to wash. You don't need me for that."

"Oh, yes, I do. The nature of J-cells is a big part of the discovery. I can't describe how they behave; only you can do that."

"Oh, all right, you big baby, if it'll stop the whining."

At that remark, he looked at her with mischief in his eyes. "Big baby, huh? I'll show you who the big baby is." He picked her up and carried her two steps into the water, where he acted as if he would throw her in. Instead, he set her back down on the grassy bank.

"There. Don't say I never did anything for you."

She slugged him in the gut, but not with full force. He laughed.

"For someone who can run like the wind, you sure don't have much of a punch."

"Oh, that was nothing. You're lucky I held back. If you had thrown me in the water, you'd still be trying to catch your breath."

He squeezed her right bicep. "I'm not so sure."

"What I lack in muscle mass I make up for with speed. Don't push your luck with me, buster."

He laughed again. "Jill used to say things like that. She said it about as cute as you."

"Adam, if you ever want to talk about her, I'm okay with that."

"That, that's thoughtful of you, Mary. I appreciate that. And I may do that sometime. You know, today would have been her thirtieth birthday."

"Oh, so today's special?"

"It is. I put flowers on her grave every year on her birthday. Did it for ten years. This is the first time I won't have made that trip."

"You don't seem, oh, sad. Subdued, maybe, at least until you tried to throw me in the water."

"I will say this. Last year was as hard as the year before, and the year before that, and so on. Not anything like that first year, but I thought this day would get easier with time. Two things have happened in the last year that have helped tremendously."

"What are they?"

"M and M."

"Candy? Chocolate candy helped you?"

"No. Melnikos and Mary. I've been so busy with the Melnikos project since finding the box. It took my mind off the past and got me back to the present. And you. You have been so great to be around. You nailed the Melnikos box science so effortlessly and helped me understand it all. Well, most of it. You were born for this moment. Who else could have done what you did?"

"Oh, anyone who knows a thing or two about molecular genetics. Don't be so easily impressed. Anyone could have done that."

"Somehow, I doubt that. And besides, you've been fun to work with, fun to run with, fun to eat with, usually with me buying, and fun to fish with. Mary, you're plain fun. I'm growing quite fond of you. If I'm replacing Jill with you, that's something I never thought would happen. Gosh, I hope that doesn't make you feel like I'm putting a lot on you. This is my struggle, but you've been an enormous help. I thank you for that."

"Adam, you are so, so humble. Who else could have discovered a box containing pieces of the very flesh of Jesus Christ and not let it go to his head? It hasn't changed you a bit. Most other guys would be figuring out ways to get rich about now, and here you are trying to give it to the world. You're amazing. And you let someone you didn't even know only a few days before come in and be a part of your project. So I'm the one who should be thanking you."

"Don't take this wrong, but I wish Jill were here to share this time with us. And I wish your parents were here to share it too."

They stared into the water, both misty-eyed.

"Did losing Jill change me into the kind of guy who wouldn't get a big head over this? I could have been a greedy, selfish, ego-driven narcissist only interested in what's in it for me. One who would sell the box to the highest bidder."

"Oh, come on, that's ridiculous. That's not you. At all. You're the last person I know who would do that."

"Okay, that was melodramatic. Losing Jill did put me in a big funk, though. For a long time. And I've been mad at God a lot. I don't know the real reason I'm not taking advantage of this discovery. Perhaps I'm a little afraid of God. I don't know. There's so much I don't know. Except I do know that I like being here with you. This feels good. It feels right."

"I like it too. I'm here in a lovely piece of nature with a pleasant guy who's almost perfect."

"Almost?"

"It's not your fault; it's that you archaeologists dwell in the past way too much."

"Mary, that's corny. I should throw you in the water for that."

"You'd regret it, Bub."

"Probably. So, you ready for a tour of Henleyville? All nine or ten houses?"

"So soon? It's too pretty here. Just a few more minutes?"

"Okay, I'm in no hurry, but you know what I wish?"

"No, what do you wish?"

"I wish I had my fishing gear here. I bet there's bass here waiting to be caught."

Mary rolled her eyes. "That's why I said 'almost perfect.'"

"What's wrong with fishing?"

"Nothing, but there's a right time and a wrong time to fish."

"And this is the wrong time?"

"Yes. Now shut up and kiss me."

That caught him off guard. He stared at the water for a moment, not sure what to do.

"Well, I'd certainly like to do that," he said. "But I'm not sure I remember how."

"That's okay. I've never kissed a guy before. On a date, that is."

"And you've never been on a date?"

"A few, but I didn't like any of them, so why lead them on with a kiss?"

"Good point. I'll shut up now."

CHAPTER THIRTY SEVEN

Clark watched a wrecking ball tear into the two-story building he'd recently purchased. An interior recycling crew had removed anything salvageable, and the exterior had nothing of value, so dump trucks hauled the rubble to a landfill. The architect estimated that the new building would cost over a million dollars, including permits, his fees, the city's fees, materials, labor, and road improvements. The plans called for the bottom floor to house a reception and waiting room area, exam and treatment rooms, and three doctors' offices. A break room with kitchen, a storage area, a lab, and more offices were slated for the upper floor. He and Vanessa scraped together everything they had for a down payment and borrowed enough money to buy the old building, tear it down, and get the new one started. To complete the inside and furnish it, they needed to raise additional money from friends, relatives, investors, whoever. If the Dallas group came through, he could repay himself the money he loaned EVI and finish the interior of the building with his own money.

For cash-flow purposes, he didn't consider J-cells a potential source of revenue. There were too many unknowns, and it was way too early in the research phase to hazard a guess on their eventual profitability, but he liked the odds. He had to figure out how to entice Mary and Adam into a working relationship that gave him a stake in the future income those cells would bring. J-cells were a long term prospect, and he treated them as such.

The next morning, he drove past the lot again and observed that the trash and debris had not been completely cleared. He also saw large chunks of concrete slab scattered about the lot. He called the owner of the rubble removal service and complained. The man assured him they'd have it done by the afternoon. Clark told him a grader would be there the next day to level the lot, and a survey crew would be there the following morning. Things needed to happen, and they needed to happen now.

Later that day, he received a phone call from one of the three prospects he had pursued for investment funds for his diabetes project. They had opted out, leaving the Dallas group and one other firm as the only potential sources of new money still in play. Time to look for money. Again. But where? He printed a list of everyone he'd ever approached for funding and reviewed it. He crossed off several because they were already fully invested in other ventures. It shouldn't be hard to sell this, who wouldn't want a piece of the action in the cure for diabetes?

He wasn't ready to panic, but his employees had grown concerned. They knew EVI needed money, and not a little, for the monkey study. Several of their smaller projects were about to expire, and without new funding, layoffs would begin in the fall. Some of his lower-level staff had begun looking for other employment, and a few had submitted applications and arranged job interviews. He thought he could hang onto most of them, but he needed financial backing. And soon.

He met with his senior staff to brainstorm new projects. The United Nations was making a push for vaccines for Third World diseases like cholera and malaria. Infectious disease was not their strength, but money was money, so they decided to prepare and submit a proposal to develop a viral-delivered cholera vaccine. Clark assigned one of his lead scientists the job of writing a proposal to test such a vaccine in guinea pigs and rabbits. The vectors EVI had developed were more useful for long term gene therapies, but they had one that was self-limiting that might work as a vaccine delivery vehicle. Stay in the animal a few weeks and pump out antigens while the host generated a long-lasting, protective immune response, then disappear. The concept worked nicely in mice, so no reason it couldn't work in higher-order animals. If funded, it would buy him time.

He reminded his EVI staff that they had submitted a grant proposal a year ago to the National Institutes of Health for the diabetes project. While it had received positive reviews, it had fallen short of the funding cutoff. It might be worth trying again. After all, diabetes is clearly a major health concern. Congress should get involved and pay for more research. Someone here has to know a congressman we can bribe. Or, rather, contribute campaign funds to.

Before he got back to the business of looking for

money, a part of the job he was on the verge of loathing, he called Mary Walsh to offer her a temporary summer position at EVI.

"Mary, Rich Clark here. I won't keep you long. I wanted to throw something out at you and let you think about an alternative to working here full time. Vanessa suggested the idea, which would have you work here for the summer. Call it a workshop. Coming out here in mid-June and staying for eight weeks would get you back to Baylor by the start of the fall semester. And if you can get Adam to agree to release the DNA sequence, I'll hire a bioinformaticist now and get him started on the J-cell genome annotation. He'll help you find significant differences with the consensus genome and pick several of those for functional studies. Publish that, and J-cells would be out there for the world to marvel at."

"You won't believe it, but that's exactly what I suggested to Adam last week. I just wasn't sure how to pay for it since our research grant wouldn't cover the work."

"Really?" he asked, pumping his fist in the air. "That's great. Yeah, I didn't sense that you were ready to quit academics."

"Well, time-sharing with Adkins has been better than I'd anticipated. I like my situation here now, so spending a few weeks in your lab seemed like a solution. I wasn't sure, though, if you'd still be willing to pay for the bioinformatics workup if I only came out for the summer."

"No, no, I'm still happy to spring for it. What's a few bucks here and there? It's part of doing business. Adam seems like a fair man, so when it comes time to granting licenses, I'm sure he'll keep us in mind."

"He's on board with sending you the sequence and me bringing J-cells to EVI. He said he'd arrange to have an MTA sent to your lawyers."

"Great. Those cells are extraordinary. Pick any area of cellular or molecular biology and dig right in; you'll be busy for a long time. I want to help you and Adam because I want to be part of the team that delivers answers to complex medical questions to the world."

"I share your optimism."

"And don't forget, I can supply expert legal, scientific, and business advice to you and Adam on how to best make that happen. Getting involved with you this way could keep some of my guys here busy for a long time. I wouldn't have to go begging for funding as often."

Before saying goodbye, he asked if she'd like to stay in one of their extra bedrooms while in LA. She expressed appreciation for the generous gesture but preferred not to impose such a burden.

On the way home, he drove by the lot and saw that the debris pile had been reduced but not completely gone. He did see a truck being loaded, so he got out and talked to a man standing nearby that he recognized as the owner of the business. The man apologized for the delay, explained the reason, and promised they'd finish before quitting time. Clark took out a hundred dollar bill and handed it to the man.

"This is for you and your crew in case you run into problems and have to work late. I wouldn't want you doing this on empty stomachs. And, if you can't get it done tonight, I can give you an hour in the morning. My grader won't be on-site until ten o'clock. We good?"

The man nodded and thanked him. They shook hands, and Clark drove away, confident that the man's word was good.

*

Vanessa continued to appear at EVI in the late afternoons and tested the new viral expression vector Clark had acquired for potential vaccine experiments. She cultured mouse, rabbit, monkey, and human cell lines and infected them with the engineered virus, keeping records of those legitimate experiments in a separate notebook. A team of EVI scientists would later manipulate the vector by adding a gene that encoded a cholera antigen that didn't cause disease. They would then infect animals with it and measure their immune responses to the bacterium that caused cholera. The ultimate experiment would be to challenge them with the deadly microorganism and measure survival rates.

Meanwhile, her research on J-cells consisted of experiments to determine growth characteristics in different types of culture media. Even after adding various compounds known to have adverse effects on mammalian cells, J-cells always outperformed other human cell lines.

In addition to working with J-cells on the side, she also manipulated human metaphase-II stage oocytes discarded from a Los Angeles in vitro fertilization clinic. She stored them in the freezer under the label DC1600-XX. It was not unusual for a physician working in the field of in vitro fertilization to make use of discarded eggs to practice techniques and to test procedures used in their clinics.

Curious about whether the hardiness of J-cells would also manifest itself in the type of experiments she did in grad school, she removed the nucleus from an oocyte with a glass pipette one afternoon, then injected it with a J-cell. She looked through a microscope and observed the two cells coexisting nicely, the smaller J-cell resting inside the larger oocyte. She transferred the oocyte into a special liquid which she pipetted into an electrofusion cuvette. After passing an electrical pulse through the liquid, she recovered the oocyte from the mixture and looked at it again under the microscope. She no longer saw the J-cell, its contents having evidently spilled through its broken membrane into the cytoplasm of the enucleated oocyte. The two had become one, and the transformed oocyte looked healthy. She added culture medium to it and set it aside. The next day she looked at it under the microscope.

"Jesus. It's dividing."

"What's that?" Bob had walked into the lab to tell her he was leaving for the day.

"Oh, nothing. I like what I see with this vector."

"Good. You seem to know your way around a lab, I'll say that. Anyway, I'm leaving. The place is yours."

"Thanks, Bob. I'm about done. Good night."

CHAPTER THIRTY EIGHT

C lark signed the MTA from Adam's attorney and overnighted it back to Texas. With the agreement in place, he contacted local colleges and universities and asked about recent Master's or Doctoral degree graduates looking for temporary work in bioinformatics. Tom Salinger had recently defended his thesis and was currently searching for such postdoctoral work in the area. The Caltech genetic analyst came well-recommended, so he scheduled a telephone interview. During their conversation, Tom convinced him that annotation of the genome and much more could be accomplished in only a few weeks by making use of high-speed computing and new, sophisticated analytic software. The young man agreed to take the job, provided there would be no repercussions if an offer for a longer-term postdoctorate position at a school or firm in the area presented itself. He countered with a substantial bonus for agreeing to work at EVI for at least sixty days, and sweetened the deal by throwing in a six-month job guarantee.

"That's hard to beat, Dr. Clark. Most postdoc positions are flexible, and if someone can't wait a few weeks for me, then I probably don't want to work there anyway."

"Well, Tom, you can start here anytime."

"Next Monday works for me, but if I get access to the sequence reads, I can get the assembly and annotation programs started this week. They can still take a few days to run. Even with the fastest computers, it takes a while to handle hundreds of millions of sequences."

"Amazing. I'll get them for you."

He contacted the Lawrence Livermore National Laboratory and arranged for high-speed, high-capacity computing time. After setting up the contract, he forwarded the login and password information to Mary. She, in turn, uploaded J-cell genomic sequence data onto a server at LLNL. Tom took over at that point and set up the program in time to get it running over the weekend. He felt pleased that something finally seemed to be working right.

*

Vanessa had transferred J-cell nuclei into discarded enucleated human oocytes with such ease that she thought she might be doing something wrong. The success rate of SCNT was typically so low that it seemed like a minor miracle to get an oocyte transformed into a viable embryo. Even if one did, embryonic development was so fraught with problems that no one would bother skirting the ethical and legal proscriptions to clone a human. Would they? She thought it too difficult to be worth the potential consequences. But J-cells worked like magic; they refused to let go of their little lives even when moved into inferior eggs from older donors. Didn't seem to matter. So many embryos had divided and reached the blastocyst stage that she didn't know what to do with them all. Having assumed a low success rate for cloning those cells, when it worked every time she quickly realized that a time-out was in order. Besides, her scientific curiosity had been satisfied—the procedure was no longer a challenge. Each cloned embryo had been frozen and stored, but now what? She had no idea what to do with them. For the time being, she decided not to return to EVI.

*

That evening, she greeted Clark and changed into her swimsuit, then went straight to the pool and jumped in. Fifteen minutes and dozens of laps later, she was still so focused on her workout that Clark's voice didn't register. He walked to the edge of the pool on her next lap and got her attention.

"You're wearing yourself out. You about done?"

"Oh, yes, I guess so."

"Want a drink?"

"I haven't eaten yet, but I don't know what I'd want. What did you have?"

"A burger at Joe's."

"Bring me a daiquiri, and I'll think about it." She turned and pushed back into the water for two more laps, then climbed out of the pool and toweled off. She sat in a chaise lounge and took a sip of the drink. "Mmmm, that's good. Thanks."

"You must have needed a good workout. Have a long day?"

"Long day? You could say that. How's my clinic coming along?"

"They graded the lot today. Surveyors come on Friday. The permit is on site. We're ready to build."

"Yeah? Great. How's the money?"

"Still waiting. It'll come."

Vanessa took a long drink. "It had better, or we'll be stuck with an empty building."

"Anything new with the hospital's IVF clinic?"

"Should be operational in two to three weeks."

"You'll get to run it, I presume?"

"Sure will," she said, taking another drink. "Talk about dumb luck. This fell right into my lap."

"Next year, you'll transition out of directing the hospital's clinic into running your own. Perfect timing, courtesy of the hospital."

"Well, they owe me, as little as they pay residents. Another?" She handed her glass to Clark.

He returned with two more. "Everything okay? First, you swim yourself into exhaustion, and then you're having a second daiquiri on an empty stomach. Something bothering you?"

"I'll be fine after this drink."

"Okay." He raised his glass. "Here's to your clinic."

"To 'our' clinic," she said, clinking her glass against his.

*

"Dr. Rodgers, you have patients in the waiting area," the receptionist announced on the intercom to her office. "Dr. Rodgers? Dr. Rodgers?"

"What? Oh, I'm sorry. I'll be right out." She stared out the window another minute and sighed. Why am I perplexed over this? They're just embryos. Maybe when we get the IVF clinic up and running, this will pass.

She escorted the Volkovs into her soon-to-be-vacated office. Nina had passed her thirty-seventh birthday, and the couple had resigned themselves to the fate of not having children if in vitro fertilization failed. She'd examined the hopeful mother two weeks earlier and sent her for blood work, and had referred Ivan to a urologist. She'd arranged their meeting to go over her blood chemistry and endocrine blood panel screening results and his urologist's report.

"Nina, the fluoroscopy showed blockage in both fallopian tubes. That can be caused by a past infection, possibly before you were married. Ivan, the urologist, has described an abnormal morphology with your sperm. It's no surprise, then, that you've been unable to conceive. Can IVF work for you? It could. If your eggs are healthy, Nina, we can attempt to fertilize them with Ivan's sperm. I may need to inject them because their abnormal shape may prevent attachment to an egg. I must caution you, however, that at your age, the number of available eggs will have diminished from what you had as a girl. Also, as women get older, their eggs begin to lose vitality, and that poses problems both with fertilization and with implantation and development. Because of these factors, IVF may be difficult, but I would not say impossible. It will be costlier due to the procedures I'll have to use, not to mention the possible repeated attempts due to the higher failure rates we typically see in situations like yours."

Tears welled up in Nina's eyes. She excused herself and walked out, heading for the restroom down the hall.

"Dr. Rodgers, I want you to know that money is no object. I can afford to pay whatever is necessary to accomplish this. Nina puts on a brave face, even at home, but I know she is heartbroken over her inability to have children."

"Why don't you two go home and think it over. And don't rule out adoption, as that is a truly honorable and vital alternative."

"Thank you, doctor. I'll call you in a day or two and give you our decision."

*

After thinking it over, the Volkovs decided to try IVF. She gave them injectable follicle-stimulating hormone and instructions on when and how to administer it to stimulate her production of mature eggs. At the appropriate time, she retrieved them from Nina's ovaries and injected the healthiest-looking ones with Ivan's sperm.

"Okay, you two. Keep your fingers crossed."

CHAPTER THIRTY NINE

C lark greeted Tom the following Monday morning, his first official workday at EVI, and set him up in a recently vacated office. The new bioinformaticist anxiously logged on to the LLNL server to see the results of the DNA assembly program into which he'd submitted nearly one billion DNA sequence reads on Friday. To his dismay, it had not finished generating assemblies the sizes of full chromosomes. He inspected the quality of the sequence data and the performance of the assembly software at LLNL before informing Clark of the progress.

"The sequence reads from Dr. Walsh are good, but there are differences between the source DNA and the human reference genome that prevent final assemblage of the fragments. That's what's slowing me down. May I ask where the DNA came from?"

"Ah, well, I can't say. I'll have to let Mary tell you about it."

"Okay. It has to be a hominid, though, based on its similarity to the human genome. Is she an anthropologist?"

"Cell biologist. Do you have an idea when we'll have a complete genome?"

"The program running now has a few hours left, but it won't give us a complete genome based on what I'm seeing. I'll ask it to start using other human genomes as templates and see where that gets us. I expect to have about ninety percent of it in large contigs by midweek."

"And the rest?"

"Depends. If we're lucky, we'll get it all, possibly the end of the week. If we run into gaps or new DNA, it could take longer. Longer still if we have to resequence, or, God forbid, get fragments that don't map to anything in the database."

"All right, we'll figure out what to do if that happens. For now, let's get what we can so we can give Dr. Walsh a few divergent genes to study. Can you annotate any of it?"

"I can do that. There are now partial chromosomal fragments long enough to make it worthwhile. I can also determine how close this DNA is to other humans. There'll be a little distance, based on what I'm already seeing in the data."

"Not your everyday, ordinary Joe Blow, then?"

"No, not at all."

*

Clark had asked his secretary to generate a list of the individual members of investor groups he'd contacted in the last three years. He was scanning it when the phone rang. Dallas. They informed him that the recent decline in oil prices had made two of their members skittish about additional investments. Unforeseen fluctuations in the market, they said. Those things happened, they said. They would have to put EVI on hold until oil prices recovered, or they unloaded a block of shares. They deeply regretted it and would get back to him as soon as the situation changed. Clark placed his head in his hands and rubbed his face. He wanted to kick the trash can, but, as a businessman, he understood those things. He would simply have to bear down and increase his efforts. Starting with the names on the list in front of him. He called the first five. Nothing. He called Vanessa, hoping she was in a good mood, hoping she wouldn't ask about the Dallas group.

The IVF clinic at the hospital opened in two days, and she needed rest. The long hours preparing for the occasion had worn her down, physically and mentally. Dr. Rodgers, therefore, prescribed for herself two days of time off with strict instructions to relax, read a good book, take several good walks, and let Clark pamper her.

"What have you been doing?"

"Reading the Haynes novel."

"Ah, the mystery. Is the plot thickening yet?"

"It's a good read so far. How's everything with you?"

"Okay, I guess. On the phone, as usual. Tom is analyzing the J-cell DNA genome. So, you want me to come home for lunch and go for a walk or run?"

"Up to you."

He interpreted the lack of enthusiasm in her response as a 'no.' "Want me to get something for dinner?"

"I don't know what I'd want by then. I haven't even eaten lunch yet."

"I could come home and give you a massage. You

seem a little tense lately; you probably have tight muscles in your neck and shoulders. I'm just the man to loosen them for you."

"I'm the doctor around here; my muscles are fine. Let me think about dinner, and I'll call you back."

He remembered when she'd practically beg him to meet her at home for lunch. They'd swim and scarf down a sandwich and have some fast romance before returning to work recharged. Is this an age thing? Are we too busy? Too many responsibilities? We need to get away for a while.

CHAPTER FORTY

✛

Clark motioned for Tom to come into his office and have a seat while he continued his phone conversation. After ending the call, he asked for an update.

"The bad news is I need a few more days to finish compiling everything," Tom replied. "The LLNL assemblages were good, but they didn't close all of the chromosomes. There are gaps."

"What's the good news?" he asked.

"The other bad news is that you'll need to do more sequencing to close those gaps."

"Bad data?"

"No, the data's fine. The problem is the genome. It's larger than the typical human genome, by about two percent. I can't map several fragments because there's no template available."

"Humans don't have that DNA?"

"We do not. At least it isn't in the database."

"All right, annotate as much of the genome as you can for Dr. Walsh. Her work this summer doesn't require a completed genome. We can hash that out later."

*

"Hello, Mary. Clark here. I wanted to let you know that the sequence assemblies are coming along. Tom has done a good bit of analysis and thinks he's found interesting genes for you to look at."

"They're not found in the human genome?"

"Right. Or else will have dramatic structural differences."

"Easily assayed?"

"Yes."

"And you have an HPLC?"

"We do, and chromatography columns, ultracentrifuges, whatever you need to purify a protein, we should have. We do a little protein chemistry around here."

"That's great. I'm looking forward to getting started. Thanks again for making this happen."

"Oh, my pleasure. You'll love it here, there's lots to do, and not only on weekends. This is California. If there's anything else you'll need, we'll get it. By the way, where are you staying?"

"Oh, I'm glad you asked. A friend from undergrad days, a girl I ran track with at Texas, said I could stay at her place. That was before she talked it over with her roommate. Long story short, that's off the table."

"So stay with us. At least until you find other arrangements."

"That's very kind of you. I'll keep looking, thanks for the offer."

*

Clark's phone vibration meant a new text. Linda let him know she was in LA, tending to her sick mother. He looked at the clock. I'd better hit the gym. Too much to think about. I need to clear my head.

After lifting weights, he hopped on a stationary bike. A bank of televisions high on the wall broadcast various shows, but a woman on the treadmill directly in front of him caught his attention. She ran several minutes at speeds he could never maintain. Long blond hair, wearing the type of tight outfit that left no doubt about her physical conditioning. He continued pedaling, hoping she'd stop soon, so he could too. Oh, what am I doing? He put the bike on a steep climb and pedaled hard for another minute, then stopped and got off. After wiping it down with a towel, he headed for the steam room. He sat alone in the hot moist air, hoping positive thoughts would capture his mind. Instead, he thought about how attractive the treadmill woman was and whether he'd see Linda while she was in town. Vanessa's having worked late every night since the IVF clinic opened didn't help. He missed her companionship. Ah, well, time to get a burger at Joe's.

*

He saw Linda seated at the bar talking to Joe when he walked in. He gave her a half-hug on the shoulders and asked about her mother.

"She's better. Had to have her gall bladder taken out. Darn thing was infected. Poor woman felt awful for days. I took her to see the doctor, and he sent her straight to the hospital. She's recovering nicely. How are things with you?"

"Things are great at work, except for the funding I can't seem to get. Science is good, money sucks. How's your work?"

"Same ol' same ol'. So, you want to get beat again?"

"Whoa, whoa, wait a minute here. When did you ever beat me?"

"I saw it once," Joe said. "Or twice."

"You stay out of this."

"Try Dallas. I beat your pants off," she said, grinning. "But the margaritas have clouded your memory, I fear."

"All right. Ganging up on me. Let's get on with a game. Joe, can I get another one?"

"Of course. You want anything to eat?"

He checked the clock on his phone. "Yes, but not yet. Let me beat your sister first, and I'll order my usual—your burger concoction thing."

"You got it, my friend."

Three games and two beers later, he ordered his hamburger and paid for Linda's barbecued pork sandwich. They bellied up to the bar to eat and enjoyed a lively conversation. He washed down his last bites with a fresh glass, and Linda did the same.

"One more game for the road?" he asked.

"One more, then I'd better check on Mom. Which reminds me, I need to stop by the drug store and get her prescription."

He got home before Vanessa and turned on the Dodgers' game. Between innings, he packed things from the spare bedroom closet into cardboard boxes and hauled them to the garage. He wouldn't normally do that for a weekend house guest, but Mary might end up staying the whole six weeks. When he finished the closet, he packed items from the dresser and put them in temporary storage as well. He repaired a broken door lock that had been neglected for at least a year and replaced a light bulb in the ceiling fan. He'd hired a carpet cleaner and a maid to get the house in shape, so the guest room was nearly ready for occupancy.

Vanessa arrived during the middle of the ninth inning. "Hey. What are you doing?"

"Clearing out Mary's room. Fixing things."

"Mary's room, huh?"

"You said you were okay with that. I can find somewhere else for her to stay if you aren't."

"No, no, that's fine. Long day, I'm tired. I think I'll shower and go to bed."

"Want me to fix you anything to eat?"

"No, thanks," she said. Her shoulders slumped and her feet shuffled as she walked. "We had pizza delivered."

"Everybody putting in long hours?"

"Still a lot to do. We found ourselves rearranging exam rooms and equipment while patients were coming in. We're getting there."

"Good. Go to bed. I'll be along shortly. The game is almost over. Good night."

CHAPTER FORTY ONE

Clark drove to the building site on his way to EVI the next morning. The lot was empty, but he could see that the excavation work had been completed and forms had been installed for footers. Drainage, water supply, electrical, phone, cable, and fiber-optic lines were in place. Concrete trucks would be rolling in soon. He pulled out his phone and called the general contractor to confirm progress and ask if snags had developed.

"We're on schedule, Dr. Clark. The foundation will be poured tomorrow and ready to build on this time next week. I'm not aware of anything that might delay us."

He stood in the vast hole that would be gone in a few days, replaced by the foundation of the clinic. Being there reminded him of his efforts to get funding for the diabetes project—below ground and unable to see a way out. But, progress is coming; keep the faith. Please, God, make it soon. Did I say that?

He went to the gym after work and lifted weights for almost an hour. The cardio room came next. He picked a familiar bike and raised the grade selector to a seven-percent incline and began pedaling. The walkers and runners on the treadmills in front of him gave him something to think about. He thought about the reasons people had for working out at the gym. The older ones probably came for safe exercise. The younger ones walked and ran faster, and may have been there for a runners' high or to keep trim. The overweight ones? Probably desperately trying to lose that extra weight, but never having figured out how to cut their daily intake of calories. Then he recognized the shapely blond from the last time he rode the bike. Now, there's a real distraction. I can see why guys get caught up in affairs. Take me, for example. Vanessa is at the hospital late every day and comes home tired. She's been distant for a while. Then an attractive young woman in a skimpy outfit exercises right in front of me. How do you spell temptation? Would I ever allow myself to get involved with another woman? We're not married, but we do have an understanding, and she's never given me a reason to suspect that she wants out. Am I still obligated to her? The blond finished her workout and left. He headed for the steam room for a short stay before showering, dressing, and driving to Joe's.

Joe greeted him with a beer.

"Salad for me, tonight."

"All right, take this list and check off what you want in it and your dressing. You on a diet, Clark?"

"No, but I did just come from the gym. Get to be my age, and extra fat doesn't burn off like it used to. Besides, salads are good for you."

"They are indeed."

"Linda still in town?"

"Leaves day after tomorrow. Mom's good as new with that pesky gall bladder gone."

"Great. Glad to hear it."

"Speaking of the devil," Joe said.

"Linda's not the devil, Joe."

"You didn't grow up with her."

"What are you two laughing about?"

"You. Joe says you mistreated him when you were kids."

"I actually said you were a devil."

"He's jealous because I knew how to get away with things. I used my pouty eyes many, many times with Dad."

"That actually worked?"

"Once in a while. But nothing ever worked for Joe, and I guess he never got over it."

"Happy to hear about your mother. So you're heading back to Texas?"

"Thanks, yes, Mom is much better. And I need to get back and make my rounds before they forget who I am."

"Here to play pool?" he asked.

"That and a free meal."

"Usual?" Joe asked. Linda nodded. "You want me to hold your salad, Clark."

"Yeah, sure, bring it when you bring her sandwich."

"Salad?" she asked.

"I've had them before."

"I'm sure."

"I know I look like I'm in great shape, but the scale doesn't lie. Two pounds. They have to go."

They played one game of pool before eating and then

called it a night. Linda needed to take her mother to a doctor's appointment in the morning, and he had gotten into the habit of making repairs or cleaning areas of the house when Vanessa worked late. He seemed to be doing a lot of that lately. She hugged him and gave him a quick smooch on the cheek.

"Linda, I told your brother I would behave myself around you. Now what'll he think?" he asked loud enough to be overheard.

"He'll think you were lying," Joe said.

"Eavesdropper," Linda scolded.

"Hey, I'm your brother; you're supposed to be on my side."

"He paid for my meal. Bye, Joe, gotta go," she said on her way out.

A few minutes later, she walked back in. "Either of you know anything about cars? Mine won't start."

He took a look under the hood and listened to the sounds the car made when she turned the ignition key. After a few tries, she stuck her head out of the window and asked what the problem was.

"You either have a bad relay or a drained battery. This your mother's car?"

She nodded.

"Let's see if we can jump-start it. I'll pull my car over."

"Know what year model this is?" he asked when the jump failed to crank the engine.

"'95, I think," she answered. "And it has the mileage to go with the age."

"There's a relay that lets power go from the battery to the starter. If that goes bad, the car won't start. They aren't expensive. I can run to an auto parts store and be back in ten minutes. If that isn't it, well, who knows, you may have an alternator problem or bad wiring. A mechanic should look at it if that's the case."

The auto parts store had the relay. Linda paid for it, and they drove to Clark's house for tools.

"I'll be just a second; my wrenches are in the garage."

"Can I use your bathroom?"

"Of course." He unlocked the front door and pointed the way. "I won't be long."

Vanessa arrived home just then but couldn't pull into the garage with his car in the middle of the driveway, forcing her to park on the street. He heard the complaints on her way into the house, and, realizing she'd run into Linda, raced to head her off. Too late.

"Hey, what the devil were you think—oh, excuse me, I thought you—who are you? And why are you in my house?"

"Sorry, dear, I tried to catch you in time, but, anyway, this is Linda. Joe's sister. Joe owns the bar and grill we go to once in a while."

"Hello," Linda said.

"I see. So you're the Linda who beats Clark at pool. Tell me, can you beat him when he's sober?"

"She's pretty good, I believe she could," he said, sensing he'd better cut his losses and get Linda out of there. "Her car won't start. We bought a relay at the auto parts store and came here for a tool. We need to get back and see if it fixes the problem."

"Oh, being a Good Samaritan again?"

"I'll be back soon; if this doesn't do the trick, she'll

need a mechanic."

"Thanks for the use of your bathroom," Linda said to Vanessa. "Nice meeting you."

Vanessa gave her an icy stare and walked away.

"Did I say something wrong?" Linda asked.

"No. I'll explain in the car. Let's go."

CHAPTER FORTY TWO

"Hey girlfriend, welcome back," Adam said, greeting Mary, who'd returned from a trip to see her brother and his family after the spring semester had ended. "How was Virginia?"

"Good. I got to see Keith. Hey, did I say you could call me that?"

"No, but as an archaeologist, I deal in facts. And that is a fact, ma'am."

"Oh yeah? Well, I'm a scientist, and I deal in empirical data. We haven't been on enough dates for you to say with statistical certainty that I'm your girlfriend."

"Yeah, but I kissed you once."

"An outlier. Establishes no trend whatsoever. And why has it been only once?"

"Good question. You're the scientist, you tell me."

"Uh, we've both been busy finishing the spring semester and preparing for fall classes since we'll both be gone for the summer?"

"Nah. We can take our work with us and do that during the summer."

"You want to do that in Cancun?"

"Technically, it isn't Cancun. It's Tulum. Will I get to Cancun on occasion? That, my scientist girlfriend, is a statistical certitude."

"Anyway, yeah, Keith is doing well. So are Kathy and the baby. That boy's getting big, not a baby anymore. We had fun. And my cousin Lizzie and her husband drove over from Virginia Beach for an afternoon. Lizzie's pregnant. She let me feel the baby kick. I'd never done that before; it was amazing. So, anything happen here while I was gone?"

"Ah, let's see. I took care of the reviewers' questions; they were minor. Then I submitted the revised manuscript right after you left. I got a note from the journal yesterday; our paper comes out in August."

"Hey, that's great," she said. "Finally. You still want to hold a press conference? In August? We both might be gone."

"It'll just have to wait."

"Let the anticipation build a few more days?"

"Well, thanks to Davison, the news is already out."

"But they'll want to see the face behind the discovery," she said. "Your face. And details only you could supply. It's a good story; they'll want to hear it. Someone will write a book about it, then a movie. Next thing you know, you'll be off to Hollywood and Paris and London and Lithuania..."

"Wait, wait, that ain't happening. Forget Hollywood. Now get me to Lithuania, I'll go for that. I've been there; they are good people. Down to earth. Anyway, we'll cross that bridge when we get to it. So, tell me what you'll do in LA for fun? Disney? Dodgers?"

"I haven't thought about it. I'll let Clark be the tour guide. But it's the same for me as for you. I'll be there to work, not play. Six weeks to get J-cell experiments done, and if I hit snags, I'll work weekends."

"Well, you can't go to California and not play a little. Just don't have too much fun without me."

"I'll be in the lab. You, on the other hand, you'll mostly be digging dirt at Tulum. Just don't dig too much sand at the beach."

"Of course not. It'll be nice to get back to real archaeology. Cancun will just be a nice weekend diversion, I suppose."

"I hope it doesn't get too hot."

"It could, but it typically isn't much hotter than here. I'm used to it, and thanks to you, in good shape. I'll be all right. Oh, the lawyer called a few days ago, he said the judge informed him the Greeks had dropped the lawsuit."

"Good for them. They should have to pay your attorney's fees; it was frivolous all the way."

"That'll take a while, but he is asking for it, thinks we have a decent chance. We'll see."

"I bet Davison had something to do with that."

"He did. The Greeks disclosed an interesting little tidbit during discovery. Turns out Davison's sister is married to a State Department employee assigned to the U. S. Embassy in Athens. Davison got his brother-in-law to persuade the Greek Foreign Ministry to pursue custody of the box. They realized early on it was fruitless. Apparently, his brother-in-law has been sent back stateside, possibly for his involvement."

"Wow, no kidding? Gee, that's too bad. You're getting

all kinds of people fired."

He grimaced. "I don't mean to. Hey, I leave for Dallas at ten tomorrow morning. How about a seven-o'clock run?"

"Well, uh, boyfriend, sure, let's run at seven. Three miles or five?"

"Let's see how we feel then."

"Fine. If you win, I'll let you call me girlfriend."

*

Three miles. She won. Again.

"I tell you what," she said. "I won't run this summer. You run every day in Mexico. That way, you might have a shot at me when you get back."

"If you weren't so cute, I'd…I'd…"

"You'd what?"

"I'd do something to wipe that smirk off your face."

"You can kiss it off, silly."

He kissed her.

"It's still there. That smirk is still there."

"That's because you didn't kiss me."

"Whoa, whoa, let's look at the replay. Yes, there it is, I kissed you."

"Well, technically our lips touched, but on a scale of one to ten, I'm giving that a one. Poor design, poor execution, didn't stick the landing…a 'one.' Sorry, it wasn't a real kiss."

"You're such a perfectionist."

"When I see you in August, I'll expect perfection."

"Well, I guess I'll have to practice on Mexican girls this summer."

"Wait, wait, that isn't what I meant. Or intended. I withdraw that last statement."

"Too late, it's already on the record."

"That's okay; you're too shy with girls anyway. I don't have much to worry about."

"Well, then how do I improve?"

"I don't know, read an instruction manual, watch a movie. Oh, never mind. When you get back, I'll teach you myself. Imagine having to teach a grown man how to kiss. What is this world coming to?"

"If I may remind you, you're the one who hadn't kissed a boy before. Maybe the problem is with you. Maybe you're the 'one,' and I'm the 'ten' trying his best to help you improve your score."

"Shall we watch the replay again?"

"How about a live kiss instead?"

"Don't push it, Bub. I need to recover from the last one."

"Well, I'll need one before I leave. I'll stop by your place at nine fifty-five, and I will get my kiss."

CHAPTER FORTY THREE

After three cycles of failed attempts at IVF, Vanessa advised the Volkovs that, despite her best efforts, her opinion was that this approach would never be successful. She saw the distressed look on Nina's face and offered an alternative.

"We can try donor eggs or donor sperm."

"How would we know what characteristics our child would inherit?" Ivan asked.

"As you may know, donated eggs and sperm are from anonymous sources. Otherwise, we'd have fewer to work with. However, that doesn't mean we don't know anything about the source. Donors are screened for certain genetic mutations, sexually transmitted diseases, chromosomal abnormalities, and such. And, of course, you'll know many of their physical characteristics, like height, weight, eye color, hair color, skin color, and racial ethnicity."

"But half of the genes would be from him or me?" Nina asked.

"Yes, they would, depending on whether we used your eggs or his sperm."

A visibly disappointed Nina walked out into the seating area and stared through the glass. Ivan then made an offer that stunned her.

"I'll pay a million dollars if you can make Nina pregnant with our baby."

Her eyes widened, and her jaw dropped.

"That's quite generous," she said, "but it wouldn't change anything I do here. You're getting my best effort and expertise and that of other leaders in this field with whom I've consulted about your case."

"I could donate the money to your husband's company or even your future clinic. I could stipulate that it only be used to further his diabetes research or as a grant to offset expenses for poor patients who come to your clinic. I'm a businessman. I know how to do things like this, and it will happen if Nina conceives."

"How did you know about Clark? And my clinic?"

"Let's just say I have sources. Look, all I want is a competent doctor for this, and you're the best around. Every medical professional I asked said you were among the best fertility docs in LA."

"I see." She didn't particularly appreciate a stranger digging into her and Clark's backgrounds, but let it go for the moment. "Now, by 'our baby,' are you referring to her being the mother or you being the father?"

"Either. Whatever works."

"Hmmm. I'm tempted." She rubbed her forehead, then shrugged. "Well, it's your money, and I could use some of it."

She isolated eggs from Nina first. Under the microscope, they appeared less than high quality, and donated sperm fertilized only two of the twelve eggs she considered the healthiest. After explaining the risk of miscarriage due to the age of her eggs, she implanted the embryos when her endometrium thickened to close to nine millimeters and displayed a trilaminar appearance in ultrasonography. Two weeks later, Nina called her office and described symptoms consistent with pregnancy. She reminded her patient of the problems that could lie ahead and cautioned her not to celebrate yet. And, sadly, after a thorough exam on Nina's next visit, she informed her that the pregnancy had terminated. More heartbreak. After a good cry, Ivan's wife agreed to try a donor egg with Ivan's sperm. That never happened as all attempts at making an embryo with his sperm failed.

"It seems that your eggs are not healthy enough to be fertilized by donor sperm and then survive implantation, and your sperm, Ivan, do not fertilize donor eggs. The only option left is embryonic transfer, where we implant a healthy, frozen embryo."

"Which would not be a descendant of either one of us."

"Unfortunately, no, it would not."

A week later, Ivan called to tell her that Nina had given up. He thanked her for trying her best.

"Damn. So close, and yet, so far,"

CHAPTER FORTY FOUR

Mary waited in a throng of travelers outside the arrival terminal. She called Clark, and the two worked out a pickup spot. She made her way to his car when he pulled to the curb and threw her luggage in the back seat. They decided it wasn't too late in the day to head to EVI for a quick orientation and a short meeting with Tom. Clark gave her the mini-tour of the building and then knocked on Tom's open door.

"Tom, meet Dr. Mary Walsh. I'm setting her up in the office next door. You two will have a lot to talk about over the next six weeks, may as well make things convenient. I'll show her the lab, and then you can bring her up to speed. Tom is an interesting guy, I've found out, but he will talk your head off if you let him. Sometimes it's even intelligible."

"I'll try to speak English, Mary," Tom said, shaking her hand.

"I'm off to a good start, thanks to you. We have exciting gene products to look at. You've done great work."

"Thank you. It's a pleasure meeting you."

"If there happens to be time left in the day after you get tired of Tom, why don't you use it to get settled in?" Clark said. "Turn on the computer, put your access card in, and change the password to whatever you like. The default is EVI. All right, let's see your lab."

He showed her the room and lab bench she'd work at during her time at EVI. He opened a refrigerator and pointed out the assay kits they'd ordered for her experiments. A freezer next to it had other kit components and assorted reagents on the top shelf.

"While I'm here, I should warm a batch of culture medium," she said, removing a bottle of the liquid from the refrigerator and placing it on her assigned bench. "No reason not to start a batch of J-cells for tomorrow."

"You don't waste time, do you?"

"I have several vials with me. Before we leave for the day, I'll inoculate flasks and get them shaking."

"Very well. Why don't I hand you off to Tom now, and tonight we can discuss the experiments you have planned."

"Oh, that reminds me. Are you sure it's still okay for me to stay with you guys? I'd be happy staying at a motel."

"Vanessa is fine with the arrangement. If something comes up, we'll deal with it. For now, you're staying with us. So, let's find Tom."

*

"When one compares a new human genomic sequence to others, there will be differences," Tom explained. "DNA insertions, deletions, rearrangements, you see them all. They can be as short as a single base pair, or as long as thousands of base pairs, and more. DNA is subject to change, that's just a feature of it. Most small changes are inconsequential, but occasionally we see an important genetic defect. Thankfully, those defects are often partly or even mostly compensated for by correct alleles on a sister chromosome. Surprisingly, with your J-cell DNA, we see ten times the number of differences we typically see in these kinds of comparisons."

"Does that include the so-called 'new' DNA?"

"No, I'm only talking about homologous regions. New DNAs are their own special category. In any event, I'm cataloging the differences between J-cell and other human genomes. At every position along each chromosome, you'll be able to compare your J-cell genome with other human genomes. You'll be able to tell at a glance which genes are unique to J-cells and which are similar to human genes but with minor changes. And you'll be able to tell if a given change truncates or lengthens an encoded protein, deletes a number of amino acids, or encodes a different amino acid."

"That's a lot of work. How long will it take you to tabulate all that?"

"Oh, a month or two. The genome is looking better all the time. I can piece most DNA fragments where they belong, but I don't think we'll have it all. At some point, one of you needs to decide on whether to pursue new sequencing to bridge a few gaps."

"I'd like to have a complete genomic sequence when we publish, so that will need to get done. Meantime, thanks for your good work."

In her new office, she fired up the computer and

logged on. She checked the link Tom gave her, opened the main folder, and browsed a few subfolders. Nice work, Tom. Impressive. She closed the folder and clicked the internal email server icon. One unopened email, from Clark: "Welcome to EVI." She sent Adam a note to let him know she was in LA and already at work at EVI. He'd told her he wasn't sure his phone would have service in Tulum, but they did have satellite internet service. Before sending the email, she added, "I miss you."

"Hey, Walsh, you hungry?" Clark asked, sticking his head in the door.

"I can wait."

"Why don't I take you to the house, let you unpack and relax a bit, then we can figure out dinner."

"That's fine, just give me five minutes to start J-cell cultures."

She logged off the computer and headed to the lab. The culture medium felt cool when she poured it into a flask, but that wouldn't bother J-cells. She pulled a vial and pipetted a small amount of the stored cells into the flask, then snugged it tightly into a clamp on the platform of a shaking incubator. She set the orbital speed, flipped the "on" switch, and left with Clark.

CHAPTER FORTY FIVE

Vanessa drove by the construction site every day on her way to work once the foundation had been poured. She likened it to a developing embryo. Nothing in its early stages gave away its specific ultimate nature. It could be a bank or a retail establishment or an office or lots of things, and it seemed to take forever for the form of a building to take shape. When it became apparent, to her at least, that a medical facility could be housed there, money problems threatened to abort its short life. Without additional financing, and soon, work on it would grind to a halt. Despite assurances from the Dallas investment group that they would soon commit to EVI, at the moment they were sitting on their hands. *Maybe it's time I took matters into my own hands.*

Arriving at the hospital early one morning, she would have the clinic to herself for another hour. She pulled the records of Ivan and Nina Volkov. *All right, Ivan, what did you mean by 'money is no object'? And why don't you have medical insurance? Why do you always pay cash? So you work at the Russian Consulate? What do you do there that is so lucrative?* She searched for his name on the internet but found no matches for one in the Los Angeles area.

Later that morning, she called the mysterious gentleman during a break. "Hello, Ivan. This is Vanessa Rodgers. I want to discuss with you an experimental procedure that will result in a baby for Nina. Guaranteed."

"Dr. Rodgers, I'm afraid it's too late, she's given up. She's in no mood to talk about it. But I am curious. How can you guarantee a pregnancy after all the failures we've had?"

"It's an experimental therapy. Brand new. Something I've developed myself. I'm confident it will work for you."

"All right, I'm intrigued. Tell me about it."

"Can you come in? It's a bit complicated. I'd rather discuss it here where I have all my resources. You'll have questions, and it would be easier for me to explain things here rather than over the phone."

"I can stop by tomorrow afternoon."

"Make it five-thirty?"

*

When the last patient left, she gave the receptionist the rest of the day off. A few minutes later, she met Ivan at the door and locked it after him, escorting him to the table in the side meeting room.

"Ivan, we haven't used a frozen embryo."

"Because the child would not be from either one of us. It would seem out of place in our home. We've already explained that to you. And in any case, that procedure is not experimental."

"No, you're right; the method is not new. It's the embryo itself. That is what's new. It's unique. It would not be related to anyone. So while the baby may not be your offspring, it won't be anyone else's, either."

"I don't understand."

"Have you heard about the Melnikos Box?"

"Of course, I read the papers."

"But you didn't read about the human tissues recovered from the whip."

"True, I missed that."

"Because it hasn't been published yet. But it will be soon. I've worked with those tissues, still alive after two thousand years, and they have remarkable properties. I made embryos from cells derived from those pieces of flesh. They're amazing. They're easy to work with, and they survive everything I throw at them."

"You cloned human embryos from ancient tissues? That's hard to believe. Let's say your claim is true, how in the world would you know what the child would look like? After all this time, it might be a monster."

"It's true we don't know the genetics of skin or hair color, height, those kinds of things. But we do know probabilities."

"I'm listening."

"First, it would be a male who would look like a first-century Palestinian."

"Wait, the Melnikos box was supposed to have been left by Pilate, the guy in the Bible. The whip would have been used on someone in his day. No. No way. Surely you aren't saying those tissues came from Jesus."

"I am."

He sat speechless, staring at her. "You can't be serious."

"Look, Ivan, am I convinced they came from Jesus? No, but they are extraordinary, and I am serious. As healthy as those cells are, and as easy as it is to make embryos, clones of Jesus, or whomever, I have to believe that they would develop into a completely healthy baby boy. You'd get pregnancy for Nina, and a healthy baby boy."

"How did you get them? Do you know that guy? Adam, something?"

"Believe it or not, he's giving them away. He gave them to Clark, who asked me to confirm the unusual findings of the cell biologist who first studied them. Clark is right now putting together proposals to use the genetic information in them to cure diseases. I want to use them to help infertile couples have children."

"How many babies have you made this way?"

"None, yet. Yours would be the first."

"No, I don't like it. It's too risky."

"Okay, Ivan. I've hit you with a lot today. I know it's not easy to comprehend, so if you change your mind, I'll be here. Oh, and please keep this confidential. I have another patient considering this option, and I don't want reporters or nut jobs bothering her if she decides to go through with it and be the first to have one of these children."

"By the way, Dr. Rodgers, we don't have pictures of Jesus. How do you know what the clone would look like?"

"Jesus grew up in Palestine, and no historical record claims he looked different than the rest of the population. He fit right in with everyone else."

"If that tissue came from Jesus."

270

"I've seen a draft of the paper coming out. They make a convincing case that it's him, even though I don't know if I believe in God or not. One thing I do know for certain, those cells are superior to any other human cell line. So whoever the original source is, he had to be a special person who hit the genetic jackpot. If these are from Jesus and he hadn't been killed, he might be alive today. I did experiments with a clone I let grow into a blastocyst. It had amazing healing properties when I damaged it with a needle. It wanted to stay alive and seemed to know how to sustain itself. Ivan, your son could live forever."

"I don't know about this. It sounds too…experimental. We would be the 'guinea pigs,' one might say."

"Yes, you would be the first."

"I'll have to think about it."

"If you're concerned with the cost…"

"I'm not. If I decide I'm interested, I'll contact you."

*

Two days later, Vanessa received a call from Ivan requesting another meeting. She met him at the door after the clinic had closed.

"So, did you decide you wanted to try this?"

"First, I want to know everything you know about this DNA. Its remarkable properties, as you said."

She told him about the experiments Dr. Walsh, Clark, and she had each done on the cells. Then she described the genome as she understood it from her discussions with Clark. She reminded him that Jesus was a remarkable human being, the debate over his divinity notwithstanding.

"I have every reason to believe your child will be extraordinary. Smart, healthy, strong, about the only thing he won't be, is a girl."

"In that case, I have a proposal for you."

She offered to make him coffee or get him a bottle of water. He declined both. She warmed a cup of coffee for herself in a microwave and sat back down. Propping her elbows on the table, she let her chin rest on clasped hands and looked at Ivan.

"Okay. Let's hear it."

"I am prepared to put two million dollars into a trust fund from which your husband can draw money for diabetes research at EVI," he said.

"Excuse me. Did you say two million?"

"Yes, and I will also create a similar account into which I will deposit an additional two million dollars from which withdrawals can be made to finance the building and furnishing of your new clinic. Or you can use it to hire staff or subsidize needy patients."

"The clinic is in Beverly Hills. There won't be needy people."

"Fine. Use it to pay off building loans. Finally, I'll put one million dollars into a Swiss Bank account in your name, and you can use that money however you like."

"I like the sound of that. But, I take it there's more to it than just getting Nina pregnant."

"I have three requirements. First, I need to see one of these babies, and he has to look normal and stay healthy for a year. I want to see him doing algebra or reading Homer at the end of that first year. I joke about that, but the boy has to be special, extraordinary even. Okay, second, Nina has to get pregnant with one of these embryos and deliver her own healthy baby. And, third, you do not impregnate anyone else with these embryos, for now. You and I are going into the baby business."

"The baby business? You want to sell babies? I hate to break it to you, but that's illegal all over the world."

"No, we don't sell babies, we sell pregnancies. This is contingent on a guinea pig pregnancy. I don't care who. Get a volunteer, a surrogate, do it however you like, but it must be a perfect baby and grow into a perfect child. There has to be a reason the wealthiest couples in the world will want one for themselves. This will take time, but if that child can, say, learn calculus or speak a foreign language by the time he's five, or never get sick, we'll have them lining up for millions of dollars a pop."

"And, what, I'd perform embryonic transfers on the customers you bring in?"

"Exactly, only you may have to go to them. This may have to be done discreetly."

"They wouldn't want the publicity?"

"In some cases, but there may be legal issues that would force us to do this outside the country. We could start a treatment center in the Caribbean. You could work there on-demand and run your clinic here for the rest of the time."

"I'm tempted. Any chance I could get some of that money in advance? EVI is barely holding its head above water, and work on my clinic will stop soon. We need money now, not a year from now."

"All right. Find a candidate who agrees to do this, and I'll set up the accounts. As soon as you have a pregnancy,

I'll put in enough money to keep EVI afloat for the short term and get your clinic back on track. We can discuss adding to it as long as mother and fetus are healthy, but the bulk of it only comes when I see a healthy baby. What do you say?"

"What if I take your money, and the first pregnancy fails?"

"It can't fail; it's guaranteed, remember? But if it does, the deal is off, of course. In that case, you can simply pay me back, and you can do that when your clinic starts making a profit. I'd want reasonable interest, of course. But, there's too much money waiting to be made. I feel confident you'll find someone who wants to make easy cash for carrying a baby."

"That's…right, I'll find someone. Okay, I'm in. I'm in."

CHAPTER FORTY SIX

Mary awoke thinking about Adam. How did such a great guy not get snatched up sooner? Must have been Jill. Memories of her must have taken him off the market, as science did me. I think Dad would have really liked him. Mom, too. Keith will like him. They'll get along great. If it continues, that is. Guess I'll just have to see how it goes. Here's hoping. She washed her face, dressed, and headed to the kitchen for coffee. She greeted Vanessa, who was lifting car keys off a hook on the wall outside the door leading to the garage.

"Help yourself to cereal or fruit or a granola bar. Milk and OJ are in the fridge. Coffee in the pot. Would you care for anything else?"

"No, I don't think so. Thank you."

"I have to run. Have a good day."

"I will, thanks. You too."

"Clark's dressing. He'll be out soon."

She sipped coffee and turned on her tablet. An email from Adam gave rise to a smile.

"Good morning," Clark said. "Ready to roll?"

"I need breakfast. They say it's the most important meal of the day."

"Oh yeah? Who is 'they'? Cereal makers? Go ahead; take your time. I usually eat a granola bar with coffee."

"I can do that."

"We can hit the road if you do."

"What do you do for lunch?"

"Depends on what day it is. What say we eat out today? Grab Tom and go to a restaurant? There are some good ones not far from EVI."

It didn't take long for her to figure out Clark's routine. She adapted her schedule around it where she could. She kept running shoes and clothes for the days he left early and jogged the six miles to their house when she finished for the day. If she worked until after dark, she planned to take a bus and walk the last five blocks. She preferred to pack a lunch, and usually did, but if the menu was to her liking and the company interesting, she ate out with EVI employees.

She went with Clark to EVI on Saturday mornings when he'd spend a few hours tying up loose ends. If she needed to work in the lab longer, she'd simply run back to the house. She'd hoped Saturday afternoons would be spent with her hosts at a ballgame, at the beach, or on the Pacific Coast Highway, but that didn't happen much. Their recent workloads meant too many neglected projects around the house and too little free time.

On Sunday mornings, she walked to a neighborhood church. Similar in many ways to the one in Waco she and Adam attended, it didn't take long for her to feel welcome and make friends. While Sunday afternoons and evenings were free for the three, she sensed that her hosts needed the downtime to relax by the pool and catch up on personal reading or the news, so she got involved with a group of young single adults from the church.

JoAnne, their leader, befriended and introduced her to the others in the group at her first meeting. A dozen regulars met after the morning service for a meal and then traveled to the weekly point of interest. JoAnne suggested that Mary pick the places they'd visit since her time in LA was limited. She agreed but asked for suggestions. One Sunday, they left right after the service, drove to Oxnard from Santa Monica, and ate lunch there, then backtracked and spent time at the beach near Malibu. Another Sunday, they parked as close to Rodeo Drive as they could and went window shopping, then took a tour on a trolley to nearby neighborhoods. They spent another fun afternoon at Venice Beach.

"Jo, I want to thank you for what you've done," she said as JoAnne pulled to a stop in front of Clark's house after another Sunday afternoon adventure.

"What have I done?"

"You've been a friend when I didn't really have one here. You made me a part of a great bunch of people. I don't know, you guys feel like family to me."

JoAnne smiled. "Christ tells us to love one another. I hope that has come through to you; it's what we intended."

"It has. Thank you."

"It's been our pleasure, and thank you for taking the time to try to explain cell biology to us. None of us get it, but it sounds important."

"Aw, you didn't get any of it? I must be a terrible teacher."

"It's not you; it's us. We're not scientists. We don't have the background."

"I know, but you're all smart. I should have made a better effort. I'll work on that for the future. Speaking of which, I can't believe I only have one more Sunday here."

"You'll have to come back and visit. At least write and let us know how you're doing."

"I'll do it. And Jo, I should also thank you for helping me get through the summer without Adam. I miss that guy."

"Hey, why don't you come out here for the wedding? We'll get you a beach. What do you say?"

"I say you're premature; he hasn't asked. And it's way too early for that."

"Oh, he will."

"How do you know?"

"I can see it in your eyes. The way you smiled when he called you last Sunday. You are smitten, girl."

"Maybe, but is he?"

"Gosh, you've got it bad. You are so head-over-heels in love you can't see the plain and obvious. Didn't you have boyfriends growing up?"

"No."

"That explains it. Tell you what. Friendly wager. Ten bucks says he proposes the first week you two get back together in Texas."

"All right, I'll take that bet. What do I have to lose?"

"Ten bucks. But so what? I'll send it back as a wedding present."

CHAPTER FORTY SEVEN

Clark whistled while he collected clothes and travel necessities.

"Suitcase?" Vanessa asked. "Going somewhere?"

"Texas. The Dallas group wants to meet."

"Can't those guys make up their minds? First, they're interested, then they're cautious, now they're interested again? Is this an oil price thing?"

"I don't know. Oil prices haven't moved much lately. It's the nature of investments. Anyway, I'm optimistic, based on the conversation."

"I can't run a clinic without equipment. Do whatever it takes to convince them. We need money."

"I could mention J-cells, and insist they keep it confidential, so it doesn't get back to Mary or Adam."

"Did your lawyers ever figure out a way to get around the MTA?"

"No, not yet. But they're working on it. If nothing else, Adam is willing to give those cells out to whoever wants them. We'd have a decent head start. That ought to be worth something to them."

"Plan to see Linda while you're there?"

"Linda? Come on. You're being silly."

"All I know is I'm about to finish residency and I want to start a clinic. I get irritable when things drag out."

"I, for one, am optimistic. I'm leaving tomorrow and returning the next day. Want to drive me to the airport?"

"Why don't you drive yourself?"

"I promised Mary she could use my car while I was gone."

"I see. She knew you were going to Texas before I did."

"I arranged the trip at work. It made sense to tell Mary to give her the option of driving my car tomorrow and Friday."

"I can take her to work. You drive yourself to the airport."

"But can you pick her up on time? Then again, she runs home a lot, so that may not be an issue. I'll ask if she's okay with that. Why don't you two make it a girls' night out."

"Somehow, I don't think she'd be much fun. Little miss goody-two-shoes walks to church every Sunday. She hasn't touched a drop of liquor since she's been here. Something's wrong with that woman."

"She's a damned good scientist, I can tell you that. She got all four experiments done in seven weeks. All showed distinct differences between J-cells and the human cell lines she tested. She's a natural. She's even written the first draft of a manuscript."

"So now the whole world will know about J-cells."

"It had to come out sooner or later," he said. "I'll have to work fast to get in front of the line for first pick on a therapy. Where is she, by the way?"

"Out by the pool, talking to Adam."

"Those two must be serious. I somehow didn't figure that one."

"You're so dense sometimes. I could see it on her face the day she arrived."

"Well, I guess I had my head buried in work. I wasn't thinking of things like that. But, I'm a guy; we miss those things. That's a female attribute."

"She's off the phone. Let's get it settled."

Mary opted to ride with Vanessa since it allowed him to drive to the airport, making things convenient for everybody. He'd take her to work the next morning, and she could jog home, wait for Vanessa, or catch a bus.

"I'll take my gear and run home. I can call her if I change my mind."

"I should be back Friday afternoon, so if Vanessa can take you to work on Friday morning, I can bring you home."

"Sounds great. Good luck in Dallas."

"I'm hopeful. Truth is, if this falls through, we'll be laying people off."

"You have a good crew. I don't want to see their faces if they get that news."

"Me either. I'd hate to lose any one of them."

*

Late the next afternoon, Vanessa arrived home to the sound of the shower running in the guest bathroom. She mixed a drink, sat in a recliner, and turned on her tablet to read messages and the news. She greeted Mary when she emerged from the bathroom and offered her a drink.

"What is it?"

"Strawberry daiquiri. Good for you; has natural fruit."

"No thanks. I'll have a little tea."

"You don't drink?"

"I don't."

"Never?"

"Never. My family didn't drink; my friends don't, and I never got into it."

"Not even at college?"

"No."

"Want to eat out tonight? My treat."

"That's kind of you, but I don't know what I'd want. I usually don't eat much after a run."

"That's why you've kept your figure. Exercise and diet."

"You keep yours well too, what's your secret?"

"Walks. Lots of them. And swimming. Lots of laps. And there's biking and running. I just like to exercise. And I watch what I eat. There's a restaurant not far from here that makes great salads. How's that sound?"

"Sounds good, let's go."

*

They ordered salads and drinks. The waiter brought Mary an iced tea with lemon, and Vanessa a Mai Tai.

"I'm curious about what attracts you to that church you walk to every Sunday morning. Do you actually believe in God?"

"I do."

"But there's no proof. I'd believe in God if there was proof."

"Yeah, that's a biggie. How does one prove the existence of God?"

"Not science."

"And not philosophy."

"So, what convinced you?"

"Well, Jesus' disciples continued to believe in him after he died. The reason for that was because they saw him after his resurrection. And they convinced many others to follow him too. A second reason is all the people who say their lives have changed after becoming believers. Can I prove God exists? Hardly. But my conclusion is that He does. So, it's a faith thing."

The salads arrived, and the topic of conversation changed.

"So, are you and Adam serious?"

"We're dating, so, sort of serious, I guess."

"Exclusively?"

"Yes."

"Well, that is serious. Thinking about moving in together?"

"No."

"Ah, you're doing it the old fashioned way, getting married first."

"What's the old saying? Why buy the cow if the milk is free?"

"Well, then," she said, suppressing the desire to seethe at the comment. "Is marriage in the works?"

"Not yet. A friend at church here thinks he'll propose

the week I get back to Texas."

"What do you think?"

"Well, we didn't hit it off at first. In fact, it took a while to warm to the idea of dating him. But once I got to know him, I found out what a great guy he is. He's fun-loving, smart, good at what he does, has a great family. We seem compatible. He likes me. I like him. All the ingredients are there. So, yes, it could happen."

"Well, good luck to you."

"You and Clark have been together for what, six or seven years?"

"Seven."

"You're making it work."

"So it seems. Hey, care to tour our IVF facility?"

"I'd like that. When?"

"How about now? The hospital isn't far."

"It is early. Yeah, sure, let's go."

She took care of the check and led Mary out of the restaurant, intending to drive her to the clinic. Once outside, she heard the sound of country music coming from across the street. She could see it had caught Mary's ear too.

"That's my bud singing there," Mary said.

"Your bud? Who's your bud?"

"Kenny. Kenny Chesney."

"I don't know him. But I have heard that song before. If you want to, we can go over and stick our heads in the door."

They crossed the street and walked into Merle's Place. A DJ played music for an energetic, young adult clientele. With line dancing in full swing, the two sat at a table to watch. A waiter soon appeared and asked if they wanted something to drink or eat.

"Bring me a Wild West Cocktail, pardner," she said, grinning.

"And you ma'am?"

"Ginger ale, please."

Before he returned with the drinks, two fellas wearing boots, jeans, and cowboy hats approached and asked them to dance. Vanessa begged off, saying she didn't know how, but Mary jumped at the chance. Three songs later, the dancing-phenom scientist returned to the table to try to convince her to join in the fun.

"That's something I've never done. You look like you know what you're doing, though."

"Texas does have a few dance halls. I can teach you the steps."

"No, no thanks. You go on back out there."

"I don't want to leave you here alone."

"Oh, looks like I have a call. It's Clark. Go on back out there," she said, shooing her toward the dance floor.

"Hey, how'd it go?"

"Uh, good news and bad news, I'd say."

"Then it's all bad news."

"Okay, the good news is they like us and have committed to us. The bad news is they have to free the money first, but EVI is officially in their pipeline. They'll cut us a check first chance they get."

"How long will that take?"

"They've initiated the process, but it could be a few weeks; no more than a few months."

"You don't have months, Clark. Your workers won't

work for free, and I need to be ordering clinic equipment."

"I know. I know. I need to get a short-term bridge loan, or refinance the house."

Vanessa looked at the ceiling and snarled. "I knew there was no God."

"No God? What do you mean? Where did that come from?"

"I'm out with Mary. We had a little talk about God. The big guy never seems to be around when you need him, like right now."

"This is a temporary setback. It's business. The money is coming. God has nothing to do with it."

"Yeah, 'cause he ain't who he says he is."

"What? You've had a drink or two, haven't you?"

"How can you tell?"

"You talk a bit like a country hick with the 'cause' and the 'ain't' when you've had a few. That sounds like country music in the background. What are you girls doing?"

"We ate at Emily's Diner and were on our way to the IVF clinic for a tour when Mary heard a song she likes. It came from the dance hall across the street, so here we are. I'm having a drink; she's dancing.

The waiter came around and asked if she wanted another drink. "Yes, I would, and another ginger ale for my friend."

"Why don't you join her?" Clark asked.

"Join Mary? Are you kidding? That girl can cut a rug. I'd look like an idiot next to her."

"Who cares what you look like? The idea is to have fun."

"You get that money, and then I'll dance."

"Okay. Well, thanks for looking out for Mary tonight."

"That's one strange woman."

"How so?"

"She's beautiful, athletic, can run, dance, she's smart, a good scientist, has a great personality, and she ruins it all by believing in God."

"Many people do. How does that ruin anything?"

"Well, look at all the evil religion has done."

"Vanessa, we don't have time to discuss this tonight. Sure there have been abuses, but Christianity has been a positive force in many ways. I'm saying that, and I'm not even a Christian. So don't be so hard on Mary."

"Mary is too good. Why did you bring her here?"

"J-cells. You know that. For the J-cells."

"Well, why couldn't an ugly scientist or a guy have brought them?"

"For God's sake, I had nothing to do with that."

"Somehow, I'm not so sure you'd have invited an ugly woman to stay with us for six weeks."

"That's absurd. You'd better go easy on the drinks."

"And that bitch believes in God. I'm surprised she went out with me tonight, she's so much better than me, the little self-righteous, church-going bitch."

"Hey, now. Where's that coming from? Vanessa, calm down, please. Can you put Mary on the phone?"

"She's out hustling guys on the dance floor."

"Right. I believe that. Look, please let her drive you home. I'll be back tomorrow night and help you forget this whole conversation. You're under a lot of stress lately. So am I. We'll unwind this weekend. Vanessa? Hey, Va…"

287

She'd hit the "end call" button when the DJ announced a five-minute break, and everyone left the dance floor.

"You ready to see the clinic?" Mary asked, looking at her phone to check the time. "Looks like Clark called, weren't you just talking to him?"

"Probably a misdial. Okay, let's go." She stumbled backward as her chair slid awkwardly behind her.

"Oh, Vanessa, let me drive, okay?"

"No. I know where it is. But first, I gotta use the potty."

She walked into the restroom and apologized to a man on his way out. He kindly directed her to the ladies' restroom as Mary watched the spectacle. "Thanks, pardner. Mary, I'll, I'll be r…I'll be right out."

"Take your time; we're in no hurry."

As they walked to the car, Mary insisted on driving and had to wrest the keys from

Vanessa.

"I should take you home. I can see the clinic another time."

"Nonsense. It's not out of the way. Broad Street is two blocks that way," she said, pointing toward the setting sun. "No, wait, that way."

"I know where Broad Street is, what's the address? I can find it with GPS."

"It's a hospital, for heaven's sake," she said, laughing. "Follow the blue signs."

"I can find it on my phone," Mary said, opening a map app.

"Wait, wait," she said, ransacking her purse. She

found a business card with the street address and handed it to her. "Here we go."

*

They arrived at the door to the IVF clinic, located in a side wing of the hospital. The nearby offices had closed for the evening, and the only activity was in the emergency room they passed on the way in. Vanessa fumbled with the keypad but couldn't get the door unlocked.

"What's your code?" Mary asked.

"No, no, I can do it," she said. "Okay, well, it used to be 4-3-3-2. Somebody must have changed it."

"Let me try," Mary offered.

"Be my guest."

The lock beeped. Mary turned the knob and pushed the door open.

"Hmmm. I think I had a li'l too much to drink tonight. Sorry 'bout that."

"That's all right. So this is your clinic? Nice."

"Uh, yeah. Something to drink? I have water, and uh, let's see, water."

"Water's fine."

After a few moments, she returned with an opened bottle and handed it to Mary, then slumped in a chair in the waiting area. Mary sat down across from her.

"So, how busy is this place? I imagine infertility is a bigger problem than most realize."

She didn't answer. She sat, motionless, and stared at Mary.

"But it must be rewarding when you help a couple conceive."

"More than you'll ever know," she said. "Do you want kids, Mary?"

"I...I..."

"More than you'll ever know, sweetheart. Not feeling well? Your eyes seem a little glassy. Why don't you come lie down on the soft table."

She tried to stand but fell back in her chair. Let's try that again. Better turn the lights out. She made it to her feet and worked her way to the door. She locked it and flipped the light switch—nobody in the hall. Okay, Missy Goody Two-Shoes, let's go. Unable to lift her from the chair Mary slept in, she slapped her to wake her up. C'mon, stand up, I can't do this by myself. That's it. Just need a little cooperation, and it'll all be over soon. She managed to steer her into the exam room and finally got her up on the table. Let's put some straps on so you don't fall off. Good. Now don't go anywhere, I'll be right back. Gotta go to the potty.

In the restroom, she washed her hands and stared at the image in the mirror. "Who are you? I don't recognize you. Tell me something. Do you know what the hell you're doing?"

CHAPTER FORTY EIGHT

"What happened last night?" Mary asked. "I don't remember a thing after dancing."

"You passed out," Vanessa said. "I brought you home and put you into bed. Your pulse was strong, breathing normal, eyes looked okay, blood pressure was good, so I let you sleep it off. How do you feel this morning?"

"Not so hot. Let me take a shower and see if that helps."

A shower and a cup of coffee helped lift the fog in her head. Saying she was hungry, she poured cereal into a bowl and topped it with milk, then sat at the kitchen table.

"Thanks for taking care of me last night. That's never happened before."

"Time of the month?" Vanessa asked, even though she'd seen a tampon wrapper in the bathroom trash two weeks earlier.

"No, that's not it. I don't know. You're the doctor; you have any ideas?"

"Yeah, take two aspirins and call me in the morning."

"I suppose you need to get to work. Can you drop me off at EVI?"

"Of course. Let me take your vital signs again and have a quick look at you, but from here, you seem fine."

"A good three-mile run would do wonders."

"I advise you to wait until after work. And then only if you're feeling better."

Vanessa gave her a quick exam and pronounced her fit, so Mary dressed and rode with her to EVI.

"Thanks. Clark can bring me home. Have a good day."

"Call if you have fatigue or other symptoms. This is probably a one-time thing. Who knows, maybe something in the salad or the dressing last night didn't agree with you? You aren't allergic to any foods, are you?"

"Not that I know of."

"All right, call me if it comes back, we'll get it checked out."

*

Mary heard a tap on her office door. Clark had returned from Dallas and asked for an update.

"I did that last enzyme assay this morning. Writing the report now. Any luck in Dallas?"

"Yes, I did. It's only a matter of time. Money is on its way."

"Great. Good for you. And for EVI."

"Yeah, I'm pleased. And your summer worked out well. All four genes characterized. Awesome."

"I got lucky."

"I couldn't have done that. Face it, Mary, you're very

good at what you do."

"I'm not bad when luck is on my side. Anyway, when I get this written up, I'll work with Tom on J-cell annotations until Tuesday. He's agreed to teach me what he's doing and to go over the structure of the database he's building. That way, when he leaves, we won't be completely in the dark."

"That makes sense. I take it you're riding home with me?"

"I am."

"Okay, see you in a bit. I have to go crack the whip."

She wrote the last section of the first draft and put it away. Thinking ahead, she knocked on Tom's door and asked about developing a website devoted to news and information on J-cells. He advised her to get someone with more experience for that but said he'd be happy to help integrate the J-cell database into it.

"I'll talk to Adam about that. In the meantime, teach me some bioinformatics." She rolled the chair from her office into his, sitting at a good viewing angle to his computer monitor.

*

"So, did Vanessa show you the IVF clinic?" Clark asked on the drive home.

"No. I wanted to see it, but we didn't make it there."

"Oh? What happened?"

"I wish I knew. I was out on the dance floor one minute and passed out the next. Vanessa took me home and put me to bed. I didn't remember any of it this morning."

"I didn't know that. You seem fine now. Were you sick?"

"I don't think so. I don't know what happened. I've never fainted before."

"It didn't happen to Vanessa too, did it?"

"No, she seemed okay this morning. At least she didn't complain about anything."

"That's good. Let's hope it never happens again. I guess you're anxious to get back to Texas?"

"Oh, yes. It's been enjoyable out here, but it's time to get back. Get back into the routine."

"I take it you have classes this fall."

"Yes, a course in cell biology, naturally. And I get to run the seminar series this semester. Those are fun."

"Graduate students presenting?"

"Mostly, but we'll mix in a faculty member or two and guest speakers if we can get them. I've made a few calls this summer."

"Any luck?"

"I'm corresponding with John Decker from Rice and Peter Siemens from Alabama. You know either of them?"

"I know John, I've heard of Peter. Isn't he studying apoptosis?"

"That's him. So we'll try to get one or the other. Or both. I enjoy talking to students about their work, so I'm looking forward to it."

"And you'll see Adam?"

"Of course."

"He's an interesting guy."

"Yeah, he is. I kinda like him."

*

Mary awoke the day of her flight and lay in bed a moment, recalling the events of the summer. Interesting. Productive. Good to get back, though. She dressed and packed her bags and went into the living room where Vanessa and Clark sipped coffee. She thanked her hosts for their gracious hospitality and gave them a house gift before leaving—a painting of Texas longhorn cattle in a field of wildflowers, in a mahogany frame. She suggested it be hung in the guest bedroom as a reminder of her stay. She hugged Vanessa, who barely returned it, said goodbye, and walked out. Clark had already put her luggage in his car, so they headed for the airport.

"I'll send you the paper after I get back and have a chance to look it over. You and Tom should be co-authors."

"Tom should; I don't have to be."

"You contributed. You know as much about these cells as I do. I'm counting on your input."

"All right, agreed." They arrived at the airport and made their way to her departure terminal. When he spotted the sign for the airline she'd be taking, he pulled over to the curb. "Here we are. Let's get your bags and get you on your way."

Clark lifted her two suitcases from the trunk and placed them on the walkway. She hugged him and once again expressed her gratitude for everything, then said goodbye. She checked her bags and went through security. Wanting to break into a run, she smiled and bounced her way through the terminal. Arriving at her gate, she took a seat near the jet bridge entrance, then texted Adam to let him know she'd be boarding her flight within the hour. His plane had already taken off so he wouldn't get her message until it landed, but at least he would know she'd made her flight when he reached Dallas.

CHAPTER FORTY NINE

Mary fidgeted in her seat, disappointed she couldn't find anything good to read. The airline's magazine didn't interest her, and she found the in-flight movie boring. She pulled out the J-cell paper to work on revisions, but the latest draft had become a blur in her head after reading it several times. The outline for the second half of the upcoming cell biology course needed attention, but that required a discussion with Adkins first. Her phone told her she still had another hour before landing.

The young man sitting in the next seat had politely tried to engage her in conversation. Unable to find another way to pass the time, she relented. He was flying back to Texas after an interview with a prospective employer outside Los Angeles. After visiting an army buddy in Dallas, he would continue on to Ft. Hood for his last month of active duty.

"Shrapnel from an IED in Nigeria got him. He didn't lose any limbs, thank God, but he needed several surgeries to repair the damage. A year's worth of rehab hasn't brought him back to normal yet. He may never get there."

"What were you doing in Nigeria?" she asked, then remembered Keith would not talk about his trips like that. "Never mind. Thank you for your service. And please thank your friend for his sacrifice. I hope he makes a full recovery. God bless him."

"How about you? Where are you from? What do you do?"

"Waco. I teach cell biology at Baylor."

"Get out. You're a college professor? You aren't old enough."

"How old do you think I am?"

"Uh-oh. Now I'm in a pickle. Don't they say you can't get into trouble if you tell a woman she looks like she's twenty-nine? But you don't even look twenty-nine. My official answer is 'I don't know.'"

"Then I'm twenty-nine."

"I can live with that. I'm almost your age."

"Which is?"

"Twenty-eight."

"What do you do in the army?"

"I can't say."

"Ah, one of those."

"One of those what?"

"My brother is Special Forces. He hedges his answer to that question. I can see by the look on your face that's it."

"Your brother is Special Forces? What's his name?"

"Keith Walsh."

"He an officer?"

"Yes, he's Major Walsh. How about you?"

"Captain. Captain James Aronson."

"Dr. Mary Walsh. Pleased to meet you, Captain Aronson."

"Likewise, ma'am. Vacationing in California?"

"No, a summer hiatus. Seven weeks in a research lab in LA."

"Enjoy it?"

"I did. But, even though it's been a good summer, I'm anxious to get back to the routine. And I've missed my boyfriend. Are you seeing anyone in particular?"

"No. I broke up with my girlfriend at Christmas. Haven't gone out with anyone since."

"Baylor has lots of cute girls. I could play matchmaker and find you a date. Interested?"

Aronson thought about it a moment. "Heck yeah. Let me give you my number." He wrote it on a napkin and handed it to her. "These girls, will they be cute and smart?"

"Of course."

She glanced at her phone. Thirty minutes to go. Should I continue the conversation or pretend to read something? He is friendly and pleasant. And active duty military.

"Where in Dallas does your friend live?"

"North of Duncanville. Gives him a short commute to the VA hospital."

"What do you guys do when you get together?"

"We'll hit a bar and go out to eat, watch a movie. I'll stay at his place tonight. If he has an appointment tomorrow, I'll drive him to the VA. If not, we'll hang out until mid-afternoon. Then I'll hit the road for Killeen."

"I'm sure he appreciates the company."

The Dallas skyline came into view, and then the runway. "Not a bad flight," she said after touchdown. "No turbulence, right on time."

"Yeah. Nice, smooth flight."

"Well, good luck to you, Captain Aronson. I have your number; I'll get in touch when things settle down."

"You're on. Goodbye, Mary."

The plane rolled to a stop, and the cabin door opened. She joined the forward-moving procession and exited the plane, stepping back into Texas.

Coming out of the ladies' room and getting back in the flow of passengers heading for the baggage area, she found herself walking next to Captain Aronson.

"Ah, we meet again. Need help with your luggage?" he asked.

"No, thank you. Adam is waiting for me. Say, how about your buddy? He's single, I take it?"

"He is, yes."

"Well, you're both invited to a football game. Our treat. Adam and I would love to have you down for the day."

"That's very kind. Thank you. You haven't told me much about Adam. What does he do?"

"Teaches at Baylor, like me."

"Biology?"

"Archaeology. He made a big discovery a year ago—great publicity for Baylor. So, tell your friend we want you to be our guests at a game. Okay?"

"That'd be great, Mary, uh, Dr. Walsh."

"It's Mary. Do you go by James or Jim?"

"Jim."

The army captain opened the door exiting the security area, and held it for her. "Thank you, Jim. Oh, and look who I see. That's my boyfriend over there in the brown shirt."

"Ah, the tall guy."

"Come on, I want you to meet him."

When Adam caught sight of Mary, he ran to her and opened his arms for an embrace. She moved forward and slid her arms around him, squeezing tightly.

"This feels like every Christmas morning I've ever had, all rolled into one," he whispered in her ear. "I missed you, girl."

"I missed you too," she said. "Oh, Adam, I'd like you to meet Captain Aronson. He's stationed at Ft. Hood."

"Pleased to meet you, sir," he said, shaking his hand.

"Jim Aronson. Pleasure's mine."

"We sat next to each other on the plane," she said. "He's visiting an army buddy here in Dallas, a wounded warrior hero."

"God bless you guys. How badly injured was he?"

"Big Mac wasn't far from an IED when it exploded. He never did know what set it off, but he took shrapnel everywhere. Except for his head, thank God, but his arms and legs took a beating. A Kevlar vest saved his life."

"Afghanistan? Iraq?"

"Africa. Chasing terrorists."

"He lives near Duncanville," she said. "Not far from the VA hospital. Jim's on his way to see him, to take him to rehab. I told him we'd get them football tickets, have them down for the day."

"Our faculty tickets? Cool, you guys are certainly

welcome to mine."

"No, I thought you could use your new clout with the administration, get the athletic director to find decent seats for these guys."

"My clout? What, did she tell you about our discovery?"

"She said you were an archaeologist and that you found something important."

"Can you walk with us to baggage claim, Jim?" Adam asked.

"Sure."

"I have a friend picking us up; I don't want to keep him waiting. Can you use a ride?"

"No thanks. My car is in a satellite parking lot. So I'm good."

"We can take you to your car. It'd be faster than a shuttle."

"All right, thank you. So, what was the big discovery?"

"Have you ever heard anyone say they've found Jesus?"

"Yeah, I have, and some of them are a bit loopy."

"I'm sure. Anyway, one could say, and not be totally inaccurate, that we found Jesus. Now before you think we're kooky, let me explain."

Adam recounted the Melnikos story and Mary's role in the discovery of J-cells while they waited in the baggage claim area. Jim said he'd heard about it but didn't know the details, and appeared to listen with rapt attention. Mary spotted her bag on the conveyor belt, and Adam grabbed it, then the second one, which followed closely behind.

"Wow. Wait 'til I tell Big Mac about this. You guys are famous. And she didn't say a word about it on the plane."

"I'm not surprised. Anyway, the crown and the whip are becoming big deals for the school," Adam said. "They want to put them on display there, but I'm thinking they ought to be in a museum where more people can see them. Now, if Baylor wants to build a museum…"

"So, what do we call your friend?" she asked. "How'd he get the name 'Big Mac'?"

"His given name is Todd, but I started calling him MacGyver when he always seemed to come up with the most ingenious ways of getting us out of trouble in the field. That got shortened to Mac, and, well, Mac is a big guy."

"So, Big Mac," she said.

"Big Mac."

"He's okay with that?"

"He is. Or was. He's gained a little weight, so, lately, I've gone back to just Mac or Todd. But he's a great guy. When you meet him, you'll see."

"I'm glad he has you for a friend."

CHAPTER FIFTY

✢

I t took two full days for Adam and Mary to catch each other up on their summer adventures. Mexico had been on the warm side, so to stay in shape, he ran in the evenings, often jumping into the Gulf of Mexico to cool off and swim until tired. She ran home from work at least once a week, and around Clark's neighborhood other evenings. He described the fun of getting back into the field and working with students; she recounted her experiences with JoAnne's group. Then she told him about the night she passed out and had to be taken home and put to bed.

"Too many margaritas?"

"Don't be silly. You know I don't drink."

"Well, then, what happened?"

"I don't know. Vanessa wanted to show me the IVF clinic. We ate dinner at a restaurant and then walked across the street to a dance hall. The last thing I remember was dancing to country and western music. I still felt woozy the next morning."

"Are you okay now? Has it happened again?"

"Thankfully, no. I feel fine. Especially now that you're here."

"Aw, that's sweet. Hey, do you remember that bike ride we went on in the spring? Past Everson Lake?"

"Of course I do. I enjoyed that."

"I did that ride yesterday and stopped at the same place where we had our picnic. I walked up the creek a ways and saw something I want to go back and check out. It may have been the site of a campfire a few hundred years ago."

"How could you tell?"

"I found a small piece of pottery with markings. It predates the arrival of the Spaniards. Anyway, I thought I'd take my tools and check it out. You interested in going along? I could teach you techniques we archaeologists use at real sites."

"Yeah, sure, I could use the exercise. I think I gained a pound or two in LA. Can't let you beat me in our races, you know."

"All right, pick you up at two? Doesn't seem too hot today, and the earlier we get started, the sooner we get back. We don't want to be out riding after dark. I don't think we'd need to be there long, and we can always go back another time if there's more to it than a campfire."

*

He put digging tools and brushes in his backpack along with snacks and his camera and a notepad. He picked her up and drove to the edge of town, where they offloaded their bikes and began the ride. They pulled off the road at the bridge and parked the bikes directly below it so they couldn't be seen from the road. He led Mary by the hand to the site.

"Okay, see that bump under the soil there?"

"No. Where?"

"Right here. Feel it with your fingers."

"Okay, I feel something. How'd you ever see that?"

"I'm good at what I do. Now, take this brush and gently move dirt away at the surface until you see something. Once we get an idea of what it is, we'll figure out how to proceed."

She did as instructed, removing soil and grass from around what emerged as part of the rim of a piece of pottery.

"So, I keep clearing dirt away from the sides?"

"Yes, you're doing fine. Keep going."

"Ooh, cool, it looks like a small vase."

"Okay. Good work. Let me get a picture before you go farther." He took the photo and issued more instructions. "All right, continue. Now that you have the outline, you can go a little faster with a trowel, unless you hit something else, then stop and I'll check it out."

She continued digging while he photographed the event. Before she got to the point at which the vase could be safely picked up, he mounted the camera on a tripod and started the video recorder.

"Almost there." She lifted the top of the vase slightly so she could get under it with a claw tool Adam brought. She worked it with her hand to loosen it from the soil and pulled it out of the ground. "Okay, I have it. You still think it's old? Seems in good shape for something hundreds of years old."

306

"Those markings there," he said, "I believe a certain Indian tribe painted them on their pottery. Is there anything inside?"

"Leaves, dirt, not much."

"Take that tool and try to work the leaves out. I want to see the inside. That could help prove its age."

The leaves came out, and Mary looked inside. She heard something move when she turned the vase. "Sounds like a rock in there."

"Well, get it out," he said.

"How?"

"Turn it upside down."

"Oh, I guess I thought there was a special tool—never mind."

She turned the vase upside down and saw a shiny object fall into the grass. When she found it, she held it up in the sunlight to get a better look. "Hey, a ring. A diamond ring. I knew this vase wasn't old. Okay, what gives?"

She turned toward him for an explanation, but he was down on a knee. "Here, let me see it," he said. When she handed it to him, he held it up and asked, "Mary Walsh, will you marry me?"

She turned various shades of red, and the expression on her face hit every look from embarrassment to laughter to serious. "You tricked me, Adam Garrett. And yes, I'll marry you. Stand up, goof."

They kissed and hugged, and kissed again. She pushed him toward the creek. He stumbled backward and never did catch his footing. Down he went, half-submerged in the shallow creek. He sat up and splashed water while shouting, "She said yes. She said yes."

"Now come help me out of the water, please," he said after settling down.

She took a step toward the water's edge and stopped. "You're a big boy, get yourself out. I'm not falling for that old trick. You thought you could take my hand and pull me in with you. Ain't happening, dude."

He splashed water toward her, but she'd retreated a few steps. He couldn't reach her, despite his best efforts.

"That'll teach you to play tricks on me."

"Hey," Adam said, getting back to his feet. "Do me a favor and turn off my camera's video recorder."

"What? You recorded that? You stinker. I may be able to erase it by the time you get out of there."

"Don't you dare. That was too good."

He dragged himself out of the creek and sat on the grass. She played the video in the shade, laughing through most of it.

"You had me. How could I not have figured that out? When did you plant that vase?"

"This morning. I couldn't leave a diamond ring out here long, that's for sure."

"When did you get it? And how did you know my ring size?"

"I actually got it in Mexico. And I talked to the jeweler about the size. We did our best."

"Well, you lucked out. It fits, and I love it. *Muy divertido. Bromista.*"

CHAPTER FIFTY ONE

Clark emerged from a meeting with the EVI accountant, having seen the writing on the wall. The announcement to the employees would come at three that afternoon. Over half of them would be let go within thirty days. The other half might make it through the end of the year. Tom would ordinarily have been on the thirty-day list as well, but an idea simmered in his head, and he would need his postdoc's expertise to pull it off. He had been given thirty minutes with the Dallas group at their next investor's meeting, one week away. Tom would be with him, and it might speed the money transfer they promised.

*

"I had to tell a bunch of good people they wouldn't have jobs in thirty days. About the hardest thing I've ever done."

"Let's sit on the patio and talk about it," Vanessa said. "Want a drink?"

"No. And I don't want to talk about it, either."

He did go outside, though, and plunked himself into a deck chair. She followed. They sat quietly, but Vanessa appeared to relax while he fidgeted.

"I can see the wheels turning. Tell me what you're thinking."

"I'm thinking that I'm getting tired. Tired of the never-ending chase for money to keep EVI afloat. I don't think I mind the day-to-day responsibilities like trouble-shooting experiments or shuffling resources around, but laying people off is hard."

"Well, you had a couple of pieces of bad luck, or the diabetes therapy would be well on its way to market."

"Yeah, but I'm supposed to be a businessman. I'm supposed to know how to stay prosperous in good times and bad."

"You're a scientist first, who studied business so you could control all phases of your research. Money is just one part of that."

"But an important part. I misplayed this, and now it's biting me in the butt."

"Oh, don't be so hard on yourself. I have confidence in you, because you know what will happen if work on the clinic stops."

"Yeah, I do."

"That's all the motivation you need."

"I do have an idea, though. I'm flying back to Dallas next week."

"You were just there. What's changed in the last few days?"

"The J-cell genome. Tom has all but finished the annotation. It's remarkable."

"Oh? How so?"

"For starters, no pseudogenes, so no gene degradation.

All functional human genes are there, but where we have pseudogenes, J-cell DNA either has a complete new gene or nothing at all. Second, every gene that's a marker for human disease is good in the J-cell genome; there are no mutations. Third, there are lots of subtle differences between our housekeeping genes and J-cells. And fourth, Tom says many unknown proteins encoded in it are likely to have regulatory functions. He thinks there are biochemical processing control mechanisms we've never seen before. I'm telling you, the J-cell genome is extraordinary."

"So, what you have is the perfect DNA template. Simply replace a diseased gene with a J-cell gene? And EVI is in the perfect position to exploit that information?"

"Exactly. That's what I'll sell Dallas on."

"I like it. But Adam owns the patent."

"He does, yes, but money talks."

"I don't know, that guy is about as crazy as Mary."

"Mary's not crazy. Neither is Adam, but I do have to get him to see what's in his best interest."

"Get the rights to those cells and you can cure diseases while I help couples make designer babies."

The conversation stopped a moment while her statement sunk in his head.

"Designer babies? Look, gene therapy is one thing, that is quite another. You're talking major controversy there."

"And why stop there? I could also help couples get J-cell children. They'd never get sick. May not ever get old, either."

"Are you out of your mind?"

"Think of how rich we'd be. It's mind-boggling."

"Your mind is boggled. Human cloning is very much verboten. You can go to jail for that."

"It'll be legal somewhere, someday. And when it is, we'll be ready for it."

"How would you be ready for it if it's banned? How do you practice?"

"I've already done it. J-cell clones, they're easy. Hard to kill those things."

Clark fixed his gaze on her, hoping to see a look on her face that said, "I was only joking," but it wasn't there.

"When you say, 'hard to kill those things' does that mean you've already done this and does it also mean you have embryos? Is that what you were doing at EVI?"

"Yep. SCNT. Somatic cell—"

"I know what it is. What I don't know is who you are. Who are you? Why did you do that?"

"Calm down. You know me, Clark. You know I did these kinds of experiments in grad school."

"Yeah, but not with humans."

"No, but, well, I experimented with J-cells at EVI, as we agreed. I determined that they really were highly resistant to stresses. So, I was curious. I had discarded eggs, and—"

"How many? Where are they now?"

"A dozen. All worked. As I said, it's hard to kill those things. They don't want to die. I have them at my office."

"You have to destroy them. And notebooks, we have to destroy them too. Wait, why are they at your office? That's an IVF clinic. Surely you weren't thinking about—
"

312

"No, of course not. I didn't want to leave them at EVI, that's all."

"Look, we're sitting on a gold mine here. We can't take chances. Promise me you'll destroy all records of cloning experiments and autoclave the eggs you transformed."

"They're technically embryos. Some people think that's tantamount to killing a human being. And they're J-cell embryos. We could be killing Jesus clones. You okay with that?"

He didn't answer. He stared at the pool and wondered how life had gotten so complicated all of a sudden.

"I need to go to the gym," he said, then left.

CHAPTER FIFTY TWO

"You know we have to do this," Adam said. He sat in her office, reviewing his lecture for the next day's class while Mary did the same.

She looked up. "Do what?"

"See if you can still beat me in the five-mile."

"Or the three-mile; take your pick. You never win, why do you think anything has changed?"

"You said yourself you gained a pound or two in LA while I stayed active in Mexico, working and running. I think you're out of shape."

"Loser buys dinner?"

"Of course."

Mary held up her hand and looked at the ring on her finger. She smiled. "This is so beautiful. Seems like everybody at Baylor knows about it. They all ask to see it."

"And you like showing it off, don't you?"

"I love showing it off."

"I thought about buying one made of lead."

"Seriously? You did not. Why would you do something like that?"

"The extra weight would slow you down on the track even more."

"Even more? You're saying I'm fat now? I may have to rethink this marriage thing."

"You? Fat? Right. Now, when we get married and the little darlings come along, then you'll be fat. And I might win a three-mile race."

"In my ninth month of pregnancy, and if I have the flu. Maybe. Now, hypothetically speaking, if I were a little out of shape and the race came down to the wire, would you let me win to make me feel better?"

"No way."

"That's what I thought. Saturday morning?"

"Ten o'clock. Football game is at two. You buy dinner afterward."

"We shall see," she said.

"By the way, good news. I talked to the athletic director. Mac is on for the coin toss on the fourteenth."

"That's awesome. I knew you had clout."

"I don't know about that, but the AD did seem eager to do it."

"But at least you had his ear. That's clout."

"If you say so. Can you talk to Captain Aronson and see if they can make it?"

"I'll call him right now."

"If they want to stay at my place that weekend, it would be an honor," he said while she punched in the number. "Tell them I insist."

She spoke with Jim, who thanked her for remembering Mac and promised to confirm their visit that weekend after consulting his army buddy.

Before leaving her office, he invited Mary to go to Abilene with him the weekend after next. It would be a one-day trip to break the news of their engagement to his parents. That settled, they agreed on a dinner date after work. He whistled on the way back to his office.

*

Saturday presented the two racers with typical September weather. It would be ideal in the morning, but get hotter and more humid as the day progressed. They agreed on five miles. After stretching and warming up, they met at the starting line of the Baylor track. She gave him a kiss for luck and then shoved him backward and took off.

"Hey, you didn't need to do that. Unless you're concerned about your conditioning," he yelled.

"You'd better stop whining and start running," she called back over her shoulder.

She jumped out to a significant lead and kept the pace until about the last half-mile. He steadily gained ground on her during the last two laps and caught her at the finish line. She kneeled on the track and breathed heavily.

"Hah, you are out of shape."

"I had you easy for four and a half miles," she said between breaths. "I guess I was too much of a tourist in LA."

"But, you did run some."

She stood and leaned over, hands on knees. "Yeah, but I don't know, too much rich food?"

"That, or I'm getting better."

"I like that explanation. Let's go with that."

"So, who buys dinner? We tied."

"I'll buy. Better yet, let me make dinner."

"No argument from me. You're a great cook. So how about a three-mile race next?"

"You saw how big a lead I had at three miles. You think you can close that gap?"

"Sure. I paced myself today. If it had been a three-mile race, I would have been right on your heels."

CHAPTER FIFTY THREE

✠

Clark drove himself and Tom to EVI from LAX. Pleased with the way the meeting in Dallas went and how well his bioinformaticist handled himself with his future investors, he offered the young man a full-time position, provided, of course, he could turn the EVI ship around and get it back on a firm financial footing.

"Great work, Tom. You helped save a bunch of jobs here, at least through the end of the year. But I'm feeling good about our future prospects."

"Thanks, boss. Just doing my job."

"They were impressed. Think about my offer. I could use you if this takes off."

"I have, and I will, but I'm not sure I'd be needed once the genome is finished and fully annotated. I wouldn't mind staying on a little longer, though. At least until a user-friendly database is up and running. Plus, I could help Mary with the website she wants to set up. After that, we'll see."

"Yeah, she mentioned it, and I agreed, it should be done."

"I don't create websites, but I know guys who do. I

suppose they could walk me through it."

"You might enjoy it more than you realize. If you manage the website and database, you'll meet and work with top scientists in genetics and molecular biology. You'd probably travel a good bit; not every lab has the computing skills to program what they need for their specific research. You'd be in demand. Get around enough, and you'll come across that ideal job. One that could mean a career. Then pounce on it. Think about it."

By the time they pulled into the near-empty EVI parking lot, the workday had essentially ended for everybody. Tom called it a day and left for his apartment. Clark went to his office for a few minutes before heading to the gym. After a vigorous workout on the treadmill and in the weight room, he headed home. Vanessa had not yet arrived, so he fixed a drink and went out to relax by the pool. This time he didn't fidget, and the sound of a door closing woke him from a brief doze. Vanessa sat in the wicker chair next to him, sipping her own drink.

"You said you had good news."

"Dallas wants in on this. Tom convinced them of the J-cell gold mine. I brought back a check for $300,000. More will be coming later."

"That's fantastic. I knew you could do it. I got so tired of driving by my clinic and seeing a foundation. That money will go a long way to getting walls up, don't you think?"

"Sorry, dear, but I'm using it for EVI. With it, I can pay salaries for two more months."

"Seriously? Those jobs are more important than my clinic?"

He turned his head and looked at her in disbelief.

"No, of course they are. But when do we continue the work on the building? I'm almost through with residency."

"You have a good job now; you can stay with the hospital a while longer."

"How much longer? What has to fall in place?"

"Mainly, we need to get Adam to turn over the rights to J-cells. A negotiator will meet with him soon to discuss terms."

"How much will they offer him?"

"They'll start at a million."

"Wow. Not bad. How much will they invest in EVI?"

"Depends on whether he accepts the offer and we get the patent outright or have to work through a licensing agreement. Everyone prefers ownership of the patent on the genome, naturally, and the amount we discussed was in the several millions."

"And if it has to go through licensing with Adam, will there be enough to resurrect EVI and build the clinic?"

"That, I don't know. We discussed it in general terms. But if it doesn't bring in enough, I expect to attract other investors who'd want in once they saw Dallas commit."

"But it would take longer that way."

"Yes, it would."

"Let's hope Adam does the right thing, then."

"Let's hope."

That hope was misplaced, however, as Adam's position hadn't changed. He was willing to let others work with his discovery under a licensing agreement only. For the small cost of a legal contract and administrative fees, anyone could make all the money they wanted to on their research and development efforts with J-cells. A representative for the Dallas group offered the authorized million dollars, but he declined. The next day, the negotiator increased the offer to two million. A week later, it went up to five million. Wanting to make sure he wasn't missing something, he referred it to a lawyer recommended by his patent attorney. He considered it for a week and was tempted, thinking of starting a charitable foundation with the proceeds. In the end, however, he couldn't get past the thought of selling pieces of the body of Christ.

CHAPTER FIFTY FOUR

Karen Lincoln, Baylor's public affairs director, called Adam to inform him that higher than expected interest had forced her to move the venue for the press conference from the anthropology department's lecture hall to the Chapel Auditorium. She met him at his office, along with Mary and Brad, who'd arrived from Lubbock earlier that morning. The four walked together across the campus and met with President Hardcastle on the stage of the auditorium before the proceedings began.

"How are you handling the notoriety, Adam?" Hardcastle asked.

"About my engagement to Dr. Walsh? I'm enjoying every minute of it."

Mary elbowed him in the ribs.

"Oh, you mean Melnikos, of course. To be honest, sir, I haven't given it much thought. The box is famous, not me."

"You're too modest, but we are thrilled about this, and so proud to have you here at Baylor."

"How appropriate that a Baptist university be in the news for a discovery that could impact the faith of many people."

"We could use the good press. Have you thought about putting it on display here?"

"Luigi tells me the lines of people wanting to see it in Rome are getting longer every day. And I've gotten inquiries from museums all over the world. What I'm enjoying right now, though, is this being right under the pope's nose. I wonder if he'll pay a visit."

"I appreciate our Catholic brothers and sisters, I do," said Hardcastle. "But I'm so glad a Baptist found the box. And a Baylor one at that."

"Well, Luigi is Catholic, and I love that guy," he said. "I'm happy that he gets to show it off first. I did tell him to send me an autographed selfie of him and the pope when he shows up."

"I'll take a copy of that," Hardcastle said.

"Me too," Brad added.

"I'll look at Adam's," Mary said.

Ms. Lincoln interrupted to explain the order of events.

"Dr. Hardcastle will greet everyone and then introduce you, Adam. At some point, you'll want to introduce Dr. Walsh and Dr. Goodwin. I recommend you do that early and then talk about the box. You can say whatever you want, but remember, there'll be questions afterward, so you don't have to cram everything in. Okay? All set?"

"One question—what are the cameras doing here?"

"Those are news organizations. This isn't being broadcast live, though, so don't worry if you stutter or stumble, it'll be edited out."

"Right."

*

They drove to Abilene the following Saturday, arriving at the Garrett home before noon to a driveway full of cars. A Highway Patrol car and a Parks and Wildlife Department truck betrayed the presence of his brothers. What are they doing here?

"I didn't expect anyone here today. It isn't anyone's birthday. Are you okay with this?"

"Oh, of course. Your family is fun. I'm fine."

His mother told him later that she'd sensed something was up when he called to let her know they were coming for a short visit. She, in turn, called his brothers and invited them to come over for the day. If she was wrong, then at worst they'd have a family barbecue. If she was right, they'd all be present for the announcement. She wasn't wrong. The barbecued ribs and chicken, beans, cornbread, and engagement announcement made for a memorable afternoon. They found it hard to tear themselves away when evening came, but Mary seemed a little tired, and they both needed Sunday afternoon to prepare for Monday lectures. Congratulations, hugs, and goodbyes sent them on their way back to Waco. Before they could get away, however, his mother stuck her head in the car window and hugged Mary.

"Mary, you seem to have come out of nowhere and put the sparkle back in my son's eyes. I'll never forget you for that. And you two being engaged means it'll stay that way, I know what you mean to him."

"All I did was fall in love with the guy. I didn't see it coming, but I'm so glad it's happened. You raised a spectacular young man; I'll never forget you for that either."

"Well, it took someone special to get him out of the funk he's been in since losing Jill. Welcome to the family."

"Mom, your eyes are misting up, and so are Mary's. Come give me a hug so we can get out of here before I can't see to drive."

CHAPTER FIFTY FIVE

On tap for the following Saturday were a race in the morning and a Baylor football game in the evening. With a three-miler at ten o'clock, Adam had plenty of time to clean his apartment and prepare for Jim and Mac's arrival at mid-afternoon. They didn't plan on eating out before the game as they were told food would be provided at the stadium.

The first order of business, then, was the race. The contestants met at the starting line. She kissed him and pushed him backward, but he was ready for that. He pulled her arms around his waist, locked his arms around her back, and whispered into her ear. "Did you really think that would work?"

"I thought it worth a try. Now, will you let me go, or do you concede the race now?"

"I don't know, it might be worth conceding. Can we stand here and hold each other for twenty minutes?'

"Twenty minutes is your time. I do this run in eighteen."

He let her go, and she took off. He took off after her.

She ran a steady two miles but hadn't built her usual lead. At the two and a half mile mark, they were even.

"This isn't right. Let's go, kick," she said, watching Adam ease ahead.

He won by twenty yards. Mary panted, and squatted down, then sat on the ground.

"Are you all right? You aren't coming down with something, are you?"

"Let me catch my breath."

They sat on the infield a few minutes, then she lay back on the grass. "Ah, this is comfortable. What a gorgeous day."

"Here, drink some water." He handed her a bottle.

"I guess I'm buying lunch?"

"You are, but you've never run that slow. Is anything wrong?"

"Well, I have been feeling a little tired lately. You won fair and square, though, so I'm buying lunch."

"Lunch, shmunch. You weren't yourself. What's wrong?"

"I don't know. I just don't know."

"When's the last time you had a checkup?"

"I have an annual physical; I guess I'm due again next month. I'll be fine."

"All right. I may be overreacting here because I've lost someone before. I don't know what I'd do if I lost you, Mary."

He sat her up and put his arms around her, and she laid her head on his shoulder.

"Thanks for being here for me. I love you, Adam."

"I love you, Mary. I'm here for you always. You stay

with me, okay?"

"I will."

*

Mac and Jim knocked on his door at three o'clock. He invited them in and offered each a cold drink and a spot on a comfortable sofa in his air-conditioned apartment.

"Mary will get here before five. We'll get you to the stadium by six-thirty. I'll introduce you to Fred Robinson, Baylor's athletic director. He'll go over what you need to know about the coin toss. It isn't much, and you can't mess it up."

"If anyone can flub a coin toss," Jim said, "it's Mac."

Mac put a couch cushion on Jim's head and pushed his face into the sofa.

"Take that back, or you'll be there a while."

"Adam, get him off."

"That's easy. Take back what you said."

"Okay, okay," he said, laughing. "I take it back."

"That's better. Please excuse my buddy, Adam. Sometimes he thinks he's back in third grade."

Adam grinned. "So, what can you tell me about Africa? I've never been there."

They talked for two hours straight. Adam told them the Melnikos story, but was in awe of the experiences his guests had in Africa and during other deployments. Their squad prevented the slaughter of villagers in Nigeria by terrorists. Not long after that, an IED ended Mac's army career.

"You look like you're getting around well for a guy who's had five surgeries."

"The VA actually has good docs, despite the bad press."

"Glad to hear that. You guys deserve the best."

Mary arrived a little before five. Adam introduced her to Mac.

"Damn, Jim, you didn't tell me she was Miss America. Oh, shoot. Pardon me, ma'am, that was improper. I meant no disrespect."

"That's quite all right. I'm used to that kind of talk from Adam."

"I believe it. I have to ask, did Jim behave himself on the plane? He told me he sat next to you. Knowing him the way I do, I don't see how he controlled himself."

"Mac, you forget that the army spent a small fortune training me to stay cool under pressure."

"Jim was a perfect gentleman. He helped make the long flight go by faster."

"Sorry, but I don't believe that," Mac said.

Jim playfully punched him in the gut.

"Anybody hungry?" Adam asked. "If you can wait, there'll be food at the stadium, but we can grab a bite to eat now."

They continued to chat while thinking it over, and the next thing they knew, it was time to head to the stadium.

*

The public address announcer informed the fans that a Mr. Todd "Mac" Starnes would perform the coin toss before the game. When he described the injuries Mac sustained in a military operation as an Army Special Forces soldier and his extensive rehabilitation, he received a standing ovation. He saluted the crowd, and when the head referee motioned to him, he threw the coin into the air. Jim stood on the sideline and watched his friend with pride, pleased with the recognition his army buddy received and appreciation from the crowd he deserved. They embraced briefly on the sidelines and then rejoined Adam and Mary. The four went to find their seats for the game.

"You sit in the upper section?" Jim asked as they headed through a ramp toward a walkway that led to an elevator.

"Sorry, this is the best I could do," Adam explained.

"Oh, no, no, I didn't mean it like that. I guess I figured hotshot faculty had seats close to the field."

"Come on, Jim. Do we look old enough to be hotshot faculty?"

"No, not really. Okay, look, I'll be quiet now."

"What he means is, he's happy to be here, sir," Mac said. "I am too."

"An elevator to get to our seats?" Jim asked.

"We usually sit on the lower level, so this is new for us too," Adam said.

They exited the elevator and walked the short distance to the suite where they'd watch the game. Adam handed a card to an usher who opened the outer door and motioned for them to go in. They entered and stood behind three rows of plush seats, most of which were occupied. Through the retractable, tinted glass, he could see that Baylor had moved the ball downfield, already in scoring position. With everyone's attention on the game, no one in the suite knew they'd arrived. Two plays later, the coach for the other team called a timeout, which momentarily quelled the excitement. The suite owner and their host for the game, Bob McFarlane, turned and saw the four during the break in the action.

"Hey guys, welcome, come on in." The gentleman pointed to four empty seats in the front row. "Please, take a seat."

Baylor scored on the next play, giving McFarlane the chance to greet his four guests properly. He'd spoken to Adam over the phone but hadn't met him. "Please, there's plenty of food and drinks in the back. Help yourself. And Jim, Mac, thank you for your service. Mac, I live in Dallas too. If there's ever anything you need, call me." He handed Mac his business card. McFarlane owned a law firm in Dallas that handled oil and gas contracts as well as commercial real estate. "I mean it, son. Now enjoy the game, we'll talk more later."

"Are these seats okay or what?" Mac asked Jim, winking at Adam.

"Shut up and sit down," Jim replied.

"Not me," Mac said. "I'm going to check out the food."

"Well, the man did say to help ourselves," Jim said. "I guess it sounded like an order."

CHAPTER FIFTY SIX

Adam walked to the track. Alone. Mary's mild fatigue had turned into a low-grade fever with chills and aches. A run, a quick bite to eat, and a trip to the doctor's office with her for a one-thirty appointment were his only plans for the day. He'd lost count of the number of laps he'd run; all he could think about was her. He tried to remember Jill's earliest symptoms, but that was eleven years ago, and the passage of time caused the details of those days to blur. Her illness came on slowly, he recalled that, and progressively worsened until it took her. This can't be happening again. No way would you let that happen again. This is a little passing virus. It'll be gone in no time. Right, God?

With little appetite, he skipped lunch and piddled around the office, organizing desk drawers and rummaging through old files. When the trash can filled up, he stared out the window. A bright, sunny day with cotton-ball clouds drifting by, the delightful weather did nothing to improve his mood. Instead, he allowed a sense of foreboding to creep in and darken his disposition.

The waiting room at the doctor's office only made things worse. He'd gone through that with Jill—spending hours waiting, and rarely, if ever, receiving optimistic news. The TV on the wall blared the sounds of a soccer match. He ran through all the channels, but nothing caught his interest, so he left it on but at a barely detectable volume. He sat, and he stared. A boy about seven years old limped into the room with his mother. She helped him into the chair opposite Adam and then signed him in and provided insurance information at the receptionist's desk. The boy looked at him, from head to toe.

"Where did you hurt yourself, mister?"

"I'm not hurt, I'm here with someone else. She's in with the doctor now. I'm waiting for her."

"Oh. Well, I hope she isn't hurt too bad."

"Me, too. Me, too. How did you hurt your foot?"

"I jumped out of a swing. And I didn't come down right."

"Ouch. How bad is it?"

"It isn't too bad. They don't think it's broken or anything."

"But they want to X-ray it to be sure?"

"Yes, sir."

"Good idea. You're brave not to be crying."

"I did a little, at first."

"That's normal. We all do that."

The mother returned. She sat next to the boy and told him the doctor would see him soon. She picked up a magazine and thumbed through it. The boy nudged her and asked if that man was the one in the newspaper Dad talked about.

"What? Oh, honey, I don't think so," she said before looking more closely. "Why, it is. It's you, isn't it? You're the one who made that discovery, aren't you?"

Tempted to say "no" and return to his brooding, he confessed. "Yes, ma'am. A box. I found an old box."

"Okay, hon, you were right. Now, let's leave the man alone, okay?"

"Okay."

"It's all right. He told me he hurt his foot jumping out of a swing?"

"At school. He's such a little daredevil. I told him this would happen someday."

"But a polite little daredevil, he called me 'sir.'"

"So you talked to this man? What have I have told you about talking to strangers?" she said, then turning to Adam, "No offense."

"None taken. That's good advice."

He picked up the magazine lying in the seat next to him and pretended to read. The boy's father arrived and consoled his son as best he could. Fortunately for the boy, the worst of the pain had passed. A few moments later, a nurse came to take him for X-rays, so the three went back with her, presumably to the radiology room. Adam resumed staring at the wall, thinking of nothing in particular, and fearing the worst. He heard the boy's father return a while later and take his seat. He assumed the X-ray had been taken, and they were now in an exam room, and either the room was too small for everyone or the man needed to make a phone call. He did pull out his phone, but appeared to be checking messages instead of making calls. Then he heard the man's voice but didn't pay attention to it until he heard his name.

"Excuse me, but are you Adam Garrett?" he repeated.

He lifted his head and saw the man looking directly at him.

"Oh, I'm sorry, you were talking to me, I thought you were making a call. Uh, well, yes, I am."

"I knew it. You look like your picture."

"Surprising how often that happens. So, who are you?"

The man introduced himself and commenced making small talk. Mary emerged from the back and rescued him. Another look of recognition appeared on the man's face, but Adam had her by the arm and headed toward the exit before the man could ask.

"Well, what did the doc say?"

"Nothing much. He said there were no local upticks in infectious diseases, and that my symptoms were too general to help with a diagnosis. He thought it likely bacterial, so he prescribed antibiotics. He wants to see me again in two weeks."

"That's it?"

"Oh, yeah, he prefers I not run until I get my energy back. I told him it would be with you, and he almost relented since I told him running with you was like a fast walk."

"Ask him to check that out when you go back in two weeks."

"Check what out?"

"That sick sense of humor you have. Ask him if there's a transplant available so you can get one that works."

She elbowed him in the ribs, then put her arms around

him and asked if that hurt.

"What, are you kidding? I barely felt that."

"Probably because I'm weak. Take me home, will you, and stop by the pharmacy on the way, you big hunk of burning cheese."

They laughed. "You meant 'love.'"

"I know. It's the fever; I have no idea where that came from."

"After the pharmacy, you want to stop and pick up some love burger for lunch?"

She hit him in the ribs again.

"Ouch, I felt it that time. You must be feeling better."

*

The fever did not let up, and she grew weaker by the day. After a week on antibiotics, she scheduled a follow-up appointment with the doctor. After seeing her weakened condition, he admitted her to the hospital for a complete examination. By the time blood work and a battery of tests had been completed, Adam had only a few minutes to see her before visiting hours ended. When he kissed her goodbye, she gave him her brother's phone number and asked him to make him aware of her situation. He'd never met him and had no idea what to expect, but the call went to voicemail anyway, so he left a brief message.

The next morning, Adam came to visit but had to wait until a doctor could come out to meet him.

"I'm afraid her condition has worsened. She's in and out of consciousness. We're doing everything we can for her. Your name is on the list of visitors she gave us, but her brother Keith is her sole living relative, so he'll have power of attorney to make medical decisions on her behalf, if it comes to that. She wanted to change that to you, but unfortunately, she weakened considerably before she could sign the paperwork. We hope this is a temporary setback, and that none of that will be necessary."

He sat next to her bedside and held her hand. She never did open her eyes in his presence, but did speak twice. "4-3-3-2. 4-3-3-2." That was it. He spoke her name, told her he was with her, and asked what "4-3-3-2" meant. She didn't respond. He felt her forehead. Warmer than it should be, but not hot. The doctors would not comment on her condition other than to tell him the obvious—she had a fever and might be in a coma. He called his mother and gave her the news. He could hear her tears even though he couldn't see them. They consoled each other for a good half hour, but it didn't help much. He dragged himself out of the room when visiting hours ended.

The next day, more of the same. He grew impatient and wanted answers, but couldn't get any. I guess they don't know either.

He left the hospital and drove home, realizing on the way that he hadn't eaten all day. He hadn't shopped for groceries in a while either, so if he wanted something, he either had to stop at a grocery store or fast-food it. He diverted from his route and drove to the restaurant that made the burgers and fries he shared with Mary in her office the day they met. He sat at a table, alone, waiting for his meal. When it arrived, he asked if they could instead pack it into a carry-out bag. He apologized for the inconvenience and left a generous tip. He drove to the pull-off overlooking Lake Everson and parked. Getting out, he found a tree to lean against. He nibbled a few fries but didn't touch the hamburger. Maybe later.

"Look, God, you and I have, how should I put it, an unusual relationship. We've been through a lot together, and I understand your ways a lot better than I did ten years ago. You know I don't expect a life of ease, but doggone it, I can't go through this again. If I lose Mary too, how do I come back from that? What's happening? Talk to me."

CHAPTER FIFTY SEVEN

Adam continued to perform his teaching duties and went to church on Sundays, but other than running at the track, did little else. Mary's condition had not improved, but neither had it worsened. The doctors told him precious little, and the nurses, while sympathetic, couldn't help either.

"Good evening, Sharon."

The woman at the information desk wished him the same as he headed into another night of apprehensive uncertainty. He'd determined the cycles of every traffic light on the route back to his apartment. He'd also calculated the optimal speed—three miles per hour above the speed limit—that would get him home in the shortest amount of time.

He turned the door key and entered his apartment, managing to close it a split second before being hurtled back into it. A muscled forearm swung up and across his throat, pinning his back against the door and closing off his airway. He struggled to breathe and free himself, but the harder he fought, the more he realized the effort was futile. He couldn't speak, but his ears worked, and he heard instructions to remain perfectly still and not to say a word, that he could breathe again as soon as he complied with those two commands. The pressure against his neck lessened, and he lowered his head and eyes enough to see the person now in control of his life.

"Keith? What the—"

"I said you weren't to say a word. Want to do this again?"

He shook his head.

"Good. Now, when I ask you a question, you answer it truthfully, and I let you breathe. If you lie to me, you may not survive what happens next. Understand?"

He shook his head again.

"First question. How do you know my name?"

He took his time, not wanting to misspeak in the slightest. "Mary…has shown me pictures…of you."

"Next question. What happened to her? Why is she in the hospital?"

"She's sick. She's in a coma. That's all I know."

"How'd she get sick?"

"I, I don't know. The doctors don't know, or at least they won't tell me. I don't know."

"I think you know," he said, pressing his arm against his neck more forcefully. "I'll give you another chance. Why is my sister in the hospital?"

"She has an infection, a fever. How she got it, I don't know. How would I? I wish I knew. I love her; we're engaged for goodness' sake. She had to have told you that."

"One more question. My sister swore she would never live with a guy before marriage. That would include you.

340

Did you rape her?"

"What? No, of course not. What are you talking about?"

"I'm asking the questions. What I want to know is, what did you do to my sister? Are you a pervert? Do you enjoy rough sex?"

He froze, staring at the man in disbelief. "What did you say?"

"You heard me. Answer the question."

"It's a ridiculous question. Look, I have no idea where this is coming from, but she's never been with a man, and I've never been with a woman. We agreed on that when we got engaged. I didn't rape her, and I resent the question."

Angered, he flailed his arms and kicked at Keith, but the grip of the Special Forces soldier grew tighter, and he lost his ability to breathe and speak once again. Just before the point of passing out, he fell in a helpless heap to the floor.

"Well, how the hell did she get pregnant?"

He heard the word, but his mind didn't register it until he'd reestablished his equilibrium and regained his wits. When it finally did, it seemed like a foreign word.

"What?" he asked, struggling to get his bearings and find Keith. "Pregnant? What are you talking about? Mary isn't pregnant. She's sick, but she isn't pregnant. How'd you get into my apartment? Leave, or I'll call the cops."

Keith focused on his face. "You didn't know. You didn't know, did you?"

"Didn't know what? Start making sense, or I'm calling the cops."

"Of course, they couldn't release that information to

you. You two aren't married; they could only tell me. I flew in last night and visited Mary this morning, that's when I found out she's pregnant."

He studied Keith's face. This guy is a highly-trained military operative who could probably pull off a lie like this, but, why? This is so…absurd. He closed his eyes to help himself think, but nothing made sense.

"I don't know why you're saying this, but she isn't pregnant. She can't be. We've never…"

"Just because you didn't know she was pregnant doesn't mean she isn't or that you didn't do it. I don't have much time, and if I find out you've lied to me, it won't be pretty."

The violence of the door slamming shut sent a jolt through his body. When the aftershocks subsided, he picked himself off the floor and wobbled to the sofa, collapsing on it. He turned his body and lifted his legs onto one end and lowered his head onto the other. He stared at the patterns of flecks stippled onto the ceiling. Random. Chaotic. That's my life, right there. Chaotic. Mary pregnant? I don't even know how to process that. Must be a mistake with the blood work. Has to be. But why did her brother break into my apartment and almost take my head off? I need answers. I need the truth. Now.

He gathered himself and drove back to the hospital. The staff at the front desk advised him that another visitor had come to see Mary and suggested he wait in the lobby.

"Is it Keith Walsh?"

The receptionist looked at her after-hours log sheet.

"Why, yes, it is, sir."

"Okay, I'll wait. Is there a doctor here? Someone who

can tell me about her condition?"

"Sure, but they may not be able to release information to you. Are you a family member?"

"No, not yet."

"I'm afraid you'll have to ask someone in her family for health information; we can't give that out. It's the law. I'm sorry."

"I'll wait here."

He didn't have to wait long. Keith strode through the lobby toward him. He stood and faced his fiancée's brother, who made a demand before he could get his question out.

"You need to submit blood for a paternity test. You didn't do this? Here's your chance to prove it."

"I don't believe she's pregnant. It's so preposterous I can't get past it. I need proof."

"You think I'm making this up? You think I have time to play games here?"

"I don't know you well enough to guess. Based on my first impression—"

"You can either do this voluntarily," he said, cutting him off. "Or I'll get a court order. If I can't get a court order, I'll draw blood from you myself."

"Fine, but first, I need to hear the doctor tell me she's pregnant."

"All right. Be here at ten tomorrow morning, and I'll arrange for him to talk to you."

"Make it ten-thirty; I have a class at nine."

"Not a minute later, you got it?"

"I got it. I got it. Why can't we do this now?"

"I want you to hear it from her primary care doc, and

he's gone for the day. So be here tomorrow morning, and you'd better not be lying to me. Now's the time to come clean."

He didn't reply. He didn't know what to think or say. He walked away. He made the trip back to his apartment in record time. Seated on the floor with his back against a wall and his feet tucked close, he rested his head on his knees. His mind raced to find an explanation, but the effort proved fruitless. His phone rang, but he didn't move to answer it. He didn't move at all. The world didn't make sense at the moment. Nothing did. I thought I knew her; how could I have been so wrong? Who is she? She'd only been in California for six weeks, how could she have gotten involved with another guy in that short amount of time? Unless it was Clark. Clark. Had those two resumed a grad-school fling? But what does that say about us? Do I even know this woman? At all? Okay, I have to get out of here. I need a run.

The lighting that illuminated the field for flag football extended just far enough so he could see to use the adjacent track. Fourteen laps later, the game ended, players scattered, and the lights went out. The overexertion he'd forced himself into during the run had provided momentary relief from the agonizing circumstances that engulfed him. The ensuing darkness brought an end to the extreme workout, and with it, a creeping sense of despair similar to the one he felt during Jill's final days. Was it the same? Or worse? His concern over Mary's health crisis had vacillated between dread and hope—hope that God would intervene. However, it was now complicated by the possibility of her unfaithfulness, a prospect that nearly incapacitated his thinking abilities. If she had a boyfriend in LA, it means I don't know her very well, and if I don't know her very well, why should I care that much about her health? But even if I may not know this person, don't I have to hope she gets well? Don't I owe her at least that much? Of course, that's the only civil thing to do. At some point, though, I'll have to quietly say goodbye. When the alarm went off the next morning, he couldn't remember sleeping a wink.

CHAPTER FIFTY EIGHT

✤

Adam listened as Mary's doctor confirmed Keith's assertion. His fiancée was indeed pregnant. He staggered out of the hospital, looking at the ground in front of him, almost running into a nurse on her way in.

"Oh, sorry," he said.

"That's all right," she replied. "Sir, are you okay? You look pale."

He continued to the parking lot without responding and fumbled for his keys. He searched his pockets several times and looked back at the hospital entrance. Then he found them. In my hand the whole time? Gosh, I'm losing it. He drove to the grassy spot where he'd proposed and sat next to the creek. Staring into the water, reflecting on the events of the last twenty-four hours, he looked for answers in the gurgling current. No luck. He lay back and looked into the sky. Nothing for him in the wispy clouds or expansive blue, either. He closed his eyes and put his hands over his ears, trying to shut out all sensory input. He didn't want to hear anything, see anything, talk to anyone. He wanted to stop existing, at least for a moment. Pregnant? Are you kidding me? That is…inconceivable. He opened his eyes and scanned the heavens again. Hey, do you have any answers? When you get time, I'd be interested in an explanation. He trudged to his car and drove back to his apartment. He took a long shower, ate a sandwich, and turned on the TV. Reruns, old movies, it didn't much matter. Life had just beaten the stuffing out of him, and all he could do was sit in a hazy fog and look for a light. Any light.

*

His running shoes sat idly in his closet, having been covered over by a tossed towel. He didn't miss them. Food container boxes piled up by the kitchen garbage can. His days consisted of microwaved meals and minimal effort preparing lectures. He never returned the call from a concerned church buddy who hadn't seen him in a couple of Sundays.

A knock on his door interrupted an episode of The Andy Griffith Show. Keith.

"Nice of you to knock this time. What do you want?"

"We need to talk. Can I come in?"

"Oh, asking permission this time? Look, I don't have anything to say to you, and the only reason I didn't call the cops on you before is that it would have been your word against mine. Get lost."

He studied the face of Mary's brother, catching the resemblance between the two for the first time. He turned away and walked into the bathroom and soaked a wash rag with warm water from the faucet. He pressed it onto his cheeks and forehead and held it there. A moment later, he dried his face and plodded back into his living room.

"You still here?"

"Tell me about California," Keith demanded.

"Why should I? You are definitely not on my good side at the moment, what with breaking into my apartment and putting me through hell."

"That was nothing. I took it easy on you only because Mary had spoken so highly of you. If she loves you, you can't be all bad."

"Then why torture me?"

"That wasn't torture. I had to put a little fear into your head to get honest answers."

"Well, I resent it, okay? Go back to the army and leave me alone. I'm not in a good mood. I just found out my fiancée is pregnant with someone else's baby. How would you feel if you were me?"

"Look, cry in your beer all you want, but what I need from you now, if you can pull yourself together for a few minutes, is information on California. Tell me everything you know about Mary's interactions with anyone she met in Los Angeles."

"Why? Do you want to see if they're sick? See if anyone has what Mary has?"

"No, her infection isn't contagious."

"Well, I wouldn't know, you never let me find out anything about her condition."

"You've had permission for three weeks. You mean you haven't seen her since I left?"

"Seen who? Mary? Apparently, I don't know her, why should I see her?"

"Because she's your fiancée, jackass. Good God, get it together, man. I'm catching a flight to California to find out who raped her. And God help the SOB when I find out who he is."

He bolted upright, nearly falling off the sofa and spilling pretzels. He looked at Keith as though he'd uttered an incomprehensible word.

"Rape? She was raped? What makes you think that?"

"Two reasons. One, I know my sister. She would never have consented before marriage. Never. Especially not with you. And two, do you remember me asking you if you liked rough sex?"

"How could I forget such a bizarre question?"

"I asked it for a reason. An MRI found a lesion in her uterus. The doc says it could have been caused by rough sex. That means forced sex, and I aim to find out who did the forcing. So, I need to know about California."

"Wait. Wait a minute. No, no, she wasn't raped. She couldn't have kept that from me."

"You just admitted you didn't know her very well."

"Well, I'm not that dense. I would have sensed it if something traumatic had happened to her. No, I'm thinking she had a history with Clark that I didn't know about. He's the one she worked with this summer. She may have been able to hide that from me, but not a violent rape."

"Mary doesn't hide things. That's not her. But, tell me about this Clark guy."

"He mentored her at Texas during grad school. I met him briefly when he stopped by on his way through Waco in April. She'd asked him to help with a publication. He seemed reasonable enough, but then again, I'm obviously not a good judge of character."

"All right, that makes him a suspect, but if he's the father, I guarantee you it would have been against her will."

"You're stuck on the rape idea. If that's true, and I don't think it is, what would you do to him?"

"Turn him over to the police, of course."

"Just like that? You wouldn't torture him?"

"Torture is illegal. But, if he happened to have a mishap on the way to the sheriff's office, well, that would be most unfortunate, wouldn't it?"

"I don't know how I'd feel about that. If I saw proof with my own eyes that he'd raped Mary, I'd probably help you beat him. I'd at least mess with his head and watch him squirm. More threat than actual torture. You, on the other hand, you'd probably tear his head off."

"I might."

"I may need to go with you to keep you out of trouble."

"I usually work better alone, but, maybe, in this case, you have a point. I may need someone to keep me from getting in a jam. Look, don't get me wrong, I don't intend to do the work of the police. I want to put together a list of names to show a judge and the reasons why we want a paternity test done. I can tell if someone is lying. Having you along to corroborate my suspicion of guilt might help convince a judge to issue a subpoena. We might get a detective to open an investigation."

"Or we could prove there was a consensual relationship with the guy."

"I'll be open to that, but that's not what we'll find.

Can you be open to the possibility of rape?"

"I'd feel like an idiot. Rape is so traumatic, how could I have not seen the after-effects in her? She would have been different, somehow, and I would have noticed. I don't think I'm that clueless at reading people. It didn't happen. But, okay, I'll allow for the infinitesimally small chance that it did."

"Fair enough. Now, I need to get moving on this. I told you before I didn't have much time, and I still don't, I rarely do. So, I'm going out there today to get started. You catch up when you can."

"I can be out there late tomorrow. I have a class in the morning, so if I get a teaching assistant to give my students their exams on Monday, that's four or five days."

"That'll do for now; it's all the time I have anyway. Now, tell me about California. Tell me her routines, who she had contact with, tell me everything you know. Start with Clark."

"Mary stayed with Clark and Vanessa. Vanessa often worked late, so Clark would have had opportunities to rekindle a relationship with Mary."

"Or attack her in his home. We'll have to be prepared when we talk to him, we both have our own suspicions. He can't run a company and be a dummy; he'll know something's up if we question him about his feelings for her."

"I have an idea about that. He wants me to sell him the J-cells patent. I've refused. What if I tell him I haven't completely ruled it out yet and wanted to see his operation first-hand."

"That could work."

"You can be a graduate student attending a conference with me."

"I'd need to be in disguise. He might see a little of my sister in me."

"Good idea. And I can do most of the talking so he won't look at you much. Oh, and, by the way, you should know the amount of his offer."

"Okay, tell me."

"Last figure was five million."

"Five million? And you turned it down? Why?"

"Long story for another day. I thought you should know there may be added tension when we meet. He still wants the rights to J-cells."

"I'll say. But, that's okay, tension can be useful. What else can you tell me about California?"

They spent the next two hours reviewing the seven weeks Mary spent in LA. He scoured her emails for details about her daily activities. He printed copies of them for Keith, deleting the irrelevant sections that reflected on their growing fondness for each other. He found Clark's phone number and the name and address of his company and gave those to him as well.

"Mary didn't mention meeting anyone suspicious?"

"No. She only complained once, and that was about Vanessa. She seemed less hospitable as the summer went along, like she didn't want her staying in their home anymore."

"Got jealous when Clark paid her too much attention? But, of course, she didn't do it."

"No. As I said, though, Vanessa and Mary went out together the night she fainted. I'd like to know more about what happened at that dance hall."

"All right. Get there when you can. I'll snoop around until you do. Send me your flight information, and I'll pick you up at the airport. And do not say a word to anybody about me being there."

CHAPTER FIFTY NINE

Adam greeted Dr. Richard Clark and introduced him to Carson Bennett. With the young archaeology professor holding the legal rights to J-cells, the CEO of EVI appeared eager to accommodate his visitors. Their gracious host offered coffee, sodas, water, and snacks as they sat in his office and chatted. He accepted a bottle of water, and Keith asked for coffee, black.

"So, what brings you to LA?"

"A conference," he answered. "The last session was this morning, but we skipped out early. Couldn't take any more talks. We weren't much interested in the topics anyway. At least I wasn't."

"Nor I," Keith added.

"I understand," Clark said. "Been in that same position myself a few times."

"Our plane leaves in the morning, and we didn't have anything planned for this afternoon, so I thought I'd drop by and see your lab. After all, you are working with J-cells. And, I thought while we were in the area, I'd talk to you about your offer to buy the patent. I wanted you to know it has nothing to do with me holding out for a higher offer. I don't want to sell, is all, but if I did, it would probably be to you. Mary thinks highly of you."

"That is as I suspected, based on what I know about you from her. For me, wanting to buy the patent is simple business. We convinced a group of investors in Dallas that those cells will change medicine. The genome is a treasure trove, and J-cells are a gold mine, in my opinion. I could have gotten a deal that would have funded EVI for years to come. I could also have paid for Vanessa's clinic, something she desperately wants. I would love to be able to give it to her. But, if I work hard and develop products under our current MTA, I'll eventually meet both of those goals. It will just take longer to get there. But I understand your decision. Speaking of Mary, I haven't heard from her in a while. I thought by now she'd have completed a manuscript on her work here this summer. Is her other research keeping her busy?"

"Well, no, as a matter of fact, she's in the hospital."

"Oh, no. What's wrong?"

"She has a serious infection; the docs think it's MRSA."

"MRSA? That's not good, but my understanding is that it can usually be treated. Has it gone systemic?"

"Unfortunately, yes. She's undergoing intensive antibiotic therapy. They're optimistic, but that's why she hasn't finished the paper."

"Oh my goodness, bless her heart. Well, she's young and strong. If anyone can beat it, it's her. We're anxious to continue and even expand her research with new possibilities my bioinformatics postdoc has turned up. I wanted to discuss it with her first, and you, too, of course."

"That's fine. I'll let her know we stopped by, and I'm sure she'll have that paper ready as soon as she's back on her feet."

Clark gave them a tour of the building and described the projects currently in progress, the most prominent being diabetes gene therapy trials. They were then shown the lab where Mary had done her experiments and the office she used. They concluded their visit to EVI with Tom, who'd actually spent a lot more time working with her than Clark.

"I'm sorry about Mary, I like her a lot," Clark said, escorting them to the front entrance. "We go back a ways. You know that. She's a great scientist, a great person. She'll pull through. She has to. Let me know if I can help, if I can do anything, anything at all."

"Uh, say, where's the restroom here?" Keith asked. "That coffee is kicking in."

As Clark pointed the way for Keith, a technician appeared and said he needed a quick word with his boss.

"Adam, give me a second, please."

"Of course."

Clark finished his discussion with the lab tech and returned to their conversation. "Sorry about that. Say, where are you guys staying? If it isn't far, why don't you come to the house for dinner tonight?"

"Well, I'll run it by Ke—uh, Carson."

"Run what by me?" Keith asked, having completed his errand.

"Dinner. My place. Or we could go out somewhere, your choice."

"That sounds great," he said. "We've eaten out three nights in a row now, not to mention lunches. We're ready for a home-cooked meal, if it isn't too much trouble."

"It would probably be something on the grill, but, no, no trouble at all. It would be my pleasure."

"That's kind of you. What time should we be there?"

"Oh, let's say six-thirty." He handed him a card with his home address printed on it.

"Will we get to meet Vanessa?" he asked.

"I don't think so; she's busy at the hospital lately. But I'll let her know you're coming. She might be able to sneak away.

"Great. See you then."

"Where you off to now?"

"Not sure. Any recommendations?"

"Depends on what you want to do. When I go to conferences, I like to walk after all that sitting. You could window shop on Rodeo Drive, walk out on the Santa Monica Pier, or the beach, or both."

"We may do that," he said.

"Nice meeting you, Clark," Keith said.

"And nice meeting you, Carson. You guys have fun. See you tonight."

*

They drove to the church Mary attended that summer. The pastor recognized Adam from the news accounts of Melnikos, and, after expressing surprise by his visit, invited them both into his office. He remembered Mary from their brief exchanges after Sunday morning services. He knew more about her, however, from having a single adult daughter in JoAnne's Sunday afternoon group.

"Mary impressed Katie with her knowledge of science, and not just cell biology," the pastor said. "The whole group thoroughly enjoyed her. Katie talked about her a lot."

"And Mary talked about them a lot too," he said. "She had a lot of fun."

"How big is this group?" Keith asked.

"Oh, it varies, but I'd say any given Sunday ten to fifteen go on their little outings."

"I bet some cute girls are in it."

"Oh?" asked the pastor. "I take it you're single?"

"Yessir."

"Well, about half are young women and half are young men, and all are single. Do they sometimes date each other? I don't know; you'd have to ask my daughter."

"Do you happen to have JoAnne's phone number? Mary asked me to say hi to her while we were out here, and to give her this." He pulled a ten dollar bill from his wallet. "This is for a bet she lost. She wouldn't say what it was about, and if I wanted to know, I had to ask JoAnne."

"I'm sorry I don't have it, but if you leave me your number, I'll have Katie call her, and then JoAnne can call you."

"That would be great," he said, writing it for him on the back of an old restaurant receipt still in his wallet.

*

They left the church before noon and drove to the restaurant Mary and Vanessa dined at the night she fainted. They each ordered a salad and, while waiting, were able to talk to the manager, who wanted to be helpful but had nothing for them. The restaurant didn't have surveillance of the dining area, and the two cameras outside the building erased recordings every seven days. After eating what turned out to be rather tasty salads, they walked across the street and ordered hamburgers at the nearly empty bar of the dance hall. They asked the bartender about the evening clientele and anything else that might be useful to their investigation. The place maintained surveillance tapes for at least ninety days, she thought.

"Yes, sir, and we have a bouncer on duty in the evenings, though we seldom have fights. But, every once in a while…"

"Can we talk to the bouncer?" Keith asked. "And can we see the recordings from August seventh?"

"Are you guys police?"

"No, we're private investigators. We're checking out a story about a possible rape that night."

"Rape? It didn't happen here. I'd have heard about it."

"We don't think it happened at all. Look, we've been hired by the father of the accused. Well, he isn't accused yet, but she's threatening. It looks like a blackmail deal to us, so if we can see how they interacted that night, it might give us an idea of what happened."

"And whether the guy should fight it or settle now?"

"Exactly."

"Can you come back at five? The boss will be here, and you can ask him about the video."

"We'll do that. Thanks."

Keith looked at images on his phone while they waited

for the burgers.

"You can sure sling it," he said. "How'd you think of that so fast? And what are you looking at on your phone with such interest?"

"These are pictures of a notebook Clark had on his desk," Keith said. "Does 'DC1600' mean anything to you?"

"No."

"How about...uh, what is that? How about...'F cells'?"

"Wait, 'F cells'? Could it be a 'J' instead of an 'F'?"

"Well, somebody drew two lines through the word 'cells' and the single letter in front of it, so, yes, it could be a 'J.' It looked like an 'F' with those two lines at the top. So, this must refer to what Mary worked with and what Clark wants, right?"

"Right. Mary resurrected what we call J-cells from the tissues we pulled from the whip. She gave them that designation. That was probably her notebook you looked at. When did you take those?"

"When I went to the restroom. Clark left his office door open. No one was watching, so I took pictures."

"What if he came back while you were there?"

"Looking for my misplaced phone."

"Oh, that's good. But what's so interesting about a notebook? It's a laboratory, after all. There'll be lots of notebooks. Why that one?"

"Clark hid it under a stack of papers when we talked in his office. He tried to do it inconspicuously. I watched his face as he did it, and I interpreted what I saw as suspicious."

"Yeah, but why would he try to hide Mary's notebook?"

"It wasn't Mary's notebook."

"How do you know that?"

"Two reasons. There was a notebook in Mary's office. She'd written her name on it and a date in June, probably when she started at EVI. The other reason is this isn't her writing."

He showed Adam one of the photos from his phone. "Does that look like her handwriting?"

"No, you're right, it doesn't. But Clark may have worked with those cells too. Which he can legally do. With an agreement in place, he wouldn't have to hide anything."

"I'm just saying his behavior looked suspicious."

CHAPTER SIXTY

✠

"Now what?" Adam asked.

"Santa Monica."

"Why? Never mind. You want to walk around there in case Clark asks what we did this afternoon."

"Now you're catching on. I've been there before, but it's been a while. I'd like to see what's changed."

They parked near the pier and walked out on it, then on the beach, and finally around town. They were discussing what to do next when JoAnne called. She agreed to meet them at the church after work, and suggested five.

"You talk to JoAnne," Keith said. "I'll go back to the bar and talk to the manager."

＊

Keith dropped him off fifteen minutes early. The pastor had not left for the day and asked him to come into his office.

"Adam, I hate to cash in unfairly on the opportunity, but, since you're here, what can you tell me about the box that wasn't in the news?"

"Oh, I don't mind your asking. Tell me what you know, and I'll fill in the rest."

He did so until JoAnne knocked on the door shortly after five.

"Am I interrupting?"

"As a matter of fact, you are. I'm picking this guy's brain about the Melnikos box. Why don't you come back in an hour."

"I'm in no hurry, pastor, why don't you two continue and I'll sit and listen. I'd like to hear this too."

"JoAnne?" he asked.

"Yes, I am, and you have to be Adam. I've heard so much about you. I may know more about you than you do."

"How might that be?" he asked, curious about the statement.

"Mary. It seems she spent a great deal of time talking to your mother this past summer when you were in Mexico. For example—"

"Wait, wait, I don't want to hear it."

"All right, you two, time for me to leave," the pastor said. "He's all yours, JoAnne. Adam, nice meeting you. Thank you for such a captivating account of your find. The best of luck with everything. Please come back whenever you're in the area."

"Thank you. I'll do that. Next time I'll bring Mary."

"So, Adam, what can I do for you?"

He gave her the ten dollars Mary had lost in their bet. After a good laugh, he engaged her with small talk long enough to discern that she could be trusted to hold their conversation in strict confidence.

"I'm afraid I have bad news. Mary is in the hospital with a uterine infection."

"Oh, no, is it serious?"

"I'm afraid it is. What's more, she's pregnant, and we think the two are related."

She gasped. "What? Mary? Pregnant? I...I don't understand."

"She's been unconscious for two weeks. She's in the best of care, and I've put the outcome in God's hands. The reason I say that her pregnancy and the uterine infection might be related is that we think she may have been violently raped. The timing suggests it happened while she was here, sometime in late July or early August."

She gasped again. Tears welled and soon rolled down her cheeks.

"I had that same reaction. It's unbelievable. I'm here with her brother, and we're looking for the guy who did it. I'm sorry to do this, but I need to ask you about your young adult group, or any other guys she encountered when she was here. Could any of them or anyone else you know about possibly have done such a thing?"

She reached for a tissue to dry her eyes.

"I know it's a hard question, but Mary is lying in a hospital bed fighting for her life. I'm sorry, but I have to ask. Take your time. I'm not in a hurry."

JoAnne wept.

"It's okay. Take your time, but think hard about it, please."

"I, I'm sorry. Mary was, she is, so special. The answer is no. I can't in my wildest imagination see any guys here doing anything like that. I've known everyone in our

Sunday afternoon group for, oh, two years? At least two years."

"All right, thank you. Now, are you aware of anyone with sexual predator status coming to this church or anyone new here, not in your group, who acted strangely those Sundays?"

"No, not offhand, no one comes to mind."

"Okay. Again, I'm sorry to have to ask these questions, but there's a rapist on the loose. Mary liked to jog; it's possible she ran home one day, and that's when it happened. It may have been so traumatic that she blocked it from her memory, and that's why she never told me. I'm sure this church is safe, so don't go getting suspicious of anybody. I appreciate your candor. One last question. Did she ever talk about going anywhere other than to or from work or here? Or meet anyone other than you guys or the people where she worked?"

She thought for a moment, then took a deep breath and sighed.

"No, not that I remember. Clark and Vanessa are all I know about."

"Okay. You have my number. Call me if anything comes to mind, anything that you want to talk about."

"Yes, of course, I'll do that."

"And keep the beach open for us," he said, hoping she believed his sincerity. "We may come back for a wedding."

*

"Any luck?" Adam asked when Keith pulled up and parked along the curb in front of the church.

"Yes. Get in. The manager let me look at the tapes

365

from that night. They stayed for about forty-five minutes. Vanessa sat at a table, and Mary danced most of the time."

"Did any guys hit on her? Or on Vanessa?"

"No, everyone behaved. Vanessa had several drinks, Mary had one, but I'm sure it was ginger ale."

"Mary didn't seem woozy or weak or anything?"

"No. I'd even say she had a good workout that night. When she wasn't line dancing, she danced with three different guys, and they each acted like gentlemen."

"Vanessa didn't dance?"

"She just sat at the table and nursed her drinks."

"So the dance hall is a dead end."

"Yes, but it does help with the timeline. Everything was normal until they left at eight-thirty. She passed out sometime after that."

"Well, one more stop."

"Yeah, remember who we are now. Let me do most of the talking about our time here; I'm probably more familiar with the area. You handle everything about Mary since I'm not supposed to know her. And my name is Carson Bennett."

*

Adam complimented Clark on the grilled Italian sizzlers he served on buns topped with green peppers and onions. They washed theirs down with lemonade while their host enjoyed a cold beer. After eating, they sat on the patio and talked for over an hour. Vanessa had not yet returned home from work when Adam suggested that it might be time to leave.

"You may have things you need to do tonight, so we

should get going. I wish we could have met Vanessa. I'd like to know more about the night Mary fainted."

"Yeah, that came out of nowhere. I was in Dallas, so I don't know the details. Let me call her and see when she'll be here."

He looked at Keith, who made circular motions with his index finger, which he interpreted as wanting him to try to stall until Vanessa got home.

"Looks like another thirty minutes. You're welcome to stay."

"Do you have anything pressing tonight?"

"No, nothing that can't wait until tomorrow."

They found things to talk about, including J-cells and what Clark thought might be a way to handle their distribution. He rattled off a number of potential uses for them and suggested again that they'd be in great demand.

"In fact, if our vaccine trials don't go well, I may be looking for work. I could manage those cells for you. I have experience with the legalities of these things. I know the marketing angle, and I know the science. I, or someone like me, would be the perfect person for that job. Think about it. And set that up before Mary's paper comes out, because once it does, you'll get so many requests for J-cells it'll make your head spin."

"Good advice. Thanks."

"Her in Texas, me here in LA. A third person on the East Coast. Then again, they can ship at room temperature, so it doesn't matter where they're stored. The bottleneck would be the legal agreements, so what's an extra day or two for shipping?"

"First things first," he said. "Let's get Mary back on

her feet and see how the paper is received and go from there."

"Here, here," Clark said. "A toast to Mary and her quick recovery."

Three glasses clinked as Vanessa walked onto the patio.

"A toast to me?" she asked. "How nice. I'll drink to that."

"Hello, sweetie," Clark said as they stood to greet her. "Come meet Adam and Carson. Carson is a grad student working for Adam. They're here for a conference."

The four sat around a table by the pool for another hour. They managed not to blow Keith's cover nor give away their real purpose for being there. They excused themselves and thanked their hosts, then left.

"I can't wait to hear your thoughts on Vanessa," he said on the way to the car.

"Oh, I don't know. She's attractive, engaging, funny at times. She works a lot."

"Yeah, she does seem driven. Knows what she wants."

"And yet, there's something about her. I can't put my finger on it."

"Did you buy her account of when Mary passed out?"

"I'm not sure. I didn't get a good read on that, but she did seem uneasy talking about it."

"More than normal? I mean, Mary had a medical emergency, anyone might seem uneasy talking about something like that."

"That's true. At least now we know it happened at the clinic. If you're going to faint, that's as good a place as any to do it. Yesterday I asked a few people at the hospital about her. None had problems recommending her as a fertility doc and said she was the best. Everyone liked her."

"Well, we know she didn't commit rape."

"Yeah. Let's sleep on it and see what we think in the morning, but I need to get back to Virginia. So, unless we come up with a lead, you're on your own here."

"I can ask around about Clark. We haven't ruled him out yet. At least I haven't."

"I have," Keith said. "I followed him after he left work yesterday. Went straight to the gym and then to a little bar and grill near his home. I convinced the guy at the bar that I was FBI doing a security clearance investigation on Clark. I told him nobody was in trouble, that I had a few routine questions to ask about someone the government may need to confide secrets in should EVI happen to win a contract. He agreed not to tell him about our visit."

"Wow, that's good. So, what did he say."

"He told me about his sister in Texas. Seems like our boy got a little drunk playing pool with her in Dallas one night. He was in no shape to drive, so she put him up in her hotel room. He behaved himself, slept in the other bed, and that was that. The guy vouched for his character too, says Clark never plays around on Vanessa, that he's devoted to her."

"Good for him."

"Bad for us. I'd considered him a prime suspect for several reasons."

"That leaves other workers at EVI. What do you think there?"

"We only talked to Tom, and I don't think it's him. Look, on second thought, why don't you go home tomorrow and gather more information by phone and computer. That way, you won't arouse suspicion here."

"Who would I call?"

"Call the Better Business Bureau and ask about EVI. Search the internet and read everything you can about them. Look for anything unusual. Look for local news accounts of sexual assaults, see if anything happened in or near Clark's neighborhood. I have to be off the grid for a while, so you'll have to do this on your own. But I'm sure you're plenty motivated. And, besides, you don't like me anyway."

"That's right, I haven't forgotten. But, you do seem skilled at these things, and you are her brother."

"Let's stop it right there. I don't want you getting all tender on me."

CHAPTER SIXTY ONE

Adam returned to Waco, having been yanked out of his malaise by Keith and the trip to California. The idea that Mary had been raped, one he hadn't fully subscribed to yet, nevertheless had enough merit to force him to consider the possibility that she might be completely innocent. That made him revisit his thinking about how well he knew his fiancée, which, in turn, led him to reverse his opinion on the cause of her pregnancy from a willing encounter to a criminal act. He concluded that, if nothing else, he owed her the benefit of the doubt, at least until the truth came out. He cleaned his apartment, restocked his refrigerator with fruits and vegetables, and tossed the ice cream and snack cakes. Wait, that's Blue Bell, can't throw that away. He dropped the five pounds he'd gained in the last month. He put more effort preparing lectures and hit the track on even days, and the gym for weights and racquetball on odd days. He made the trip to Abilene to inform his parents of Mary's pregnancy. They cried together, which had a cathartic effect on him. He resumed visits to the hospital, and on a late October afternoon, her doctor stopped by her room to talk.

"Keith authorized us to use all necessary medical procedures to treat Mary. We've been unable to contact him to give him an update on her condition, but he also has given us permission to give you this information. So, I'll give it to you, and you can tell him when you can. Here's where we are. She's been in a coma for four weeks. Antibiotics aren't working. Her fevers come and go, but her brain function is what we're beginning to be concerned about. We've done CT and fMRI scans, and, putting together everything we know, we think neurotoxins are attacking her brain. We see abnormalities in those scans, not extraordinarily so, but we see differences nonetheless. We think we need to be more aggressive with the lesion in her uterus, as that is likely the source of the toxins. So, the first step is to go in and cut it out. Hopefully, we'll get it all, but we'll culture it to see exactly what we're dealing with and what antibiotics it's susceptible to in case a few bacterial cells get left behind."

"This procedure, will it harm the baby?"

"There is risk, yes, but the surgeon will insert a camera to guide him to the spot and avoid the fetuses."

"Fetuses? As in more than one?"

"Keith didn't tell you?"

"He doesn't talk much. At least to me."

"Well, there are actually three, and they each look healthy. Now, if we don't get the whole infection and the antibiotics don't work, we can be more aggressive. We can bring in new ones, try different combinations, and find something that works. However, that could mean more risk to the little fellas. We'll do all we can to save them, of

372

course, but our priority is Mary."

"Three?"

"Three. Each doing surprisingly well. Adam, are you okay?"

"It's all been a lot to process, and now this. Three babies. Wow."

"One last thing, if none of that is successful and she remains in a neurotoxin-induced coma, we may need to perform a hysterectomy. We'll do everything we can to avoid that, of course, but it may be necessary to save her life."

"Oh, gosh, I hope it doesn't come to that."

"As do I. Let me hasten to add that I'm consulting with several specialists, so it isn't only me making these calls. In fact, I've talked twice with an infectious disease expert at Johns Hopkins. He has Mary's scans and medical records. He monitors her progress along with the staff here, and concurs with the treatments she's been getting."

"I can't ask more than that. Thank you for all you're doing for her. I hope you don't mind me asking questions as the days go by."

"Not at all, it's a sign of your great concern, which I can see in your eyes. We're pulling for you, and the best way to do that is to get this young lady back on her feet. We've scheduled her procedure for tomorrow morning, first thing. Can you be here?"

"I can."

*

Adam waited for Mary in the recovery room. He looked over his notes for the next day's lecture to pass the time.

When they wheeled her in and got her situated, he held her hand and prayed. The surgeon appeared and asked to speak to him in an adjacent office.

"Everything went well. We cut out the lesion, and the microbiologists are culturing it to identify the bug that's causing Mary so much trouble. With luck, this will be the end of it, but we have seen instances of reseeding."

"Reseeding?"

"Yes, another lesion might pop up nearby, so don't be overly alarmed if that happens. When we identify the strain of bacteria, we'll have a better shot at knocking out such a recurrence with specific antibiotics."

"That sounds hopeful. How about the babies?"

"Well, they complicated the procedure, but all three are in good shape. I'm a little surprised the infection hasn't hit them, too. They seem to be little troopers, fighting for their lives as hard as Mary."

*

The next day he observed a difference in her appearance as he held her hand. She looked better to him, somehow. More peaceful. When the nurse came in to tend to her, he asked about her temperature.

"No fever last night or this morning. That's a good sign."

"It sure is."

"Now get out of here so I can give her a bath," she said, winking at him. "You two aren't married yet."

He smiled as he walked out. He went home and packed a lunch for a bike ride to the lake. He leaned against the trunk of a mesquite tree near the water as he nibbled on his sandwich. Not as warm as it has been. Fall is here. I hope she's home by Christmas. Oh, Jill, I know you'd want that too, that would be so like you. Strange how I get the best loves in the world but can't hang onto them. Is that my destiny? Not complaining again, God, but when you made Jill and Mary, well, even you would have to admit they're two of the best ever. And me, an average Joe, I get to love them and have them love me back. But dammit, God, why do I have to lose them? Would I be better off not having met either of them? Or maybe it's them who'd be better off never having known me.

*

Her fever returned the following week. An MRI showed not one but two new lesions in her uterus. To counter them, one of the three antibiotics she'd been taking had been dropped, and a new one that worked more effectively against her particular MRSA strain had been added. That reduced her fever for three days, but then it returned once more.

"This is a tough case, Adam," the doctor said. "These bacteria are apparently developing resistance to one or more of the antibiotics. They have remarkable survival abilities. They can encase themselves in a biofilm that reduces the effectiveness of the drugs by preventing them from reaching their surface. We may try to remove the lesions again, but my consulting specialist recommends more efficacious antibiotics. Unfortunately, they have teratogenic potential, so I want to hold off on that if we can. Let's give her another day or so and then decide. In the meantime, rest assured that the minds of the best infectious disease doctors around are focused on Mary."

He left the hospital and drove to his office to prepare another lecture. After an hour of staring at his notes, he wandered outside to the oak tree he and Mary used to sit under after a run. He leaned against it and thought how nice it would be to have her there with him, stretching and laughing and cooling down after a five-mile race. Even if he lost for the umpteenth time, he'd be so happy. You'll make it, girl. Hang in there.

The antibiotic regimen, however, failed to control the infection, so they opted to remove the new lesions. He waited for her in the recovery room, once again. The surgeon explained that he'd cut away the lesions and sutured the cuts, then vigorously scraped the lining of her uterus a centimeter or two around the spots. He avoided the placentas, but suggested that this might be the last opportunity for such a procedure since things were starting to get crowded in there. Mary seemed restless back in her room, but a nurse told him that it was not unusual after surgery. He found her resting more comfortably the next day, and the nurse informed him that the fever had once again resolved. The doctor had more good news—the babies had come through the procedure with flying colors. After the visit, he left for the track and ran a fast five miles for Mary. Things are looking up. This has to be it. This will be the end of that nasty infection. Come on, girl, come back to me.

*

A week later, the fever returned. The doctor said her brain scans troubled him, and that it might be time for the hysterectomy.

"We can't afford for her to become bacteremic. We think the antibiotics are keeping the infection limited to the uterus, but if it gets out, it could result in sepsis and septic shock. She won't survive that. I'm sorry, but we may have to do this. I finally got through to Keith, and he has authorized the procedure. I'd like you to be on board as well. Can you do that?"

"How old are the babies?"

"About twelve to thirteen weeks. They're too young to save. I'm so sorry. If you want time to think and pray, please take it, but we need to schedule this soon."

"No, you warned me about this possibility. I've prayed about it. It's hard; it may be the hardest thing I've ever been a part of. It's different from losing my childhood sweetheart Jill, somehow. I knew her so well, but even though I've only known these guys a few weeks, they've grown on me. And even though they aren't mine, I love them. It's a sad day, but I've resigned myself to trust your judgment."

"They aren't yours? I guess that's none of my business, but I can see that it doesn't matter to you. Good for you. I'm glad these boys were loved while they lived."

"Yeah, well, they're completely innocent. They had nothing to do with how they got here. They deserve a chance at life. I'd do anything to save them, but...let me know when to be here."

"I want to look at her chart again this afternoon and then huddle with the staff, but if nothing changes, we'll probably schedule this for tomorrow morning."

*

Adam waited once again in the recovery room, a bittersweet experience. The surgery would mean he'd have Mary back soon, but his heart ached for the three tiny ones who would soon be…gone. He thought it strange that she'd never have an awareness of them. How would she have reacted to them? It would be up to him to tell her. He dreaded it, but as his mother said, she's strong, she'll get through it. The surgeon approached and asked to speak with him in the office. Uh-oh. Where's Mary? Why is he here now, and she isn't? What's happened? Oh, no. Oh, my God, no.

"We've postponed the surgery. Before administering anesthesia, she developed a rapid heartbeat and spiked a severe fever. We gave her antipyretics and waited, but she's still febrile. At least her pulse has returned to normal. We'll try again tomorrow morning. She's back in her room if you want to see her."

His stopped heart beat once more. The lump in his throat dissolved. He resumed breathing. He hurried to her room and took her hand, and asked her not to scare him like that again.

*

The next morning, he greeted the staff and took up his usual position in the recovery room. Once again, the surgeon came in without Mary. This time, he informed him, the operating room lighting had gone out just before the procedure. Initial efforts at restoring it had failed, and since the operation had not begun, hospital protocol required that it not be performed under emergency lights. Each of the other operating rooms was occupied, so her surgery had to be delayed until the afternoon.

He left for a run, followed by lunch. When he returned, he sat with Mary and told her it would all be over soon, that they'd be back together again. She wouldn't be able to have children, but she'd be alive and the light of his life. A nurse entered the room and informed him that the surgery had to be postponed again. It seemed that the surgeon had badly sprained his ankle at a lunchtime basketball game.

*

The next morning, he returned to the hospital earlier than the scheduled time for the hysterectomy to avoid a thunderstorm. He talked to Mary until the surgeon entered the room and greeted him.

"Think this will happen today?"

"It will. We'll be taking her back soon. How are you doing with all the weird things happening?"

"Anxious, I guess, to get Mary back, that is. Sad for the babies. So, mixed emotions."

"Well, we apologize. Nothing like this has happened in my twenty plus years of practicing medicine. I'll see you in recovery."

"How is your ankle?"

"Not too bad. I got ice on it quickly, which kept the swelling down. I have it wrapped, so I'll be okay. Thanks for asking."

He watched him limp away, happy that the injury wasn't worse. A few minutes later, a surgical tech wheeled Mary to the operating room. Once again, he waited in the curtained-off area where Mary would be brought after surgery. He pulled a notepad out of his backpack and settled in to prepare his next lecture.

A loud noise startled him. It startled the staff as well—a siren outside the building. A voice came over the loudspeaker, instructing everyone to shelter in place due to reports of a tornado in the area. He looked around and decided the nearby office would be the safest place. Others had made that same decision and huddled under desks or in the closet. While working his way there, the power went out, and emergency lights came on. He found a chair to sit in as the closet and desk kneehole were already occupied. Twenty minutes later, a security guard entered the area and announced the "all clear." Power remained out, however, so Adam left the hospital after Mary had been safely returned to her room. The tornado touched down outside Waco and spared the Baylor campus. The university did not suffer the power outage other parts of the city, including the hospital, had experienced.

That afternoon, he drove to the lake with fishing gear and found his favorite spot along the bank near a rocky overhang. The lake had its deepest point fifty feet offshore. He attached his favorite spinner to the swivel and launched it out into the aqua green water. A four-pound smallmouth bass hit the lure on his first cast.

"Okay big fella, go back out there and enjoy life. All right, God, what is happening? Are you doing something here? I don't suppose you've got a way to save both Mary and the babies, do you? I'd love that. Oh, would I love that. But, I guess I'm too used to disappointment to have much hope for it."

He switched gears and changed to live bait with a

bobber set at six feet. He used a knife and dug around in the dirt behind the rocks until he found an earthworm. Once on the hook, he threw it out and watched the bobber for a moment, then called his mother on his cell phone. She answered but asked him to hold while she turned down the volume on the T.V.

"That sounded like Billy Graham," he said.

"It is. Sarah Newly gave us a box of old VCR tapes. I was surprised our player still worked. Anyway, I'm watching, well, mostly listening to one while I clean the house."

"I always admired that man. Great guy. Anyway, do you have a minute?"

He had to pause twice to reel in a fish but managed to tell her everything that had happened in the last week. The conversation with her comforted him, bringing a peace he hadn't felt in a long time. After the call, he put the lure back on the line, but nothing bit. During those fruitless casts, his mind went back to the voice he'd heard in the background earlier during the call to his mother. A voice of conviction, but not harsh, not overbearing. More of a matter-of-fact, authoritative voice. Then his mind replayed the scripture he'd heard. "The wages of sin is death, but the gift of God is eternal life through Jesus Christ our Lord." He knew that verse well, having memorized it as a kid. That afternoon it became the song he couldn't get out of his head.

Later that evening, he sat on his couch and thought about that verse again. And then it hit him. "The wages of sin is death…"

CHAPTER SIXTY TWO

Adam called Keith and made a peculiar request.

"You want some of Mary's blood?"

"Yes. There's a frozen sample at the lab you used for the paternity test. I checked with them yesterday. They need you to call and authorize me to pick it up."

"And do what with?"

"Let's say it's a hunch. If it pans out, I can tell you who the rapist is. Please trust me on this."

"All right, you've earned it. When would you know something?"

"Later today. I have everything set up."

"Call me tonight and explain. Have they rescheduled the hysterectomy?"

"Yes, tomorrow morning. I also need you to send me the pictures you took of Clark's notebook. And call the lab, I'm headed there now."

He rushed to the lab and obtained the tube of blood, which they'd put in a plastic bag with crushed ice for him. He drove to the campus and walked it into the biology building, where he met Ed in the lab on the second floor.

"Here you go. You have everything you need, right?"

"I'm good to go. I'll call you when it's ready. It'll take a few minutes to thaw reagents and prepare DNA from the blood, but the reactions go fast. I'll know whether it's positive or negative in an hour on our real-time PCR thermal cycler. I'll call you when I have an answer."

"Thanks so much, Ed."

*

Back in his office, his mind bored in on the implications of a positive PCR result. Wow, what would I do with that? Good news for Mary. Better news for the babies. This is overwhelming. "You have to help me with this, God. This is so much bigger than me. I am not equipped for this. Just sayin'."

He called his attorney and asked him to send a copy of the MTA with Clark. He then printed the photos Keith had sent and walked back to the biology building. He found the office of Dr. Patricia Koning and knocked on the door. He showed her the photos Keith had taken of pages from the notebook in Clark's office and asked her to interpret them. She read through the data making "ooh" and "ah" sounds.

"Where'd you get this?"

"I can't say at the moment, but I'll fill you in you when I can. Do you know what kinds of experiments are being described here?"

"There are two. One is testing the growth of several mammalian cell lines in a number of different culture media. This DC1600 line looks impressive. But the more interesting part is the cloning experiment. Someone is using a technique called somatic cell nuclear transfer to make a clone of DC1600. This could be therapeutic cloning using embryonic stem cells. I can't say because I don't know what the recipient or the donor is. But it is mammalian. Heady stuff. I have to ask again, where did you get this?"

"All I can say for now is that I didn't get it from anyone here."

"Not surprising. No one here is doing that type of research. Fascinating technology. Promise to come back and tell me more about this when you can?"

"I will. Thank you."

He flew down the steps to the second floor and pushed open the door to Mary's lab. Ed was talking on the phone.

"Ah, there you are." He hung up the phone. "I left a message for you telling you that the sample you gave me definitely has J-cell DNA. So, here's how it breaks down. Your sample has both modern human DNA and J-cell DNA. My human blood control sample was negative for J-cell DNA but positive for modern human DNA, as expected. However, that same control sample to which I added a small amount of J-cells tested positive for both modern human DNA and J-cell DNA. So, it reacted the same way as your sample. I did each reaction in triplicate. So, where did that blood come from?"

"I can't say right now," he answered on his way out the door. "But thanks, Ed."

Back in his office, he downloaded the MTA from his attorney and compared Clark's handwriting on it to that in the notebook.

"Gotcha."

*

"All right, Adam," Keith said, "you have five minutes. Convince me why I should call off the hysterectomy. Go."

"Ed proved the babies have J-cell DNA. Mary is pregnant with clones of Jesus."

He heard a clanking noise and then silence. The connection with Keith was broken. He dialed back, but it went to voicemail, so he disconnected on his end, but before he could redial, it rang.

"Keith? What was that? What happened."

"I dropped the phone when I thought I heard you say Mary was pregnant with clones of Jesus. What did you actually say?"

"That's exactly what I said."

"What? No way. That's preposterous."

"Ed tested her blood and found traces of J-cell DNA."

"Whoa, hoss. Hold on a second. How can you be sure J-cell DNA came from the babies? Ed could have made a mistake."

"He did multiple samples and included controls. He knows what he's doing. The only way for Mary to have their DNA in her blood is to be pregnant with a baby, or babies, who have J-cell DNA. Not only that, those babies are keeping her alive."

"Okay, now I'm really confused."

"And I know who did it."

"Who?"

"It's obvious. Think about it."

"Uh…Clark?"

"No. The handwriting in the notebook wasn't his. I

had an expert look at the notes, and they described mammalian cloning experiments. Vanessa did her PhD thesis in that field. It's her. She drugged Mary the night she passed out, probably there in the IVF clinic. Then she impregnated her with embryos she'd made from J-cells. And I'll bet she was drunk at the time, filled with rage for some psychotic reason, and didn't use sterile technique. That's where the uterine infection came from."

"That bitch. Oh, wait until I get my hands on her."

"I know, I know, but calm down. I know you want to knock her into next week, but let's deal with Mary's situation."

"Listen to you, keeping a cool head. I'm impressed."

"I could be Special Forces someday, huh?"

"Right. Anyway, what does this mean for Mary? Is being pregnant with those babies safe? I mean, I've heard horror stories with animal experiments."

"Mary is safe. In fact, she's the safest person in the world right now. It's like being in the eye of a hurricane, sort of."

"How do you figure that?"

"Ever read a Bible?"

"Actually, yes. I read it in college for an English course, or at least parts of it. I pick it up now and then. Why?"

"A Biblical principle is at work here. The New Testament author Paul wrote in his letter to the Romans 'the wages of sin is death, but the gift of God is eternal life through Jesus Christ our Lord.'"

"Yeah, I remember reading that. And?"

"And, focus on the first part of the verse."

"'The wages of sin is death' part?"

"That's right. Basically, it's saying that if you sin, you die. Now, turn that around. If you don't sin, you don't die. It's a simple principle. Got it?"

"Yeah, I do, but this is taking longer than five minutes, and I'm still confused."

"Can you spare another five?"

"I'll adjust, go ahead."

"So, let's go back to the Garden of Eden. Something happened to Adam and Eve when they sinned. They lost God's protection. Their bodies deteriorated as genetic mutations changed their genomes. Their descendants inherited weakened bodies, and none of them, none of us, have ever been able to avoid the consequences of weakened genetics. We've inherited their weaknesses, including their rebellious natures. The Bible says we're sinners. We're under a curse, we all eventually die. Jesus could not have been a descendant of Adam and Eve because he would have been prone to sin, so he came with new genetics. Paul called him 'a new man' in his letter to the Corinthians. So, the babies in Mary's womb are also 'new men,' or will be. You know what I mean. They do not have sinful natures, and when they're born, they won't be prone to sin. Like Jesus, they won't be subject to death. They are now, and after they're born, will still be under God's protection. So, there won't be a hysterectomy. There won't be an abortion. The babies will be born alive. And I believe Mary will survive long enough to give birth to them, which is why it's crucial to cure the infection before that happens."

"One little problem with all that. Jesus, the non-sinner, ended up dying."

"Yes, but the principle wasn't violated."

"Yeah? Why not?"

"You remember when Jesus was on the cross? Well, he was sinless up until the last minute of his life. He wasn't going to die, and he could have come down any time until the moment the sins of the world were transferred to him. He voluntarily accepted those sins. It was actually his main mission. Jesus was God himself—that's the Trinity, another theological concept. But it's kinda cool that if punishment had to happen, he wanted to be the one punished. The one thing Jesus was reluctant to do was to take our sins, because up until then, he was holy and not acquainted with sin. That experience of knowing depravity and rebellion and the guilt that goes with it all—but also the separation, brief though it would be, from his Father— is what troubled him in the Garden of Gethsemane. In any event, he allowed himself to be nailed to a wooden cross and suffer for a number of hours. That way, when the world's sins were transferred to him, something only God could do by faith and make it happen, his body was so weak he couldn't come down from the cross even if he wanted to. God turned his back on him at that point, and no angels would come to his rescue, so he was on his own. It was as though Jesus sinned all our sins, and since the wages of sin is death, he deserved to die. And he did. That's how believers can know their sins have been forgiven— because theirs were transferred to Jesus, one who could never die. His death is proof that the transfer happened. We don't own them anymore."

"Sounds like it makes sense, but I'll have to think about it. For now, let's go with what you say. If the babies will survive, no matter what, why would it matter if I call off the hysterectomy? How do you square that?"

"It won't matter, because something else will happen and prevent the procedure as it has for five straight days now. But, it would save the hospital time and money not to have to go through more futile preps, delays, and especially reschedulings for staff and operating rooms."

"All right, I'll call the hospital and authorize you to act on my behalf on this one decision. If you can convince the doctors, I'll consent to whatever they decide. I have to go. Good luck, and good luck to Mary and the boys. Do we know they're boys?"

"They're boys. Definitely."

*

That's an interesting theory, Adam, but we're dealing with medical realities here, and the life of one of our patients is at stake," Dr. Phillips said. "We can't possibly consider it when deciding the best course of care for her. The fevers are still spiking, her CT and EEG scans haven't improved; nothing has changed. We simply must perform the hysterectomy if she's to have any chance at emerging from the coma."

"But please understand that when it doesn't happen for whatever reason, and it won't, those babies won't be denied their chance at life."

"They're immature fetuses, thirteen weeks along at the most, and they've been assaulted by bacterial toxins and antibiotics almost their whole existence. I'd be surprised if any survive to term even if we don't do a hysterectomy. For whatever reason."

"They've been assaulted by those things for weeks now, and their heartbeats are strong and regular. And they're growing. They've done well to this point. They'll continue to thrive. I'm just trying to save the hospital the expense of setting up an operating room that won't get used, not to mention the wasted time of the surgeons and nurses."

"You think the mishaps in the last week are explained by your theory?"

"Absolutely."

"I appreciate that, I do, but I'm still obligated to treat her as I see fit, and my medical opinion is informed by the best infectious disease experts in the world. I think we'll take our chances. I mean, you can't seriously believe we'd take your theory into account when deciding how to treat a patient, can you?"

"No, I actually don't. I'd do the same in your position. But, when it doesn't happen and you see Mary's condition improving, or something you can't explain medically, I advise you to take the fates of the babies into account."

"Interesting. I guess we'll each have to play our parts and see how this turns out. Hey, if Mary and the babies survive this ordeal I'll, be the first to shout and jump for joy, but I don't see it happening. I'm sorry."

"They'll survive, count on it. And we might want to have other kids when she gets well. We may even name one of them after you."

"I'd be honored."

"Oh, and, again, please don't discuss this with anyone else."

"I'll keep it between you and me. And Adam, I'm pulling for you to be right."

CHAPTER SIXTY THREE

Adam sat next to Mary and explained his theory.

"So, it's a win-win. You get well, or at least have time to fight off this infection, and the babies— Oh, wait until you find out about the babies. Won't you be surprised. I didn't do it; you know that. But now I know who did. You would have figured it out too, sooner or later. Knowing you, probably sooner. I need to be able to prove it, though. That part I haven't figured out yet. Your brother wants to kill her. Well, not kill her as in make her dead, but I think he wants to make her suffer. I just want you well. Anyway, they'll be coming for you again soon. Hopefully, you'll be right back after the next snafu. In fact, here comes the doctor now."

"Good morning Adam."

"Doctor Phillips."

"Adam, I've postponed the operation, not because of your theory, mind you, but because her fever subsided overnight, and her EEG yesterday showed improvement. I talked to the night shift nurse, and she said Mary was less restless. So, I'm giving it twenty-four hours. We'll monitor her condition closely and do another scan this afternoon. If we continue to see improvement, we'll hold off on the hysterectomy."

"And this has nothing to do with my theory?"

"Absolutely nothing. But, can I tell you a little secret?"

"I'm all ears."

"Somebody double-booked the operating room. We're trying to figure out how that happened. The other surgery was more pressing, so I offered to wait until this afternoon. However—"

"Let me guess. The surgeon had golf plans for the afternoon."

"Close. He had already scheduled two operations at Scott & White and couldn't get back in time."

"But holding off on the hysterectomy has nothing to do with my theory?"

"Hey, could there be a little divine intervention here? I don't know. But, she does seem better. And who am I to go against, well, let's just say the mysterious healing hand of…"

"Of?"

"Yes."

"All right, doctor. Thank you."

He sat with Mary for another hour, then stopped by the track on the way to his office for a two-lap walk. He imagined her by his side, hand-in-hand, enjoying the beauty of the day with him. *Those times will return. We'll be pushing a stroller for triplets, but we will do this again.* The phone in his pocket vibrated.

"Keith, have you pulled out her fingernails yet?"

"What happened to a simple 'hello'?"

"I could ask you the same question. That would have been the civilized way to greet me when we first met."

"Okay, I might deserve that. With my sister lying unconscious and pregnant in the hospital, I may have had a short fuse that day. Look, we need to talk about what to do with Clark and Vanessa."

"Besides wringing their necks?"

"Yeah, after that."

"You're including Clark in this too?"

"He had the notebook on his desk," Keith said. "He's part of it. Anyway, I can't decide what to do. I see two options. One, we let the police handle it as most sane people would do, or, two, we investigate it ourselves. There are pros and cons either way."

"I agree. The minute we take it to the police, Clark could get wind of it, and the evidence disappears."

"Yeah, it doesn't take much time to burn a notebook and flush embryos down a toilet."

"Uh-uh. That won't happen."

"Oh, yeah," Keith said. "Forgot."

"But, what if the police did it right and executed a search warrant and got the evidence? When it goes to trial, it becomes a giant publicity circus. I mean, human cloning, medical rape, clones of Jesus. Geez, what a spectacle that would be. It would tear Mary apart when she needs time to recover from this whole mess. And then there's the teasing, and worse, that the boys will face when they get older. They would be stigmatized for life."

"So, even if we went out there and recovered the evidence and got it to the authorities, without getting caught, an iffy proposition, but let's say we pulled it off, there's a huge downside."

"But, if we do nothing," he said, "she gets away with it and could do it again."

"Okay, it's clear we don't know what to do. Can you talk to your brother? He might have an idea."

"I'll talk to David. He'll be cool. He'll have solid advice."

"All right. You're on your own a while. I have to be gone for a week. By the way, Phillips tells me he's delaying the hysterectomy because Mary's improving. How does she look to you?"

"Noticeably better, I'd say. I like what I'm seeing."

"Fantastic. All right, I'll call when I get back."

*

The next day, Adam asked the nurse if Dr. Phillips had made a decision about Mary.

"He's still satisfied with her progress, says he'll hold off another day. Oddly enough, we had a cancellation this morning for one of the operating rooms. Figures, doesn't it?"

"Yeah, it does. But I'm not complaining."

"Nor am I," she said, looking at her patient. "You go, girl."

He went back to his office for a while and then gave his archaeology lecture. After class, he called Brad and asked if he had time to discuss his predicament.

"I need your input on my life, why it sucks, and how to make it better. Got a few days to talk?"

"I will in an hour. Can I call you back?"

"Of course."

He changed into his running clothes and ran three miles, then showered and pulled out his lunch. PB&J with chips and an apple. Needing to outline his spring semester lectures, he broke out a new yellow legal pad and commenced constructing a syllabus.

True to his word, Brad called back within the hour, and the two discussed Mary's plight. After expressing his regrets and giving him encouragement to soldier on, he offered his thoughts on the matter.

"This is a quandary. What if you turned it over to the police and asked a judge to issue a gag order on all the participants, and then be prepared to assume new identities if it leaked out?"

"We're the victims; we shouldn't have that burden put upon us."

"I know, but that's how witness relocation programs work. Those people are innocent too, and their lives get completely turned upside down."

"It would mean Mary couldn't do science, or me archaeology. That would be tough on us."

"Well, you'd have to weigh that against the future difficulties the boys might face. But I'm not sure that's necessarily the certainty you make it out to be. If you live low-key lives and ask the schools to avoid talking about the boy's status, I mean, I think we're getting better at that in this country."

"I don't know, I see a bullseye on them when they get older."

"But if what you tell me is true, then they'll be all right, won't they?"

"They would be under God's protection, yes, but that

doesn't mean their lives would be easy. I wouldn't want them to have to face idiots out to make names for themselves their whole lives."

"Didn't Jesus have an unremarkable childhood before he began his controversial ministry?"

"Good point. We don't know much about his youth. There's no record of his childhood other than his mom and dad taking him to Egypt when he was very young. When he was a little older, he had discussions with scholars in the synagogue. Smart kid. But that's it. So are you suggesting we shouldn't be too worried about it because God will help these kids when they need it? Am I overreacting?"

"You might be. And don't forget, there's a criminal out there who may feel free to strike again if you don't do something about it."

"That won't be easy. This is a unique crime. I mean, have you ever heard of someone committing in vitro fertilization assault? Is that even a crime?"

"I've heard of doctors convicted of using their own sperm, but not someone impregnated that way against her will. But there has to be something in the penal code to cover it. Anyway, let's say she, they, destroy the physical evidence and it comes down to the circumstantial. If I'm a juror, it would seem clear to me that she did this. But let's say a jury acquits her, do you think she'd ever even think about doing it again? In fact, wouldn't that have a huge negative impact on her business? She ought to go to jail, I know, but she wouldn't get off scot-free. She will pay the price."

"So, you'd lean toward turning everything over to the police and letting them handle it?"

"At first blush, yes, but you're there on the ground, and you know everyone involved. I'm merely a spectator with no skin in the game, so I'm probably not the best one to ask. Why not talk to a lawyer? They'd have to keep it confidential, and contrary to popular belief, they do know a thing or two about the law."

"I know. I'll think about that."

"Look, kiddo, call anytime, I'm always here for you."

"Thanks, Brad."

CHAPTER SIXTY FOUR

✛

Adam grew more hopeful over the next week as Mary's vital signs, blood workups, and brain scans suggested that the worst had passed. The infection seemed under control. Finally. He couldn't wait for her to regain consciousness so he could talk to her again.

"We can take the hysterectomy off the table, for now, at least," Dr. Phillips said. "She isn't out of the woods yet, but her brain scans are clearly better. And there's been no fever lately. Her condition has stabilized, and, I dare say, even improving."

"I like your thinking, Doctor. So, what did the trick? Antibiotics?"

"I'm sure they played a major role. But she's had time to respond to the bug and the neurotoxins. We have a two-front assault—her immune system and the antibiotics. But I must caution you, Adam, bacteria can mutate and gain resistance to drugs. They can also change their outward appearance so that antibodies don't recognize them anymore."

"Just when I felt better about her chances. Now you

tell me this ordeal may not be over."

"You should be optimistic because the odds of this bacterial strain overcoming both the drugs and her immune system are small. It can happen, but I'd put my money on Mary recovering. I wasn't so sure two weeks ago."

*

When he came back from Christmas break and visited the hospital, he learned that Keith had been there earlier in the day. He kissed Mary and talked to her, then told her he had to go find her brother and make a decision on what to do about Clark and Vanessa.

"Too bad you have to find out the truth about them. I know you admired Clark, but this world, I'm sorry to say, has some bad folks in it. You've had pain in your life. I wonder how you'll react to this, this evil, especially when something good like three baby boys resulted from it. Isn't that like life? On the good news front, Dr. Phillips says you might come out of the coma any day now. Don't disappoint him, or me, okay?"

*

He drove the familiar route home and saw Keith waiting for him outside his apartment.

"Why didn't you wait for me inside?"

"I don't have a key."

"So?"

"Aren't you over that yet? Look, we need to decide if we want to deal with them or let the police do it."

"I say we turn our evidence over to the police and let

them handle it. I'm prepared to deal with the fallout from the publicity. I may have overreacted about that."

"Not to mention that it would be several years before it becomes an issue for the boys. They wouldn't understand it until they were old enough to be in school, by then much of the notoriety should have died down."

"And your sister is strong, she'll deal with it, don't you think?"

"She will, but we'll be there for her when she needs us."

"We will indeed. All right, then, I've written a description of the genetics of the babies and an explanation for why we believe Vanessa did it. I've included copies of the notebook pages you sent me. Anything else we should add?"

"We need a statement from the hospital that the infection likely started about the time she became pregnant," Keith said. "I'll take care of that."

"How about waiting until Mary regains consciousness before we talk to the police. That will give us a chance to ask her what she remembers about the night at Vanessa's clinic."

"Good idea. The doctors say it's any day now. We can wait a few days."

"So, you staying long?"

"No, I can't, unless she comes out of the coma before tomorrow morning."

*

Mary did not awaken, so Keith returned to Virginia. Adam resumed his routine when the spring semester began—class in the morning and the hospital in the afternoon. He went to visit after a run and lunch on the second day of classes. She'd been taken for a scan, he assumed, so he waited in the room for her return. When he'd been there an hour, he went to the nurse's station and asked where she was.

"She's not in her room? Should be by now. The orderlies took her downstairs for a scan at one o'clock. That was two hours ago. I'm surprised she isn't back yet. I'll call and see what the hold-up is."

He took a seat in the waiting area and watched the nurse tracking down Mary's whereabouts. He heard her make several phone calls, each a dead-end. She eventually called a hospital administrator who appeared with two security guards less than a minute later. They huddled out of earshot, and when that meeting broke up, the administrator approached him.

"Dr. Garrett, please come with us."

"Where's Mary?"

"Please come to my office, and we'll discuss it there."

"No. Right here is good. Where is she?"

"Sir, please."

"Fine, but you'd better have a good explanation."

*

"Dr. Garrett, we need to ask you some questions about the abduction of Mary Walsh," the detective from the Waco Police Department said. "Would you like an attorney present for this?"

"No, I would not like an attorney present. I want you to find Mary. And I want you to tell me how a comatose patient gets abducted from a hospital in broad daylight. With security cameras everywhere. No, I don't know anything about it. Nothing at all, so don't waste time on me."

"Sir, you wouldn't believe how many times people tell us that and then provide important information anyway. I assure you we're doing everything we can to find her. We have our guys out looking for her. We have the State Police on the lookout. The FBI has been notified. We'll find her, but time is critical. We want to find her in a few hours, not a few days. So, tell me about Mary."

*

"Adam, you want to know who I just talked to?" Keith asked. "The FBI, that's who. Why didn't you tell me about this?"

"I tried to leave a message, but your voicemail was full. What, are you out of the country again?"

"I can't get away for a few days. Anything new?"

"All they would tell me is that, according to a hospital security video, two unidentified men wheeled her from her room to the morgue. Those same two men put her into a vehicle waiting outside a ground floor exit. That's all I know."

"Yeah, they won't tell you much, that's how they do things. How are you holding up?"

"Not so well. Just when Mary starts improving, she gets kidnapped. This is all…this is too much. I need it to end."

"I know. Me too. Look, I'll be down as soon as I can, but it'll be a few days. I want you to call me the minute you hear anything, anything at all. In fact, call every hour even if you don't have anything. I'll get there as soon as I can."

"There's nothing you can do here; you may as well hang tight there. I'll keep you informed."

"No. I'm either coming to Texas or going to LA."

"LA? So you think Clark and Vanessa had something to do with this?"

"Of course they did."

"I thought of them too, but that's so hard to believe. You should know I told the police everything."

"Everything?"

"Yes, we discussed this. I want Mary back so much it hurts, so I told them everything."

"Do you think they'll act on it? Send someone to talk to them?"

"I hope so, but the guy kept looking up at me when we talked. He'd be writing down whatever I said and then look at me crossways. I caught him rolling his eyes once. I'm not sure he believed a word I said."

"Well, I can't say I blame him. I mean, this is bizarre. What would you think if a stranger told you that his fiancée was pregnant, but not with his kids, and, by the way, the kids are clones of Jesus Christ?"

"Yeah, I probably should have left that part out. But he said that sometimes tiny details make a difference. So I didn't leave anything out."

"Did you tell them what to look for? Their notebooks and such?"

"Yes, but they can't go barging in without a search warrant."

"Why don't you see what your brother can find out about what the police or FBI or whoever is running the investigation turns up in LA? I'm concerned they won't push hard enough when they find out Clark and Vanessa are model citizens with no prior criminal history. We may have to do this ourselves."

"Yeah? How?"

"We'll figure it out. You want Mary back, don't you?"

"Stupid question, Keith."

"Sorry. Look, I'll get free as soon as I can, and we'll find her. Whatever it takes. Call me when you know something."

"Okay."

*

"What the hell, Ivan?" Vanessa said. "The FBI was here asking questions. This was you, wasn't it? Why?"

"I'm protecting our interests. The hospital wanted to do a hysterectomy. They may have autopsied the babies to see what effects the infection and antibiotics had on them. Then they'd want to know why they were still healthy and viable in spite of those assaults. They'd eventually figure out what you did, and that would be the end of it. I don't want to take risks, but don't worry, she has around-the-clock care.

"By whom?"

"A nurse, and I have a doctor on standby. She'll be fine."

"Where is she? Never mind, I don't want to know. Look, don't harm her, or our deal is off."

"I assure you that is not my intention. Stay calm.

404

Everything is under control."

"How do you know she's carrying more than one baby? You must have someone at the hospital."

"I do."

"What happens after she gives birth?"

"Depends."

"On what?"

"How reasonable she's willing to be."

"She's stubborn. You won't be able to buy her off."

"Well, she may find herself in a rural village in Siberia. She can raise the boys there."

"You can't be serious."

"Let's see how she wants to play this. We don't need to get ahead of ourselves. Money has a way of talking sense into stubborn heads. And don't worry, she will not be harmed."

"She'd better not be."

"In any event, we've confirmed the pregnancy. Money is now in your accounts as agreed. In fact, I'll deposit another half-million since I acted unilaterally here. You'll get the rest when she delivers healthy babies. By the way, why did you implant three embryos? Afraid one or two wouldn't make it? You're fortunate I'm going to overlook that bit of imprudence."

*

Adam's calls to Keith dwindled to twice daily, then once a day. Two weeks had passed since her disappearance. He heard the frustration in her brother's voice growing with every call.

"I'm going to California," Keith said. "I can't wait any longer."

"And do what when you get there?"

"I'll buy Vanessa a cup of coffee and politely ask her where my sister is."

"Right, but we need to do something. David tells me the FBI had a field agent in LA talk to Clark and Vanessa, and that nothing came of it. I think Vanessa worried that the babies could be used as evidence against her, and that's why she took her. I'm concerned about Mary's safety."

"You said the babies would be protected."

"And I believe they will, but they'll be viable outside the womb soon, if not already. The hourglass is running out for her.

"I could use your help in LA again. Can you get away?"

"Later this week, I can put together a few days. What do you have in mind?"

"Evidence. It's in his office, her clinic, their house. It's there somewhere. I need to get into those places and find it."

"Break in, like you did at my place?"

"You left your door unlocked."

"Right."

"I merely turned the knob, and it opened."

"Right. Hey, if you need more help, I may be able to get it. Two army guys we met recently. One's in Dallas rehabbing a combat injury. He's an electronics and IT expert. The other is good at everything else, like you."

"What makes you think they can get away? Or would want to help?"

"Mac, the IT guy, was medically discharged last year. He's getting around better but still in rehab and still unemployed. Jim was stationed at Ft. Hood, but I think his enlistment has ended. They may want something to do. It's worth a shot."

"Let's say they're available, why would they join us?"

"Because they fell in love with Mary, as I did. Don't get me wrong, they're perfect gentlemen, but she went out of her way to make them feel special. The attraction was mutual. We got Mac to do the coin toss at a Baylor football game last fall."

"Oh, those guys. Yeah, she mentioned them during the last phone conversation we had before she got sick. We could certainly use the help. Go ahead and call them, but don't say too much over the phone. Can you meet either of them in person?"

"I'll try. If they're interested, can I give them your phone number?"

"Yeah, sure. Let me know how it goes."

CHAPTER SIXTY FIVE

✠

Adam flew into LAX on a Sunday morning in mid-February and rented a seven-passenger minivan. An hour later, he spotted Keith near the curb of the terminal. The two drove to a motel near the hospital where Vanessa worked. After a few minutes relaxing in the rented room, they drove to electronics, hardware, and specialty stores where they purchased one or two items at a time, moving from store to store in different shopping areas. By the time Jim and Mac arrived that afternoon, they had gathered most of the gear they would need for the job. Mac examined everything and made a list of additional items they could pick up the next morning.

After dark, they borrowed license plates from an abandoned truck in a rundown neighborhood and drove to the hospital. Each in disguise, they entered it one at a time and scouted the place. Mac made his way to the emergency room waiting area, pulled a laptop from his backpack, and hacked into and inspected the hospital's main server. Thirty minutes later, they left and returned to the motel, restoring the van's legal tags in a side alley on the way. They removed their disguises and found an all-night restaurant to discuss plans over a late dinner.

The next day, they purchased the additional electronics equipment Mac wanted and finalized their primary and backup plans to get into the hospital's IVF clinic. They tested and adjusted communications gear, and each put on disguises consisting of beards, mustaches, wigs, glasses, and various types of headwear. They ate a light meal, swapped license plates again, and drove to the hospital before dark, with Keith at the wheel.

They dropped Adam off at the front entrance. From inside the building, he watched them pull into a parking space at the edge of the main lot that offered a view of a side exit door—the one that Vanessa most likely used when she left work. He then headed for the IVF clinic, walking past it toward the unoccupied restroom at the far end of the wing.

"Two females standing near the door. Vanessa is one, the other is older. It looked to me like they were about to leave. They had purses in hand, and one fumbled around in hers, possibly looking for keys. One other office in this wing has lights on."

"Copy that." Keith's voice sounded clearly in his ear. "Wait two minutes and walk back past the clinic toward the front lobby. Give us another status report before you reach the end of that hallway. Remember, it's a blind spot. Head to the waiting area and take a seat in the back."

At the two minute mark, he left the restroom and walked back through the hallway. He reported that the older woman had left the clinic and Vanessa stood over a desk looking at papers. The occupant of the other office in that wing remained seated behind a counter. From his vantage point in the waiting area, he saw Vanessa leave the IVF clinic and head for the exit. Keith confirmed her departure. After another ten minutes, the last person walked out of that wing and left the building through the same door Vanessa had used.

"I see someone leaving through the side door," Keith said. "Acknowledge when you can."

Adam confirmed that the lights in every office along the IVF clinic corridor were off. As he walked toward the front entrance to leave, he passed Mac limping his way to the emergency room waiting area. He continued due north through the parking lot and opened the sliding door of the van and climbed in.

Mac's mission included finding an inconspicuous seat in the back of the emergency room waiting area, hacking into the hospital's surveillance controls, and upon Keith's command, temporarily disabling the recording system for all cameras inside and outside of the building. Furthermore, he had to do it in such a way that if security discovered the missing time frames, it would look like a computer glitch.

"Making progress, Mac?" Keith asked.

"Almost there. Need another ten."

As they waited, Keith went over Adam's assignment for the fourth and fifth times. Several minutes later, Mac's voice came into his headset.

"Mission accomplished. Ready here."

"Roger that," Keith said. "Are you getting video feeds from us?"

"Affirmative. Both chest cameras working. Hospital

feeds looking good too."

"Okay, Adam," Keith said. "You're up."

Upon exiting the van, he walked back through the hospital entrance and past the information desk to a gift shop, where he pretended to look at greeting cards. A few minutes later, a door in the back of the main lobby swung open, and a man in uniform walked out. He put the card in his hand back in the rack and followed the security guard into the cafeteria. He watched the man pick up a tray and load it with food.

He relayed the information to the others. "Server room empty. Security guard one eating dinner."

"You confirm, Mac?" Keith asked.

"Affirmative. Server room empty."

"Okay, turn off the system recorder, and let's get to work."

He found a seat on a bench that had a view of both the emergency room and the walkway leading to the IVF clinic. On his cell phone, he watched the split-screen video feed of Keith picking the exit door lock, then entering the hospital with Jim. Mac and Adam both confirmed they had a clear path all the way to Vanessa's office. Once there, Keith opened his tool pouch and placed two small, metal lock picks into the keyed portion of the keypad door lock. He wiggled the picks and nodded to Jim to turn the handle when he thought he had it. They tried again, then a third time.

"Security guard two on the move," Mac said through the comm lines.

"I have him," he said. "Headed your way, boys, let's hurry it up."

"Trying, lock not cooperating," Keith said.

"Okay, passing me now, and...heading in your direction," he warned. "Thirty seconds."

His pulse quickened, but he didn't hear panic from Keith, Jim, or Mac. "You guys get it yet? He's fifteen seconds away from the hallway."

"No luck...abort," Keith said.

"Try 4-3-3-2," he said a little too loudly through his microphone.

Keith had put his tools away, and they were about to run for the far restroom to hide, but 4-3-3-2 on the keypad worked. They entered the clinic and shut the door as the guard turned the corner and walked down the hallway, checking doors along the way. Keith and Jim crawled behind the front counter and hid. They heard the doorknob to the IVF clinic jiggle twice, then silence as the security guard proceeded down the hall.

"Where did that come from?" Keith asked. "You holding out on me, boy?"

"I got it from Mary. I'll tell you about it later."

"Mary?" Keith asked. "Yes, you will. All right. Hold positions. Let us know when it's clear again."

The guard finished checking the wing and reversed course, working his way back through the hall and heading for the hospital administrative area.

"Everything okay, Mac?"

"Affirmative. All clear. Go to work."

*

"We looked everywhere," Keith said after they returned to the van. "Nothing. No notes, no logs, no vials, no nothing.

We photographed the rooms, Vanessa's office, her desk, the inside contents of her desk drawers, the receptionist's desk, her drawers. We found nothing having anything to do with Mary."

"Could be in the correspondence on her hard drive," Jim said. "We'll have to wait for her to login first, and when she does, we'll get her."

"And you got a camera set up?" he asked.

"We did," Jim answered.

"How does that work?"

"Tiny camera and microphone in the ceiling tile," Jim said. "Painted white to blend in with ceilings. One in her office and another in a conference room. Voice and motion-activated. Fresh battery ought to last a few months. The unit will record and then send video and audio to a Bluetooth receptor in one of their computers."

"But the camera stores video files and doesn't download them to the receptor until a computer is turned on," Mac explained. "Then we have a back door hack in place to access that data. And the hard drive too, of course."

"What happens if a computer crashes, or they get a new one?"

"She has three computers, and each has a receptor. One is Vanessa's, one is in the assistant's office, and one is out front, presumably used by a receptionist. If we lose all three, then, yes, we're out of luck."

"But that won't happen in the next few weeks, at least, and it might be enough to get the goods on them," Keith said.

"And what happens when they see your receptor and get suspicious?"

"They're inside computer cases. They'd have to take one apart and know what they were looking at," Mac answered. "Even then, with nothing to arouse their suspicions, they'd think it was part of the original hardware."

"Worst case scenario," Keith said. "The camera is discovered, and they figure out they're being spied on. Mac knows how to make sure they can't trace anything to us."

"And that receptor can intercept internet traffic? Emails and such?"

"Of course. What do you think we are, amateurs? If she contacts anyone about the kidnapping, we'll know it."

"By the way, is this legal?" he asked.

CHAPTER SIXTY SIX

S itting in the van in the motel parking lot, Adam recounted the day Mary spoke the door code twice before lapsing into a coma.

"Obviously, it didn't make sense at the time."

"It does now," Keith said. "She must have been conscious when Vanessa took her there."

"Odd that Vanessa spoke it out loud," Jim said. "Who does that?

"Many people do it without thinking," Mac added. "I see them. You can get PINs that way. Some say it out loud, others you can read their lips."

"I'm guessing she was drunk and couldn't punch the numbers in correctly," Keith said. "Which proves Mary's presence at the IVF clinic."

"Just visiting?" he asked. "Getting a tour when things took a turn?"

"Let's speculate later," Keith said. "Right now, we need to focus on EVI. What do you guys think? Ready to hit it? Easy alarms and cameras at the front and rear doors. Shouldn't be that hard."

"How do you know that?" he asked. "You were there only once."

"You can see a lot if you know how and where to look. And what to look for."

"What are the chances," Jim asked, "that they've installed more sophisticated alarms or surveillance cameras since you were there?"

"That's possible," Keith said. "Especially since they were questioned by the FBI. But it's an older building, and anything like that would have been retrofitted and easy to find. We'll know soon enough if that's the case, or if they've hired a nighttime security guard."

"How will you get past the cameras?" he asked. "And the alarms?"

"Fire escape on the side," Keith responded. "One of us will boost the other up so he can lower the fire escape ladder. We'll go in the first door we come to, provided it isn't alarmed. If it is, we'll figure out plan B. Mac, do you have everything you need for another camera?"

"I do," Mac said, "but it would be easier for me to get it ready in the room."

"Good," Keith said. "I say we go to EVI after midnight and look for security. If it's clear, Jim and I go in and look for that notebook. We photograph every page if it's there. Then we look for anything useful in Clark's office. We'll do the same in the lab and install a camera in his office before leaving. Adam, you can sit this one out, no sense risking your getting caught."

"Not a chance," he said. "If nothing else, I can drive better than Mac. No offense, but Keith, if you need a quick getaway, you need me."

"He's right," Mac said. "And no offense taken, brother."

"All right, Adam. All right," Keith said. "Park the van a block away. Jim and I will hop out and get to the building. Keep the engine running until we signal. After we're in, if something goes wrong and we're discovered, drive away. Got it?"

"Why would I leave you there? I don't think Mac would do that either."

"We'll take care of ourselves; you head for the motel if this goes south. We'll get back on our own. Promise me."

"Okay, Keith, okay."

*

Just before one in the morning, he and Mac watched the video feed on his cell phone as Keith and Jim picked the lock of the fire escape door on the second floor. The two made their way into EVI. A few minutes later, they worked the lock on Clark's office door. Keith found the notebook, but it had been moved from the desktop to a locked drawer. They photographed every page. They also took pictures of the notepad on Clark's desk, filled with bits and pieces of disjointed information and doodles. Jim began installing the camera in the ceiling while Keith looked through the other desk drawers and a filing cabinet. He then inspected the office Mary had used that summer. It looked the same. The notebook she'd used remained neatly placed in the middle of the desk. He took pictures of the last twenty pages, then moved to the lab, where Mary conducted her research. He started on one side of the large room and looked through every bench drawer and on every shelf of the cabinets along the wall, then worked his way across the lab.

"Camera's working," he heard Jim tell Keith. "What can I do here?"

"Look in the refrigerators and freezers for anything labeled DC1600 or J-cells, or anything that has Clark's or Vanessa's name or initials."

At two-thirty, he spotted the signal from a dark driveway next to the building: two short flashes from a small LED flashlight followed by a third flash two seconds later. He started the engine, pulled into the street, and drove toward the EVI building in the next block. As he did, a late-model sedan turned onto the street three blocks away and approached them from the opposite direction. He did not stop at the appointed place but instead drove past the oncoming car and watched it disappear in his rearview mirror. At an intersection two blocks later, he turned left and circled back to his original parking spot. A minute later, he spotted the flashes again. This time he drove past EVI and stopped in front of the adjacent building for the three seconds it took Keith and Jim to jump in the back doors. Despite his racing heart, he steered the van away at the posted speed limit and navigated the five miles to the abandoned truck to return the plates, then made his way back to the motel without attracting the attention of law enforcement. Safely in their motel room, they discussed the events of the evening.

"So, nothing at Vanessa's clinic," Keith said, "and nothing at EVI, other than the biologicals that establish their opportunity to commit the rape. The notebook, vials of J-cells, it's as though they weren't concerned, other than locking the notebook in a desk drawer. No security precautions. If they were raided today, they'd be toast. What am I missing? Why aren't they worried?"

"They're allowed to have J-cells," he said. "It's the oocytes and embryos that would be a problem."

"Didn't find them," Jim said.

"We'll monitor their correspondence and look through their hard drives," Keith said.

What about their house?" he asked.

"I don't think we want to do their house," Keith said. "They're home at night, and I don't want to risk being seen there in the day, even with disguises. I saw an alarm by their front door the night we had dinner there, which makes that harder to pull off."

"So, is that it?" he asked. "Are we done here?"

"No," Keith said. "Let's get some sleep, and in the morning, we need to figure out how to tap their cell phones. We'll need access to install Mac's spy app."

"Clark goes to the gym a lot," he said. "Can you get into his locker?"

"Sure. The trick would be keeping other patrons out of there long enough to do the job. Good thought, that's a possibility. Let's sleep on it."

*

The next day, while the others kept watch outside the gym Clark frequented, Keith applied for a free one-week introductory membership. Using the name Terrance Lamar, "Terry" toured the facility and secured a locker for his workout clothes. When Clark failed to show for a late-day workout, they changed targets and drove to the hospital where they waited for Vanessa to leave for the day. Adam waited inside the hospital and alerted the others when she departed the clinic and approached the exit door. He discreetly followed her outside, keeping enough distance between himself and her to avoid detection. He ducked behind a truck as she entered her vehicle, then watched as Jim deliberately rode a cheap, thrift-store used bicycle into the side of her car as she pulled out of a parking spot. Both apologized profusely to the other. Jim claimed he was uninjured, but the bike had suffered a fatal blow, or so he explained to Vanessa. He declined her offer to drive him somewhere, asking her instead if she had a phone he could use. He tapped the virtual keypad ten times and, while talking to an unused phone number about the accident, turned his back to her and pretended to examine the bike more thoroughly while downloading Mac's spyware from a micro USB flash drive. He thanked the nonexistent person on the phone for agreeing to come and get him, then thanked Vanessa for the use of her phone. Keith downloaded the same app onto Clark's phone the next afternoon and promptly cleaned out "Terry's" locker.

They returned the rental van to the airport the next morning. He took the same flight to DFW as Jim and Mac while Keith flew to Dulles. While he had a lecture to give the next day and Keith had military obligations, Jim and Mac planned to examine the phone calls, video feeds, and hard drive contents of the computers in Clark's and Vanessa's offices from Mac's apartment in Duncanville.

CHAPTER SIXTY SEVEN

Mary blinked her eyes twice. She squinted and blinked again, then stared at the ceiling, struggling to remember who she was. Her eyes darted around the unfamiliar room, which made her wonder where she was. She tried to maneuver herself into position and get out of bed, but nothing moved. Legs, arms, shoulders, nothing. What the heck? She waited a minute and repeated the effort. Several repetitions later, her right arm obeyed and moved up and toward her left side. A strange bulge in her abdomen, however, blocked its progress. She probed the prominence briefly with her fingers before the arm tired and dropped back to the mattress. What was that? She lifted her head long enough to get a snapshot image of it before her neck muscles fatigued. She displayed that image in her mind's eye for a moment, and when the realization of what it meant dawned on her, she shrieked Adam's name.

A woman ran into the room. "You're awake. Finally. Good to have you back with us. How do you feel?"

She studied the strange person next to her bed. "Am I pregnant?"

"Yes, ma'am, you most certainly are."

"How did that happen? Where am I? Who are you?"

"Keep quiet, please, or the guards will come."

"Guards? What the…seriously? Who are they guarding? What's going on?"

"You've been in a coma. I don't know how long, and I don't know how you got pregnant. You don't remember your husband or boyfriend? That's usually how it happens."

"I know how it happens, thank you. And I know this happened without my consent. A coma? How?"

"I don't know. Can you remember anything?"

"I remember being sick, fevers, headaches. I remember being in a hospital, but I don't remember being pregnant. Where am I? Where's Adam?"

"I can't tell you that."

"Why not?"

"I don't know anything to tell you. They hired me two weeks ago to be your nurse. That's all I know."

"Who hired you?"

"A doctor's office called, then I met a man who paid me upfront for one month. I'm sorry but don't know anything about him."

"Well, who can tell me something? Anything. Get them in here. And take this tube out of my nose."

The door opened, and a man dressed in army fatigue pants and a flannel shirt, wearing an old baseball cap, came in. The AR-15 he carried startled her.

"What the—"

"Shut up," he said.

"Shut up? You shut up unless you can tell me why I'm

here. And if you can't, get out and find somebody who can. Now!"

The man looked at her and shook his head. He waved at the nurse. "Let's go."

She heard the sound of the door being locked after the two closed it behind them.

"Hey, get back here. Get this tube out. Hey. Come back."

The commotion and shouting made her head throb, so she tried to sit up in the bed to get relief, but her atrophied muscles wouldn't allow it. Her abdominals didn't have the strength to pull her upper body forward, and her arms weren't strong enough to do it on their own. The extra load she carried presented another impediment, not only with the added weight but also the change in her physique. Moving around with a baby inside would be something she'd have to adjust to. For the moment, though, she could only lay there like a big lump of dough. A fly buzzed past her head. She made a move to swat it, but her arm stopped short of reaching into the air. Wow, I am so helpless. That ends now. She lifted her right hand and let it fall back onto the bed. She did the same with her left hand. Her legs were a different story. Neither raised off the bed. Too heavy. All right, muscles, you're all getting stronger whether you want to or not. Let's try it again. She repeated the routine twice more before her energy level fell to zero. She rested and gasped for air. Didn't I used to run miles at a time? Effortlessly? And now I can't even lift a leg. Or swat a fly.

She grimaced as she moved her hands to her face. This tube has to come out. Why didn't that nurse pull it out? I don't need it anymore, do I? She turned her head to the side and found relief from the headache. A minute later, she rotated it to the other side and saw a metal water pitcher on the stand next to her bed. Oh great, now I'm thirsty. Why did I have to see that?

She repeated the exercise routine several times, rested a moment, then went for the tubing. Her right hand crawled along her torso toward her head until it reached her face. She touched the plastic with her fingertips but couldn't tighten her grip around it. Okay, left hand. Get up here and help. Her other hand moved into position behind the tubing and next to her right hand. She clamped both hands around the plastic nasal feeding tube and moved her arms downward until a searing pain made her stop. Ouch. Oh, that hurt. The next effort hurt as much as the first, but her hands had progressed noticeably farther down her torso. Ah, can't be too much left in there. One more yank and she accomplished her first goal—the tubing was out. She laughed with delight, but the resulting pain brought that to a halt. Okay, take a break. The pitcher is next. After some rest.

The first activity in months exhausted her, and she fell asleep. She awoke in a sharper mental state, her brain outpacing the rest of her body in recovering some semblance of function. Wow, what a strange dream. Me. Pregnant. And unmarried. But it was so real. She moved her right arm toward her abdomen to dispel the silly notion that the dream could actually be true. But, as she slid her hand up her side again and felt the bulge, the confirmation that it wasn't a dream caused an eruption of emotions. How? Tears left her eyes and rolled down her cheeks onto the sheet. How did this happen? She lay still and stared at the ceiling again while more tears flowed. "Momma. Oh, Momma, I need you. I need you so badly. What do I do? How do I get my life back?"

*

She woke after a brief nap more sober-minded and more determined to extricate herself from the situation she found herself in. I need out of here, and I need answers. Okay, okay, think. How do I get out of here? Her mind wanted to wander instead to the question of whom to blame for the pregnancy. Adam? No, he was serious about waiting, it wasn't him. A guard? Wait. First things first. Get back to how I'm getting out of here. Focus. I'll find out how this happened later. Right now, I need my strength, so that's first. The water pitcher caught her eye and reminded her that she was thirsty. Okay, I guess that's really the first thing. Come on. I can do this.

Encouraged, she launched her second venture of the day. She pushed with her right leg and right arm against the bed and contracted her abdominal muscles, slowly rolling onto her left side, facing the bedstand. She took a deep breath and then worked her right arm toward it, sliding her hand onto the wooden surface before stopping to rest. She grunted as she lifted her fingers to grasp the handle of the pitcher, but the clumsy effort sent it crashing to the floor with a loud, head-splitting clanking sound. She winced and fell slack, head throbbing, her arm and upper body exhausted from the effort. The door flew open. A guard cursed her and called for the nurse.

"Hey, hey, what are you doing? You're lucky that

pitcher was empty, or the guard would be mad. Are you thirsty?"

"Yes, and do you have anything for a headache?"

She swallowed the Tylenol tablets and washed them down with a long drink of water, then fell asleep. The sensation of a wrap tightening around her upper left arm woke her up. She tried to pull away but didn't get far.

"It's okay, it's okay. I only need your vital signs."

"Oh, sorry. You startled me. How long did I sleep?"

"About an hour."

"An hour? It seemed like only a minute. I've lost all sense of time, I guess. The room does look darker now, not as bright as before."

"Yes, the sun is setting soon. It will take you a while to readjust to the land of the living. Take your time."

"Speaking of time, tell me how long I've been here. And tell me where this is. Or did I ask you that already."

"You did, but that's okay. You were asleep when they bought me here two weeks ago, that's all I know. I don't know what happened to you; I only take care of you. You didn't have bruises or other signs of trauma, so I don't think you were hit in the head."

"Can you at least tell me what state I'm in? Is this Texas?"

"Oh, *si*. And I can tell you that your blood pressure is good, your pulse is strong, and your temperature is normal."

"Can you help me sit up?"

"*Si.*"

"I feel so weak. And I used to run like the wind. Will I ever do that again?"

"You're young, and healthy. Right now, you need to get strong again for the baby."

"Ah, the baby. I don't suppose you know when I'm due?"

"I don't know, one month? Maybe two? You have time to get back on your feet before the baby."

"Oh, I'll get back on my feet all right, and when I do, I'm out of here. Now tell me why I'm being held against my will. And take this tube, this catheter out, it's uncomfortable."

"*Si*, I can take the catheter out, but I cannot tell you why you're here."

"Why not? I'll find out eventually."

"Because I don't know. All I know is I come here every day and take care of you. I am a nurse. I keep you well."

"Then tell that man with the rifle to come in here. I want answers."

"Those men are mean, you don't want to make them mad."

*

That made her mad. She vowed again with greater resolve to break out and run for freedom, if only to get answers. Well, not only for that. A new life grew inside her, and she made another vow. She would not deliver her baby in that house. She did her exercises and then tried to move her legs to the edge of the bed. Still isn't happening, but better than before. I have to keep going.

"You know what this is for?" the nurse asked, entering the room with a bedpan.

"Of course. I guess this has been a routine for us over

427

the last few weeks?"

"Well, we've used diapers until now. I have a chair you can use too. Would you like to try?"

"I'd love to. I'd love to sit up, that is, but both would be nice."

The woman fetched a portable potty chair and helped her into it.

"Ah, I never thought sitting up would be so, so, oh, this feels great," she said, struggling to maintain her balance. "Hard to do, though."

"I help you, so you don't fall, now do your business."

She did, and thanked the nurse for taking care of her. Despite not knowing the reasons for her continued confinement, she knew the woman had not participated in her abduction.

"Can I sit in that chair for a while?" she asked, pointing to an upholstered chair in the corner of the room.

"Are you ready?"

"If you'll help me."

The nurse put her hands under Mary's arms and lifted, but her legs were too weak. She left and returned with a wheelchair.

"Let's take baby steps for now. You sit in this first. Get used to it, and when you are ready, you can begin taking steps."

"I used to run. Miles and miles and miles. Now I can't even stand."

"You will. You're young. And strong. And you look like you have determination. You will walk again, and you will run. Be patient. Take one step at a time."

"You're right. I'll take my time."

*

After a week of exercising all her muscles and taking in more calories than the nasal tube used to supply, she managed to move off the bed and into the wheelchair on her own. She added wheeling herself around the room to her workout program. I'll be doing wheelies soon.

After supper one evening, and with the lights out, she got into the wheelchair and rolled toward the door. With her feet stretched out in front of her and making no noise, she pushed a rug against it so that it blocked the light coming in from the hall. She reached for the light switch and flipped it on, waiting for someone to come. No one did. She wheeled herself to the closet and opened the door. Inside, on the floor, she found a stack of magazines, all issues of Popular Mechanics. Yes. Something to read. She grabbed the issue on top and thumbed through it. Well, better than nothing. Where's the article on homemade guns? She looked up and saw another stack of magazines on the shelf above. Do I want to try to stand? She decided against it, not knowing for certain whether she could stand and pull them off without making noise. Not wanting to risk losing the only freedom she had, she settled for Popular Mechanics.

A week later, she took her first step. By herself. She feigned weakness when the nurse offered to help, thinking there might be a benefit to not letting anyone think she'd soon be strong enough to walk. And keep walking. To freedom. She studied every noise, whether coming from inside or outside the house. She often heard two men talking, and determined that there were always at least two guards. Whether they were always the same two voices, though, she couldn't tell. She heard the sound of a car engine and wheels crunching gravel just before the nurse came to check on her each morning and after leaving for the day. At other times she heard the sound of a muffler that needed replacement. A truck the guards drive?

The window in her bedroom had been boarded shut, but peering through a crack in the wooden slats, she could see a line of trees in the distance. The half-mile of ground between the house and the trees looked like cattle pasture, with piles of evidence strewn about. She even thought she'd heard the beasts near the house a time or two. The presence of a few mesquite trees here and there and the rolling hills in the distance suggested she was in Texas Hill Country. This is my turf, idiots. When I get out of here, you'll never find me.

CHAPTER SIXTY EIGHT

✛

Adam had finished reading an online article about a recent discovery of artifacts in west Texas and downloaded another when his phone rang. Hoping to see the word "police" on his caller ID with news about Mary, it displayed a Dallas area code instead.

"Hello?"

"Adam, it's Mac. We have a lead. Can you come up? Keith is on his way from Virginia; he'll be in tonight."

"Oh, wow. Fantastic. I'll be there in an hour. No, make it two, I'll drive the speed limit. No, make it three, I need to take care of something. What is it? Is it a good lead? Wait, it must be if Keith is coming."

"Slow down, hoss. It's a good lead. Take your time; you'll get here before Keith."

"This is great. Thanks, Mac. And this is something you can't discuss over the phone?"

"That's right. Oh, and Jim says to bring us a pizza."

"Tell him to get a job. No, don't say that. Tell you what, I'll call you guys when I'm a half-hour out. You order one, and I'll pick it up. Oh, Mac, did I say thanks? I'd about lost all hope. I haven't heard from the police in at least a week. I know you wouldn't call on mere speculation, so this is great. This is fabulous. I'm excited. See you guys soon."

He rushed home and packed a few clothes and a toothbrush and hit the highway, heading north. After clearing town, he dialed Brad's number.

"We may have something, finally. I may need you this week. I'll call when I know more, but Mac sounds confident. I'm on my way to Dallas right now. You know where the apartment key is, my notes and materials are on the coffee table, but wait until you hear from me. I appreciate this."

"Finally. This sounds hopeful. No problem with the classes, I have your back. Let's keep our fingers crossed. Good luck, Adam."

Before reaching the Dallas city limits, he called Mac and got directions to the restaurant. He found the place and went in to pay for the large pepperoni and mushroom pizza, then continued on to the apartment and knocked on the door. Keith greeted him.

"About time, what took you?"

"I had to stop for pizza. Hey, what are you doing here? Mac said you'd be in tonight."

"I caught a military hop to Dyess instead of flying commercial. Borrowed a car, and here I am."

"What's he got?"

"I don't know, I just arrived myself, but it must be good. Let's go find out."

Jim divided the pizza and served drinks while Mac described the context for the conversation he'd recorded.

"Vanessa is on the phone with an Ivan Volkov. His wife, Nina, is a patient. This is from this morning. Listen."

Ivan: Good news. She's out of the coma.

Vanessa: Thank God. How is she? Is she lucid? Does she know who she is?

Ivan: She's fine; her brain is working. She'll be okay. And the babies are fine.

"Oh my God," he said, jumping out of his chair. "Oh, my God. Mac, you genius. Jim, thank you. Guys, this is awesome."

He gave his wounded warrior hero friend a big hug and slapped a high five with Jim. Mac asked him to keep the noise down so the neighbors wouldn't complain. He approached Keith and extended his hand, but Mary's brother barged past it and embraced him.

"Thank you," he said, looking at Keith. "Thank you all. Wait. There's no doubt it's Mary, is there?"

"What are the odds?" Mac asked. "No, it's her. I understand your caution, but it's her. There's more, but it isn't important. We have our smoking gun."

"We have our smoking gun, all right," he said. "Now let's kill this guy."

"Slow down, let's be smart about this," Keith said. "Do we know where he lives?"

"Mac traced the number to an office in LA," Jim said. "So I staked the place out when I was there. I followed a man who left that office and got the address for the single-family home he went to."

"When were you in LA?" he asked.

"Three days ago. Job interview in Anaheim. Mac caught some suspicious chatter between this guy and

Vanessa, thought it worth checking out, so I drove up. She called him Ivan in a previous call, and the only Ivan in her records is the husband of a Nina Volkov."

"Do we know anything else?" Keith asked.

"A conglomerate owns that house," Jim said. "One we can't find anything out about."

"Really?" Keith said. "A shell corporation? What's going on here? Who is this guy?"

"Let's go ask him," he said. "I don't suppose you bugged his office."

"Didn't have my team with me."

"What kind of building is it?" Keith asked.

"Single-story brick with three other offices. Connected to several shops on the other end."

"What type of lock on the door?" Keith asked.

"Keyed." He showed them photos of the building he took early the next morning before returning to Texas.

"I don't see outside surveillance cameras," Keith said.

"Neither did I," Jim said. "It looks like we could get in and out okay."

"All right, who can go?" Keith asked.

They all said yes.

"Let's get out there, then. Do you have another camera, Mac?"

"I have several. I assume one with a mic?"

"Yes. Let's try the ceiling again. So, guys, I should take the car back to Dyess. If I can catch a hop to Edwards before noon tomorrow, I'll return it tonight. If not, I'll fly out of DFW and get the car back when I can. I'll see you boys out there."

"Before we split up, what did we decide about turning

what we find over to the police?" he asked.

"The problem with that is their tapped phones and the cameras in their offices," Keith answered. "We can't explain that. What we need is evidence apart from those bugs."

"Not to mention the documents we downloaded from Vanessa's hard drive," Mac added. "You open a big can of worms when you have medical information you aren't supposed to have."

"Yeah, big no-no," Jim said. "We can't get around that. None of us would be doing this for anyone else but Mary."

"Let's find her first," Keith said. "If we get evidence independent of the bugs, we'll give it to the police. If we decide the police have a better chance of finding Mary, we'll give them our information, consequences be damned."

"I can probably scrub traces of our clandestine activities, but, if not, I'm with Keith, we suck it up and turn it over."

"I'll take the fall, guys, I can't let you do that, you've already done so much," he said. "I can't begin to thank you enough."

"Let's get out of here before he gets all tender on us again," Keith said.

"You know, before this is over, I may get to like you, brother," he said.

"Oh, shoot, too late, there it is," Keith said

*

Mac and Jim flew out together, Adam caught a different

435

flight an hour later. Keith beat everyone to LA and picked up the others at LAX. They arrived at Ivan's office at four and staked it out. Their target was the last to leave the cluster of offices at six-thirty. They followed him to his home and kept vigil there until well after dark, then returned to his office. With everyone in disguise, Adam kept vigil in the shadow of the entrance to one of the offices while Mac kept lookout in the rental car. He saw Keith and Jim pick the lock on the glass entrance door to Ivan's business and disappear inside. Thirty minutes later, they reemerged and got back in the rental car to plan their next move.

"I say we get a room and divide the document photos and look for clues," Keith said. "If we don't find anything, we'll see what he wants to tell our camera in the morning."

"And if he doesn't go to the office or doesn't talk about Mary?" he asked.

"Then we go home and wait. I know what you want to do, but it's too soon for that. Let's give it a few days. If we get nothing in, say, a week, we come back and make him talk."

CHAPTER SIXTY NINE

✠

"I'm getting tired of this food, Maria."

"How did you know my name? I never told you."

"I heard a guard call after you the other day. You'd left, but I guess he didn't know that. Back to the food. You should let me come out and cook sometime. I promise I won't try to run away. Besides, how far could I get seven months pregnant and barefoot? And barely able to walk. Let me work in the kitchen. I need to get out of this room. Please?"

"Oh, I don't know."

"It wouldn't hurt to ask, would it?"

"No, I suppose not. Okay, I go ask."

The nurse returned and gave her the good news. "They say it's okay, but if you try anything, no more."

"Great. Can I give you a shopping list? I make a great hamburger stroganoff."

She wrote down the recipe she'd learned from her aunt. Something was missing, however, and try as she might she couldn't remember what it was. Her memory and thought processes had returned, for the most part, but she had occasional lapses.

"Give me a second. I don't want to leave anything out."

"Take your time; I'm in no hurry. I can stop by the store on my way here tomorrow, but if you can't remember something, we can do this the next day."

"No, give me a minute. Let me think my way through the steps. This is good exercise for my brain, thank you for asking the guards."

"Oh, *de nada*."

"Aha, I have it," she said, scribbling onto the paper the last ingredient. "Yes, now it's all there. Here's the list."

"Good. You can make this meal tomorrow, then."

"Will you be here to help me around the kitchen? I don't think I can stand long," she said, not being totally honest. After Maria left in the evenings, she had been stretching and doing yoga. She'd done sit-ups, push-ups, and squats while the guards watched TV. She even jogged in place when they watched a sporting event with the sound up. She wondered whether they drank much at night and if it would give her a chance to escape. Or make things more dangerous.

"Of course, I'd be happy to help you."

"One more thing. Can I get different clothes? This hospital gown is getting old. And it shows too much."

"I'll see what I can do."

*

The next afternoon, she prepared hamburger stroganoff, but sat in the wheelchair as much as she could get away with. She had Maria drain and rinse the cooked noodles and also had her stir the seasoned ground beef she'd heated in a skillet. Same for the sautéed mushrooms and the sauce. She poured the sauce over the meat and stirred in the mushrooms, let it simmer a minute, then spooned the mix over the noodles. Maria served the guards who ate their meals in the living room watching TV while they ate at the kitchen table. Her creation was a hit with everybody. She even surprised herself. Two days later, after Maria's meals that were nothing special, the guards urged her to try another dish. She responded with chicken quesadillas. When they asked her a third time, she requested a charcoal grill. They found one in the shed and cleaned it, then lit the coals. She prepared a dozen beef shish kabobs and cooked them to perfection, with Maria's assistance.

"You are a fabulous cook, Mary, how did you get so good?"

"Oh, watching my aunt, I guess. And in college, I didn't want to eat out much, so I practiced what I'd learned from her."

She became a fixture in the kitchen, but always asked Maria for help.

"Why don't you make that hamburger meal again?" the nurse asked. "It was so good."

"Do you still have the list of ingredients?"

"I do."

"You're on."

*

The next afternoon, she tried on one of the dresses Maria had brought her. A little loose, but it would do. She then asked the nurse if she could be allowed to sit outside for a few minutes. She'd be barefoot and in the wheelchair and couldn't walk far if she wanted to. The guards hesitated, but relented and told her they could reward her for the work she'd been doing in the kitchen. They let her know she'd be watched the entire time and not to try anything.

Seated in the wheelchair at the back of the house, she took a deep breath and exhaled in a deliberate, slow release of air. She looked at the sky and clouds as if it were a new experience. She smiled with delight when a mild breeze ruffled her hair. Ah, this is so nice. She waited until the noise inside the house indicated that she could get up and walk away for a minute. Her destination: a decaying pile of cow dung fifty feet away. The prize: a cluster of mushrooms she'd spotted while grilling the shish kabobs. Twenty seconds got her to the pile. Ten seconds later, the fungi were in a zip-lock bag in a dress pocket. Another twenty seconds got her back to the wheelchair. She collapsed into it as the door opened. Did they see me?

"Mary, it's time to start supper," Maria said.

"Coming," she said, wiping her hands on her dress.

"Were you trying to stand?" the nurse asked.

"I—yes, but I didn't want to get into trouble, so I sat back down. Let's make dinner."

They repeated the process of browning the beef, boiling and draining the pasta, slicing and sautéing the mushrooms, heating the sauce, then mixing everything together in a frying pan. Maria excused herself to use the bathroom, and when she left, Mary broke out the bag of mushrooms hidden in her dress pocket. She rinsed and sliced them into pieces, then mixed them into the pan with the rest of the ingredients. The blue color that appeared in the stems where they'd been sliced told her they might be *Psilocybe cubensis* mushrooms. She picked as many of the store-bought mushrooms out of the skillet as she could and stuffed them in the plastic bag before the nurse returned to the kitchen.

"Why are you smiling? Is this your best meal yet?"

"Mmm-hmm," she answered, hiding the bag in a side pocket. "I think so. I only wish I could join you, but my hormones are acting up. My stomach is queasy. You enjoy. Can you save me some, please? I may feel like eating later."

"Of course. Why don't you go lie down?"

"I will." She sat in the wheelchair and rolled herself into her bedroom, leaving the door partly open. She wanted to hear everything that happened during the meal, and especially afterward.

Sounds of pots, pans, and dishes being cleaned came from the kitchen. Now she could only wait, but she used that time to formulate an escape plan should she get the opportunity. A half-hour later, she sensed that the mushrooms might be working. The conversation, normally barely audible from inside her room, grew louder with interspersed bouts of laughter. By the time the sun set an hour later, the three were clearly under the influence of psychoactive compounds. The sounds of cans being crushed meant the consumption of beer. She heard the front door open and slam shut as the frivolity moved outside. Even through the walls, she could hear laughter, a noise somewhat like a wolf's howl, then a rhythmic sound, like a stick beating on an overturned trash can. Shouting and laughter continued for another hour. The loud noises gradually subsided, and a door slamming shut told her they'd moved back inside the house. Snoring sounds signaled that the window of opportunity to escape had opened.

They hadn't bothered turning off the lights, which made leaving easier. She tiptoed past her new friends, one guard slouched in an easy chair, the other stretched out on the couch, and Maria asleep on the love seat. She grabbed the flashlight off the kitchen counter and headed for the front door. She took Maria's purse from the hook next to the door and opened it, finding car keys and a cell phone. Each guard had a phone, and now they were hers. She eased herself through the door and walked gingerly to the Honda Civic parked behind a pickup truck, using the flashlight to trace a path clear of rocks or other small objects she didn't want to step on barefooted. Before getting in the car, she pointed the flashlight down the gravel driveway and could see that it intersected with a dirt road fifty yards away. She slipped into the driver's seat of Maria's car and adjusted it for her taller, and now heavier, body size. She examined the four keys on the chain and found one with a Honda insignia on it. Sliding it into the ignition lock, she turned it one click and saw the instrument panel light up. Yes. Okay, good. She turned it back to the off position and got out of the car.

Okay, okay, now what? She wanted to drive away then but resisted the temptation and took precautions. First, the pickup truck. She popped the latch and struggled to lift the heavy hood, but managed to get it high enough to work the support rod into its slot. Pointing the flashlight into the engine compartment, she yanked out the distributor cap wire and two spark plug wires for good measure. She put those in the back seat of Maria's car, then headed to the house. She eased the door open and peeked in. All three still asleep. She grabbed a Glock 9mm pistol that sat on the floor next to the easy chair. A second Glock lay on the coffee table next to the couch. Both went into a backpack she found hanging on another of the hooks near the front door. She put a bottle of water into the backpack and, before leaving again, took both AR-15 rifles resting upright against the wall in the corner of the room. The weapons went into the backseat, and Mary climbed into the front. "You ready?" she asked, looking at her belly. "Let's get out of here."

The engine purred when she turned the key. With her foot on the brake, she shifted into reverse, then paused, glancing toward the house. Seeing no movement inside, she backed down the driveway until she reached the T-intersection. She got out and shone the flashlight in both directions, but saw no traffic or lights either way. This is the middle of nowhere. Most of the tire tracks went the same direction, that would be the way she'd go.

A half-mile later, she stopped at a locked gate. Visible in her headlights was a chain wrapped around one end of the gate. A heavy-duty combination lock secured it to a fencepost. She got out of the car and peered over the fence. The beam of the flashlight lit up nothing but gravel road as far as she could see. No crossroads, no signs, nothing but fence posts and barbed wire. And a drainage ditch to boot. Maria's car won't make it through that. She shook the gate, hoping to find it flimsy and something she could crash through, but as she did, a bright flash briefly blinded her.

When her pupils had re-dilated, and she could see again, she found the culprit. A camera had been mounted on the top of a post just beyond the gate, and, judging by the look of the concrete at its base, had been recently installed. You guys did this for me? How thoughtful. Too bad it has to come down. She couldn't reach it, however, so she retrieved an AR-15 from the back seat. Holding it by the barrel, she thrust the stock at the camera and caught it flush, loosening it from its metal bracket. A second whack sent it flying through the air and crashing near the gate post. She picked it up and examined it. A simple game camera, but the device attached to its top gave her cause for concern. Uh, oh. This flashing LED isn't good. A transmitter? If it's an alarm, it probably woke everybody in the house. They're probably scurrying around looking for their weapons. She shook the gate again and determined it to be too sturdy to crash through with the Civic. Now what? She thought again about driving through the fence. If she angled it properly, she might be able to half-pipe the ditch, but the problem would be the approach. Hitting the fence at an angle would likely bounce the car back into the field. If not, it could become disabled when the high tension barbed wire flew every which way on impact. Hitting it straight on would not give her enough distance to get the car turned to avoid getting stuck in the ditch.

She tried the guards' phones, but both required a password. She dropped them on the ground and smashed both with the rifle butt. Maria's home screen lit up, but the app she tapped did nothing. No signal? She held it up and whirled in a circle, but to no avail. "What do you want to do here, little guy? Crash the fence? What if the car gets stuck? I have no shoes. We have to get out of here. Let's see what's at the other end of this road." Dust and gravel flew behind the car as she sped toward the house, fearing the guards may have heard the alarm and ran to the road looking for her. I'm not stopping, guys.

CHAPTER SEVENTY

✛

Seeing no one in the road ahead, she slowed just enough to get a good look at the house. No activity. Well, that's good. But they could be blissfully sleeping through the alarm. Hope I didn't give them too many mushrooms. Nah. Too bad if I did. She slowed as the road transitioned into two grassy ruts and then stopped another quarter-mile later in front of a barbed-wire fence. She saw nothing beyond the fence in the headlights except rugged terrain and a few scraggly trees. Opening the door, she stepped out and checked for a cell phone signal. Still no luck. Where are we? She grabbed the top strand of wire between barbs and tugged, then pushed on the wooden fence post. Hmmm. Not sure if we can get through this. Might tear up the front end. Still… "How about the truck, little guy. I think you might be a boy as active as you are. You'd like trucks. Should we? It would certainly be better over there. Higher ground clearance, four-wheel drive." She got back in the car and grabbed a Glock. Racking the slide to load a round in the chamber, she set it on the passenger seat. "All right, let's go back and check the house for the keys. Maybe there was no alarm. We'll know soon enough. If they're up and looking for me, I have their weapons, and I know how to use them. I'll protect you, little guy."

She turned the car around and headed back to the house, stopping after turning into the gravel driveway. Waiting there a moment to see if anyone appeared in a window or a door, she let the car creep to a spot halfway between the road and the house and stopped again. With the engine running, she kept an eye on the house and tried Maria's phone again. No luck. With headlights off, she eased the car closer to the house, warily watching for signs of life. She parked next to the truck and reinstalled the wires she'd taken off its engine. She moved the two rifles from Maria's backseat into the cab, leaning the barrels against the passenger door with the gunstocks resting on the floor. She dumped the contents of the backpack—a knife, two boxes of ammo, cigarettes, matches, and the other Glock—onto the passenger seat, then took the empty pack and the loaded handgun and tiptoed to the window at the back of the house. Peering inside, the sight of the three sleeping soundly caused her tensed shoulders to relax. She took in a deep breath and blew it out through pursed lips. "Let's go," she whispered.

She opened the screen door and slipped inside. Scanning the front room where each of the sleeping beauties remained in dreamland, she hoped to find keys to the Ford Ranger pickup sitting in the driveway. Seeing none, she set the empty pack on the floor and searched the pockets of the pants lying on the floor next to the guard on the couch. She turned and looked at the other guard, who still had his clothes on, wondering if she could search his pockets too. *I could whack him over the head and knock him out, but that might wake his buddy up. I could whack him too, or shoot him.* She moved closer and pointed the gun at his head with her right hand, then slid her left hand down to his waist and felt each pocket in turn. Nothing. *In the truck somewhere?*

Keeping an eye on the sleepers, she took the backpack into the kitchen and filled it with food and bottled water from the pantry and refrigerator. On her way to the truck, she thought of things in the house that might be useful should she break through the fence and find herself still in the middle of nowhere. *Gotta see if those shoes fit, but first things first.*

She set the backpack on the passenger seat of the truck next to the rifles and looked for keys. She found a set on the driver's side floor mat below the front edge of the seat. One of them fit the ignition. She left it in place and retreated back inside the house. She picked up the sneakers belonging to Maria and tried them on. *Tight, but they'll have to do.* She grabbed a second backpack and, after throwing out packs of cigarettes, she added to the knife, matches, and ammo already in it a pair of binoculars and another flashlight she'd taken from a shelf on the wall near the kitchen table. *What else? What else?*

She went into the bedroom and took a sheet, a thin blanket, and a pillowcase and stuffed them into the backpack. She headed to the bathroom but froze when the man on the couch stirred. He settled into a new position and began snoring again—what a wonderful sound. A roll of toilet paper, a hand towel, and a first aid kit from the bathroom each went into the backpack. One more thing. She gathered the men's boots and jackets and the one pair of pants and took them to the truck, tossing them into the bed. That'll slow them down. Some. Okay. Gotta go. Anything else? No, don't think so. Gotta go. She turned off the lights inside the house and walked out.

She opened the door to the truck and was about to hop in the driver's seat when she realized it was more of a climb than a hop. While she contemplated a maneuver to get herself in the driver's seat, it dawned on her that she should disable Maria's car. The nurse might have a spare key in a magnetic case attached to the underside, or one of the guards might know how to hotwire a car. She couldn't find a distributor cap, so she pulled four spark plug wires and tossed them into the truck.

She found a handhold above the door and grabbed it with her left hand and the steering wheel with her right, then hoisted herself, big belly and all, up and into the seat. Whew. Can't rest now, though, let's roll. She turned the key. Nothing happened. What? She pressed her right foot on the brake pedal and turned it again—still nothing. The wires are back on, is one loose? Ah, look at that—a third pedal. Of course. Like Uncle Frank's old Ford. When did I drive that last? Five, six years ago? I can do this. The gear locations were stamped on the shift knob.

She pressed down on the clutch with her left foot and moved the gear lever into neutral. The key turned, and the engine roared to life. She shifted into reverse and let out the clutch. The truck jerked backward, and the engine stalled. She looked at the house and waited a minute. All quiet. She went through the process again, but this time eased the clutch out more slowly, and back the truck went. She continued into the road turning the rear end toward the south gate, shifted into first gear, and drove north.

CHAPTER SEVENTY ONE

Whe n she ran out of road and ruts, Mary steered the truck left and drove along the north fence, looking for an unlocked gate. If she could get off the ranch, she figured the odds of finding a path or trail or dirt road that led to a public road were good. Stopping at a homestead on the adjacent property concerned her as its occupants might be friendly to the owner of the house in which she'd been held captive. Then again, who has kidnappers for friends? Nevertheless, she decided to stay clear of houses on her way out. If it got to the point where she had no choice, she'd take a chance. She might even have the element of surprise working in her favor. After all, who expects a pregnant woman to be toting a loaded handgun?

The wheels hit jarring holes and bumps in the pasture, but nothing the truck couldn't handle. She drove until the fence that formed the western boundary of the open grazing area stopped her. Beyond it, she saw what looked in the dark like a stand of mostly oak and mesquite trees. From the times her captors allowed her outside, she'd observed that trees populated the western edge of the property as far as she could see. She turned the truck around and headed back toward the end of the dirt road and drove past it another hundred yards before stopping at a pond. She saw that the fence continued another fifty yards or so until it cornered out and turned back south. She turned the steering wheel to the right and eased the clutch out, letting the headlights follow the adjoining fence into the distance until she lost sight of it over a hill—no gate, and more trees. Well, I guess it's plan B. Shifting into reverse, she turned the wheel and backed the truck until she faced the trees in the west. She eased forward, looking for the clearest path on the other side of the fence she could make out in the darkness. "Here goes, hold on." She turned the truck toward a fence post and hit the gas. The bumper made short work of the fence as it keeled over and collapsed behind her. She drove another thirty feet and stopped to survey the wreckage. Strands of barbed wire had curled in chaotic fashion behind her, but she'd made it past their grasp.

The terrain looked daunting, but she couldn't stop. Daylight approached, and the guards would soon emerge from their mushroom-induced stupor. It wouldn't take long to see that she'd taken the truck and figure out which direction she went. Tracking her would not be hard, either, but she had their weapons and their shoes, and, most importantly, they had no phones.

She needed rest but pushed on. After driving a hundred yards across the rocky landscape, she reached a shallow creek. With the truck's headlights illuminating the upstream geographical features, she liked what she saw.

The scattered presence of small stones visible throughout the stream bed told her its depth would not be a problem. She turned the front end downstream only to find a narrowing of the waterway and the presence of trees along the banks as far as she could see. No, don`t think so. She engaged the four-wheel-drive knob and pulled into the creek, heading upstream in first gear. The truck's springs squeaked, and its suspension grumbled bump after bump after bump. She'd traversed at least fifty yards through the shallow water when she decided to pull out. The stream had gotten wider and, not seeing as many rocks, she suspected deeper. Trees lined the banks ahead, and since an opening on the other side had presented itself, she drove up the bank and headed cross-country again, hoping to find a road. Any road. None appeared, so she maneuvered the truck up a hill and stopped to get out and look around. Nothing. Nothing but a gray horizon to the east. She tried Maria's phone, but still no signal.

Sunrise about an hour from now. Do I hide or keep looking for a road? She headed down the other side of the hill toward a stand of trees and found a gap wide enough to get the truck through. After a sharp right to dodge an oak tree and then a left to avoid another, she stopped in front of a sapling. Getting out of the truck and shining the flashlight past the small tree, she discovered a juniper thicket that would do a decent job of hiding her and the vehicle. She drove over the young tree and watched it snap back up in the rearview mirror, then pulled into the cover of the junipers.

Sunlight crept over her face until its brightness and warmth woke her. She didn't know how she fell asleep in the bed of the truck but assumed it had to be due to sheer exhaustion. Rubbing her eyes, she sat up to survey her surroundings. The junipers would do a reasonably good job of hiding her from a ground search, but the glaring weak spot was overhead. Unfiltered sunlight told her that. A plane or helicopter could easily spot the truck from the air. Okay, first things first. She took the larger of the two knives she'd apprehended from the guards and cut down a number of tree saplings. She dragged them to the truck and lay them on the hood, roof, and bed for camouflage. That's better.

She opened a bottle of water and drank lustily from it. "Sorry about that, you were probably getting thirsty," she told the baby. "Well, drink up." She took a can of beans from the backpack and opened it, washing them and a few crackers down with the rest of the bottle of water—an apple made for a tasty dessert.

She debated whether to drive around or scout the area on foot. The truck's engine, however, could probably be heard at least a half a mile away, and noise was now an enemy. She did have their weapons, however, and a head start. The extra load she carried had made walking harder for her the last few days, and she didn't feel she had anywhere near the energy or strength she used to have. She opted to take her chances in the truck and turned the key. A clicking sound was all she heard. She waited a moment and turned the key again. More clicking. She released the hood latch and got out. Sliding the saplings off the hood, she lifted it and set the support rod. The connections between cable clamps and battery terminals seemed tight enough, but corrosion was evident, and the battery looked several years old. Wiggling them didn't help. "Guess we walk." She closed the hood and spread the saplings back across it, then prepared to hike out.

That decided, she emptied one of the backpacks and filled it with enough food and water to last a day. To those provisions, she added the binoculars, a knife, one of the Glocks with a full clip inserted, a jacket, and Maria's phone. She would walk for two hours in a direction that roughly continued her trek away from the ranch house. If she didn't find a house or a road or some sign of civilization, she would return to the truck to eat and rest, then try a different direction in the afternoon. She locked the truck and walked north.

The rocky terrain and her physical condition took their toll on her stamina, reducing the distance she covered in the two hours she'd allotted for the trek. When the sun had made its way directly overhead, she stopped to eat more beans and crackers, and to consider whether she ought to risk it and continue on. *Surely I have to come across somebody this afternoon.* She realized though that the "somebody" might be one of her captors. She turned on Maria's cell phone and looked for a signal. Nothing. She powered it down and headed back to the truck. *What is this place? No roads, no houses, no cell phone signal? Must be a huge ranch. State park? Wildlife refuge? I may never get out of here.*

After nourishment and rest, and no sign of pursuers, she set out in an easterly direction with a full backpack. A half-hour later, a clap of thunder rumbled behind her. She turned and studied the sky. Dark clouds in the distance looked menacing. A cool breeze hit her, and, worse, the storm's movement indicated it would pass her way, and soon. She pulled the jacket from the pack and put it on. It reeked of cigarettes and made her stomach queasy, but the wind helped—a little. Assessing the situation, she decided she couldn't make it back to the truck in time, so she quickened her steps and looked for shelter. That pace did not last long, however, as the effort tired her.

She staggered along in fits and starts, but kept moving. A large rock formation emerged from the hillside in front of her, forcing a detour. When she reached the downhill side, she stopped to catch her breath and removed the backpack to get to a water bottle.

The sound of more thunder made her eager to resume the search for shelter. She slung the pack upward but failed to secure it around her shoulders, forcing a second try. Preparing for the attempt, her eye caught a darkened spot on the front side of the huge rock she'd bypassed.

With the sun hidden behind thick clouds, she dismissed the possibility that it was merely the shadow of the Ashe juniper guarding its front. Curiosity took over and drew her closer.

Working her way around the tree brought the mysterious structure into view—an opening in the rocky hillside that beckoned her further. She stepped inside to a large, spacious room, easily large enough to wait out the storm in. It even had a skylight, a hole two feet wide that not only let light pass through but, she soon found out, rain as well.

Fortunately, rainwater that found its way through the ceiling channeled toward what looked like a passageway to the interior of the hill. She explored the rest of the room with a flashlight and was delighted to find carve-outs and cubbyholes in the walls. She crawled into the largest one and leaned against a side wall. She fell asleep sitting up.

CHAPTER SEVENTY TWO

✛

The four watched Ivan Volkov enter his office the morning after Keith and Jim installed hidden surveillance and computer-hacking equipment. He made no phone calls nor sent any emails mentioning Mary, at least not before lunch. They followed him to his home when he left his office at noon and parked nearby, watching the place for over an hour.

"Can we bug his house?" Adam asked.

"It would take a while to put together the electronics," Keith said. "Not to mention figuring out how to get inside. I say we stick to the plan. We have eyes and ears in his office, so let's go home and see what happens for a few days. If we don't get any leads, we'll come back and talk to the guy. And Vanessa."

On the flight back to Texas, they contented themselves with reading through the documents downloaded from Ivan's office computer when he logged in that morning. They each fell asleep reading the tedious material and had to finish at Mac's apartment. They found nothing useful. Mac downloaded the morning's camera recordings and phone calls, nothing there either. Keith and Jim discussed tactics and technical gear they might need if they went back to LA in a few days. Adam called Brad to give him an update.

"We're still examining documents, but we believe we have the right guy."

"That's fantastic. Now what?"

"We're trying to decide. I'll be back tonight, unless we get something definite."

Mac's animated whooping stopped all activity in the room.

"Gotta go, Brad, Mac's got something."

"Guys," he said. "Check it out."

He turned his laptop around so the others could see the screen. Ivan stood behind his desk, his face contorted, mouth open wide and speaking into his phone. Mac hit the play arrow.

Ivan: "What do you mean, escaped? How could you let that happen? What kind of idiots did you hire?"

Ivan: "Ha, that's good. Took their boots. Unbelievable. Morons. All right, get there as soon as you can. Find where she got through the fence and track her down. For your sake, it better not be along the road, but the ditch probably scared her away. If she went out on the north side, she won't get far; it's too rugged. Call me when you get there."

"This next one is an hour and twenty minutes later," Mac said, hitting the play button.

Ivan: "Okay, good. I'm sending help. Where should they meet you?"

Ivan: "No, no, Lago Vista is fine. They're three hours

out, but I hope they won't be needed, so find her and get her back to the house. And don't harm her, do you understand?"

"Yes, yes, yes," he said, the sound echoing off the walls. "Yes. She escaped. Yes. I love that girl."

"Yes we do," Keith said.

They exchanged high-fives. He shook his fist in the air.

"We have you now, jerk," he said.

"When did he make that last call?" Keith asked.

"Thirty minutes ago," Mac said.

"Okay, okay. We aren't too far behind. Anyone know where Lago Vista is?" Jim asked.

"I do," he said. "Half hour west of Austin."

"What's there?"

"About seven thousand people, give or take. It's in the Hill Country on Lake Travis. She won't be there, of course."

"No," Keith added. "That's where they're meeting, so their man on the ground can lead them to what I bet is a remote ranch, at least by the sound of it."

"And I'll bet that ranch butts up against the Balcones Canyonlands," he said. "That could be the rugged terrain Ivan referred to."

"Isn't that a wildlife refuge?" Keith asked.

"It is. It's also a good place for Indian artifacts."

"So, you've been there?" Jim asked.

"I have. Much of it's for the birds, so to speak. The public isn't allowed in most of it. I've gotten permission, with help from my brother John, to explore the non-public areas."

"That could be an advantage if she's there," Keith said. "But we don't know that yet. Mac, can you remote in to Ivan's office on the road?"

"Of course."

"Okay, let's pack up, boys," Keith instructed. "We're going to Lago Vista. It'll be dark by the time we get there, so let's figure on a motel and getting an early start in the morning unless Mac comes up with something definite. Jim, do you know anybody in Killeen that can lend us weapons?"

"How about a tank?"

"Nah, take too long to get on site. Whatever you can scrounge up, though. Adam, I don't suppose you have a shotgun at your place? Or know anybody in Waco who does?"

"No, but my brother David can get SWAT gear and meet us there."

"No sh— Ah, yes, the state trooper. Hmmm. Is he a 'strictly-by-the-book' guy?"

"Ninety-nine percent of the time he is. Are you asking what I think you're asking."

"I am."

"He'll work with us. And my other brother John knows Central Texas like the back of his hand, plus he carries a sidearm and keeps a rifle in the rack inside his truck."

"Adam," Keith said. "I knew we kept you around for a reason. Get on the horn and recruit those guys. Tell them to meet us in Lago Vista tomorrow morning. As for the rest of us, let's pee and flee. Adam, you and Jim should take your cars too, we may need eyes in several places. We'll meet in Leander in four hours and go from there."

"David can have half a dozen state police meet us there, plus local cops."

"That's awfully tempting, but we wouldn't know where to send them. And if this guy senses extra heat and gets to her before we do, he'd move her somewhere else. We'd have to start over. Right now, we have the element of surprise. I say we keep it that way a little longer. Does your brother drive an unmarked car?"

"He does. John doesn't, but it's a Parks and Wildlife truck, not police."

"Well, we need him. Let him know we're keeping a low profile. Mac, bring all your electronic toys."

CHAPTER SEVENTY THREE

✠

Mary awoke to the sound of water droplets splashing into the small puddles that had collected on the floor of the cave. Light coming through the hole in the roof illuminated the interior of the cavern more so than when she'd first entered it, the worst of the storm having now passed. The drizzle eased to a light mist and then stopped completely. She got out of the cubby and stepped out of the cave.

"What do you think, little guy?" Ooh, a kick. And another. She rubbed her tummy. "Does that mean hit the road? I wish I could, I do, but I only have so much energy. And I can only walk so far in these tight shoes. So, we have to look at priorities. Number one is safety. Those guys will come looking for us soon. They'll find the truck, so if we want the rest of the food and water, we need to get it today. Now, in fact. This cave is safe. We'll be okay here tonight. Tomorrow we'll leave and either find help or a phone signal. We're gonna make it. First, though, let's make a bed."

Working her way past the juniper guarding the

entrance to the cave, she paused to scan the area for signs of life. Satisfied it was clear, she moved down the hill with an empty backpack to a stand of oak trees. There, she filled the pack with fallen leaves and hauled them back to the cave, where she spread them out on dry spots on the floor. Three full backpacks later, she pronounced the job finished. How long will I have to stay here, anyway?

She ate more beans and crackers. After taking a long swig of water, she put the rest of the bottle in the backpack along with a Glock, the binoculars, and Maria's phone, and set out for the truck. An hour later, she approached the juniper grove one step at a time, scanning the area with binoculars between steps. Seeing no one, she took off the backpack and set it on the ground. She removed the Glock and raised it, then entered the small clearing expecting to be ambushed. All was quiet, though, with no sign that anyone had been there. Satisfied she was alone, she unlocked the door and moved everything to the lowered tailgate. Dividing the supplies into two piles, she filled the backpacks. The late afternoon air remained cool after the storm, allowing her to wear the jacket rather than try to stuff it into the crowded pack. A Glock and ammo went into a side compartment along with a flashlight. She left an AR-15 and an ammo clip behind the driver's seat of the truck cab, out of view as best she could. Shutting the door gently, she locked it and hid the key on the ground behind the right front tire. She slung the heavier backpack around her shoulders and adjusted it. The binocular strap then went around her neck. After scanning the woods, she picked up the second pack, the rifle, and the other handgun. "Ready? We may have to stop a few times, but I need this gear. So no complaints. Okay?" She began the journey back to the cave as the sun sank toward the hills behind her.

The extra gear and provisions took a toll on her energy reserves, forcing her to stop twice to rest, snack, and rehydrate. The extra calories burned on the walk made her hot, and the jacket held the heat in. She didn't care much for the odor anyway, so off it came. Preferring to toss it, but concerned someone might find it, she tied it to a loop on the bottom of the backpack she wore.

When she reached what she thought was the cave's location, the landscape looked different. She set everything down and took off the backpack. Is it because things look different in twilight? She pulled the flashlight out and took another drink of water, then looked in all directions again. Okay, now, don't panic. Don't let this little guy think you're worried. "I'm only resting, again." Think he believed it? Geez, I'm already deceiving my kid. I'll make a great mother. How in the world did I become one in the first place? Someone has some explaining to do when I get out of here. This just doesn't make any sense.

In her head, she replayed her first trip there, then the one back to the truck, and now this last one, trying to compare distances, directions, and times to get a feel for where she was. Am I lost? Why didn't I tie a ribbon on that juniper outside the cave? Because I didn't have one? I'll go with that. I hate to use the flashlight, but I may not have a choice soon. A raindrop smacked a boulder near her, then another. She told herself again there was no need to panic. She untied the jacket from the bottom of the backpack and wrapped it over her shoulders. A flash of lightning lit the sky, and thunder followed four seconds later. She heard a steady rain hitting trees on the hilltop she'd just traversed. Another bolt of lightning danced across the darkening sky, and in that flash of light, her eye caught a lone juniper on the slope behind her. Is that it? Did I walk too far? Oh, thank God, I think that's it. It is. "Hey, kiddo, we're back, you can relax now." She made it into the cave with everything just as the heavens let loose.

Inside, she set her gear down away from the entrance and the area below the skylight in the ceiling to keep it all dry. With the help of the flashlight, she gathered the leaves she'd spread earlier to prepare a bed in the largest cubbyhole the cave offered. The blanket went on top to add a degree of stability and to hopefully delay the onset of whatever dampness remained in the leaves. She filled the pillowcase with the remaining leaves and tossed it to the back of the cubby, then set the sheet to one side of the blanket, ready to be spread out over her body to provide whatever warmth it could. I'll probably wake up a little damp, but that's certainly better than soaked in that deluge outside. She placed a bottle of water, Maria's phone, the Glock, and toilet paper on her bed next to the sheet. With advancing pregnancy, she had to relieve herself more often during the night, so each of those items served a purpose. She ate crackers and drank water while waiting for the rain to stop so she could go outside one last time before trying to sleep. When the rain finally subsided, with flashlight and toilet paper in hand, she ventured out, did what she had to do, and returned to the relative comfort of her lodgings. "Okay, you, bedtime." She wiggled her way into the cubby, managing to keep the bedding mostly in place.

"This is firm, are you okay with that? If we stay another night, scratch that, we aren't staying another night. Sweet dreams, little guy." She plumped the makeshift pillow under her head and snugged the sheet around herself, then fell asleep.

*

Rays of sunlight falling through the ceiling and the east-facing front entrance surprised her when she awoke. Wow, how did that happen? She turned Maria's phone on. Six-fifteen. Six straight hours, awesome. Ooh, but I need to go. She went outside and saw the sun peeking over a distant hill. Beautiful. Just beautiful. As she finished and turned back toward the cave, a noise stopped her. A hum. The unmistakable sound of a helicopter. Getting louder. Heading right at her. She ducked back into the cave as it passed directly overhead. She grabbed the binoculars and the AR-15 and, chambering a round, stepped outside the cave entrance. She heard the chopper again in the distance, apparently flying a grid, no doubt looking for her. She leaned the rifle against the rocky front of the cave and hid behind the juniper. The sound from the south grew louder. When it came into view, she fixed the binoculars on the aircraft, looking for identification markings. Nope, not the police. It made another pass farther east. Fourth and fifth parallel passes confirmed that the search for her had commenced. She went back into the cave and collected all the ammo and the extra Glock and set them by the entrance. This was now her home, and she would defend it. She knew how to use an AR-15, and, if it came to it, a pistol.

The helicopter continued flying the area, but the noises from its engine and rotors diminished and then went silent. Now what? I don't want to be stuck here today. She heard another humming noise in the distance, this one higher-pitched—an engine. Chainsaw? ATV? She eased her way through the entrance and scanned the hill below. Seeing nothing, she took another step out and pointed the binoculars southward toward the noise—an ATV. The driver appeared to be conducting his own grid search. He crisscrossed the area methodically, and did not seem to be in a hurry. She checked the juniper branches she'd cut and placed in front the entrance for cover, then went back inside to wait out the search. The humming moved back and forth, getting louder and louder, until it sounded as though it were right outside the entrance. To her relief, the ATV bypassed the cave and continued the search up the hill. She grinned and switched the safety back on. Your lucky day, whoever you are. She stepped outside, staying out of sight, and saw that the driver wasn't wearing a helmet. She focused the binoculars on his face and recognized one of the guards from the ranch house. Surprised you still have a job after letting me escape. The noise dissipated, and moments later, it, too, went quiet.

CHAPTER SEVENTY FOUR

M ary wanted to leave the cave in the worst way. She made the decision, however, to lay low for several hours, and, not having anything to sit on, she came to appreciate the invention of chairs. She passed the first hour cross-legged in the cubby, trying to read the Spanish language newspaper she'd found in Maria's car and brought along thinking it might come in handy for a fire. Many of the words and grammar came back to her, and she got the gist of several of the articles. When she wearied of that, she took inventory of everything in the cave, even the rounds of ammo for the AR-15 and the two Glocks. She figured she had enough food for two more days, if she rationed, but water was getting low. It might not last another day.

It had been more than three hours since the searchers left the area. Getting restless, she decided to go for a slow, careful walk and look for a phone signal, a road, a house, or even the creek she'd driven across two days prior. She loaded empty water bottles into a backpack along with Maria's phone and flung it on her back. She carried a

Glock in one hand and binoculars in the other. Upon leaving the cave, she headed south across the open ground, scanning the terrain with every step. She climbed a hill and stopped at its highest point to rest and survey the area. No people, no houses, no roads, but a line of trees about a half-mile further south suggested the possibility of that creek. After trying the phone again, she continued her methodical march toward the potential source of water.

Just before the tree line, she heard a faint sound and paused—gurgling water. Around the next hill, she found the source of the noise: a natural spring. A small pool of the clear, cool liquid collected before it spilled over the lip of a rocky ledge and trickled down the hillside into a gully. She scooped a handful into her palms and tasted it. Ahhh, this is good. She took another drink and wiped her mouth, then studied the setting for future reference. She filled the empty bottles and prepared for the return to the cave when she heard a rustling noise. She froze, not moving until a second sound revealed the direction of the disturbance. With a slow, deliberate motion, she turned her head toward it while reaching for the Glock. Her eyes found the culprit, and she relaxed. Deer. Two. No antlers. A doe and a fawn. How cute. She watched them forage the area beneath a pecan tree, and after they'd moved on, visited the spot herself. Pecans lay on the ground, by the hundreds. She cracked one open and inspected it. Rotten. She found another; same thing. A third, though, looked okay. She tasted it. Mmmm, I believe I could subsist on spring water and pecans. These are delicious.

"But you need variety, don't you," she said to the traveling companion lodged within. "How about venison?

Nah, you're right, too much noise. Let's hope it doesn't come to that. I can look for blackberries. Wrong time of year, though, birds will have picked them over. You probably didn't get much variety back at that house, did you? You don't seem too worse for the wear, always kicking. Why don't you take a nap, read a book, or watch TV?"

She gathered all the pecans she could and put them in the backpack. On her return to the cave, she looked for more producing trees and kept her eyes open for berries, but found neither. Back in the cave, she poured the pecans onto the raised surface of the cubby next to the one she slept in and sorted them into two piles, one for clearly bad ones and another for possibles. She cracked open a few of the possibles, all but one were edible. Finally, a break. A source of food and water. "Well, kiddo, we're good for as long as—I know, I know, you need a hospital, and sooner than later. All right, I'll find us a way out of here tomorrow."

*

She made it through the night. Again. "Wow, two in a row, I guess this bed suits me. Us. Even though it's on the firm side. Or else I'm too exhausted not to sleep seven straight hours. My bladder doth complain, however. Okay, outside, let's go. Oh, look, another beautiful sunrise in Central Texas. All right, little guy, you want to get out of here? Let's go. Let's grab a bite to eat and leave these luxurious accommodations. I say we head north and stay out of sight on our way to freedom today. With the pecans and water we found yesterday, we can travel farther, and I believe we'll make it out."

She prepared a backpack while munching beans and crackers. She chose north because higher elevation meant a better view and a better chance at a cell phone signal. Before departing home, sweet home, she hid a Glock and an ammo clip under the leaves of her bed. Picking up the other handgun and the AR-15, she left the cave and began the walk to freedom. An hour into the walk, she spotted what had to be the highest peak around and headed straight for it. Having been delayed with stops for snacks, rest, and bathroom breaks, she didn't arrive until late morning. She found a grassy spot and sat down, removed the backpack, and took a long drink of water before surveying the countryside.

CHAPTER SEVENTY FIVE

Adam felt cautiously optimistic when they left the motel before dawn. After breakfast at a local restaurant in Leander, they drove in three vehicles to Lago Vista. He, Keith, and Jim each drove pre-planned routes within a ten-mile radius of the sprawling little town. Mac's job was to ride with Jim and monitor Ivan's computer and the surveillance camera with microphone in his office. An hour later, they gathered in a Lowe's Store parking lot and discussed the situation.

"David can't make it until this afternoon," he told them. "He's in court this morning, but he'll be here as soon as he can. John is on his way."

"No hurry anyway, we have no idea where to look. This is frustrating. Nothing new, I take it, Mac?"

"Ivan is in his office. It's early there, but as soon as he got in he called his man here. I didn't get a location, but this is a good sign."

"I don't like our tactical disadvantage," Keith said. "We need weapons, and we need information."

They were considering various strategies when John arrived.

"Hey, look who's here," he said as his brother pulled into the lot. He introduced him to the others and brought him up to speed on the situation. While Mac kept his eyes glued to his laptop, the other four racked their brains trying to figure out how to even begin looking for the house Mary was being held in.

"Mac, anything new?" he asked. "We're getting nowhere."

"As a matter of fact, yes. I heard another conversation. There's good news and bad. The bad news is Ivan's men are out looking for Mary."

"And the good news?" he asked.

"Well, we may have a location for the house."

"That's not good news," he said. "that's great news. How'd you find it?"

"Ivan told his contact that he'd 'strap those guys to that old windmill and use them for target practice if she gets away.' I thought I'd look at satellite imagery for windmills near houses within driving distance of Lago Vista. They aren't easy to spot because they don't have a big footprint, but they're tall and their shadows are a giveaway. I found several and narrowed those down to the best two possibilities. Both are ranches on roads with a drainage ditch next to a fence on one side of the property and rugged terrain on the other. I got addresses and looked up the owners. One belongs to a young couple with kids, and the other belongs to an elderly man who now lives in a nursing home in Austin. I'm guessing that's the one. It butts up against the Balcones, as Adam thought. It's worth a shot, and I say we check it out."

"Let's split up and check them both out," Keith said.

"Great work, Mac, we may have caught a break. So, show us where these places are."

They studied the map on Mac's laptop, concentrating on the terrain surrounding the elderly man's property. With trees bordering the ranch on the east and west, the only way off the property in a truck, other than through the main gate, was through the fence into the wilderness area north of the house. They split into two groups. Adam and his brother John visited the young couple's house and ruled it out. They drove to the vacated house and parked well up the road from the main gate behind the other two cars. Mac informed them that Keith and Jim had found the house empty and were looking for a break in the fence.

"I see them," he said.

"And I think I see a busted fence post on the north line," John added, having spotted the damage through the scope on his .22 rifle. "Looks like they're heading back."

"That's it," Keith said when he and Jim returned. "We found an I.V. stand and other medical equipment in a back bedroom. This has to be it. You're a genius, Mac."

"Yeah, and we found where Mary broke through the fence on the north side of the property," Jim added.

"Yeah, she's on the run."

"So, do we bust in there and follow Mary's tracks, or go around and backtrack this direction?" he asked.

"Two sets of tracks lead through the barbed wire fence," Keith answered. "Ivan's men are already trailing her. I believe they'd spot us, and we probably don't have the firepower to take them on. I say we go around to the other side of this place and come back in this direction. We'll either find Mary or catch them by surprise and take them out. Mac, can we do that?"

"I see a road about five miles north of here. It may be a dirt or gravel road by the looks of it."

"That's good," Keith said. "We don't want a lot of traffic anyway. Let's saddle up."

They drove to a spot north of the refuge and pulled off the dirt road onto a wide, flat area that Mac determined was due north of the ranch. Keith assessed the situation and devised their plan.

"We're about four miles north of the ranch house. Mary is somewhere in between. Mac will stay here and coordinate communications from John's truck, and he'll meet David when he arrives. The rest of us will work our way south on foot and find her. We may encounter hostiles, in which case our only weapons are John's service revolver and his .22 varmint rifle. But we also have the element of surprise if we stay quiet and watch our step."

He listened as Keith gave a quick tutorial on stealth maneuvering and how to stay inconspicuous while moving through the woods. Mac manned the radio comm controls and tested everyone's headsets. He confirmed a good satellite signal and said he'd be able to continue monitoring the camera in Ivan's office on his laptop. He also offered to get his drone in the air and put it through its paces. He explained that the UAV was a pet project he'd worked on in his ample spare time but hadn't fully field-tested yet. Keith said he wanted to keep their presence undetected by Ivan's men as long as possible, but if they made a sweep through the area and reached the house without finding Mary, they'd launch the drone.

John gave the rifle to Keith and kept his revolver.

Keith and Jim fanned out to the east while John and Adam moved out to the west. They covered nearly a mile of territory along their line. The march southward commenced.

CHAPTER SEVENTY SIX

✛

A jet airplane in the distance caught her attention. She followed its path and determined it to be on approach for a landing. While watching the plane, she spotted a patch of blue on the ground about a mile away. Bluebonnets. Gorgeous. A few minutes later, a second jet streaked across the sky. Definitely an airport over there. Don't see any roads or houses. What is this place? State Park? Balcones Canyonlands, maybe? And the airport is Bergstrom? Two jets in ten minutes—that has to be a city. She turned on the phone and waited. What's this? A signal? Oh, thank God. Finally. She touched the phone app and punched in 911. A message appeared that read "Network and data usage suspended. Please contact service provider." Seriously? Great, I just sent them an invitation to come and get me. She flung the phone as far over the other side of the hill as she could, then picked up her gear and took off, heading north again.

A faint whirring buzz in the distance, a sound unlike the ones that came from the helicopter and the ATV, stopped her. A higher frequency engine made the noise, which came from above. The pattern it made suggested that another methodical search was underway. She pointed the binoculars toward the sound and spotted a drone. She scampered down from the peak and hid behind the first shrub she found, a sumac that barely covered her outline. The buzz moved toward her position and circled overhead. She kept still until a sharp pain caused her to double over before she could catch herself. She grabbed her bloated belly and winced, then moved back behind the shrub. Too late. The drone stopped circling. It descended to within thirty feet of her and remained stationary. Now what do I do? Make a run for it? I can't outrun that thing. Give up? What choice do I have? She figured she had a few minutes before anyone would reach her there, but if she couldn't lose the drone, it wouldn't make any difference. But I can't give up. I can make a break for the cave if I can get that down. Glad that she'd brought the AR-15 along, she reached for it and took aim.

*

Their line had advanced about a mile south when Jim reported that he'd seen a drone in the air to his southwest. They each ducked behind cover to avoid being spotted and then watched as it circled high overhead a half-mile away.

"Mac, that isn't yours, is it?" Keith asked.

"Negative."

"Is yours ready to launch?"

"It can be in two minutes."

"Get it ready, and stand by."

"Roger that."

They watched the worrisome flying machine soar and

swoop as it appeared to scan the area. It descended and circled over one spot, then hovered in position.

"They've found something," Keith said. "Mac. About a mile and a half due south of your position. Go look."

*

She heard another sound, one not too different from the buzz coming from the drone hovering overhead. Another one? A second drone approached and moved to a position at the same altitude and ten feet behind the first one. Great, now I have two to shoot. Fine. She took aim at the one in front as it moved lower and to her right. That's it, come on down, closer, come on. The second drone followed the first, remaining behind it. Takes two of you, eh? Then she saw a beam of light from the second drone shining onto the first one. A laser? Thin, wispy smoke wafted from the middle section of the one in front, dispersed by the whirling blades, until she heard the snapping sound of breaking plastic and watched it plunge to the ground. What the...? The remaining drone flew directly upward for about two hundred feet and hovered, rotating through two revolutions before returning, only she was no longer there. She'd moved to a nearby rock and crouched behind it.

*

Mac had launched his baby and sent it straight south, finding his prey nearly stationary above a hillside. He'd closed in on it from behind and informed the others that the unknown drone hovered about twenty feet above someone hiding behind a small tree.

"That's got to be Mary, let's go get her," he said.

480

"Hold on," Keith said. "And keep your voice down. Mac, can you identify?"

"Not yet. He or she is crouched behind a tree. The drone is descending and moving left; looks like it's trying to get a better angle to see its target. I'm moving down and behind it again. The hunter is now the prey. All right, let's see if this works,"

"See if what works?" Keith asked.

"Laser. I'm firing it into the back of this thing. Smoke is rising and…and…down it goes. One enemy drone bites the dust."

"You shot it down?" Keith asked.

"Melted some plastic, maybe fried a circuit board. Either way, it's out of the sky."

"That's good, but the bad guys have to be on their way. Let's get there before they do. Mac, can you look around and see what's coming?"

"On my way."

The quadcopter ascended hundreds of feet vertically and scanned the landscape.

"I don't see anything, but the laser must have sapped my power because the battery needs recharging. I'll swap it, but I want to see if I can communicate with Mary first, if that's her. And…yes. Guys, that's Mary. And she looks mad. She's pointing a rifle at me. Or my drone, that is."

"She's armed?" Keith asked. "Awesome, that helps the odds. Let's move out, boys."

Mac hit the three-sixty button twice to try to get her attention with flips and avoid bullets fired at his UAV. He then made a series of arcing maneuvers while remaining in front of her.

"What are you doing, Mac," Adam asked, stopping for a second to watch the maneuverings of his drone from a distance. "Is that thing out of control?"

"Negative. I'm trying to figure out a way to let her know we're friendly before she shoots me. Okay, let's try something else here."

*

Mac thought he had enough battery power left to make an attempt at getting Mary to realize she had help. It would require making his drone vulnerable to her skill with a rifle, however, and that put him in a dilemma. It may be better to have eyes in the sky than risk it being shot in order to comfort Mary. With power draining away every second, he had to make a quick decision.

"Look, pal," Mary said. "I don't know why you zapped the other one, but I can't take chances with you. Sorry, nothing personal."

Her trigger finger squeezed slightly, then stopped. The drone had closed in on her and had done two three-sixty flips right in front of her. It then made back and forth curves in the air as though tracing the arc of a pendulum bob. Do I shoot, or is that a message? It stopped moving and hovered nearly motionless, as though giving itself up. Then she heard the noise. Music? She heard it repeat the same electronic notes. I know that melody, "The Eyes of Texas." From a drone? She lowered her aim, and when she did, it went up two feet and came back down the same distance, repeating the movement three times. Then it played the music again. That has to be a message, but it's so crazy. She moved forward a step and mouthed the

482

question, "who are you." It did a flip. Hmmm. Does that mean continue? All right. She then mouthed, "police." It flew a few feet sideways and returned, making the same horizontal movements twice more. That must mean no. Keith? Oh, be still my heart, please be. She mouthed, "Keith." It flew up and down three times and played the Eyes of Texas again. Tears welled up in her eyes as she patted her heart. She mouthed, "Oh, thank God." It did a flip. More? Uh, oh. Adam? She mouthed his name and got the up-and-down movement that meant "yes." With a questioning look on her face, she spread her arms and held her hands facing upwards, then pointed to her belly. She mouthed the word "who?", then collapsed in pain. She recovered and stood again, holding her midsection. She mouthed the word "hurry." The drone did another up-and-down movement and flew straight upward, hovered a moment, then descended to the east where she lost sight of it behind a hilltop.

*

"Keith, she knows you're here."

"Awesome, Mac. We're on our way."

"Adam, she knows you're here too, and she wants to know how she got pregnant."

"Tell her it wasn't me."

"Sorry, no time, I have to get my bird back before it dies. And by the way, she says 'hurry.' She looks like she may be having a baby today."

He flew it upwards three hundred feet and scanned the area again.

"Two ATVs headed in her direction," Mac warned.

"Two men each with weapons. You guys need to hurry it up."

His drone fell like a rock and took a course straight at the lead vehicle, dodging trees and hills and then whizzed by the driver's head. He flew it straight up and orbited directly overhead to assess the results. The ATV must have swerved sharply to avoid the drone because it had flipped onto its side and slid into a tree with the two riders on the ground nearby. The second vehicle screeched to a stop next to the downed ATV. The two men aboard helped the first pair to their feet, but not without difficulty. Both appeared groggy. One limped, but the other couldn't stay upright, he sat on the ground and held his head.

"Bought you boys some time, it looks like one of the ATVs is disabled, but I'm out of power and have to return to base. Good luck."

"Thanks, Mac," Keith said. "Get back in the air when you can."

"Two minutes to swap batteries, then I'll join you as soon as I can."

CHAPTER SEVENTY SEVEN

With renewed hope, Mary strapped on the backpack, grabbed the rifle, and descended the hill toward the cave. She figured she had the firepower to protect herself in it until Keith came to the rescue. Moving at what seemed like a snail's pace, she reached level ground and made it to a stand of trees. She found a thicket of junipers to hide in and rest. Listening intently for her captors, she recognized a familiar noise— an ATV. Behind her, probably headed for the spot where the drone went down. She peered through the trees and spotted the four-wheeler sliding to a stop at the bottom of the hill she'd just left. Two men jumped off, and with guns drawn, charged up the hill. She waited for them to reach the top and then took aim at the ATV gas tank with the AR-15. The bullet found its mark, and fuel flowed freely. A second shot and the vehicle burst into flames. The two men fired in her direction, forcing her out of the trees and looking for something to hide behind. She headed for a boulder, and, hearing an odd noise and feeling a sharp pain, reached for her abdomen. She heard further shots, but they were of a different caliber and direction. The men on the hill stopped shooting at her and turned their fire in the opposite direction. A firefight. Keith?

The pain stung like a needle. A contraction? Is that what they feel like? She soothed her belly with a hand rub and felt moisture. Blood? Was I shot? She lifted her hand and saw the bright red color. She slid her hand under her shirt and probed the injury. A puncture wound, oozing blood. How far is the cave? Oh, God. The baby. Was he hit? "Keith, get here quick, please."

*

Keith and John exchanged fire with the two men who'd hidden behind rocks on the hill Mary had vacated. Adam and Jim watched helplessly. The four were forced to retreat, however, when their ammo dwindled and two more men arrived on their left and opened fire. They ducked for cover and waited. Meanwhile, Mac had his drone back in the air.

"Keith, I see two on the hill to your south hiding behind rocks, and two more fifty yards east of them hiding behind trees. And uh-oh, bad news, two more are coming on an ATV, two hundred yards out."

"They're coming from the east?"

"Affirmative."

"Understood. Heard from David?"

"He called John's radio ten minutes ago, says he's close."

"Call him back and tell him we're outnumbered, it's time to call in the troops."

"Do you see Mary?"

"Negative. I'll fly over that way."

"Guys," Adam said. "I can't wait. I have to go find her."

"All right. If Mac tells you to hide, though, take cover. Got it?"

"Got it."

"Okay, Adam, head west a hundred yards to get around a big hill, then go south," Mac instructed. "She's likely moving west or south. When I find her, you shouldn't be too far away. The others will try to hold off these clowns as long as possible."

"Good luck, guys," he said, turning to run.

"Adam," Keith said. "Keep your head down."

He took off running like he'd never run before. A moment later, Mac's call stopped him cold.

"Uh, oh. I've found her, but she's having a hard time moving, clutching her stomach, and I see blood on the front of her shirt. She may be having the baby. Adam, where are you?"

"Past that hill, moving south."

"She's a hundred yards south of where we first spotted her. Hold on, she's looking at me. Now she's pointing at her belly. I don't think it's the baby; she may have been shot."

At that, he took off again, making a beeline in her direction, taking him near the two shooters on the hill. Keith crawled up the rock face he'd hidden behind and settled on a ledge. He spotted a shooter pointing a rifle in Adam's direction. He aimed the .22 at him and fired, hitting him in the shoulder. The man collapsed, writhing in pain. Adam continued sprinting while the injured man's partner and the other two began firing back at Keith, who'd ducked back behind the rock face.

"The third ATV has arrived, guys," Mac announced. "The riders are talking with the two on the hill. They're leaving now, and, looks like they're heading in Mary's direction."

"How close?" Keith asked.

"A hundred yards from her last position, but I've lost sight of her."

When the ATV passed a stand of junipers and approached a large oak tree, Adam stepped out from behind it and swung a thick tree branch he'd found on the ground at the head of the driver and connected. The ATV spun out of control and flipped onto its side, sliding along the hardpan a good twenty yards. Both men had been thrown from the vehicle. One didn't move. The other scrambled to his feet and staggered away. He caught him and delivered a second blow across his upper back. The man fell hard, moaning but not moving. He pulled the injured man's belt through the loops of his pants and wrapped it around his wrists, pulling it tight and latching the buckle. He repeated the process with the unconscious ATV driver, then sprinted toward Mary's last known position.

"Wow, Adam, nice," Mac said. "Two more bogies out of action. I'll keep an eye on them."

"Where's Mary?" he asked.

"Sorry, I don't see her, but I'm looking. Keith, David is two minutes out. And reinforcements are on the way."

"Tell him to call for a Medevac. Mary may be hurt."

"Copy. Sorry, Adam, still don't see her anywhere. I

need a battery change soon. I'll take one more pass and bring it home. I can be back out in two."

*

Mac had swapped batteries in his drone and sent it back out when he heard the vehicles approaching.

"Hooah. The cavalry's here, boys," he reported. "An unmarked car with a whip antenna and flashing lights and two State Police cars just showed up."

He eased himself out of John's truck and waved at the officers, keeping his hands above his head.

"David Garrett?"

"Yes. Who are you?"

"Todd Starnes. Adam is looking for Mary. Your brother John and two others are pinned down about a hundred yards south of here. I count four guys, but one's hurt. Adam took out two others who'd gone after Mary. Want to look? I have a UAV overhead."

"Show me."

He pointed to the positions of the two pairs of shooters on his monitor.

"And that's Keith there. He's Mary's brother, active duty. And that's Jim. Jim is ex-military; we served together. John is over that hill a ways, and out of view. They're down to one or two rounds. I have an extra headset, want to talk to John?"

"I do, but a drone? Comm gear? Who…Never mind, we'll talk later. Yeah, let me have it."

"Okay, bro," David said through the headset mic. "What did you get yourself into this time? I take it these aren't ordinary poachers. Where's Adam?"

"He went to find Mary; she may be wounded," John replied.

"All right, let's wrap this up. What do you suggest?"

"Keith, what do you suggest?" John asked, redirecting the question.

"David Garrett, Keith Walsh here. So glad you made it. How many are with you? And how are they armed?"

"Full tactical gear, Kevlar vests, we're ready."

"All right. Send one with a rifle west a hundred yards and south about a mile. There's a ridge he can climb and look down on their position."

"The he's a she, by the way, Tanya, and she's a great shot."

"Happy to have her. Get her moving."

"On my way," she said. Mac had synced their comm units, allowing everyone to communicate.

"I also have Mark Harris here with me."

"Okay. You two move east a hundred yards and then south a half-mile. That'll put you on their flank. Mac will provide a lookout in case they move."

"On our way. Chopper coming for Mary. How is she?"

"I don't know, I haven't found her yet," Adam said, with a degree of panic in his voice.

"Adam, keep looking," David said. "We'll have these guys pinned down in a crossfire shortly. We'll be there to help real soon. I promise."

"Glad you're here, Dave, but hurry it up."

"Will do. Go find Mary."

*

David and Harris worked their way to the side and a little behind the other two shooters, finding cover behind a large boulder.

"You, men, we have you surrounded," David shouted. "Throw down your weapons and come out with your hands on your heads."

"I don't think so," one of them said, firing a round in response.

They returned fire. The partner of the man Keith wounded turned his rifle in their direction also, but fell to the ground, a bullet sent his way from Tanya. He never knew what hit him. Tanya ran to the hill and handcuffed the dead man's injured partner. He screamed in pain.

"Oh, I see you're wounded," Tanya said. "Sorry about that, but it wasn't me. Hang tight; an ambulance is on the way. You'll live."

The officer turned to her right and pulled the dead man away from the rock he'd tried to hide behind. She found the two men still firing at David and Harris in her scope, and put one of them in the crosshairs and squeezed. When he fell, the last man standing threw down his rifle and surrendered.

"Hands on your head," David shouted. "Walk this way."

The man complied and was handcuffed. The firefight was over.

"Mac, anything else out there?" Keith asked.

"Negative. You guys okay?"

"We're good," Keith said. "Great work, everybody. Thanks, David. I'll go find Mary. Mac, have you heard from Adam?"

"Negative, nothing for ten or fifteen minutes."

"Ah, that's not good. Can you do a quick scan of the area here and then send the drone to his last position for a look?"

"Roger that."

The sound of helicopter rotor backwash in the distance alerted them to the Medevac's imminent arrival.

"There's a clearing not far to the southeast of her last position," John said, recalling what he could about the area from previous visits. "Tell them to set down there."

After directing the chopper to the landing zone, David surveyed the wounded. "What's their status?"

"We have one dead," John answered. "Another has a serious chest wound. A third has a bullet in his shoulder. He'll live, but the one shot in the chest needs a hospital. Jim is working on him now. Two more with unknown status. Adam clocked an ATV driver with a tree branch and caused them to flip into the ground. They're maybe a hundred yards due south."

"Call an ambulance. The Medevac EMTs can treat them, but Mary gets the chopper. Mark, find the two guys Adam took out and secure them. Let me know what shape they're in."

CHAPTER SEVENTY EIGHT

Adam saw movement at the edge of a small clearing just as a figure disappeared behind a thicket of brush. Was that Mary? Or…? He ran toward a hill that overlooked the area and worked his way to the top. Staying behind the cover of a large boulder, he peered around it to see if he could identify the person leaning against a live oak. That has to be Mary. He moved to his right and partly down the hill to get a better look. When he emerged from behind a rocky outcropping, the figure was gone. He surveyed the area and listened for footfalls. Nothing. He crept down the hill, pausing every few steps. When he reached the live oak, he noticed a red splotch on the ground below it. No sooner had he realized it might be blood and that Mary's situation might be dire than he heard the command to freeze and get on the ground. A woman's voice. Mary's. He turned and saw a gun pointed at him.

"I said fr…Adam?" Mary yelled before crumpling to the ground.

"Mary!" He ran to her and sat her up, cradling her in

his arms. "Mary, it's over. You're safe. How bad are you hurt?"

"I've been shot. In the stomach. And I'm about to have a baby."

"A Medevac is here. They'll get you to a hospital. How bad is it? Can I see?"

She pulled her shirt up to expose the wound. "It's not me I'm worried about. This baby may be hurt. Maybe hurt bad."

"The baby will be fine. You'll be fine. Can you wait here while I go get the medics?"

"No. This baby is coming. Now." She moaned and grabbed her belly. "Do something."

"Right here? In the woods?"

She panted rapidly, then relaxed. "I need to have this baby and see how badly hurt he is. There's a cave just down the hill there. Take me. Quick."

He took the Glock from her hand and snugged it between his waistband and his back, slung the backpack over his shoulder, then helped her to her feet. "Wow. You're big. Wanna race?" The look on her face answered his question. "I don't mean now; let's have the baby first."

"Adam, shut up."

"Right." He picked up the AR-15 and helped her down the hill. "Where is this place?"

They reached the rise in the hillside and went around it to the cave's entrance.

"There," she said, pointing at a juniper.

"I see it. Nicely hidden. But is it big enough…"

She'd gone into another bout of moaning and belly rubbing. Feeling helpless, he tried contacting Mac, but the

494

headset only put out a high-pitched hiss. Fiddling with the controls didn't help. Still rubbing her belly, Mary straightened and led him inside. She sat on the edge of the cubby she'd slept in the last two nights, letting her feet dangle a moment before laying back on the leaves.

"Give me some water. Please."

"Nice place you got here," he said, handing her a bottle. "A little food, water, a nice bed. And did you steal those guns?"

"Confiscated."

"There is something we need to discuss."

"How I got pregnant."

"Well, yes, let's start there. Just how did this happen? You have a boyfriend in LA?"

She reached under the leaves and pulled out the Glock she'd stashed before leaving that morning. She tapped the end of the barrel in the palm of her other hand. "I'd be careful about now, if I were you."

She gave him a look he couldn't interpret. Nor did he want to.

"Of course I don't have a boyfriend in LA. I hoped you'd know. Did you do this? No, I can't believe that." She handed him the gun and appeared to be in pain again. "This is not fun. Oh, it hurts."

"What can I do?"

"Take that sheet and tear off a bandage. Or see what's in the first aid kit I brought. See if you can tape something over this hole in my stomach. The bleeding has slowed, but I may be about to bust it open again."

He rummaged through the kit and found what he needed. He splashed water on the wound and dabbed at it with a piece of the sheet. "Looks clean." He dried the area and applied antibiotic ointment, then put a piece of gauze over it, followed by several strips of tape to hold it in place. "That won't last long, but you're right, the bleeding has slowed. Let's worry about the babies now."

"Babies? What do you mean, babies? There's more than one? How do you know?"

"Try three. And I know because I was with you in the hospital for months on end."

"Three? Oh, goodness. Oh, man, another contraction."

When it passed, and she rested again, she asked who the father was, and just how did they find her in the middle of Texas. Before he could answer, she felt an overwhelming urge to push. The look on her face told him the arrival of the three boys was imminent. She moaned, then yelled, then assumed the birthing position.

"All right, Adam, here we go."

She strained and pushed and then relaxed. "False alarm, I guess, but he's coming. Don't go anywhere."

He laughed. "I'm not leaving you. Ever."

"Who did you say the father was?"

"I didn't because I don't know. I guess, ultimately, it's God. Mary, you're having J-cell babies. Uh, oh. There's that look again. Seriously. I—"

"Never mind, he's coming. For real."

"Okay. So push."

She did. And cried. And pushed some more. Out came number one. Adam held him in his hands and inspected him closely. "I don't see signs of an external injury." He wiped him with one of the pieces of bed sheet he'd prepared and reexamined him. "Yep, he looks good, and he's breathing nicely. Let's get ready for the next one." He ripped two strips off the end of the cloth he used to clean the newborn and used them to tie off the umbilical cord. He took the knife from Mary's backpack and cut the cord between the strips.

"Hurry, Adam."

"Ah, I see a head. Okay, I'll lay this one down next to you, just don't roll over on him." Two minutes later, number two came out. He got the same treatment as number one. Finally, number three entered the world. Mary looked relieved. Tired, thirsty, but relieved. She held the first two babies and smiled.

"Aw, they're adorable." She stroked their cheeks and spoke softly to them. "They are…amazing. Now, what do you mean they're J-cell babies? Or did I hear you wrong?"

"You heard right. You're looking at clones of Jesus. But right now, I need to tend to Number Three here. He has a hole in his leg."

"Oh, no. How bad is it?"

'I can feel a bullet. It isn't bleeding too badly, thank God. Guess it's been what, twenty minutes since you were shot?"

"Something like that. Maybe more."

"Well, he needs a doctor. You need a doctor. I'll see if I can contact Mac and let him know where we are. But this headset may be broken. I'll have to go outside and look for them. First things first, though. All right, you little hero, let's get a bandage on that, okay little guy? Then we'll get you to a hospital. You know, you may have saved your mother's life." He looked down at the precious newborn. "So, I already love you, Number Three."

"His mother?" she asked. "Wow, that's going to take some getting used to."

"All right, hold this one too, and I'll go find the others. They can't be too far away."

He ran outside and looked around but saw nothing. Then he heard it. A drone in flight overhead. He ran back up the hill a short distance and got into its line of sight. The drone dropped and hovered in front of Adam, then played music. He grinned and waved at the camera, then made a rocking motion with his arms overlapped near his waist to indicate a baby. He held up three fingers and then both thumbs up. The drone did a three-sixty and played more notes. He gave him a "follow me" wave and ran back to the cave.

*

By the time the others found the cave, Adam had converted it from a labor and delivery room to a nursery. He'd wrapped the babies in pieces of bed sheet while Mary talked to and caressed each of them. He kept an eye on the wounds in Mary's abdomen and Number Three's leg.

"Am I glad to see you guys," he said to Keith, David, and John. "But especially you." He shook the EMT's hand and pointed to his patients. The medic checked Mary's vital signs and hung an I.V. for her, then examined the babies.

"The color on this one isn't good," the EMT said. He set up an I.V. for him too and had Adam hold the fluids. "Must have lost blood. These little fellas don't have a lot to begin with. Good thing you got to him when you did. How did he get hurt?"

"He was shot," Mary said. "Probably a ricochet. I remember hearing rocks fly up off the ground in front of me and then a stinging in my gut."

"Poor little guy," the medic said, feeling around his calf muscle below the entrance wound. "Not the way you want to start out your life, but he may have saved one of the other boys, maybe you too, ma'am. We have us a little hero here."

"My words exactly," Adam said.

"Ah, there it is, a hard lump. I think we'd better get you to the hospital and get that piece of lead out. What do you say? And our new mother, Mary, is it?"

"It is."

"You have an abdominal wound? Can I see it?"

"Uh, yeah, but first, I need some privacy, please?"

"Yeah," Adam said. "Everybody out."

"You too, Bub. We aren't married yet."

"Oh for goodness' sake. What just happened here? Do you think I did it with my eyes closed?"

"Out."

"Come on, big bro," David said, laughing with the others. "Let's give them the room."

The EMT cleaned and re-bandaged Mary's wound and prepared the four for transport to an Austin hospital. He hollered for the others to return so he could assign duties for loading his patients onto the chopper.

"I take it you're the dad?" the medic asked Adam.

"Yeah, Adam, explain who the dad is," Mary said.

"Uh, well, no, I'm not the dad. But she is my fiancée. It's a bit of a long story."

"Well, you can tell it to me on the flight. You're going

with me. My partner is tending a wounded man who shouldn't be left alone, and I don't think an ambulance will get here before we leave. So, you get to take his place. By the way, you did a great job here. Have you had training?"

"I have. Neighbor's calves. Not with people, though."

"Well, really good work. Okay, guys, I'll go get a transporter for the little guy with the bullet in his leg and a stretcher for his mommy. Maybe the stretcher first. I'll need two of you to carry one baby each. You decide. I'll be right back."

"Hey, everybody," Adam said. "Let's get a picture for Mac and Jim. That okay, Mary?"

"Heck no. My hair is a mess, and I don't have my makeup on. No way."

They each stared at her in disbelief. She couldn't keep a straight face very long, and the grin gave the ruse away. "Okay, get the picture, but make it snappy. I need to get to a hospital."

John produced his new iPhone and set it up. He offered to print the best one and send it out as a Christmas card. There were the usual jokes about the lack of three wise men in the group. And just where were their gifts? And the animals?

"Hey, you guys, come see me in the hospital, okay? I want to talk to all of you and thank each of you personally. Even you, Adam."

"I'm going with you, remember?"

"Oh, yeah. Keith? Give your sister a hug. Can you come to the hospital?"

"Uh, we need to decompress a little, been a long day."

He kissed her forehead and hugged her neck. "I think I'll grab some chow and crash at a local motel, then come see you in the morning after things have settled down. That okay, sis?"

"Of course. David? John?"

"I need to get back to San Angelo," David said. "But I'll keep in touch and get back here as soon as I can."

John said he also had business to tend to but likewise promised to come back soon.

"That's fine, guys," Adam said. "We have a lot of catching up to do anyway. We'll get started tonight. Hey, can one of you call Mom and Dad?"

They both said they would.

"All right, you guys, come see us when you can," Mary said. "I want to thank each of you in person. Now get me out of here. Please."

The EMT returned with a stretcher and asked the guys to help load Mary onto it. They carried her to the helicopter and lifted her up and onto the supports where the medic secured the straps. He grabbed the infant transport incubator and took it to the cave, then placed the injured baby inside. He attached the I.V. to the hook mounted on top, tucked a small blanket around him, and pronounced him ready for travel. "Now, if my volunteers can bring the other babies, we'll be ready to go," he said, then left for the chopper. A rough and rugged Special Forces soldier and a state trooper each carried tiny, newborn babies as though they were priceless Ming vases. The EMT laid them both in a wicker basket with a pillow at the bottom. He'd taken it from a nurse's station on his way out of the hospital when he'd heard there might be more than one neonate to transport. He worked blankets in and around the infants to cushion them from the basket sides and from each other. Adam's only job was to hold that basket and make sure they didn't fall out. Mary appeared alert and stable. Adam had a tight grip on the basket. When they each gave a thumbs up, the EMT signaled to the pilot that they were ready for departure. The flight captain raised the collective and increased throttle. They lifted off, disappearing through a cloud into the heavens.

CHAPTER SEVENTY NINE

✢

"Well, here we are again," Adam said, holding her hand and stroking her cheek. "You, lying in a hospital bed, sleeping, and me sitting next to you, worrying. The doctors say you're fine, though, so I'm a lot less worried today than I was the last time you were in a hospital. They say, for what you've been through, you're in remarkable shape. I told them it's a testament to the condition you were in before this happened. All that running I made you do. And that you're young. I wish you didn't sleep so much; I want to talk. Then again, I understand. You've been through quite an ordeal, so we'll talk when you've rested."

He went downstairs to the lobby and made phone calls to his brothers. They'd both filed reports on the incident in the Balcones Canyonlands and gone home, promising to call later and get back to see them when they could. He also phoned Keith to tell him Mary was resting comfortably and that the babies were fine. He and Jim and Mac were on their way to a local motel after a steak dinner and would be at the hospital the next morning.

He returned to Mary's room and made himself comfortable in the recliner next to her bed. A knock on the door woke him. The face was familiar, but he had to rub his eyes and refocus on the visitor.

"Jill? Sweet-J? Is that you?"

"Hello, Adam."

"What, how—?"

"You look good."

"And you look…you look extraordinary. How are you?"

"Couldn't be better. You?"

"I don't know. Things are a little fuzzy," he said, glancing at Mary before looking back at his childhood sweetheart. "Where have you been? Seems like a long time since I saw you last. So, you want to go fishing or something?"

"Fishing? No thanks."

"But you always wanted to go fishing."

"That's because it was with you, dummy. I never liked it that much."

"Oh, sorry. Well, what do you want to do? Come in, have a seat, let's catch up on things."

"I can't. Adam, I need to tell you, I have a new love interest."

"Is that why you left?"

"No, you were my only love. I so much wanted to stay with you; it just didn't work out."

"Who is this new love interest? Do I know the guy?"

"You do. You've known him for a long time."

"Oh? What's his name?"

"He's standing next to you."

504

"There's no one in here."

"Take a look."

He turned his head and saw a figure that also looked familiar but at the same time like no one else he'd ever seen. "Do I know you?"

"You should. I've known you your whole life."

"What's your name?"

"Let's just say I am who I am."

His eyes grew wide. "You're…"

"I am He."

"Right here in this room?"

"Where else would I be?"

"Well, why are you here?"

"Why are you here?"

"I'm here because Mary is here. She needs me. I love her and want to protect her. And I like being with her."

"That's exactly why I'm here. I love you both and want to be with you both. By the way, great job rescuing her. Well done."

"Uh, thanks. I had lots of help."

"That's how it almost always works. Nice job with the boys, too, though I wasn't worried about them. You know me, I don't worry much."

"Because…"

"That's right. They're under a whole different system of protection. Wait until you see them grow up. They'll be the spitting image of me."

"Well, duh, aren't they clones?" he asked, feeling more comfortable with Jill's new love interest.

"Yes, and they'll be such handsome little devils. Why are you grinning?"

"Three reasons. First, the word 'devils' seems out of place, somehow. Second, you have a sense of humor I didn't know about. And, third, weren't you supposed to have been nothing special back then? Having no 'form or comeliness,' no 'beauty that we should desire you?' If you weren't anything special back then, why should the boys be now?"

"You didn't know I had a sense of humor? Seriously? Did you hear the one about me, Peter, and Moses playing golf?"

"Yes."

"Okay. Well, how about Moses, Peter, and I walk into a bar."

"Heard it."

"Here's one I bet you haven't heard. What did Martin Luther say when I asked him if he wanted to spend eternity without me?"

"I assume he said 'no.'"

"He said, 'Hell no.'"

"Hmm. Oh, I get it. I get it. Your sense of humor is rather dry. Anyway, speaking of the boys, how am I, uh, we, that is," he said, motioning toward Mary, "how are we supposed to raise them? They aren't like other babies. They don't cry at all. Why is that?"

"Crying is something done in the other kingdom. It's a throwback to babies selfishly looking out for themselves. These boys aren't selfish. They will be unlike anything you've ever experienced."

"Exactly. I don't think we're qualified to raise them; they're too special."

"Who should raise them if not you? Where are the perfect parents?"

506

"Abilene."

"Yours are special; I'll give you that."

"Back to the boys. How do we raise them?"

"One day at a time. Don't worry. I'll be there to help."

"Like all those other times you were there to help?"

"Exactly."

"Lucky me."

"Are you complaining?"

"Yes. Will it do any good?"

"No."

"That's what I thought. Say, before you go, tell me. How did life on earth begin? And is my theory about Adam and Eve anywhere close to what actually happened?"

"Why do you want to know?"

"I'm naturally curious."

"Why else? Be honest."

"I don't want to be under an illusion of how things began. My work sort of depends on that kind of knowledge."

"And?"

"And, what? Oh, I suppose you mean I might feel smug about being the only person alive who knows exactly how life started? Do you think I would exploit that knowledge?"

"I could tell you, but I'd have to kill you."

"Wait. What? No. You're joking. You have to be. You had me there for a second. Glad to see you're enjoying your newfound sense of humor."

"Adam, did I tell you I like you?"

"You said you loved me."

"I do love you, but I also like you. You know why I like you?"

"Hmm. No. I can understand the loving part, you're supposed to do that, it's your nature. But liking someone means you enjoy spending time with them. I mean, actually enjoying it, not just putting up with…me."

"Well, for me, the two can overlap, one of the perks of being God. But I like you because you're tenacious. You don't give up. You keep coming after me. I can work with that."

"Are you kidding? I was ready to quit on you many times. Losing her," he said, pointing to Jill, "tore the heart out of my chest. And when I finally get over the worst of that, I fall in love with someone else, and then my heart gets broken again. And twice, first with the pregnancy, and then with the kidnapping. Three times if you count the coma. I'd had enough. I wanted out."

"Wanting out and even saying you want out are different than actually getting out. But you persevered—one of the things I've been working on in you—and you didn't walk away. No, Adam, you and I are friends. You know I will never leave you, and now I know you will never leave me."

He focused on the man's face. In it, he could see the best qualities he'd ever admired in others—integrity, purity, courage, strength, enthusiasm for life, only all together in the same person. And his eyes. His eyes spoke another language. One he somehow understood. As he stared into those eyes, he sensed the forming of a new and deeper bond.

"Thank you for letting me be here with you in the first place, and without feeling talked down to, or as though you were holding my weaknesses against me. And after all the times I disappointed you. And complained. So, are we good?"

"Well, one of us is."

"Ah, got me there. There is none good but…you."

"Look, if anyone ever asks you that question, if you're good, that is, tell them you're with me."

"Ah, of course. You're my righteousness. You are so interesting to talk to. Can we do this again sometime? I want to know so much more."

"I'm always here."

"Adam," Jill said, stepping into the room. "She's lovely. Has anyone ever told you she looks like me?"

"Only everyone who knew you," he said, turning to face his high school sweetheart again.

"You two make a great couple."

"So did we. So did we…"

CHAPTER EIGHTY

✛

"Huh? What?" Adam asked, rubbing his eyes.
"I asked you about breakfast. Were you snoozing?"

"No. I mean, was I? Wow, was that a dream?"

"You did seem animated in that chair."

"Yeah, I guess I dozed and had an amazing dream."

"Better not have been about another girl," she said, grinning.

"Oh no, of course…I mean, well, yes. Jill. I dreamed she came into this room."

"Well, that must have been awkward. How did you explain me?"

"I didn't have to. She…she gave me her blessing to love you."

"Oh, Adam," she said, her eyes glistening. "Seriously?"

"Yes. And, what's more, Jesus was there. Here. Right in this room."

"Why didn't you wake me up?" she asked. "I would have loved to have talked to him."

"Huh?" he asked, scratching his head. "No, wait, you

were awake. Jesus did speak to you. After he and I finished talking, he walked over to your bed. He held your hand and stroked your cheeks. Then he whispered something into your ear."

"You didn't hear what he said?"

"No, Jill was talking to me then, but right before you woke me, I saw him kiss your forehead."

She looked at him and smiled. Her expression turned more serious as she studied him.

"What?" he asked.

"What have I gotten myself into with you? I mean, I've only known you for what, two years? And look at what I've been through already."

"You? Look what you've been through? How about me? I mean, there I was, minding my own business, working on a cool discovery until you came along and turned it into, oh, what would you call it? I don't know, but if you hadn't found those chunks of tissue, none of this would have happened. We'd be living normal lives."

"So, this is my fault? You came to me first, remember? You wanted me to send your samples for carbon dating, which I did. Remember? Then you wanted me to look into that piece of tissue, which I'd put away and forgotten about. I did what you asked, Bub. So don't blame me, dirt digger."

"But did you have to be so good at what you do? And so absolutely adorable? It's your fault for making me fall in love with you."

"You got me there. So, do we blame God for this?"

"That's who I usually blame. No, no, we don't blame God. We don't blame anybody. This is life. People do crazy things. Sometimes we just get the brunt of their craziness. We have to get through times like these and not let them get the best of us."

"You don't blame God for bringing us together?"

"Good question. It's hard to imagine Him not having a role in this. I've tried to figure out things like that for a long time. I told my class that God lets the rain fall on the just and the unjust, and I think that's right. The difference is that we get better after the rain, others just get wet. Anyway, I'm happy, no, ecstatic, that you're alive and that you're here with me now. I've been waiting for this moment for so long."

"Yes, we've both been through a lot," she said. "And now look at our situation. Three boys who aren't ours but for whom we are now responsible and have to raise."

"And without the benefit of a honeymoon. I would have liked to have had some time for you and me."

"Me too, but now that you mention it, we aren't even married. Can I take it the engagement is still on?"

He stood and approached her, then kissed her passionately on the lips. "Don't read too much into that."

"Yes is only one word. Is that reading too much into it?"

"No. I mean, yes. Of course the engagement is still on. Do you want to talk about a wedding?"

"Are you kidding? Of course I do, but first, I want to know more about what happened. I don't remember anything after going to see the doctor with a fever."

"You don't remember me beating you in a three-mile race?"

"That never happened. But, I need to know what did.

512

I get the gist of it, but I need details."

"Well, I guess we have time."

He spent the next hour filling in those details for her. The picture he painted for her included the breaking of his heart by God for letting her get deathly ill, and then the devastation that hit him like a ton of bricks when he thought she'd gotten pregnant by another man. He praised her brother for his extraordinary efforts at getting to the truth of her pregnancy. He told her that her kindness to Jim and Mac had been repaid many times over, that they'd gone way above and beyond the call for her. When he described what had happened to her in Vanessa's clinic, as best as he could piece it together, she cringed.

"Do you remember any of that?"

"I think I do. I was in a fog, but I remember parts of it. Going to her office. I remember thinking she'd had way too much to drink, and yet I was the one who couldn't walk straight. And I don't know why I couldn't fight her off when she put me on the exam table. I can't believe what she…"

"We think it's how you got the uterine infection that caused the coma. The doctors said you could have died."

"It may be better that I don't remember that part. What do you think is wrong with Vanessa? How could she do something like that?"

"I wish I knew. She's a talented doctor. I'm not a psychiatrist, but, what? Money? Respect?"

"Jealousy? She was jealous of me for some reason?"

"For some reason? Are you kidding? Mary, you're much prettier than her. You have a much better personality. You're a lot smarter."

"Wait, thank you, but she's brilliant. I could tell that

talking to her at their house. No, I am not smarter than her."

"Well, no way is she smarter than you."

"Oh, you're sweet to say that. So, what happens to her?"

"Right now, we haven't made that decision."

"Why not?"

"Partly to protect the boys. Partly to protect you. Keith and I are thinking it might be best to limit the criminal fallout to the guys who kidnapped you."

"So, she gets away with it?"

"Not if you don't agree. It'll be your call."

"How hard will it be to prove she did it?"

"Well, that's another reason we haven't gone forward with our statements. We sort of took a few liberties to get the goods on her. But we do have them. We can absolutely nail her."

"I suppose Keith's career would be in jeopardy if that came out?"

"It would, yes."

"So, we hold onto it for now and let her know we're watching?"

"Exactly. It would be a second chance for her."

"And Clark, too, I suppose."

"EVI is struggling, but we haven't pulled the plug on his J-cell research yet. He got funding from a Dallas investment group for it, and I think it's what's keeping him from going under. I may let him continue under the MTA for a while, but he'll be on a tight leash, and I'm so glad you're back to help keep an eye on him. He stole our J-cells, but the human cloning was all on Vanessa. He didn't know what she was doing. No one would fault you for wanting to see her in jail. She should be."

"So, I get impregnated against my will, resulting in not just one, but three children, none of whom are mine. I get a life-threatening infection. I get shot. And I should let bygones be bygones?"

"Well, you still get me."

"I get you? That's it? That's all? You think that's worth it?"

"Keith gets to keep his job."

"Oh, well then, in that case, I'm sold."

"Only one thing left to decide, then."

"And that is?"

An RN knocked on the door and asked Mary if she was ready to nurse one of the babies.

"Oh, hi," she replied. "I'll try, but can someone show me how to do it properly? And will I have enough milk for all three?"

"We may have to supplement. I'll get you started, and I'll have our specialist stop by when she can. But you've done great up to this point. I think you're a natural. Anyway, do you want Adam to stay?"

"Heaven's no. We're not married. He'll have to wait before he sees anything."

"Once again, do you think I closed my eyes when I delivered the boys?"

"I heard about that," the nurse said.

"I suppose by now the whole world has," Mary said. "Okay, he can stay, but I want to cover up."

"We can do that. All right, I'll be right back with Number One."

"Number One?" she asked, turning to Adam. "Think we can come up with a better name for the kid?"

"Oh, I don't know, 'Number One' is growing on me."

"Yeah, I like it too," she said, grinning. "But the other two might get jealous."

"No, they won't. They'd be happy for him. That's something we'll have to get used to. These guys won't be like any other babies, ever, except for Jesus himself."

Another knock on the door interrupted their conversation.

"Hey, sis, can I come in?"

"Keith. Get in here and give me a hug."

He nodded at Adam on his way in, then hugged Mary and kissed her on the cheek.

"You look great, sis. Do you want me to run this guy out?"

"Keith, no. Don't be silly."

The nurse brought Number One into the room and instructed the gentlemen to leave.

"I'll let you back in when she's situated. Now, scoot."

When they were allowed back in, she asked about Jim and Mac.

"Downstairs, in the lobby. They said you could only have two visitors at a time."

"That's nuts," he said. "I'll be right back."

A few minutes later, he returned with the two in tow. Keith stood outside the door and signaled for them to stop.

"Ah, Number Two is in there now?" he asked.

Her brother nodded. He asked Jim and Mac to wait around the corner. When the nurse left and was out of sight, he retrieved them and brought them into Mary's room. Her face lit up on seeing them, but she excused herself from hugs until the nursing chores had ended.

"Oh, guys, thank you so much. You risked your lives for me. I'll never forget you for that. Jim, Mac, you're both awesome. Thank you."

"Aw, shucks," Mac said in a farmhand voice. "It weren't nothin'."

"Yeah, happy to help," Jim added. "Even better is how things turned out. Adam says you and the boys will be fine. That makes my day, my year, and maybe even my lifetime."

"Oh, I love you all. Adam, Keith, Jim, Mac," she said, pointing at each one in turn, unable to hide a grin. "You were there for me. And it's so great to be back…in my hospital room again. That's what I kept saying to myself the whole time I was in the coma, 'there's no place like the hospital, there's no place like'…hey, where's my little dog, Toto?"

"Nothing doing, my little pretty." the nurse said, entering the room carrying the last of the boys. "Dogs aren't allowed in this room. You'll have to settle for Number Three here. Speaking of numbers, why are there four men in this room? The limit is two. And I want it down to zero while we swap babies. Now, everyone who isn't female, git."

They got.

CHAPTER EIGHTY ONE

✠

The pastor greeted Adam and Mary, along with their respective families. Jim and Mac made the trip to LA, as well.

"Mr. and Mrs. Garrett, welcome to Los Angeles, and to our church. What a pleasure to meet the parents of this young man," he said, pointing at Adam. "He's had quite the adventure over the last two years."

"He has indeed, Pastor Smith," Alice replied. "As has Mary."

"Indeed she has," the pastor said as he put his arm around her shoulder and hugged the young woman. "It's great to see you again, Mary. We're so glad you're safe and sound. What an ordeal."

"It was, but it's over, and I'm thrilled to be back here. Thank you for praying for me."

"Certainly," he said, removing his arm and taking a step back. "So, are you the future Mrs. Garrett? Or is it Walsh-Garrett? Or Dr. Walsh? What will we call you?"

"I'm honored to take the Garrett family name, pastor. But I do still have a few hours to decide." She winked at

Adam and grinned.

"Indeed, you do. I just need to know what to say when I pronounce you two husband and wife."

"Yes, sir. So, is your daughter coming? I want her up front with JoAnne and me."

"How thoughtful. Yes, Katie will be there, and I'm sure she'd be thrilled to stand with you. JoAnne tells me their whole young adult group is going. That's their outing today."

"Well, they're all invited."

"It'll be fun, and it looks like great weather for a beach wedding. Hey, the service is about to start. I need to get inside. Oh, and our nursery is down the hall and to the left."

"Oh, that won't be necessary," she said. "These little guys will be on their best behavior."

*

Mary nuzzled Number One during the final prayer and, while kissing him, noticed movement in the balcony. The person walking toward the exit caught her completely by surprise. Handing the baby to Adam, she slipped out of the row they sat in and walked toward the rear of the church. She took a route calculated to intersect the path of the individual, apparently trying to leave. She rounded the corner of a hallway and surprised the oncoming woman, who stopped and threw a hand over her mouth.

"I'm surprised to see you here, in church. You seemed hostile to Christianity every time the subject came up. What gives?"

A tear streamed down the woman's face. She swiped

at it and rubbed it away, but another replaced it, and then another. A steady trickle of tears turned into a torrent, accompanied by loud sobs. Mary put her arm around Vanessa's shoulder and led her to a private room. Closing the door behind them, she helped her onto the overstuffed sofa and brought her a box of tissues. The distraught woman seated before her endured several moments of what appeared to be severe emotional anguish. Mary sat next to her and put a comforting hand on her shoulder.

"I…Mary, I am so sorry. What I did was, is, beyond words. I know you can't forgive me, but what I can't figure out is why you haven't had me arrested. I'm ready to go to jail. I deserve it. So, why are you delaying this?"

"It's complicated."

"No, it's really quite simple. In fact, I've thought about turning myself in if I don't hear from the police soon. I need to pay for my crime."

"Okay, we can agree that what you did deserves punishment. In fact, you could spend the rest of your life in jail for what you did. Adam and I discuss it often. Part of us wants to turn you in, but another part doesn't."

"I don't understand."

"As I said, it's complicated. We have the boys to think about. Because of who they are, we want to keep them away from the publicity that would stir up. But, I have to ask, what's happened to you? Why are you here?"

"What's happened to me? Well, start with Clark. He left me. Then there's the clinic. The building is up, but Clark doesn't seem interested in finishing it, so that dream is over."

"Wait a second. Does Clark know what you did?"

"He knows. I told him. I hoped coming clean to someone would ease my guilty conscience. It didn't, but it did drive Clark away. Now that you're here, maybe I can get this resolved one way or the other."

"I hope so. I don't want you to suffer. But, again, why are you here?"

"Well, after you were rescued and I hadn't heard from Ivan, I hoped it was all over. But it wasn't. The guilt became unbearable. I was even okay with dying because that would bring relief. One day the pastor from this church saw me standing outside, staring at the ground, so he invited me in to talk. I remembered walking around the neighborhood that afternoon, but not stopping on the sidewalk in front. I obviously did, though. We didn't talk long, and I didn't tell him much, but that night I cried myself to sleep. I came back the next day and opened up to him, and we've been meeting once a week since. It's been cathartic. Talking to him reminded me of things the sisters in high school tried to teach me. I think I'm even beginning to understand some of it. Mary, I don't laugh at you anymore. Or Adam. Or Christians. I let ambition and greed get the best of me, and it blinded me. I hit rock bottom, and I hit it hard. But, now I see again, or maybe for the first time."

"What do you see now that you didn't before?"

"For starters, I see just how utterly awful I was. I still can't believe what I did. That was evil. Pure evil. But now I also see the exact opposite. I see love. I see it in the person Pastor Smith talked about in his sermon. Sometimes I get so overwhelmed when I think of where I was and where I am now that I have to get out of there before I disturb everyone around me. Which I did today. His portrait of Christ was so beautiful that I started to cry and had to leave. But then I ran into you, and well, it's all too much. Oh, Mary, I am so sorry. I know it's asking a lot, but I think if I can somehow make things right with you, if that's even possible, I may be able to find my way out of the mental mess I'm in. Can you forgive me someday?"

"Done."

"Done? Just like that?"

"Just like that. Well, I admit I don't feel like it right now. At all. But, you've asked; it's the right thing to do; so, at this point in time my official position on the matter is that I have forgiven you. Besides, who am I to hold onto wrong done to me when I myself have been forgiven of so much?"

"Yeah, the pastor said something like that the other day, though it's hard to imagine you needing much forgiveness. You're a good woman, Mary."

"Adam explained it in a way you'll appreciate. He said the tissues we recovered from the bone shards in the whip are proof of God's love. He's made forgiveness and reconciliation with him and others possible by the suffering he went through. What a tragedy more people don't take advantage of it. Anyway, as far as I'm concerned, you and I are reconciled."

She sobbed again, tears of relief and joy rolling down her face. "I, I don't know what to say. I feel like you've given me a new lease on life."

"The One whose DNA you cloned has done that for you, not me."

"Yeah, I guess that's right. That's going to be a whole

'nother mess to work through. What was I thinking? But at the time, it was just extraordinary DNA. Now…"

"There are worse things in life besides working through your wrongs with a God who's eager to help. Oh, and, by the way, you don't have to worry about the Russian, either."

Vanessa stared at her in disbelief.

"How do you know about Ivan?"

"Adam and my brother Keith did everything they could to find me when I disappeared. They recruited two ex-soldiers and had a darned good team. How they found out about you and Ivan, or whatever his real name is, I'm not at liberty to say. He and Nina have disappeared. Our best guess is they're in hiding in Russia somewhere."

"Thank God for that. That's a relief. He was, well, he was threatening at the end. What a mistake, getting mixed up with that guy. But I did, I got greedy. I only have myself to blame. So, when do you think you'll decide? I don't know whether to sign another contract with the hospital or turn myself in to the police."

"Yes, about that. We have a proposal."

"If I can do anything, anything at all, I will. Name it."

"For starters, give me the remaining J-cell embryos and promise not to make more."

"Oh, of course, that's easy. What else?"

"Keep your job at the hospital, but we want you to volunteer your medical skills at a free clinic."

"Mary, that's a great idea. I should have thought of that. If I hadn't been so focused on myself, on my career, I might have already been doing that. Great idea, I'll do it. I'll look into it tomorrow morning."

"Good. Send us monthly reports of your hours there, and we'll hold off on filing charges. And let us know how working with those patients affects you."

"Oh, of course, absolutely. There has to be a need for a maternal medicine doctor. Thank you for that, Mary. I really wish I'd thought of it before. God, I'm so blind."

"One last thing. Come to our wedding this afternoon."

"Your wedding? Today? Aw, that's great. Congratulations, I mean it, but…I can't. Why would you want me there, anyway?"

"I want you made whole with everyone. Come early and talk to Adam and Keith. Ask their forgiveness; they'll help you through it."

"Oh, my, would that be terrific. But I don't think I could get up the nerve."

"And you should meet the boys. You had a hand in their creation.

A knock interrupted the conversation. She opened the door.

"Adam. Hey, what's up?"

"I wondered where you'd gotten off to. Anyway, JoAnne invited us to a potluck lunch in the Fellowship Hall. They're about ready. And we need to feed the babies. Diapers are changed, thanks to Mom and Dad."

"Adam?"

He looked at the woman standing behind Mary and scratched his head. "Well, I'll be. This is unexpected. To say the least."

"I'll go take care of the boys," she said. "Vanessa wants to talk to you. Okay?"

"Uh, sure."

He hugged her as she walked past, then turned to face the woman who had caused so much turmoil in their lives.

CHAPTER EIGHTY TWO

P astor Smith called the ceremony to order. The crowd of fifty listened to the music of a guitar and the sounds of the accompanying ocean waves. A young woman sang, and then Carl walked Mary toward Adam and Pastor Smith. Keith stood next to Adam with David, John, Jim, and Mac standing with him. Mac held the controls of the drone flying overhead recording the event. Alice, holding Number One, moved next to Mary, followed by JoAnne, holding Number Two, and Katie, holding Number Three.

As he was about to begin, Mary whispered in Pastor Smith's ear, who nodded. She looked back and found Clark, then motioned for him to come to the front. He looked embarrassed but dutifully came forward. She whispered in his ear, and he left, moving at a near trot toward a nearby pavilion. There he took the hand of the woman sitting at a table, helped her to her feet, and escorted her to the proceedings. The two stood in the back behind the rest of the assembled guests. When she finally lifted her head, Vanessa saw Mary smiling at her, and tears came flooding back again.

"How in the world did you do that?" Pastor Smith whispered to Mary.

"That, pastor, is grace. God's pure grace."

GET IN TOUCH

You can get in touch with J B Bonham online at www.JBBonham.com and find out more about his books and upcoming releases.

Made in the USA
Monee, IL
18 January 2021